W9-ARI-143

Caught by Surprise

This Large Print Book carries the
Seal of Approval of N.A.V.H.

APART FROM THE CROWD

Caught by Surprise

Jen Turano

THORNDIKE PRESS
A part of Gale, a Cengage Company

Farmington Hills, Mich • San Francisco • New York • Waterville, Maine
Meriden, Conn • Mason, Ohio • Chicago

Scripture quotations are from the King James Version of the Bible.
Thorndike Press, a part of Gale, a Cengage Company.

Thorndike Press® Large Print Christian Historical Fiction.
The text of this Large Print edition is unabridged.
Other aspects of the book may vary from the original edition.
Set in 16 pt. Plantin.

**LIBRARY OF CONGRESS CIP DATA ON FILE.
CATALOGUING IN PUBLICATION FOR THIS BOOK
IS AVAILABLE FROM THE LIBRARY OF CONGRESS**

ISBN-13: 978-1-4328-5560-4 (hardcover)

Published in 2018 by arrangement with Bethany House Publishers, a division of Baker Publishing Group

Printed in the United States of America
1 2 3 4 5 6 7 22 21 20 19 18

For David Turner

Even though I was convinced you got far more than your fair share of attention as the baby of the family, which was probably why Gretchen and I tormented you so much, you still — and I'm not exactly sure how — turned out to be charming, well-adjusted, and . . . completely normal.

Love you!
Jen

Chapter One

September 1883 — New York City

The first inkling Miss Temperance Flowerdew had that her rather mundane day was about to turn anything *but* mundane happened when a closed carriage trundled up beside her, keeping pace with her every step as she walked down the sidewalk adjacent to Broadway.

With her thoughts consumed by the watercolor lesson she was soon to teach at Miss Snook's School for the Education of the Feminine Mind, she gave the carriage only the most cursory of glances and continued forward. However, when the door to the carriage suddenly burst open and a masked man bounded out of it, Temperance stopped dead in her tracks and turned her undivided attention to the scene unfolding directly in front of her. For the life of her, she couldn't comprehend why a member of what was obviously the criminal persuasion would behave in such a blatant fashion in the midst of a public sidewalk.

Before she could come up with a reasonable explanation, though, the masked man set his sights on her, and then, to her utmost horror, he lurched her way and grabbed hold of her arm.

The next thing she knew, she was hanging upside down over a very broad shoulder, the breath stolen from her lungs, right before she was tossed unceremoniously into the carriage. Wincing when she landed on a seat bereft of much cushioning, she managed to get a less than impressive "help" through her constricted throat. Scrambling for the door opposite of the one she'd been tossed through, her scrambling came to an abrupt stop when the masked man grabbed hold of her foot. He then kept a firm grip on that foot even as he went about the tricky business of closing the carriage door while she twisted and turned in a desperate attempt to get free.

The door shut with an ominous click, and darkness settled over the interior of the carriage, the lack of light adding a substantial amount of melodrama to what was already a very dramatic situation.

As the carriage surged into motion, a burlap bag that smelled strongly of onions was pulled over her head and something that felt quite like a very sharp knife pressed into her side.

"If you know what's good for you, you'll not make another peep," a voice rasped as the carriage picked up speed, the driver evidently not having a care where he was driving since Temperance could hear the yells of people trying to get out of the carriage's way.

For the briefest of moments, Temperance was more than willing to abide to the demand of keeping silent. But when her scrambled thoughts began to settle, she realized that if she did remain quiet she'd be spirited down Broadway with relatively few people aware of her troubling plight. There was little likelihood anyone who realized she'd been abducted would be able to follow her since they'd all been on foot. With that in mind, she opened her mouth and managed to get what sounded exactly like a croak past her lips.

Her croaking came to a rapid end when the bag was pulled off her head and a cloth that smelled revoltingly sweet and was saturated with some type of liquid was pressed over her nose and mouth. Temperance's stomach immediately began to roil. Unable to dislodge the cloth or the man as the carriage continued to careen wildly down the street, she soon found her thoughts growing fuzzy and her limbs turning alarmingly numb. Before she knew it, her eyes fluttered shut, and everything faded straightaway.

"I done told you, Eugene, that a person really can't be trusting those remedies sold at those apparition shops. Why, that lady has been senseless for hours. We ain't gonna get paid the rest of our money if we get to Chicago and discover she died along the way. Besides, I didn't sign up for no murdering of a young lady. That would go against everything Pastor Roy used to preach to us when we was young'uns."

Forcing her eyes open even though they seemed less than willing to cooperate, Temperance blinked a few times, confusion coursing over her as her gaze settled on thin slices of light drifting through what looked to be small holes. A distinctive rumbling sound met her ears, but because her thoughts were incredibly muddled, she couldn't remember when she'd heard that rumbling before, or what it signified.

"She ain't dead, Mercy. I checked her no more than ten minutes ago, and I told you I heard snores coming out of the coffin. And not that I want to squabble with you, but I'm fair to certain that Pastor Roy wouldn't have been approvin' of us stealing that lady from the street either, or whiskin' her off to Chicago. I might be wrong about this, but kidnapping a person is almost as bad as murderin' them."

Drawing in a breath of stale air, Temperance froze in the act of releasing that breath when she realized the word *coffin* had been used, which almost seemed to suggest she was currently residing in one, although . . . that couldn't be right, unless . . .

"And because talk of Pastor Roy, God rest his soul, is making me uncomfortable," the man continued, "allow me to change the subject to something a little less troubling. *Apparition,* a word you just spoke, Mercy, ain't the right word. Apocalypse shop is where I got that sleeping potion, but I'm beginning to think I may have been a little heavy-handed with it. The owner of that shop didn't mention a thing about it makin' a person senseless for so many hours, but that's what it's done."

"If she ain't dead, that senseless state she's embracing might very well be a blessing in disguise — unless she never comes to, that is," said the voice belonging to a person Temperance thought might be Mercy. "I doubt she would have climbed into that coffin on her own accord, let alone allowed us to nail the lid of it closed over top of her, or waited quietly while we drilled more air holes through the wood. That might have made it all kinds of tricky to get her on this here train. She weren't nearly as accommodatin' as we was led to believe she'd be. And she sure didn't come along with us peaceful-like, which made the use of that coffin a brilliant idea on your part."

At the mention of the word *coffin* again, all the breath seemed to get sucked right out of Temperance's lungs as the truth of her situation settled over her.

She'd been abducted, stuffed into a coffin, and someone had apparently nailed the lid shut after they'd gotten through with stuffing her inside a place a living person wasn't supposed to be. They'd then, if she was following the conversation correctly, hauled her onto a train and were taking her off to Chicago for some unknown reason.

Panic, and a large dose of it, had perspiration beading her forehead.

Trying to push aside the panic, Temperance forced air back into her lungs, breathing in and out as she tried to puzzle out why someone would want to nail her into a coffin or abscond with her in the first place.

She was not a lady who possessed a fortune, having become a poor relation to her distant Flowerdew relatives when her parents died unexpectedly a few years before. She'd been left destitute, a circumstance that had been next to impossible to comprehend given the vast family fortune she'd always believed to be in fine form, but a fortune that had turned out to be anything other than fine.

Unaccustomed to having limited funds at her disposal, she'd found herself forced to accept the hospitality — and grudging hospitality at that — of Mr. Wayne Flowerdew, her cousin twice removed. He'd been the gentleman who'd tracked her down in Paris, given the direction by her father's business associate who'd known she was spending a few years enjoying a grand tour while perfecting her craft as an artist.

To say she was taken aback to discover a gentleman she barely knew waiting for her in the house she was renting in Paris was an understatement. But then, after Wayne Flowerdew made himself quite at home in the charming parlor her rented house offered, he'd changed her world forever with the unfortunate news he'd come to deliver.

Her parents were missing in the wilds of South America, presumed dead. They'd been murdered, witnesses claimed, by a tribe of vicious savages.

Shaken to the core by the idea she would never see her beloved parents again, having never once considered that the adventurous life her mother and father enjoyed would end with their deaths, she'd been less than prepared to deal with the next disaster flung her way — one centered around the fact that the family fortune was no longer intact.

That information had been delivered to her by Mr. John Howland, a gentleman she'd learned was her father's most trusted man of affairs. He'd met Temperance and her cousin at the New York Harbor and ushered her directly to his office off Fourth Avenue. Explanations Temperance barely understood immediately commenced, but when Mr. Howland was finished, Temperance was aware of some life-changing truths: her parents were dead, the family fortune had been lost to an ill-advised investment opportunity, and the family house in Connecticut had been sold to settle the most pressing of her father's debts.

Mr. Howland, evidently not being a gentleman who knew how to deal with a young lady who'd been brought up in the lap of luxury but was now nothing more than a pauper, launched into what he seemingly thought would be a small measure of consolation. A few personal belongings had been saved for her, those belongings having already been delivered to Wayne Flowerdew's residence.

When she'd finally had the presence of mind to inquire why Wayne Flowerdew, a gentleman she barely knew and only a distant relative to her, had become such an integral part of her personal misfortunes, she'd learned that her father had written a special clause in his will, entrusting his cousin with the guardianship of his only daughter if anything of an unfortunate nature happened to him or Temperance's mother. That guardianship was to stand until she reached the age of twenty-five, unless she got married before reaching that age, in which case it was apparently assumed her husband would look after her interests.

Before Temperance could contemplate the sheer horror of that idea, Mr. Howland professed his deepest sympathies regarding her plight, rose from his chair, took hold of her arm, and escorted her directly out of his office, leaving her standing on the sidewalk with her unwanted guardian.

As the door to Mr. Howland's office shut behind her, Temperance vowed then and there that she was going to, from that point forward, put her past ways aside, deciding that embracing an adventurous attitude was entirely overrated and led to despair and heartache in the end.

No longer would she flutter through life from one journey to another, experiencing all the many amusements the world had to offer. Instead, she vowed to adopt a retiring nature, one that would see her safely removed from the dangers adventurous sorts faced far more often than she'd realized.

That vow, oddly enough, turned out to be remarkably easy to maintain.

Wayne, while willing to offer her a roof over her head, if only to stave off judgment from the society he longed to impress, informed her in no uncertain terms that he was appalled he'd been given the task of watching over her until she reached the age of twenty-five. He didn't even bother to hide the fact that he only agreed to fetch her from Paris because he thought her fortune was still firmly intact, a fortune she would certainly want to share with him because he'd been named her guardian.

Because she was imposing on his hospitality, and with no money to ease the bother of that, Wayne determined she'd have to earn her keep. True to his word, she'd barely unpacked her steamer trunk before Fanny Flowerdew, Wayne's simpering wife, called her to the drawing room for a bit of a chat — one that detailed what would be expected of Temperance until she reached the age of twenty-five, or found a gentleman to marry, an idea Fanny thought was next to impossible.

From that point forward, and over the years Temperance had lived with the Flowerdews, she'd spent her days and nights at the beck and call of Wayne and Fanny's daughter, Clementine. Clementine was a young lady with grand social aspirations, which is exactly why the Flowerdew family had abandoned their house in upstate New York only a month after Temperance began residing with them, taking up residence on the far end of Park Avenue, one that was not quite the toniest of addresses, but acceptable all the same.

They'd immediately set about getting Clementine introduced to high society, her acceptance into that society aided by the assistance of Mrs. Boggart Hobbes, or Aunt Minnie, as the family fondly addressed her. Aunt Minnie was a leading society matron who was also Fanny's aunt, but any affection Temperance might have believed would come her way was put firmly to bed when Mrs. Boggart Hobbes stated most emphatically that Temperance was not to address her as Aunt Minnie, but was expected to maintain a formal attitude between them since they were not related by blood.

With Clementine being soundly embraced by the crème de la crème, Temperance found herself in the unenviable role of Clementine's chaperone and lady's maid when it became known she had a flare for styling hair.

Given Clementine's questionable nature, Temperance had clung fast to her vow of abandoning an adventurous nature and embraced an air of meekness and reserve, qualities that served her well as she negotiated the unpleasant realities of her new life.

It had only been recently that Temperance's life had begun taking a happier turn, a direct result of being invited to attend Miss Permilia Griswold's June engagement celebration. It was at that very celebration she'd enjoyed an unexpected encounter with one of her dearest friends from childhood — Mr. Gilbert Cavendish. She'd not seen Gilbert for far too many years, having been separated from him when he went off to college and she went off on her grand tour. Add in the fact she'd then been thrust into the retiring role of poor relation, which did not encourage her to seek out former friends, and it was little wonder so much time had elapsed since she'd last seen her friend.

Unsettling as it had been to realize how long she'd been parted from Gilbert, it had been more unsettling to accept the ugly truth his reappearance in her life brought to her attention. While she'd embraced the idea of living a less-than-adventurous life, she'd sacrificed her true sense of self, becoming a woman she didn't even recognize and a woman Gilbert had certainly never known.

A new vow had arisen as that evening spent in Gilbert's company wore on, a vow to reclaim at least a little morsel of the woman she'd been before her life turned upside down. She'd recognized that a meek existence did not suit her in the least, which was fortunate indeed because the very day after the engagement celebration, Wayne sent her packing. He stated it was past time she earned her own way in the world, even though she was not quite twenty-five yet.

The reasoning behind her abrupt departure centered squarely around the idea that Clementine, her less-than-pleasant cousin, wanted Gilbert Cavendish for herself. Oddly enough, Clementine was worried Temperance would stand in the way of her acquiring the attention of Gilbert because she believed Temperance's friendship with Gilbert was a direct threat to Clementine's plans of becoming Mrs. Cavendish.

The thought of Gilbert had Temperance's lips curving, until a loud argument between her abductors pulled her directly back to her troubling situation — that being she'd been abducted and was shut inside a coffin.

"You've clearly not been listening well enough at that fancy church Mrs. Baldwin made us attend, back before she released us from service, Eugene. *Apocalypse* is the word preachers use when they're talkin' about the end of the world, so it's not what that shop was called where you bought the sleeping potion."

"That might very well be, Mercy, but it ain't like a person can hear the sermons well, not back where members of the serving sort are required to sit in that fancy church. But that's not gonna help us know what word I was really fixin' to use. I sure do hate when a word is on the tip of your tongue, but you just can't spit it out. It's maddening, it is."

"It's *apothecary,*" Temperance called

before she could stop herself, the words echoing eerily around the interior of the coffin.

Dead silence was all that greeted her until someone cleared their throat.

"You reckon' that's God talking to us, Mercy?"

"Don't be an idiot, Eugene. The voice came from the coffin."

"Ah, right. That makes more sense, but if that there lady has woken up from her stupor, you'd best stop calling me Eugene. I'll be . . . ah . . . Thurman and you can be . . . Dolly."

"I ain't being no Dolly. I knew a Dolly years ago, and she was a nasty piece of work. I'll be Vivian because that's a right fine name and I always wanted me a right fine name."

Wanting to laugh even though she was in a most precarious situation, Temperance resisted that urge right as heavy footsteps began trudging her way. The next thing she knew, an eye was peering at her through one of the holes that had evidently been drilled through her prison to allow her to breathe.

"How ya feelin' in there?"

"How would you feel if you were entombed in a coffin while you're still living?"

she shot back.

The eye disappeared, replaced with a different eye, one obviously belonging to the other kidnapper. "You being in that coffin is all on account of my, er, partner being heavy-handed with a sleeping potion. Just so you know, if you hadn't put up such a fight, he wouldn't have been forced to use it."

"Surely you're not about to blame me for my current predicament, are you?"

" 'Course I am. You've given us all sorts of trouble, and it was only because me and Eu . . . er . . . What did you say your name was going to be again?"

"It's Thurman and you're Dolly."

The eye disappeared. "I'm Vivian."

"That's a high-society name."

"Since we're about to stay at that high-society Palmer House hotel, Vivian's as good as any name."

A second later, the eye returned to peer down at her. "Where was I?"

Swallowing yet another unexpected laugh, Temperance cleared her throat, realizing as she did so that her throat was remarkably dry, probably since she'd apparently been rendered unconscious for hours upon end.

"I believe you were about to impart the inspiration behind spiriting me out of New

York in a coffin."

"So I was, and that inspiration was all due to Thurman remembering what happened to the unfortunate A.T. Stewart."

"Are we talking about the A.T. Stewart who was the founder of A.T. Stewart & Company?"

"That's the man."

"I don't believe Mr. Stewart sold coffins at his store," Temperance said slowly.

"Of course he didn't. Eugene, I mean Thurman, thought of him because we once heard tell that Mr. Stewart done got his body stolen and held for ransom."

"I'm familiar with what happened to poor Mr. Stewart, although I do want to point out that his body wasn't stolen *in* a coffin, but stolen *from* a coffin, which was then left behind," Temperance said. "I also feel compelled to point out that Mr. Stewart, God rest his soul, was dead when his body was stolen and held for ransom. Obviously, I'm not dead, and I do hope you're not intending to kill me to remain true to the ransom scenario that followed Mr. Stewart's abduction."

"We're not intending to kill you," Mercy returned. "But getting back to Mr. Stewart — you don't mean to tell me that some fool broke into his vault and took only his body, do you? I've been close to a deceased person before and the smell is most unpleasant."

Feeling slightly reassured by the notion her abductors didn't seem keen to kill her *and* seemed squeamish about horrible smells, Temperance lifted a hand, pushing on a coffin lid that refused to move. "I'm afraid that's exactly what happened to Mr. Stewart," she finally said, annoyance flowing over her that she had in fact been nailed securely into her prison. "Although I believe the criminals who stole his body have yet to be found."

"That's good to know," Mercy muttered.

"I'm sure you are comforted by the idea criminals occasionally do roam free. But, getting back to my specific situation, while I'm not exactly in a position to argue with the manner in which you chose to spirit me out of the city, allow me to point out what I see as a flaw with your plan. I'm, thankfully, not dead, and as such, I'm afraid I have certain needs that a corpse would not have, such as the need to use a retiring room. I'm also going to need to be fed at some point. In addition to those concerns, I must tell you that the walls of my prison will soon begin to close in on me, and when that happens, I know I'll be unable to stifle the screams that my fear of being in closed confines is certain to bring about."

"It wouldn't be a wise choice for you to start screamin'."

Exasperation had Temperance rolling her eyes, not that anyone could see that, but it did seem to suit the moment. "Since I'm enclosed in a coffin, I'm not certain there's much you're going to be able to do to stop my screams, not if you truly don't mean to kill me."

"Seems to me like we got ourselves a smart one, Vivie."

The eye disappeared once again. "It's *Vivian,* and it don't matter if she's a smart one. What does matter is we've got to figure us out a new plan of what to do next."

For the next few minutes, all Temperance could hear was the sound of muffled voices that occasionally rose above a whisper as what was undoubtedly an argument turned increasingly heated. Finally, and after one of her abductors let out a snort of disgust, heavy footsteps trudged back to the coffin and an eye appeared back at the hole.

"We're going to let you out, but no funny business. We might not be keen to murder you, but giving you a few knocks over the head won't bother us a'tall."

With those less-than-comforting words, someone began applying what had to be a crowbar to the coffin, but before the lid could be lifted away, the man now going by the name of Thurman began to speak.

"We best be putting on our disguises, Mercy. It won't do us no good if she gets a look at our faces."

"It also won't do us no good if you keep forgetting to call me Vivian."

"It's not going to do either one of you any good if I end up losing my last meal due to the queasiness I'm beginning to feel over still being stuck in this box," Temperance yelled.

"Give us a moment."

A moment was all it took for her abductors to evidently don their disguises, and with a sense of relief slipping over her, Temperance watched as the lid was pried away, squinting when light immediately blinded her. Raising a hand to shield her eyes, she pushed herself to a sitting position, then felt her mouth drop open when she got her first look at her surroundings.

She was in a Pullman car, and a nicely appointed Pullman car at that.

An honest-to-goodness chandelier hung directly above her head, while a divan upholstered in green velvet, paired with matching chairs on either side of it, was placed directly underneath the side window of the train. The bright sunlight streaming through that window suggested it was either late morning or early afternoon. Switching her attention to the other side of the room, she found her abductors watching her warily.

One of the abductors was a large man, the one who'd abducted her off the street, his face hidden beneath the same mask he'd had on when he'd jumped out of the carriage back on Broadway. The other abductor was clearly a woman, small in stature and thin, with a face covered in fake whiskers, those whiskers having been slapped on her face rather haphazardly since the mustache she was wearing was lopsided and her beard was hanging from the edge of her chin.

"Goodness but you look a fright," the woman said as she looked Temperance up and down, scratching her nose as she did so. "There's a retiring room just behind that small door over there, and there's a washstand right outside the door. You might ought to make use of it."

Temperance inclined her head. "Sound advice to be sure, but first I'm going to need help getting out of here."

The large man, evidently named Eugene even though he was trying to go by Thurman, nodded and shuffled across the room on heavy-soled boots. He came to a stop right in front of her and surprised Temperance by presenting her with his hand. Taking that hand, she struggled to push herself past the high walls of the coffin. Her struggle was interrupted when Eugene plucked her straight up into his arms and set her down. He steadied her when her legs wobbled, then took hold of her arm and practically pushed her across the Pullman car, stopping in front of a narrow door she assumed led to the retiring room.

"Just give a holler if you need anything else." With that, he turned around and strode to the other side of the car, presenting her with his back — a chivalrous response even though the retiring room was equipped with a door.

Thankful she was being allowed a moment of privacy, Temperance slipped into the small retiring room, closed the door firmly behind her, and immediately began trying to plot out an avenue of escape.

Chapter Two

After spending as long as she dared in the tiny retiring room the Pullman car offered, Temperance was forced to concede defeat in formulating a viable escape plan.

The reality of her situation was that she was on a rapidly moving train. The chances of survival if she did fling herself out the door of the train were not in her favor, which made her current situation very bleak indeed.

However, because she was not a lady prone to wasting her time dwelling on futile matters, Temperance decided the only prudent option was to wait until they reached Chicago and then hope an avenue of escape would present itself.

Deciding a sensible use of her time would be to wriggle out information from her abductors, Temperance reached for the door handle and stepped from the retiring room. Her gaze slid over the well-appointed interior and settled on her two captors. They were sitting at a small table covered in fine linen, slurping their way through steaming cups of tea held in delicate china teacups.

Frowning, she took a single step toward them, then paused. "Forgive me for disrupting your tea, but isn't it a little unusual for kidnappers to whisk their captives away in a private Pullman car? My father, God rest his soul, purchased a Pullman car for his personal use, and I distinctly recall him remarking that the cost of such luxury was prohibitive."

Mercy stopped slurping. "Don't be nosey. It ain't becoming in a woman, and besides, the less you know, the better it'll go for you in the end." She gestured to the pot sitting on the table. "Tea?"

Temperance lifted her chin. "I'd rather have answers."

"Answers ain't what I offered you. If you don't want tea, that's all well and good, but it is delicious. Thurman just fetched this pot from the dining car. From what I've been told, tea is a drink best served hot."

"Unless it's iced tea," Eugene added before he returned his attention back to his own cup. He evidently found his tea delicious as well since he began smacking his lips after every slurp.

Realizing her captors were not in an accommodating frame of mind to provide her with answers to her many questions, while also realizing her throat was remarkably dry, Temperance moved to the washstand. She took a moment to scrub her hands under the flowing water coming from the spigots, noticing as she did so that she'd lost her gloves somewhere along the way. After splashing a few handfuls of water over her face, she patted dry with a fluffy towel she found on the shelf underneath the basin, then set aside the towel and dared a look in the mirror.

The image staring back at her was not unexpected given what she'd been through over the past hours.

Her hair, not quite black but darker than brown, was flattened on the right side of her head, while strands on the left side had escaped their pins and were sticking out in a haphazard fashion. Her forehead sported an angry-looking scratch, and her ivory skin, something her mother always claimed lent Temperance the appearance of a porcelain doll, was blotchy and anything other than porcelain-like.

Dark circles rimmed the delicate skin underneath green eyes, that, upon closer reflection, were bloodshot and itchy, no doubt a direct result of being enclosed in a dusty coffin.

Dropping her head, she refused a wince when she took in the sight of what had been a lovely periwinkle walking dress, but was now a mess of wrinkles and dirt.

A trickle of temper stole through her as she lifted her head and settled her attention once again on the two people who'd been responsible for ruining one of the dresses she'd only recently purchased, using money she earned from teaching.

"I do hope that along with having the funds available to travel in style, you also have funds at your disposal that will see me compensated for the damage done to my garment. I doubt it'll ever look the same, and I'll have you know, I've worn it only a handful of times."

Unfortunately, everything she said was completely ignored since Mercy and Eugene had pulled out what looked to be a veritable feast from a wicker basket, complete with bread, cheese, fruit, and a variety of covered dishes.

The sight of that feast caused her stomach to rumble. Accepting yet another defeat, Temperance squared her shoulders and marched her way across the Pullman car. Darting around the coffin, she pulled a chair up to the small table and took a seat, finally attracting the attention of her abductors as she got settled.

"Did you not see the hairbrush?" was the first question Mercy asked, her gaze fixed squarely on Temperance's head.

Temperance forced a smile even as she took a linen napkin, snapped it open, placed it over her lap, then nodded. "I did see the brush, but I simply have more important matters to deal with than setting my hair to rights. If you've forgotten, I was stolen straight off the street as I was making my way to Miss Snook's School for the Education of the Feminine Mind. Because I have yet to puzzle out why you would have done such a peculiar thing, making certain that every hair is in place is not high on my list of priorities."

Mercy set down a piece of cheese she'd been about to eat. "You don't have even a single hair in place, if you want my honest opinion." She frowned. "But hair aside, why would a lady like you be visiting a school like Miss Snook's? From what I've heard, that's a place that teaches folks new skills so they can earn themselves an honest wage. Gets them out of those positions in the big houses where a poor soul is expected to toil for hours and hours for next to no money."

She shot a look at Eugene, wincing when he sent her a scowl in return. "Not that *we* know anything about those sorts of poor souls."

Accepting the cup of tea Eugene was sliding her way across the table and pretending she didn't notice the tea was sloshing over the rim and staining the fine linen, Temperance raised the cup, took a larger sip than was considered proper, then took another as delicious warmth soothed her dry throat and began settling a stomach that was slightly queasy. Before she could answer Mercy's question, though, Eugene spoke up.

"I done bet she offers up her time at that school like some ladies offer up their time feeding the poor, Vivian. That's probably why we was instructed to take good care of her and treat her with a good dose of respect because she's one of those rare ladies who are kind and not full of themselves."

Temperance took another sip of tea before abandoning her cup. "First of all, enough of this Vivian and Thurman business. I know you're really Eugene and Mercy, siblings as well if I were to hazard a guess given the amount of bickering between you. It's confusing an already ridiculous situation by having the two of you using assumed names.

Second, I hardly believe you've taken good care of me since you, Eugene, threw me over your shoulder and tossed me into a carriage, and none too gently, may I say. Also, nailing a lady into a coffin is not what one might consider to be an act of great respect. I'll probably suffer nightmares for years after what I've experienced at your hands."

Eugene's eyes narrowed behind the mask he was wearing. "You don't strike me as the nightmare suffering sort. And just so you know, it's not gonna do you no good to point out things such as figuring out our names. That could get you killed good and proper, it could."

"It'll be difficult to kill me now that you've invited me to join you in tea," Temperance said, accepting a plate filled with cheese and bread that Mercy was shoving her way. "And, if I've figured out anything at all, it's that you two don't seem to be very experienced at this abduction business, which makes me wonder what you did to get released from your positions at Mrs. Baldwin's house in the first place."

Mercy leaned forward. "We never mentioned nothin' about us working for Mrs. Baldwin."

"Before you realized I was awake, I heard

the two of you talking. I distinctly recall one of you saying something about having a hard time hearing the sermons at the fancy church Mrs. Baldwin made you attend before you were released from service. I know for fact the Baldwin family enjoys services at Grace Church, which is about the fanciest church New York City has to offer."

Silence settled around the Pullman car as Mercy sat back in her seat but not before she sent Eugene a look that could only be called significant, a look that had him leaning forward.

"You're an odd sort of society lady, ain't you?" Eugene asked as Mercy immediately jumped back into the conversation before Temperance had an opportunity to respond.

"She is odd, Eugene, and nothin' like them society chits we're used to. Now that I think on it, I find myself wonderin' why it is that she ain't experiencing those fits of the vapors young ladies seem to enjoy, 'specially since we done stole her and are whiskin' her away from her home, something I don't reckon' society ladies experience often or at all."

Seeing absolutely no benefit in engaging in the conversation because trying to defend a person's oddness never amounted to anything productive, Temperance spread some butter on a piece of bread, popped it into her mouth, then stifled the urge to take the entire loaf and wolf it down. Swallowing the bread, she took another piece, noticing as she did that Eugene and Mercy didn't appear bothered in the least that she wasn't participating in what was turning into a rousing conversation. In fact, they almost seemed to have forgotten she was sitting with them at the table.

"Remember when Miss Martha saw Miss Cathleen wearing that hat with the peacock feathers and ripped it straight off her sister's head?" Mercy asked as she tugged up a beard that was slipping. "Why I ain't never seen young ladies dressed in the first state of fashion rollin' about on the floor like they was doing, biting and scratching in a way that said all that money Mrs. Baldwin spent on their education hadn't been money well spent at all."

"You know I never got to see what went on in the big house, Mercy. Not when I was always tending to Mr. Baldwin's prized ponies down at the livery stable."

Temperance picked up her tea. "Miss Martha Baldwin and Miss Cathleen Baldwin are difficult young ladies to be sure, but why did Mrs. Baldwin release you from service? She always seemed to be a most reasonable sort, and not one who'd dismiss members of staff for anything other than a most grievous offense."

Mercy and Eugene exchanged nervous looks before Eugene cleared his throat and settled back in his seat. "You're being nosey, again, and like my sister said, nosiness ain't becoming in a lady."

Temperance took a sip of tea, then set the cup aside. "Very well, since you obviously don't care to discuss your personal business, tell me this. What are you supposed to do with me once we reach Chicago, and how long do you believe it'll be before we reach our destination?"

Eugene folded his arms over his chest. "That's still being nosey."

"Perhaps, but our time will pass faster if we engage in idle chitchat, and a subject such as the time of our arrival is hardly an incriminating topic."

"She makes a good point," Mercy said, helping herself to more cheese, which she promptly stuffed into her mouth.

Eugene tugged a battered watch out of his pocket, took note of the time, then stuffed it back into his pocket. "We still have a few hours to go before we reach Chicago. As for what we're supposed to do with you, we've been instructed to see you to the Palmer House, where we'll find a room reserved for us under Mr. Randolph Smith and wife."

Frowning, Temperance considered that bit of nonsense. Helping herself to another piece of bread, she took her time eating it, then blotted her lips with the linen napkin and met Eugene's gaze.

"Why would someone hire you to steal me away from New York, in a private Pullman car no less, and then put us up in one of the most luxurious hotels in the country? It makes no sense, not if I assume I've been stolen to be held for ransom, although . . . that makes no sense either, unless . . ." She set aside her napkin as the only logical explanation to explain this mess sprang to mind.

"Unless what?" Eugene pressed.

"Unless you've snatched the wrong lady by mistake."

Silence descended over the Pullman car until it was broken by the sound of Eugene's and Mercy's laughter.

By the time they managed to collect themselves, Eugene had turned away from Temperance, having removed his mask in order to wipe at eyes that had evidently begun watering, while Mercy was hiccupping into a linen napkin, shaking her head as she let a few lingering chuckles escape.

"We ain't stolen the wrong lady," Mercy finally said.

"How do you know for certain?" Temperance shot back.

Wiping her eyes with the napkin, Mercy set down the linen and caught Temperance's gaze. "Because we were told your name, and after we done asked around about you, we was told you could be found moseying down Broadway most mornings on your way to whatever it is you do on Broadway."

"But why would anyone want to have a wallflower abducted, especially one who has no fortune, family, or very many friends for that matter?"

Eugene set his mask to rights and swiveled around to Temperance. "You ain't no wallflower, missy, and I know you have family because that's where we sent the note, explaining to your father and mother that you'd been snatched."

Temperance's mouth dropped open as truth settled firmly around her. "Goodness . . . you have made a mistake, haven't you?"

Eugene scowled back at her. "Why do you keep insisting we made a mistake?"

"Because both of my parents are dead, which would have made sending them a note regarding my abduction a little tricky."

Eugene and Mercy sucked in sharp breaths at the same exact time. Mercy rose to her feet, not even seeming to realize her beard was now hanging by a mere whisker from her chin.

"What's your name?" she asked in a voice barely more than a whisper.

"I'm Miss Temperance Flowerdew."

Mercy's eyes widened to the size of saucers. "Surely not."

"I can assure you, I'm well aware of exactly who I am, and I am, indeed, Temperance Flowerdew."

Mercy exchanged a horrified look with Eugene, before she swallowed and lifted a trembling hand to her throat. "On my word, Eugene, we did done snatch us the wrong lady, and we're gonna be in all kinds of trouble now."

Chapter Three

Mr. Gilbert Cavendish was a gentleman who believed in adhering to the strictest of schedules.

That adherence was exactly why he was feeling out of sorts, having been forced to abandon his plans to race to the rescue of an honest-to-goodness damsel in distress.

As a gentleman, Gilbert had been powerless to refuse the pleas of Mrs. Wayne Flowerdew, whom he'd been encouraged to address as Fanny, especially after he learned her daughter, Miss Clementine Flowerdew, had been abducted.

There he'd been, perusing his appointments for the day before he headed to his office, when Tobias, a man he'd recently added to the ranks of his household staff, stepped into Gilbert's library, announcing in a voice no louder than a whisper, that something odd was afoot.

That oddness turned out to be the arrival

of Fanny, who'd swept into the library in a flurry of rustling fabric. She'd immediately begun wringing her hands as she begged him to assist her with a most troubling matter.

At first, he thought the matter would have something to do with securing her an invitation to the engagement ball of Miss Gertrude Cadwalader and his very good friend Mr. Harrison Sinclair. Invitations to the ball were difficult to come by because Gertrude wanted it to remain a somewhat intimate affair, so members of society were now itching to get their hands on the coveted invitations. That meant Gilbert found himself most sought-after these days.

Granted, he'd become increasingly sought-after when word began to swirl through society he possessed a half brother who went by the illustrious title of Earl of Strafford. Interest in Gilbert by the lady set had also increased when it became known he'd recently begun building a mansion on Fifth Avenue, even though that mansion was not completed and was barely habitable at this point in time. Now though, with his friendship to Harrison Sinclair and his lovely fiancée Gertrude Cadwalader being much remarked upon, he was finding himself in more demand than ever. That situation was becoming more concerning by the day as invitations to the many society events kept piling up, and sorting through all those invitations with his secretary took precious time out of his busyschedule.

However, when Fanny had burst into tears right before she collapsed in a heap of sobbing hysteria, Gilbert realized Fanny's visit did *not* merely concern securing her an invitation, and he had abandoned all thoughts of his schedule and rushed to assist the distraught woman crumpled on his newly purchased Aubusson carpet. After plucking her off the floor, which was no easy feat because Fanny was not what anyone could consider a waifish sort, Gilbert sent Tobias off to fetch tea, waiting until Fanny had been plied with a full cup of that tea before he'd cautiously approached the topic of her obvious distress.

Whatever he was expecting the poor lady to say, it was not that her daughter had been snatched straight from the street as she'd been making her way to Ward McAllister's Family Circle Dancing Class, or that she was currently being held for ransom.

Pressing a crumpled note into his hand, Fanny sniffled into a handkerchief while Gilbert read the contents, having to read the ransom note three times before the reality of the situation truly sank in.

Miss Clementine Flowerdew, a young lady he'd been acquainted with for only a few months, having met her in June, truly seemed to have been kidnapped. To make the situation even more disturbing, her abductors were whisking her away to Chicago, an unlikely spot, in Gilbert's humble opinion, to hold a lady for ransom since getting there was almost a day's journey by train, and certainly lent the already disturbing situation a most peculiar air.

After allowing the details of the ransom note to settle, he'd lifted his head, finding Fanny watching him closely, the color having returned to her pale cheeks, a direct result of the second cup of tea she'd been enjoying. Because she seemed to have pushed her hysteria aside, he broached the most logical of questions — that being why she'd chosen to seek him out regarding the abduction and the demands being made instead of her husband, Wayne.

Dabbing at eyes that immediately began watering again, Fanny launched into a lengthy explanation, mingled with a few pauses when she dissolved into hysterics again, stating that Wayne was out of town and that she was unable to withdraw the amount of money from the bank being demanded for Clementine's release without her husband's permission. She then ended her sad tale of woe with another wringing of hands, begging Gilbert to assist her in what she felt was a matter of life and death for her one and only daughter.

Unable to turn away a lady in clear distress, Gilbert abandoned New York for Chicago on the first available train. He'd not, however, been spending his time since arriving in the Windy City negotiating the release of Clementine. Instead, he'd been forced to wait in the impressive lobby of the Palmer House for further instructions to arrive.

Keeping a firm grip on the battered satchel that was holding the money he'd withdrawn from his own account to secure Clementine's freedom, Gilbert pulled out his pocket watch yet again, apprehension running through him when he noticed he'd been lingering in the lobby for over two hours.

Deciding he would wait for an additional hour before he bowed to the inevitable and sought out assistance from the authorities, even though the ransom note had specifically demanded that no authority figures were to be contacted, Gilbert tucked his pocket watch away and lifted his head.

Allowing his gaze to drift over the many

guests strolling around the vast lobby, his attention was suddenly captured by a woman slipping through the crowd, a woman who reminded him of his very dear friend, Miss Temperance Flowerdew, who was Miss Clementine Flowerdew's cousin, thrice removed.

Craning his neck when the lady stepped behind a gathering of well-dressed women, Gilbert strained to catch sight of her again, freezing on the spot when the lady reappeared and he realized that she didn't simply resemble Temperance — she *was* Temperance.

Having absolutely no idea what Temperance could possibly be doing in Chicago because he'd been told back in June by Mr. Wayne Flowerdew, Temperance's cousin twice removed, that Temperance was on an extended visit to the beaches of Florida to pursue her love of painting ocean scenes, Gilbert moved to intercept his friend. His feet slowed to a stop a second later when an unwelcome thought began to form, one that *might* explain what Temperance was doing in Chicago, but . . . no . . . it was too outlandish an idea to accept, even for a lady known for pursuing an adventurous lifestyle, although . . .

Before he could finish the thought, Temperance caught sight of him, and with a widening of her eyes, she changed direction and charged his way, her brisk pace sending ribbons that seemed to be coming undone from her wrinkled walking dress fluttering behind her.

By the time she stopped directly in front of him, alarm had replaced any confusion Gilbert was experiencing because Temperance, even being a woman who'd always been rather blasé about her appearance, at least while they'd been growing up, was looking nothing less than frightful.

Her dark hair was sticking up on one side of her head, while being flattened on the other, and an angry scratch marred the pale skin of her forehead, which, now that he considered it closer, was smudged with dirt. Her walking gown was not only wrinkled and losing its ribbons but stained with dirt as well. Because she was smiling back at him, though, he got the distinct impression she wasn't under great duress, which made it all the more confusing to understand her genuine air of neglect.

It did not surprise him in the least when she moved closer and pulled him into an enthusiastic hug, something she'd done often throughout their youth, even though she knew full well he really wasn't what a person could call the warm and cuddly sort. Temperance stepped back, her smile turning into a grin. "Good heavens, but I'm delighted to see you, Gilbert. You would not believe the time I've had of it lately, but tell me, what in the world are you doing in Chicago?"

Taking hold of her ungloved hand and pressing a quick kiss on it, Gilbert tucked it into the crook of his arm. "I think a far more important question is what brings you to Chicago, and what, pray tell, has happened to you?"

"I asked first."

"True, but because you're looking downright concerning, which is saying something since I did grow up with you and you were known to take the term *disheveled* to an entirely different level, I'm going to have to insist on a few explanations."

For a second, Gilbert thought Temperance was going to refuse, especially since her jaw immediately set in a manner he was all too familiar with and could only describe as stubborn, but then she blew out a breath.

"I doubt you'd look much better if you'd suffered through the ordeal I've been through, what with the general mayhem I experienced at the hands of inept members of the criminal persuasion."

The thought that had begun festering the moment he'd seen her took that second to fully materialize. "Do not tell me that you've inserted yourself into a disturbing situation that a woman has no business inserting herself into, have you?"

When Temperance's only reply to that was a single blink, Gilbert blew out a breath. "Honestly, Temperance, one would have thought you'd outgrow that sense of adventure you always embraced while we were growing up. While it was charming in our younger days, although a touch disconcerting at times, you are no longer a green girl fresh out of the schoolroom. You should know that involving yourself in a situation that's fraught with intrigue and danger is quite beyond the pale. Why, it could have resulted in greater harm being done to your person than simply suffering from an unfortunate hairstyle and ruining what I'm sure at one time was a charming walking dress."

Without bothering to afford him a single retort to what he thought was a perfectly reasonable point, Temperance removed her hand from the crook of his arm, spun on her heel, and marched off across the marble floor of the Palmer House lobby, moving at a remarkably fast clip.

Knowing there was no choice but to follow her, even though dealing with Temperance when she was annoyed was a task not to be undertaken by the faint of heart, Gilbert trudged across the lobby, inclining his head time and time again to ladies who were clearly of the society set. Striding past a doorman, while assuring the man he did not need assistance with his satchel or leather traveling bag, he continued forward, finding that Temperance was already striding down the sidewalk. That she didn't bother to glance over her shoulder to see if he was following her was a less-than-encouraging sign.

Breaking into a run, something that caused his traveling bag to continuously bump against his leg, Gilbert finally caught up with Temperance right as she stopped in her tracks, her attention settled on a bakery where a delicious scent was wafting through the front door. Turning, she settled her attention on him.

"While I am presently more than put out with you, Gilbert, which is exactly why I quit the hotel before I did something untoward such as take you to task in the midst of the well-heeled guests, I'm also famished. Would you be a dear and extend me a small loan — one that I will repay you at my earliest convenience but will allow me to purchase a sticky bun from that delicious smelling bakery? I assure you, if you do me this tiniest of favors, there's little likelihood I'll follow through with my urge to lecture you, saving us what will surely amount to a squabble in the process."

"Do not say that you charged off to Chicago without having the foresight to make proper preparations, such as visiting your bank to withdraw funds that would see you well fed throughout the duration of your trip, did you?"

Tilting her head to the left, which had unpinned hair falling over her eye, Temperance peered at him through that hair for a long moment before she frowned. "And to think I've actually spent quite a bit of my time since we last spoke in June missing your company."

"You were missing me?"

"*Were* being the key word." She crossed her arms over her chest. "Honestly, Gilbert, I must tell you that I find it offensive you'd immediately assume I deliberately set off for Chicago without making proper preparations."

"You just asked me for a loan, which does seem to suggest you didn't prepare well."

"I didn't prepare at all because I wasn't planning on traveling to Chicago in the first place, hence the reasoning behind my lack of funds."

"I'm afraid I'm not following you."

"Clearly, although I would have thought that mentioning an encounter with members of the criminal set would have given you an inkling that I'm not in Chicago because I wanted to take a bit of a holiday."

"I never said you were here on holiday."

"Then why, pray tell, do you think I'm here?"

"I would have to believe you're here for the same reason I'm here — Clementine."

"What does Clementine have to do with anything?"

He took a step closer to Temperance, a risky move if there ever was one because her green eyes had begun flashing. "Forgive me. I've seemingly jumped to the wrong conclusion regarding why you're in Chicago. And while I know I should broach the subject of your cousin somewhat delicately, to save time, I'll simply be direct and spit it out." He drew in a breath and quickly released it. "Clementine's been abducted, hence the reason behind my presence in Chicago. I've been set the task of negotiating her release."

Temperance's mouth made an *O* of surprise. She blinked, blinked again, and then she did the very last thing he'd been expecting — she dissolved into laughter.

It wasn't a nervous laugh, the type a person releases when faced with unpleasant news, but more on the lines of a laugh that was filled with genuine mirth, which made no sense at all given the troubling news he'd just delivered.

A full minute later, Temperance swiped a hand over her watering eyes, gave a last hiccup of amusement, then beamed a grin his way.

"Oh, but this is marvelous, and certainly answers a myriad of questions I wasn't afforded the courtesy of having answered by the inept members of the criminal persuasion I mentioned before."

Gilbert frowned. "I don't understand how disclosing the concerning fact that your cousin has been abducted can possibly be a source of amusement for you. I also don't understand how learning she's been snatched could possibly answer any questions you may have since you were evidently not aware of her abduction in the first place."

Waving that aside, Temperance took him by the arm and propelled him directly toward the bakery, seemingly not bothered that his traveling bag was wedged in between them and kept bumping into her with every step they took. "Buy me a pastry, or three, and after I've eaten, I'll be much more capable of trying to make sense of what has now turned into a rather unusual situation."

Gilbert stopped walking. "Did you not catch the part of my explanation where I stated that your cousin has been abducted? I don't feel as if this is exactly the moment to be enjoying pastries. We need to get ourselves back to Palmer House. I'm currently waiting to receive further instructions at the hotel, which will hopefully allow me to proceed quickly with the nasty business of securing your cousin's release from her dastardly abductors."

Increasing her grip on his arm, Temperance prodded him into motion again, but not in the direction of Palmer House. Instead she practically shoved him toward the bakery, emitting what sounded like a grunt in the process.

"And we'll return to the Palmer House as soon as I've had something to eat. That'll allow me to puzzle the situation out more sufficiently because you must remember how I think best when I'm not famished. It'll also allow me to think while not attracting too much attention from the fashionable set roaming around the Palmer House lobby." She brushed aside a strand of hair that was blowing in front of her face. "As you pointed out, I'm not in what anyone might consider a well-groomed state, which will certainly draw unwanted notice from the guests at the Palmer House, as well as make it difficult for me to concentrate on the curious business at hand."

"But your cousin must even now be suffering from extreme anxiety due to her abduction. By us making a detour so you can enjoy pastries, we're prolonging that sense of anxiety."

Temperance stopped walking. "The only anxiety I fear dear Clementine might be experiencing is due to learning someone *wanted* to abduct her. If I'm right about what has happened, and believe me, I do think I am after what you've just disclosed, Clementine is still in New York, probably locked behind closed doors with an entire brigade of guards keeping watch over her until more is learned about what was clearly a bumbled attempt to snatch her out of New York and hold her for ransom."

"I'm afraid you have me at a complete disadvantage."

"I'm not surprised, but again, I'm about to faint straightaway from hunger. Further explanations will need to wait until after

I've eaten because I fear I will not do justice to what amounts to nothing less than a riveting tale of abduction, coffins, and inept criminals."

As they reached the front door of the bakery, Temperance waited for him to get the door for her, then breezed past him, turning to grab his arm again before she pulled him directly up to a glass counter filled with scrumptious-looking pastries. Turning, she caught his gaze, her eyes now sparkling with delight.

"Shall I order a variety for us and we'll share, just like we used to do when our parents would take us on holiday to Sarasota Springs?"

Never able to resist Temperance when she was smiling and in a pleasant frame of mind, Gilbert nodded. Although now that he thought about it, he'd never been able to resist her even when she'd been in a mischievous and certain-to-get-them-in-trouble frame of mind either. He then watched as Temperance went about the business of choosing the perfect pastries.

Less than five minutes later, and seated at a small table tucked into the back of the bakery, his traveling bag and satchel stashed underneath that table, Gilbert shook his head as Temperance devoured pastry after pastry, quite as if she'd missed every meal for a week.

"You're going to make yourself sick," he finally said when she reached for a pastry stuffed with cherries. She used a knife to cut off a piece of it, then promptly stuck that piece into her mouth.

Swallowing, she shook her head. "You're forgetting that I've always had an unusual ability of consuming vast quantities of food without having that consumption affect my figure." She smiled. "My mother was always concerned that I would one day lose that ability and thus my slenderness, but that's yet to happen so I'm perfectly willing to enjoy food to its fullest, at least until the day comes when I begin to grow overly plump. Although, because I have experienced times when food has not been available as often as I'd like, I'm not certain plumpness will be a good enough incentive to encourage me to abandon my love of a great dish."

Gilbert leaned back in his chair. "When were you deprived of food?"

Wiping her lips with a linen napkin, Temperance shrugged. "That's of little consequence right now, Gilbert, especially when we have more delicious topics to delve into."

"Do not say you're still hungry and would

like me to fetch you more pastries."

"I'm saving room for the dinner you're certain to invite me to join you in later, so no, I'm not trying to angle for additional pastries. The deliciousness I'm referring to has to do with a matter of intrigue I've been involved in — one that centered around an abduction, although not Clementine's, a stint in a coffin, and two peculiar members of the criminal class who go by the names of Mercy and Eugene."

With his lips curving over that outlandish, obviously overdramatic, statement, Gilbert settled back in the chair. Popping one of the few pieces of pastry left into his mouth, he considered Temperance as he savored his treat. Swallowing, and then taking a sip of the milk she'd insisted he purchase along with the pastries, he shook his head. "I always wondered what would come of your parents encouraging that vivid imagination of yours, but a stint in a coffin?"

"It was apparently the only solution Eugene could come up with after he doused me too liberally with a sleeping potion and I became senseless for hours."

Something uncomfortable settled in the pit of Gilbert's stomach. "Someone doused you with a sleeping potion?"

Temperance nodded. "I'd started putting

up a fuss, you see, after I was snatched straight off the sidewalk as I was making my way to Miss Snook's School for the Education of the Feminine Mind."

"Why would you have been going to a school that I've heard caters to working women?"

"I think you're allowing yourself to become distracted with mundane details, Gilbert. In case you didn't hear me, I just told you I was abducted and drugged. Nevertheless, because I know it's difficult for you to move forward in conversation when something had captured your interest, I teach classes in painting, sculpture, and music at Miss Snook's school."

"Since when?"

"Since Wayne Flowerdew decided I'd overstayed my welcome at his house and encouraged me to leave that house the day after Permilia Griswold and Asher Rutherford's engagement celebration back in June."

"While I'm sure I have no idea how you decided Wayne Flowerdew, a gentleman I've found to be quite pleasant, wanted you out of his house, allow us to first address the idea of you seeking out employment. Why would you have done that?"

Temperance's shoulders sagged just the

tiniest bit. "How is it possible you haven't heard about the abysmal state of my finances?"

"Your finances are in an abysmal state?"

"I'm poor as a church mouse."

"Since when?"

"Since the family fortune was lost due to a bad investment, a sad state I learned about not long after hearing that my parents were dead."

He narrowed his eyes. "And why didn't you notify me about your lack of finances the second you learned such distressing news?"

Temperance shrugged. "Considering you and I had not been in close contact with each other while I was on my grand tour, I had no idea where I'd find you. The last letter I'd received from you was months before my parents died, and at that time you'd been traveling through India, pursuing new business opportunities."

"You could have sent word to my mother."

"I do not have your mother's current address, nor have I heard from her since before my parents died. Besides, my being rendered penniless is hardly the type of news one wants to impart in a letter."

Gilbert frowned. "My parents and I were under the impression you'd elected to remain in Europe after your parents died. Although I did conclude you'd apparently grown weary of Europe, which I assumed was the reason behind you returning to New York and taking up residence with your cousins."

"If I'd have known what was waiting for me back in the states, I may very well have stayed in Europe. But after I traveled from Paris to New York, which is where I learned I'd been rendered a pauper, I didn't have the funds available to return."

"You could have mentioned your unfortunate change in financial circumstance when we finally reunited this past June."

Temperance waved that aside. "An engagement celebration was hardly the place to burden you with the woes of my life."

"I've always thought of you as the little sister I never had, albeit a frequently absent sister. As such, I also expected we'd share the burdens of our lives with each other."

"I didn't want you to pity me."

Gilbert reached over the table and took hold of Temperance's hand. "You always were incredibly proud, so I can't say I'm surprised by your reasoning. May I dare hope you found life with your Flowerdew relatives somewhat pleasant?"

"You obviously don't have the true measure of my Flowerdew relatives because pleasant isn't a word I'd ever associate with them."

Gilbert rubbed his finger over the top of her hand. "Wayne Flowerdew lent me the impression he's very fond of you. He made a point of proclaiming how much he missed you in Newport this summer season after he and his family repaired there."

"I was not invited to travel to Newport with them, but was, instead, told to find another place to live while they were gone for the summer."

"Surely you're mistaken about that."

Temperance withdrew her hand from his and looked a touch grumpy. "I'm not mistaken, and truth be told, it's entirely *your* fault I was told to depart from the Flowerdew house with so little notice in the first place."

"My fault?"

"Indeed."

Chapter Four

"I don't believe the word *indeed* sufficiently explains how I'm at fault for your getting cast out of the Flowerdew residence," Gilbert said, leaning back in his chair.

The edges of Temperance's lips curved. "You might have a point, but further explanation will need to wait until we're back on our way to the Palmer House. We have an abduction to figure out, and now that I'm sufficiently fed, I can lend my full attention to that disturbing situation."

"I'm reluctant to admit this, but I almost completely forgot about the abduction, ransom, and why I'm in Chicago in the first place," Gilbert said, rising from his chair to move next to Temperance. After helping her to her feet, he bent over, slung the strap to his satchel over his shoulder, picked up his leather traveling bag, straightened, and grinned. "I've also apparently forgotten that you and I tend to get distracted quite easily from matters once we get sidetracked by other riveting subjects, such as lost fortunes and evictions from residences that I'm evidently to blame for."

Heading for the door, Temperance took Gilbert's offered arm and moved through the bakery, stepping outside and onto the sidewalk. Turning in the direction of the Palmer House, she glanced to Gilbert and found him watching her expectantly.

"You really don't have the least little idea of why you're responsible for my being tossed out of the Flowerdew home, do you?" she asked.

"Will you get annoyed with me again if I admit I've been wondering whether you were asked to leave because of your questionable temperament?"

"I've never had a questionable temperament, although I will own up to the idea I was coddled and cossetted before my parents died."

"Spoiled as well."

She refused a smile. "Well, quite, but after I lost my parents, I adopted a more reserved nature, one that served me admirably as I took on the role of unwanted poor relation."

"As I mentioned before, Wayne Flowerdew never lent me the impression he was anything other than fond of you."

"Because it would not serve his agenda if he allowed you to believe anything other than that."

"His agenda?"

Temperance stopped walking. "Do not tell me that you have yet to discern that Wayne desires for you to become his son-in-law, while Clementine is determined to become Mrs. Gilbert Cavendish."

"Given that my mother drilled caution in me about young ladies and their schemes, as well as their matchmaking relatives from the time I could barely walk, of course I know Wayne, along with Clementine, are more than willing to have me set a matrimonial eye Clementine's way."

Temperance sighed. "Since you accepted Wayne's invitation to spend time with them at their rented cottage in Newport, should I assume that you're actually thinking about Clementine in a somewhat permanent and romantic way?"

"Perhaps I should have stuffed you with more pastries since you're still not thinking clearly."

Temperance considered that for all of a second. "If you're not interested in forming a romantic alliance with Clementine, why in the world would you have accepted

Wayne's invitation to join them in Newport?"

"I thought you'd be there. We'd barely had any time at all at Asher and Permilia's ball to catch up with each other. Because of that, when Wayne extended me an invitation to join him in Newport, I decided that would provide me with a most relaxing atmosphere to hear all about the adventures you enjoyed during the years we'd been apart." He shook his head. "I was most disappointed after I arrived at Wayne's cottage to learn that you'd decided to summer in Florida. I was also completely taken aback to discover you'd made that decision because of a certain young gentleman Wayne said had captured your heart — a gentleman you neglected to mention to me when we were first reunited."

Temperance felt her mouth drop open. "You were *not* told that."

Gilbert quirked a brow. "Should I assume there's no young gentleman you've set your sights on down in Florida?"

"Since I'm hardly young, being almost twenty-five, I doubt I'd set my sights on a young gentleman in the first place. But because I've been a little occupied these past few years with attending to Clementine's every demand, I haven't exactly had time to *get* a gentleman in my sights, let alone pursue one."

"Well, good," Gilbert surprised her by saying.

"How is it good that I've not had time to form an alliance with a gentleman?"

"I always assumed I would be part of the process of you selecting a beau. Frankly, I was a little disappointed when Wayne mentioned this apparently imaginary gentleman because I hadn't been given the opportunity to share my opinion of the man with you, or . . . hire a team of Pinkerton detectives to investigate him."

"When and if I *do* meet an interesting gentleman, you will not hire the Pinkertons to investigate him. However, the very idea Wayne went to such lengths to lie to you about where I was this summer and what I was doing explains exactly why I was told to remove myself from their house."

"I might need a little more to go on than that."

"Clementine and Wayne evidently concluded I was going to stand in the way of what they wanted — that being you."

"I made it more than clear, especially to Wayne, that I was not in the market for a wife, even though, being the gracious gentleman my mother raised me to be, I did point out how delightful I found Clementine, even if she wasn't for me." He started walking again. "In fact, when I stopped by the Flowerdew residence just a few days ago, looking to see if you'd returned from Florida, I made it a point to reiterate my thoughts about marriage after Wayne kept pointing out all of Clementine's many attributes, many of which I'm certain are somewhat debatable." He smiled. "He was so determined about the matter that I fear I may have brought out the largest weapon I have at my disposal."

Temperance returned the smile. "You brought out your mother."

"Guilty as charged. But after I explained to Wayne that my mother is vastly opposed to me forming an alliance with a member of society, and Clementine is certainly a member of that illustrious club, he seemed to reconcile himself to the idea that I was not going to be joining his family. We spent the rest of our time discussing my business ventures and what plans my stepfather and I have for growing our exportation prospects."

"And was Wayne impressed by your plans?"

"I'm not sure he was impressed with my plans, but he did seem to be rather enthusiastic about the type of growth I expect the business to obtain over the next few years. He peppered me with a variety of questions pertaining to that growth and was very complimentary regarding what he claimed to be my impressive business acumen."

Temperance stopped in her tracks again as an unpleasant thought sprang to mind. "Would you say he was overly complimentary about the success of your business?"

"He may have been a touch more enthusiastic about my business than I was expecting him to be, especially since it's a rare day indeed when people hang on my every word when I'm discussing exports and imports." Gilbert's smile turned rueful. "I'm sure you must recall how I can occasionally wax on and on about export details that tend to have most people turning a bit glazed in the eyes."

"I well recall that habit of yours and am sure I've sported that glazed look a time or two when you've gotten a tad carried away. But hearing you apparently did not bore my cousin to tears is disturbing to say the least and explains much." With that, she tugged Gilbert back into motion again, moving down the sidewalk at a rapid clip as she tried to sort through thoughts that were only now beginning to make sense.

"You know it's very annoying when you don't bother to expand on those random thoughts that seem to strike from out of nowhere, don't you?" Gilbert asked, pulling her directly out of those random thoughts.

Temperance gave his arm a quick pat as they came to a stop in the front of the Palmer House. "I'm sure it is annoying, but I don't want to say more until I'm perfectly certain I'm on the right track. For now, what I need you to do is go to the front desk, tell them you're Mr. Randolph Smith, and that you and your wife have a reservation."

"Why would I do that?"

"Because before my two abductors abandoned me after they discovered they'd snatched up the wrong person — although they should have mentioned that they'd snatched up the wrong Flowerdew, which would have clarified the situation for me — they told me that there's a room reserved for them at the Palmer House under Mr. Randolph Smith and wife. We need to see if there really is such a reservation, and if there is, we're going to see if any clues can be found in that room."

"I was supposed to be left instructions at the front desk," Gilbert argued.

"Well, yes, but since I'm going to assume

those instructions were meant to be left by Eugene and Mercy, my erstwhile kidnappers, I don't think we can expect any further instructions to show up since those two people are more than likely on their way back to New York by now."

"They simply left you in Chicago?"

"They abandoned me at the train station without a single cent to see me through my stay in Chicago or to see me back to New York."

Gilbert pulled her toward the doorway, thanked the doorman who was already holding the door to Palmer House open for them, and ushered Temperance inside. Glancing around, she smoothed a hand over hair she knew was looking anything other than tidy, then nodded toward the front desk.

"I'll wait for you behind that fern," she told Gilbert with a wave of her hand toward the fern in question. "Remember, you're Mr. Randolph Smith, here with your wife."

"Should I expect to have to pay for the room reserved for this Mr. Smith and wife?"

"I have no idea. Eugene and Mercy were rather reluctant to divulge much to me, especially after they realized they'd abducted the wrong woman."

Gilbert raked a hand through his hair.

"Seems a bit odd that kidnappers would coddle their victim with a luxurious stay in a hotel that caters to a wealthy clientele."

"I'm afraid, if I'm surmising correctly, matters are about to get even odder."

"But you're not going to explain that curious remark yet, are you?"

"Not until I have further proof."

"Delighted to learn your propensity for being exasperating hasn't changed much since we've been apart," Gilbert muttered before he turned and began moving through the crowd. His easy gait and confident manner caught the attention of more than one young lady, and as Gilbert inclined his head time after time to the ladies now fluttering lashes rather flirtatiously his way, Temperance smiled.

There was something about Gilbert that drew feminine attention. It wasn't that he was always the handsomest gentleman in the room, but he possessed an air of confidence that always drew the eye.

His ordinary brown hair was kept short, a length he'd always preferred because he said it was easily managed, while his clothing was always made from fine fabrics, but cut in a style that lent credence to the idea he was a serious man of business.

He never wore fancy cufflinks or diamond

stickpins, and his gold pocket watch, while of the finest quality, was not engraved with an elaborate design but carried for the sheer practicality of telling time.

When three ladies strolling around the lobby stopped in their tracks and glanced Temperance's way, looking her over quite as if she were a bug they were horrified to view, Temperance recalled that she was not dressed appropriately for her current surroundings, nor was the dirt staining her clothing what one expected to see at the Palmer House. Waiting until the ladies released sniffs and marched away, she slipped behind the fronds of the fern, peeking through to observe her surroundings when her curiosity got the better of her.

She'd never been to the Palmer House, although she understood it was said to be one of the most extravagant hotels in the country.

Being six stories tall and filled with art from Paris, chandeliers with garnets embedded in the crystal hanging from the high ceiling, and expensive furnishings were scattered about the first-floor grand lobby, Palmer House was an impressive sight indeed. Craning her neck, she let her gaze linger on a ceiling fresco, the many different scenes pictured there leaving her with a distinct longing to abandon her hiding spot, move to the very middle of the lobby, then stretch out on the floor and spend the next few days considering every inch of painted space.

Smiling at the thought that guests at the Palmer House would not appreciate stepping around a lady lying about on the floor, Temperance forced her attention from the ceiling and took in the rest of the room. Large pillars rose from the ground to meet the ceiling that was at least two stories tall. Mingling around the pillars were well-heeled guests, all of whom were there to see or be seen by the crème de la crème of Chicago society.

"You were right. There *was* a reservation for Mr. Randolph Smith and wife."

Temperance jumped and raised a hand to her throat. "You just scared me half to death."

To her annoyance, Gilbert grinned. "I'd quite forgotten how you tend to get swept up in your surroundings and become oblivious to everything else around you. What has captured your fancy this time?"

Pushing aside her annoyance because it was decidedly comforting to be around a person who knew her so well, Temperance nodded toward the ceiling. "I'd heard that

Bertha Palmer, Potter Palmer's wife, was an admirer of art, and she spared no expense with decorating her husband's hotel. If we have time later, after we've seen to collecting any clues we can about my abduction, I would like to take a few hours to roam around this place. Rumor has it Bertha acquired a few works from Claude Monet, and I do enjoy that gentleman's work."

"I'm sure a tour can be arranged, although it might have to wait until we find you some different clothing to wear. I hate to point out the obvious, Temperance, but you're sticking out like a sore thumb." He frowned. "Now that I think about it, we might draw undue notice if we're seen moseying up to Mr. Smith's reserved room together. Would you mind staying put while I give the room a gander? I'll be back with a report post-haste."

Temperance took a step away from the fern, noticing as she did so that they were already beginning to draw attention from another gathering of young ladies, all of whom were looking her up and down, evidently finding her lacking given the less-than-pleasant expressions on their faces.

"That might be for the . . ."

"Ah, Mr. Smith. I see you located your darling Mrs. Smith."

Refusing a grimace when the gazes the ladies were still directing her way seemed to sharpen, Temperance forced a smile and turned to a bellhop who'd materialized behind Gilbert. That man was already in possession of Gilbert's traveling bag, although Gilbert still had his satchel slung over his shoulder. Inclining her head to the bellhop, she pretended not to notice that he was considering her with what appeared to be horror in his eyes, although a second later, he blinked, and the horror disappeared.

"If you'd be so kind to follow me, Mrs. Smith, I'll see you and your husband to your suite. I do believe you'll be very pleased with the rooms that have been reserved for you."

Seeing absolutely no escape, and knowing she would draw more attention to them if she didn't fall into step behind the bellhop, Temperance took the arm Gilbert thrust her way. With her head lowered, she moved across the lobby, stepped into the elevator, then spent the ride perusing the floor, trying to draw as little attention as possible from the bellhop and elevator operator. With a ding, the elevator stopped at the third floor, the door opened, and after stepping out into a long hallway, Temperance followed the bellhop, nodding her head every now and again as he dispelled little tidbits about the hotel.

"After the first Palmer Hotel burned to the ground mere days after it opened, Mr. Potter Palmer built this practically fireproof hotel in its place, opening only one year later." The bellhop stopped in front of a door with gilded molding and smiled. "Your suite," he said, brandishing a key with a flourish. He opened the door and gestured them inside. "The concierge wanted me to assure you that all of your requests have been seen to, Mr. Smith, and we wish you and your lovely wife a wonderful stay with us at Palmer House."

As Gilbert discreetly passed the bellhop a few bills, Temperance moved further into the suite, not turning around until she heard the distinct click of the door shutting behind the bellhop.

"That was an unforeseen twist of events," Gilbert said, repocketing his wallet before he let out a whistle and began walking around what was clearly the sitting room of a very well-appointed suite. He nodded to a crystal vase filled with fresh flowers. "It's interesting, isn't it, how someone seems to have spared no expense in this abduction fiasco?"

Temperance nodded as she moved across the room, stepping through a door that led to what was clearly a bedchamber, complete with a canopy bed draped in ivory fabric. "What a magnificent bedchamber."

"I'll take your word for that because it would hardly be appropriate for me to join you in there."

Shaking her head at that bit of nonsense because she and Gilbert had been in many a hotel suite together throughout their privileged youth, Temperance took a moment to survey the room. Her attention immediately settled on a freestanding wardrobe, one that had a large red bow tied around the handles. Knowing she was probably not going to like what was inside of that wardrobe, but knowing there was only one way to prove the ridiculous conclusion she was beginning to draw regarding the entire abduction debacle, she stalked across the room and untied the bow.

Giving the handle a yank, she was not taken by much surprise when she discovered a beautiful yellow gown made up of luscious silk, which just happened to be the signature color of her more than troublesome cousin, Clementine.

Chapter Five

Everything considered, Gilbert thought Temperance had handled the almost undeniable proof that her cousin was responsible for the unfortunate events Temperance had experienced after being snatched from the streets of New York City rather well.

Admittedly, he'd had to wrestle the yellow gown away from her because she'd seemed intent on ripping it to shreds. But after he'd made the logical point about her not having anything that wasn't covered in dirt to wear, and the yellow gown would do in a pinch until he could take her shopping, she'd abandoned her attack on it. She'd then requested he make himself scarce for an hour or two so she could set herself to rights and collect her temper in the process.

He'd not been surprised by the request. Temperance had always been one who appreciated solitude, using it to study the world around her and gather thoughts she'd once told him always seemed prone to scattering every which way. Knowing time by herself was exactly what she needed, he'd taken a few moments to switch his travel-worn jacket for a fresh one and change his tie, then left their suite of rooms, telling her he was off to find a barber since he'd been without a shave for almost two days.

Now, sitting in a most comfortable barber chair with a warm, moist towel wrapped snuggly around his face, he turned his thoughts to comprising a plan that would see them back to New York as quickly as possible. Once there, he needed to figure out how best to go about dealing with Wayne, Fanny, and Clementine Flowerdew once and for all.

That Temperance's relatives would go to such extremes to see his name attached to Clementine's should have been shocking. But because he was a gentleman with a vast fortune at his disposal, he was somewhat accustomed to ladies going to unusual lengths to attract his notice. Still, none of those ladies had gone so far as to create an elaborate abduction ruse while they were in pursuit of attracting that notice.

Calling himself all sorts of a fool for not realizing the moment Fanny Flowerdew threw herself on his Aubusson rug that he was being cast into a play he did not want to be cast in, Gilbert reached up to adjust the towel on his face, stilling when the gentleman sitting in the chair next to him began to speak.

"I must say, Mr. Potter Palmer certainly knew what he was about when he included this barbershop in his hotel," the man began. "It allows a gentleman some male time, which I most heartily appreciate, what with all the ladies I've been surrounded with ever since we arrived in this windy city from New York."

"You here for the Chicago Literary Club weekend?" the barber who'd only recently been shaving Gilbert asked.

"My wife and her friends said they couldn't miss it." The man heaved a sigh. "Being fond of the latest novels of the day, my darling Myrtle was adamant about attending an event where the most intriguing novels are slated to be discussed for hours on end. Add in the troubling notion she's also convinced it's necessary to become involved in clubs outside of New York, there was no dissuading her from traveling to Chicago — an up-and-coming city, or so I've been told, that is already enjoying a boon to its social standing in the country."

He heaved another sigh, this one more

dramatic than the last. “When word got out that Bertha Palmer was hosting the Chicago Literary Club at this very hotel, there was practically a stampede at the train station as my wife, along with all her friends, began scooping up tickets to assure they wouldn’t miss a prime opportunity to mingle with their societal Chicago sisters.”

“At least the literary weekend provides you with an excuse to travel,” the barber said.

“I’d be content to remain back in New York at my club, thank you very much, especially because my attendance is being demanded later this evening at what sounds to be a most tiresome dinner sponsored by the literary club. There’s nothing worse for a man’s digestion than having to plod through a meal while snippets of literature are read aloud as the courses are being served.”

The barber chuckled. “I know it’s small consolation, but because that dinner is to be held here at the hotel, you’ll not find a better meal served. Mrs. Palmer Potter is very particular about keeping up appearances, so you should at least enjoy your meal, if not the literature being shared.”

Making a note to himself to avoid the Chicago Literary Club dinner because it seemed as if it was to be attended by numerous New Yorkers, Gilbert shifted in his chair, drawing the immediate attention of his barber.

"I say, Mr. Smith. Are you ready to get on your way?"

Before Gilbert could respond, his rapidly cooling towel was taken away, a splash of lime water was patted over his face, and with a beaming smile, the barber gestured to the mirror. "Is the cut and shave satisfactory, Mr. Smith?"

Glancing in the mirror, Gilbert nodded. His brown hair, which possessed a bit of curl, was now combed perfectly into place, and his face sported not a single whisker. Turning his head to see if his sideburns were evenly matched, he stilled when he found the man sitting beside him frowning back at him.

Regrettably, the man turned out to be none other than Mr. Frank Miller, a gentleman Gilbert knew because he'd once exported Mr. Miller's cotton wares to his contacts in England.

"Mr. Miller," Gilbert began, knowing there was no help for it but to greet the man. "Here for the literary weekend, are you?"

"I am, but I think a more interesting question is why you're in Chicago and why you're going by the name of Mr. . . . *Smith.*"

Having no idea how to respond since he certainly wasn't willing to disclose the true reason behind him being in Chicago, which would certainly draw far too much notice because it wasn't every day a woman was abducted, Gilbert pushed himself up from the barber chair. Inclining his head toward Mr. Miller, he summoned up a smile.

"It might be best if you and I simply pretend you're unaware of my presence here in Chicago and leave it at that."

Mr. Miller inclined his head in return. "Understood, although I should point out that it might have been more prudent for discretion purposes if you'd chosen a name other than Smith." He shook his head. "That's a name rife with implications, if you get my meaning."

Pretending he didn't see the wink Mr. Miller sent him, or the telling look that accompanied that wink, Gilbert kept his smile firmly in place. "Do enjoy your dinner this evening, Mr. Miller."

"Enjoy your evening as well." Mr. Miller winked again. "Although allow me to bestow a word of caution — be careful wandering around the hotel. Many of the guests are from New York, and the ladies of New York are *well* aware you're not Mr. Smith. Being ladies, I'm sure they'd be all aflutter with the idea you're here under an assumed name, and . . . they may not understand your need for discretion the way I understand it."

Feeling as if he'd just made a complete muddle out of everything, especially after Mr. Miller sent him a third wink, Gilbert thanked the barber, who was watching him curiously, then strode from the barbershop. He barely glanced at the barbershop floor he'd been told to notice from a member of the hotel staff — a floor that Palmer Potter had embellished with genuine silver dollars cemented into the stone.

After he reached the lobby, he glanced over the crowd. When he didn't recognize a single face, he strode for the front desk, knowing that after his encounter with Mr. Miller he needed to get Temperance out of Chicago with all due haste.

Abandoning his role as Mr. Smith since he'd never been a gentleman comfortable with subterfuge and wasn't willing to continue with a farce not of his making, Gilbert introduced himself to a young man working the front desk and laid out exactly what he needed. Ten minutes later, and impressed by the young man who'd known exactly how to go about scheduling a private Pullman car if one had the funds to schedule such a luxury, Gilbert was feeling more at ease, knowing he and Temperance would be on their way back to New York later that night.

"Is there anything else I can do for you, Mr. Cavendish?" the young man asked.

"If that's Mr. Gilbert Cavendish," another man behind the front desk said, "we have a telegram waiting for him."

Gilbert nodded to the man who'd mentioned the telegram. "I am Gilbert Cavendish."

Nodding in return, the man moved to a large wall filled with cubbyholes, plucked out a telegram, then walked back to Gilbert, handing him the missive. "Was there anything else you needed, Mr. Cavendish?"

Gilbert leaned over the desk and lowered his voice. "While I know this may sound slightly peculiar, you wouldn't happen to have a telegram waiting for a Mr. Randolph Smith to collect, would you?"

Not so much as blinking, the man returned to the cubbyholes, looked them over, then shook his head. "Nothing for Mr. Randolph Smith, although . . ." He plucked out an envelope, then another, and another. Turning, he caught Gilbert's eye. "We do have messages for a Mr. Herbert Smith, Mr. Charles Smith, and Mr. Thomas Smith."

Swallowing a laugh over the fact Mr. Miller had been quite right about Mr. Smith not being a wise choice to use when a person was intent on discretion, he thanked the man for his assistance, thanked the other man for arranging to have a Pullman car attached to one of the trains returning to New York later that night, then tucked his telegram into his jacket pocket. Walking across the lobby, he kept his head down, breathing a sigh of relief when he reached the elevator without drawing anyone's notice.

After telling the elevator operator he needed to go to the third floor, he stepped to the back, dropping his head again when he was suddenly joined by a group of ladies. Pressing himself against the wall, he soon found himself privy to their conversation, one that centered around a literary lecture they'd recently attended.

"I must say I've never looked at Charlotte Brontë's novel in quite that way," a lady said. "It now seems to me as if Miss Brontë was a troubled woman, possessed of a questionable . . ." The lady stopped speaking, then cleared her throat, that clearing apparently responsible for having all the feet in the elevator turning his way. Gilbert then felt what he imagined was every eye in the elevator settle on him as he tried to press himself even further against the wall, keeping his head lowered.

A second later, whispers began circling around the elevator, and he swore he heard a whispered "Mr. Cavendish."

It was the longest elevator ride up three floors he'd ever taken, especially since he was not a gentleman prone to neglecting his manners. However, in this particular instance, he could not acknowledge all the ladies, nor could he admit he was Mr. Cavendish because that would certainly stir up the hornet's nest, and he'd had quite enough drama for the day.

Finally, and with a loud ding, the elevator shuddered to a halt, the operator called out "Third floor," and keeping his head bent, Gilbert made his excuses as he stepped around the ladies, forcing himself to walk ever so slowly down the hallway instead of breaking into a run.

He knew full well, what with all the giggles and whispers that followed him, that the ladies were now leaning out of the elevator watching him walk away. Reaching the suite that had been reserved for Mr. Randolph Smith and wife, he shoved the key into the lock, twisted the knob, and practically fell into the room, shutting the door swiftly behind him when another bout of giggles met his ears. Turning, he took a step into the room then stopped when he noticed Temperance.

"Ah, Gilbert, there you are. I was becoming worried."

For the briefest of seconds, Gilbert simply considered Temperance, who was stretched out on her back on the rug in the middle of the sitting room, hands folded behind her head. His gaze darted to the ceiling and his lips began to curve. Tiny prisms of light were dancing over the ceiling, the dancing a direct result of the intricate chandelier hanging in the middle of the room swaying slightly due to the breeze that was wafting in through an open window.

Temperance had always been a lady prone to fresh air, hated to be inside for any length of time, and the notion she'd been captivated by the sight of the light display, a display most people, including himself, wouldn't have noticed, left him grinning. That grin, however, began fading when he returned his attention to where she was still lying on the floor, the sight of her leaving him feeling curiously disconcerted.

The skirt of the yellow gown she was

convinced had been left for Clementine was spread artfully around her, the hem of that skirt not quite long enough to cover feet that were encased in white stockings and crossed at ankles that were surprisingly well-turned out. Two elbow length gloves were spread out beside her, as if waiting for her to remember to slide them up her arms, and when she suddenly propped herself up on her elbows, he noticed she'd arranged her hair in a most delightful manner. Her dark tresses were swept to the top of her head, and she'd somehow managed to get curls to cascade from that knot, some of which were caressing cheeks that were slightly pink, probably the results of the bath she'd told him she was determined to take.

Shaking all thoughts of baths firmly aside because that train of thought was leaving him feeling more than unsettled, Gilbert realized that while he'd been gawking, Temperance was rising to her feet and looking at him with a great deal of concern in her eyes.

"Please do not tell me I truly had a reason to be worried and that another disaster has happened," she said, gliding across the room to stand directly beside him.

Unfortunately, when she reached out and placed her hand on his arm, a shock of something unexpected traveled through him, and because he was so taken aback by that shock, he found himself incapable of forming so much as a single coherent word.

He'd never, not once in his twenty-seven years on this earth, felt a shock when a lady touched him, and that it came at the hand of one of his very oldest friends, well . . . it was cause for concern.

"Perhaps you should sit down," Temperance said. "You look as if you're about to get sick."

Because he still seemed incapable of speech, and because Temperance was now watching him rather warily, as if she truly did expect him to toss up his accounts right there in the middle of the sitting room, Gilbert walked over on somewhat unsteady legs, he was sad to say, to the nearest chair and took a seat.

Temperance, instead of sitting down in the chair placed next to his, plopped straight back down on the floor directly beside his unsteady legs, the fabric of her skirt billowing out around her.

The sight of her sitting on the floor, a place she'd always favored over chairs and a sight he found comfortingly familiar, had breath returning to his lungs and words, thankfully, coming out of his mouth.

"I see some habits never die," he said.

She ran a hand over the rug. "I always feel more settled when I'm on the ground for some unknown reason, something you should probably try at some point in your life, such as now, since, clearly, you're unsettled about something."

When she set him an expectant look, and knowing exactly what she meant without her having to say a single thing, Gilbert pushed out of the chair and slid to the ground, stretching his long legs out in front of him as Temperance beamed a smile of approval.

"There, isn't that better?"

"Will you become annoyed with me if I say no?" he countered.

"If you say no, I'll conclude that you're simply being ornery because you've never enjoyed admitting I'm right. Nevertheless, that has nothing to do with why you look as if you've just escaped from an encounter with unsavory sorts."

"I didn't encounter unsavory sorts, merely ladies of the far-too-inquisitive type in the elevator." Gilbert shook his head. "I'm afraid those ladies are gathered at the hotel for a literary weekend, many of whom traveled here from New York, at least according to a gentleman I spoke with while I was getting a shave."

To Gilbert's concern, Temperance's eyes began sparkling. "There's a literary gathering here this weekend?"

"Yes, but no, you can't attend it."

Her eyes went from sparkling to stormy in a split second. "That's unfortunate because I do enjoy gathering with literary sorts, but . . ." She brightened. "I suppose you're right, so I'll have to settle for you telling me all the particulars of this gathering — is it a frequent event, or is it one of those gatherings that only happens every year or so, and are there specific genres that are discussed, or is it more on the lines of everyone discussing the most popular works of the day?"

"You do recall that I've never been a gentleman prone to being overly inquisitive when it comes to idle chitchat, don't you?"

Her face fell. "You didn't find out all the pertinent details of this literary event even though *you* must recall that I'm a lady possessed of a most curious mind?"

"I'm afraid I was much too busy fending off the curious questions that were flung my way by Mr. Frank Miller, a member of New York society who, unfortunately, recognized me. Add in the pesky notion that he made certain to tell me that the hotel is filled to the brim with New York society members, and I'm afraid I never once considered that you'd become put out with me for not discovering more about a literary gathering. I was much more occupied with thoughts of what would happen if any of those society members became aware of the fact you and I are alone together in this hotel, which will send tongues to wagging for certain."

Temperance lifted her chin. "There is absolutely nothing for those tongues to wag about. It's not as if we planned to meet up here together or planned to share space in this suite of rooms."

"True, but we're here, and alone together, and . . . that man who recognized me as I was getting a shave, Mr. Miller, heard the barber address me as Mr. Smith, which then caused Mr. Miller to, well, forgive me, come to the troubling conclusion I might be using an alias because I'm here with a . . ." Gilbert stopped talking, trying to decide how to continue without offending a dear friend who was also, unquestionably, a lady.

To his surprise, Temperance leaned forward, placing a hand on his arm as her eyes crinkled at the corners. "Oh dear, you have had a time of it, haven't you?"

"I don't believe you're grasping the gravity of this situation. Mr. Miller has concluded I'm here with a, well . . . no need to get into that. But if you're recognized and seen with me, your reputation will be destroyed forever."

"We'll simply have to make certain we're not seen together. And, as there's no reason for you to continue as Mr. Smith, you shouldn't be put into such an uncomfortable situation again while we're in Chicago."

"Would you be surprised to learn I already abandoned the alias of Mr. Smith when I had a man at the front desk make arrangements to secure us a Pullman car? I told him to reserve the car for Mr. Cavendish. I have to imagine that might have been a bit perplexing if someone behind the desk thought I was Mr. Smith."

Temperance sent him a commiserating smile. "You were never good with chaos, Gilbert, or abandoning a well-kept schedule, two circumstances you've been forced to deal with today. It's little wonder you're agitated."

"I'm not agitated."

"Of course you are, but getting back to this Pullman car, when do we leave?"

"In a few hours, although I will need to check back with the man at the front desk to make certain everything went as planned. I'm afraid I became somewhat distracted with finalizing our travel plans because I learned a telegram had been delivered for me — the real me, as in Mr. Cavendish, not Mr. Smith."

"Who sent you a telegram?"

Realizing he'd completely forgotten the telegram up until now because of the unusual shock he'd experienced earlier, but unwilling to admit that to the *source* of the shock, Gilbert stuck his hand into his pocket and pulled out the telegram. It took him all of twenty seconds to scan, and then another twenty seconds to ascertain he'd read it correctly. Lifting his head, he frowned.

"It's from Fanny Flowerdew, advising me that Clementine has been recovered."

Temperance grinned. "Has she now?"

"Indeed, although why you find that amusing is beyond me."

"Because I can't help but wonder how long Clementine was forced to stroll along a sidewalk, waiting to be abducted. What did she do after she realized their plans had gone awry?"

"I'm sure I have no idea. I can't even begin to wonder why they came up with such an outlandish plan in the first place." Gilbert tilted his head. "Are you so very certain your cousins were responsible for setting up this abduction scenario? Could there be the slightest chance Clementine really was supposed to be abducted by some dastardly criminal, but you were simply taken by mistake?"

Temperance pushed herself up from the floor, moved across the room, picked up something from the seat of a chair, then returned to join him again. Holding up what appeared to be strips of yellow velvet, she rolled her eyes.

"I found *these* tucked into the wardrobe, and if I'm not mistaken, dear Clementine was supposed to be tied to a chair, where you would then discover her. You'd then be unable to help yourself from appreciating the charming picture she presented, what with her being in a yellow dress with matching bindings no less. That appreciation, I'm sure my relatives were hoping, would then have you declaring your undying devotion to Clementine."

"Surely not."

"I'm afraid that's probably exactly what they were hoping would happen." Temperance pressed her lips together for the briefest of seconds. "Unfortunately, they hired the ineptest criminals I've ever encountered. Because of that mistake, the two of us have now become embroiled in a very tangled web of nonsense, the most nonsensical of that being the idea I'm apparently being cast in this farce as some type of —" she leaned toward him and lowered her voice even though it was only the two of them in the room — "fancy piece."

"Now there's a term I never thought to hear slip past your lips. Should I claim shock that you're familiar enough with the term to understand its meaning?"

She waved that away even as she moved to plop down beside him on the floor again. "I'm very well traveled, Gilbert, and I'm almost twenty-five." She caught his eye. "Although I have to admit I never thought I'd be placed in a situation where someone might mistake me for a man's mistress."

"Which is exactly why we have to leave Chicago as discreetly as possible to avoid any situations where our reputations might be put into jeopardy."

Temperance abandoned her spot on the floor again, holding out her hand after she'd shaken out the folds of her skirt. "You'll hear no arguments from me about that."

Taking her hand, Gilbert rose to his feet. "We should leave this suite separately."

"A prudent choice," she said. "And since I do know we'll be on a train for hours on end, I'll leave you to your privacy so you can set yourself to rights, or whatever it is you need to do to prepare for another long journey."

"You'll stay out of trouble?"

"I'll be on my best behavior, even though I would so love to take a little stroll past Marshall Field & Company. I've been told it's quite a delightful shop, almost as lovely as our very own Rutherford & Company."

"Dare I hope you'll refrain from wandering over to Marshall Field & Company while you wait for me, something I know might pose a problem for you since you've never been one to resist the temptation of a delightful shop?"

She gestured to the yellow gown she was wearing and smiled. "I'm hardly dressed for a shopping expedition because this is clearly a dinner gown, not a walking dress, so yes, I'll resist the urge to see the store. You'll also be relieved to learn I have every intention of returning to my favorite fern and lurking behind it until you come fetch me."

Sending him a smile that had his heart, curiously enough, kicking up a beat, Temperance turned on a stockinged foot, slipped on her shoes instead of the yellow satin slippers that had been in the wardrobe with the yellow gown, then sailed from the room, leaving Gilbert behind.

Because he well remembered that Temperance's good intentions could be forgotten the second something captured her fancy, such as a pretty picture, an unusual piece of furniture, or once, a fly that whizzed by her face that she decided she needed to catch, he made short shrift of collecting his belongings and setting himself to rights. Striding through the suite and down the hallway, he checked his pocket watch, hoping the scant amount of time they had remaining in Chicago before their train departed would not see them involved in any further shenanigans.

Chapter Six

Deciding to take the stairs because she would soon be sitting on a train for far too many hours, Temperance hurried down the three flights, reaching the main floor a few minutes later. Moving to the door she hoped led to the main lobby, she eased it open and stuck her head through it, drawing her head back almost immediately when she noticed a group of young ladies gathered a few feet away.

The very last thing she wanted to do was draw attention her way as she slunk out of the stairwell, or worse yet, have any of the ladies from New York recognize her, which would assuredly lead to unwanted questions.

It wasn't that she was overly concerned for her own reputation, especially since she no longer traveled in society and had reached an age where the status of spinster was warranted. But . . . Gilbert's reputation was another matter altogether. His generous nature had already been sorely abused by her own relatives, and she would not further abuse that nature by bringing even a whiff of scandal to his name.

How she was going to handle her relatives and the disgraceful behavior they'd displayed, she couldn't say. She was confident, though, that Miss Henrietta Huxley, a delightful and eccentric older lady who'd taken Temperance under her wing, was going to have all sorts of ideas.

Miss Henrietta Huxley was a woman of indeterminate age, although given her white hair and the snippets of history she'd disclosed in conversation, Temperance thought she might be approaching seventy. Miss Henrietta, along with her slightly younger sister, Miss Mabel, were known throughout New York as the Spinster Sisters. After they'd failed miserably with making their debuts in their youth, they deliberately stayed clear of high society for decades. But, after becoming acquainted with Temperance's good friend Permilia Griswold, the two sisters had decided to abandon their reclusive ways. They'd recently concluded it was their lot in life to assist ladies in need. Besides donating their mansion on Broadway to Miss Snook to use as her new location for her school that catered to uneducated women living in New York, they'd set their sights on more than a few wallflowers, determined to see them well-settled in life.

Temperance had found herself in the sisters' sights, and if she wasn't much mistaken, Miss Henrietta had probably already sought out the services of the Pinkerton detectives to locate Temperance once it became clear she'd gone missing.

Deciding to ask Gilbert to loan her funds to send Miss Henrietta a telegram, allowing her to know she was still amongst the living, Temperance stuck her head out the door again. After ascertaining that the ladies she'd first spotted had moved on, she scanned the rest of the lobby, breathing a sigh of relief when not a single familiar face could be found. Walking through the door, she moseyed her way as casually as she could across the marble floor. She slipped behind her fern of choice and then began one of her favorite pastimes: watching people as they went about their business.

Having traveled extensively throughout the world before her parents died, Temperance was not surprised in the least by the jewels and fashions she saw paraded before her. She'd always been fascinated by how people strove to impress one another by donning as much wealth as they could possibly manage. Clearly, the Palmer House was an establishment where people went to be seen, and they did not disappoint, especially since they were wearing the latest fashions from Paris, evidently purchased from shopping expeditions that had taken place during the spring.

Furs, diamonds, and expensive silk swirled around the lobby, and Temperance's fingers itched for a pencil and pad of paper to sketch out the fascinating scene unfolding before her. That itch disappeared straightaway, though, when she suddenly spotted a group of society ladies she'd seen often in New York City, all of the ladies members of Mrs. Astor's New York Four Hundred. Shrinking back behind the fern, she held still as a statue, praying the ladies wouldn't move closer, or worse yet, spot the yellow of her gown and decide to investigate why a lady would choose to lurk behind a fern.

"I'm off to return the key to the front desk. I'll be right back."

Swallowing the shriek that had almost burst out of her mouth, Temperance looked up and found Gilbert peering back at her through the fronds. "Really, Gilbert, you should know better than to sneak up on a person when they're trying to remain undetected." She frowned. "But why in the world are you going through the bother of returning the key? You could have simply left it in the room where one of the more than proficient members of the staff would have found it come morning."

"Hotels expect their guests to return the keys, as well as allow them to know they're departing earlier than anticipated. I also tidied the room a bit, and remembered to stuff the dress you wore here into my traveling bag."

"Since I'm convinced that walking dress is beyond saving, you could have left it in the trash where I do remember putting it. As for returning the key, I'm not sure why you'd go through the bother since it wasn't our room and you might draw unwanted attention from guests lingering around the front desk."

Gilbert immediately turned stubborn. "It's expected."

Remembering far too well how Gilbert had always been a man determined to adhere to the rules, Temperance abandoned the argument that was on the tip of her tongue. "Since you'll take to brooding if I dissuade you from returning the key, and I don't care to spend the trip from here to New York with you in such a trying state, by all means, return away."

"I don't have the habit of brooding."

"A topic we'll certainly debate at a more opportune time, this not being that time. If it's escaped your notice, you're complicating our plan of me remaining hidden because I'm sure the guests in the lobby are beginning to notice that you seem to be engaged in a conversation with a plant."

"A most excellent point." Spinning around, Gilbert strode away without another word, leaving Temperance smiling even as she shook her head.

Less than five minutes later, he returned, presenting her with his back as he began mumbling out of what must have been the side of his mouth, that circumstance making it all but impossible to understand what he was trying to say to her.

". . . had to pay for the room . . . unbelievably rude of . . . round the back . . . carriages for rent . . . meet up in . . ."

Without waiting to see if she'd understood the end of his conversation, which might have been instructions of how they were going to proceed, Gilbert sauntered away from her.

Waiting until she couldn't see him, Temperance slipped out from behind the fern and skirted around the lobby, doing her very best to avoid the different groups of ladies mingling about. Relieved when she reached a back door, she sent the doorman a nod of thanks and walked outside, releasing the breath she hadn't realized she'd been holding once she reached the sidewalk. Catching sight of Gilbert standing by a hansom cab, she took two steps in his direction, but found herself unable to take another when someone came up beside her, took hold of her arm, and gave it a good shake.

"What, pray tell, are you doing in Chicago, Temperance, and why were you sneaking around the lobby like a common thief, and . . . why does it appear as if you're off to meet up with that gentleman over there? I distinctly heard that man claim to be a Mr. Smith when he was returning his room key only moments ago, but I now recognize him as being none other than Mr. Gilbert Cavendish."

With apprehension stealing up her spine, Temperance turned and found herself pinned under the glare of Mrs. Boggart Hobbes, Fanny Flowerdew's aunt and well-known society matron of the New York social set.

Two hours later

"We'll have to get married as soon as we

reach New York."

Temperance abandoned the plates she was placing around the blanket she'd decided would work in a pinch to hold the picnic supper they'd purchased before traveling to the train station. Setting her gaze on Gilbert, who was slouched in a chair on the other side of the Pullman car, she felt her lips begin to curve.

That he was agitated, there was no question, especially since his recently well-combed hair was decidedly mussed, and he'd even gone so far as to untie his tie, giving him a somewhat derelict appearance.

"We're not getting married, Gilbert," she said for what felt like the hundredth time in the past ten minutes.

"We were discovered by a New York society matron, at a hotel no less, without benefit of a chaperone for you, and discovered after that society matron overheard me returning a key to a room that had been reserved for Mr. Smith and *wife.*" He began drumming his fingers on the arm of the chair. "We've stepped far beyond the proprieties this time, Temperance. And, given that we're even now chugging our way to New York in a private Pullman car, and again without benefit of a chaperone, well . . . I think that's reason enough for you to realize we need to exchange some vows. We'll also need to exchange those vows as quickly as we can because I'm all but convinced that gossip about our time in Chicago will spread rapidly through New York, as well as to every other large city in the country."

No matter how hard she tried, she couldn't hold back a grin. "I don't believe we're interesting enough to command the attention of the entire country."

"This is not amusing, Temperance. You and I have been well and truly caught in a most outlandish situation, one that demands we do what's expected and get married."

Temperance moved to stand in front of Gilbert. Leaning down, she patted his arm, quite like she used to do when they'd been children and had gotten into one unfortunate scrape after another. "We can't get married, Gilbert. We'd be at sixes and sevens with each other before the last vow was spoken. I am far too carefree for your schedule-loving life, and you're far too structured for mine. Why, I'm sure if we were to marry, you'd soon be a prime candidate for the Long Island Home Hotel for Nervous Invalids. I, on the other hand, would be a prime candidate for the nearest jail since I'm sure I'd be tempted to do some manner of bodily harm to you at some point in time."

"We aren't going to have a choice in the matter, not once word gets out about this adventure we've shared."

"We've shared many an adventure together, Gilbert, none of which ever demanded we speak any vows once we completed them." She smiled. "If memory serves me correctly, we've spent numerous hours in hotel rooms together throughout the years, as well as spent hours together without the benefit of a chaperone."

"We were children when we spent time alone in hotel rooms, and the only reason we weren't chaperoned at all times is because you were always incredibly proficient at losing whatever poor governess your parents hired, of which, if you've forgotten, there were many."

"I did seem to have a knack for becoming parted from my governesses, didn't I?"

"You also had a knack for not adhering to the rules, something that always had me wondering how you managed to get through that finishing school your parents insisted on sending you to without getting expelled."

She turned and moved back to her picnic setting. "I'm perfectly able to abide by all the rules of decorum, and have done so admirably over the years, especially while living with my Flowerdew relatives. But, as I mentioned before, I've decided to reclaim my true self, and that self demands I occasionally abandon some of the more ridiculous etiquette rules. Life is too short to be constantly stifled by expectations set by people who've decided they're superior to the masses, and people who hold fast to that superiority by creating an attitude of snobbery they expect their peers to embrace."

Gilbert nodded to the picnic setting she was creating. "Should I assume you're now under the belief that sitting at a table harbors a sense of snobbery, which is why you're now expecting me to dine with you on the floor instead of making use of a perfectly fine table and chair?"

Temperance plopped straight down on the blanket. "Not at all. I simply thought that it would be more amusing to enjoy a picnic dinner on the floor since I've never picnicked on the floor of a Pullman car. Since you're clearly not keen to embrace a sense of amusement, feel free to enjoy your meal at the table."

Blowing out a breath, Gilbert pushed himself out of the chair and joined her on the floor. "You know I'm not about to refuse your offer of a picnic dinner, especially when I know it will hardly benefit me to annoy you right before you and I speak vows that will tie us together forever."

"We're not getting married."

Gilbert accepted the plate she thrust his way. "You can keep saying that, but we were discovered in a compromising situation, which means we have no choice but to get married."

Temperance lifted her chin. "Just as I occasionally choose to ignore the more ridiculous social etiquette rules out there, I'm choosing to ignore what's now expected of us. I plan to continue on with my lovely new life, make my own way in the world, and become independent for the first time in, well, ever."

"You were independent before your parents died."

She shook her head. "While I did believe that at the time, I now know I was anything but independent because I had the benefit of my father's fortune to back my extensive travels and lifestyle. Now, though, I'm earning a living on my own, and that is something I intend to continue doing."

"You cannot be earning a very substantial wage by teaching at Miss Snook's school."

"It's not substantial, but it's enough." She smiled. "I've learned to adopt an incredibly frugal attitude, one I never imagined I'd adopt in previous years, but one I'm proud of all the same." Her smile widened. "And because I've become friends with Miss Permilia Griswold, a lady who takes the word *frugal* to an entirely different level even though she has quite the fortune behind her, I've even learned how to haggle."

"I'm not certain how you expect me to respond to that."

"You simply say 'How lovely,' or better yet, 'Now I understand exactly why you don't want to marry me,' and we'll move the conversation forward to more important matters."

"You don't want to marry me because you're afraid you'll have to stop haggling?"

Temperance slid a slice of meat pie on her plate, did the same for Gilbert, then rolled her eyes. "I don't want to marry you because being forced to marry was not what I had in mind whenever I've turned my thoughts to marriage."

Gilbert picked up his fork. "What did you have in mind?"

She wrinkled her nose. "Because you were the boy I made rescue me time and time again from the castle my father's butler built for me, I would have thought you'd know exactly what I've always had in mind as pertains to marriage."

Gilbert wrinkled his nose right back at her. "You want someone to build you another castle in a tree and then rescue you?"

"Don't be daft. I simply want some type of fairy tale, castles not necessarily required."

She was not amused when he suddenly grinned, shook his head, and, without another word, began eating his pie, his lips annoyingly enough, continuing to twitch.

Jabbing her fork into her own pie, she took a few bites, then frowned. "How did you imagine the circumstances of your own marriage unfolding?"

He paused with his fork halfway to his mouth. "I imagined it would unfold like a business deal."

"A business deal? You must be jesting."

"How can you be surprised by that?" he asked, setting aside his plate and fork. "You, more than anyone, know how I enjoy an organized life, and what could be more organized than approaching marriage exactly how I approach making deals? I figured I'd meet a young lady through mutual business contacts. She'd probably be a daughter of one of my more prominent business partners, and by marrying her, she'd get the protection of my name and comfort of my fortune, and I'd get additional business by joining my business with that of her father's."

"That's a barbaric way to consider marriage."

"It's a moot point now, Temperance, since our fate was sealed the moment Mrs. Boggart Hobbes overheard me returning the key for Mr. Smith *and* witnessed me paying for a room that she then figured out you and I had shared."

Temperance resettled herself on the blanket. "I've been thinking about Mrs. Boggart Hobbes, and I have to tell you, I don't believe she'll spread a single snippet of gossip about what she thinks she uncovered about us."

"How did you come up with that?"

Shrugging, Temperance reached for a piece of bread. "Because she didn't confront me in the hotel, but waited to stop me until *after* I'd removed myself from the crowd of guests assembled in the lobby. She's also remarkably fond of Fanny and Clementine, dotes on them no less. Because of that, I believe she's privy to the idea Clementine fancies you. The last thing she'll want to do is disappoint her darling Clementine by making certain the object of Clementine's affections has to marry someone else — especially me."

She took a bite of the bread, letting her thoughts travel for a moment before she swallowed and frowned. "I must say, though, that encountering Mrs. Boggart Hobbes certainly does shed additional light on why Chicago was chosen as the destination of an absurd abduction plot. In all likelihood, Clementine and her parents knew Mrs. Boggart Hobbes was traveling to Chicago this weekend and staying at the Palmer House. I imagine there was some plan afoot that would find you and Clementine bumping into Mrs. Boggart Hobbes at some point during your stay in Chicago. That tricky business would have forced you into a matrimonial corner, allowing my cousin to achieve what she desired while also allowing her duplicity in the matter to go unnoticed since she would have played the role of victim to perfection." She caught Gilbert's eye. "Do know that I *would* have stepped in on your behalf. I'm not sure how I would have gone about doing that, but I wouldn't have allowed you to tie yourself to a shrew like Clementine."

Gilbert inclined his head. "That's kind of you, but tell me this — Clementine is an attractive lady and can also be quite charming when she sets her mind to it. Why do you believe she resorted to such subterfuge to secure herself a groom? She must have more than enough suitors paying her court to find one actually willing to marry her."

"Clementine is not accustomed to disappointment, Gilbert. I'm afraid that after she lost any chance she had of winning Mr. Harrison Sinclair's affection, what with him falling in love with Gertrude Cadwalader, she was determined to avoid another bout of disappointment again, this time in regard to you."

"Clementine fancied Harrison before she took a fancy to me?"

Smiling, Temperance reached out and smoothed her hand down his arm. "I'm afraid she did. In fact, she even went so far as to steal a painting from Harrison's yacht, intending to frame Gertrude for the theft." She sat back as her mouth then made an *O* of surprise.

"What is it?" Gilbert asked.

"That's it, that's why they resorted to such drastic measures. They must have discovered that painting is no longer in their attic because I found it not long after it was stolen and returned it. Why, I imagine that finding the painting gone and having you show up at the Flowerdew residence, wanting to speak with me, not Clementine, and then reiterating to Wayne that you were not in the market for a wife, exactly explains why they came up with an abduction scheme."

"I'm not certain that explains anything, at least not in a way I can understand."

Temperance tapped a finger against her chin. "Clementine must have been worried she would soon find herself carted off to jail, so she needed you to marry her, which would then afford her protection against being arrested because you're friends with Harrison Sinclair, the owner of the painting she arranged to have stolen."

Gilbert poured wine into a glass, took a sip, then shook his head. "How is it possible I forgot what an interesting place your mind is?"

Temperance held out her glass, waited until he poured her some wine, then saluted him with the glass. "Outlandish as everything I just said sounds, I'm right. I know I am."

"Even if you are right, and even though it does appear we were the victims of a ruse gone horribly, horribly, wrong, we'll still have to be married. We've broken practically every rule of expected behavior. And even though we didn't set out to break those rules, we will have to accept our new lot in life, and try to manage the best we can as husband and wife."

Temperance took a sip of her wine. "You should mind that glib tongue of yours, Gilbert. If you keep plying me with such romantic turns of phrase, such as 'manage the best we can,' I'm sure to dissolve into a swooning heap right in the midst of our picnic and agree to marry you."

Gilbert choked on the wine he was sipping. Sputtering for a good moment, he set the glass aside, then narrowed his eyes on her.

"Should I assume from the level of sarcasm in your tone that you believe I've gone about this marriage proposal business all wrong?"

"I don't think anyone in their right mind would consider what you've gone about as being even remotely close to a marriage proposal."

Nodding as he seemed to consider that, Gilbert cleared his throat, rose to his feet, shuffled about for a second, then knelt on one knee directly beside her.

"Right then, I should try a different approach."

Not having the least little idea how to respond to that while resisting the impulse to laugh, since Gilbert sounded exactly as if he was about to launch into a very dry and boring speech, Temperance soon found her hand taken in his. Gilbert then raised that hand, pried the knife she'd been holding away, then cleared his throat again. "You were clearly expecting some sort of romance, even though you and I have been friends forever, and here I've simply stated that we'll get married without reciting a single snippet of poetry, or . . ." He brought her hand to his lips and placed a surprisingly lingering kiss on her fingers. Lifting his head, he smiled. "Is this more on the lines of what you expected?"

"I can't say it is."

He released what sounded exactly like a grunt, kissed her fingers again, this time lingering over each and every one, then caught her eye. "I'm not much for flowery words, as you very well know, but I would be quite pleased if you, Miss Temperance Flowerdew, would do me the very great honor of agreeing to be my wife."

Even though she was oddly charmed by his woeful attempt to provide her with a romantic gesture, and even though tiny little prickles of something peculiar were now traveling up her arm from the fingers he'd just kissed, Temperance pulled her hand out of his and gave his face a bit of a pat, one that was slightly harder than was strictly necessary.

"While I do thank you for that, I must point out that a romantic gesture, which is apparently calculated on your part to convince me to agree to a plan that I'm not keen to agree to, is not very romantic, so . . . no, I won't marry you, and I'll thank you to not ask me again."

Chapter Seven

Gilbert wasn't exactly surprised that Temperance had turned down his offer of marriage. He was, nevertheless, even hours after he'd gotten down on one knee and been rejected, surprised by how disgruntled he felt over her refusal.

While he understood and agreed that he and Temperance were opposites in every sense of the word, being told he was essentially too stodgy and lacking in the romance area for Temperance's taste rankled.

Granted, he *was* slightly stodgy and not what one would consider proficient in the art of romance, but he'd been told by numerous people he was considered quite the catch, and he'd been pursued by the lady set for years.

Using a fine pen to scrawl exactly that on the list he'd begun to make under the heading *Reasons Why a Lady Would Want to*

Marry Gilbert Cavendish, he lifted his head when less-than-ladylike snores began rumbling around the Pullman car . . . again.

Swiveling around in the chair, he smiled at Temperance, who was sound asleep on the fainting couch, a blanket pulled up to her chin while snores that seemed impossible for such a slender woman to make erupted out of her mouth.

There was something delightful about watching Temperance sleep. She was not a peaceful sleeper, something he'd forgotten, and had spent the last several hours mumbling in her sleep, tossing the blanket off her every other hour, then mumbling more and flailing about as she went about recovering that blanket when she'd apparently taken a chill.

"Do not tell me you've been making it a habit to watch me as I sleep."

Unwilling to admit exactly that, and annoyed with himself for forgetting that Temperance was a person who could be snoring one minute and completely coherent the next, he oh-so-casually began pushing his uncompleted list underneath the satchel he'd placed on the table.

"Is that one of your lists?" she asked, and before he could finish hiding the evidence, she was standing directly behind him, peering over his shoulder.

"I don't believe bringing attention to the idea you're considered quite a catch is the best way to convince me to marry you."

Picking up the satchel and placing it directly over the list, Gilbert made the split decision that a distraction was desperately needed. He nodded to where a covered tray sat on an abandoned chair. "I took the liberty of traveling to the dining car while you were sleeping. There's a meal still warm under that dome waiting for you."

Temperance stopped peering over his shoulder. "You are a *dear* man, and I may have to forgive you for asking me to marry you after all."

"And reconsider your refusal?"

Walking to the tray, she lifted the lid, sighed in delight over the feast laid out there, then shot him a grin. "Providing me with a meal is hardly incentive enough to marry you, so don't go putting *Provides a Lady with Food When She's Hungry* on your list."

His hand stilled in the process of retrieving his list. "I wouldn't dream of adding that to my list. Although I do believe putting something to the effect of anticipating your need to consume vast quantities of food, and often at that, would be appropriate. It would also be appropriate to add that since I still seem to know you so well, if we married, we'd avoid experiencing any nasty surprises about each other, such as the fact that you still snore like a lumberjack."

She popped a piece of buttered bread into her mouth, pulled up a chair next to the table the tray was on, took a seat, and frowned after she swallowed. "It's rather indelicate of you to mention my snoring, or to compare me to a lumberjack." She nodded to where his list was hidden. "If anything, you should add, and only for future reference as you go about finding a wife who isn't me, that any mention of snoring is best kept unmentioned."

"I didn't say I found your snoring annoying."

Buttering another piece of bread, her brows drew together. "How comforting. Exactly how long were you watching me snore, or better yet, how long was I sleeping?"

"About ten hours, and before you get your back up, I wasn't watching you the entire time because I slept numerous hours as well, until the snoring finally got so loud I couldn't sleep any longer." He smiled. "That's when I decided I needed to find something to occupy my time, and what better way to do that occupying than to —"

"Make one of your lists," she finished for him before she dove into her meal, not speaking until every morsel on her plate was gone.

"That was delicious," she exclaimed, looking somewhat longingly at the empty plate before she put the lid back over it and patted her stomach. "I'm feeling much better. And now, with my thoughts becoming clearer by the second, allow me to return to the point you made about us not discovering nasty surprises about each other because we know each other so well." She caught his eye. "I'm sure there's much about you I don't know because we have been apart for years. I'm also certain there's much about me you don't know as well."

Gilbert leaned back in his chair. "We still have a few hours before we reach New York. Divulge away. What nasty surprise might I not know about you?"

"Why do I have to go first?"

"Because you brought it up."

"That hardly seems fair."

Gilbert smiled. "You can't think of any nasty surprises I wouldn't know about you, can you?"

Blowing out a breath, Temperance looked out the train window, seemed to consider his question for a long moment, then turned back to him. "I gave up playing musical instruments publicly because I didn't appreciate the pressure of being expected to perform on demand, nor did I appreciate the expectation of playing only the most complicated of pieces from masters such as Beethoven, Bach, or Mozart."

Of anything Gilbert had been expecting Temperance to disclose, that hadn't crossed his mind. "What would you have preferred to play?"

"I tried to play a few original pieces here and there, but the audiences assembled to hear me play were so critical of my efforts, and I was still relatively young at the time, that I lost all pleasure in performing. I turned to painting and sculpting instead, a pursuit that still brings me criticism at times, but not on the scale my music did."

"I thought you told me you teach music lessons at Miss Snook's School for the Education of the Feminine Mind."

"That's different. Those women have never been exposed to music, and are much more open to experiencing music in all its forms. They have no preconceived ideas about what good music is and what isn't. That means I have more freedom in choosing what to expose them to, taking great pleasure in watching them embrace a song simply because it's beautiful over embracing it because they've been told it's beautiful and they're expected to enjoy it."

Gilbert frowned. "Do you ever think you're doing the world a disservice by not sharing the musical talent God gave you with the masses?"

Temperance returned the frown. "I've recently come to believe that God may have given me my talent to share with my *students,* giving them a glimpse of a world they never knew existed before, and thus improving their world in the process."

"An interesting belief, although I'm not certain I agree with it." He leaned forward. "If you would have returned to music after your parents died, you would have had no need to move in with your Flowerdew relations. If you've forgotten, you were once in demand."

Temperance shrugged. "Only because I was a novelty and audiences enjoyed exclaiming over a child capable of playing multiple instruments and playing those instruments somewhat well." She settled back in the chair. "I'm no longer a child. And even though I did think about returning to music for a very brief moment after I found myself destitute, I realized that I didn't have the luxury of time to bring rusty musical skills back to snuff."

"I'm sure your abilities were never that rusty."

"Which is kind of you to say. But even if that were true, after my parents died, the music that always filtered through my mind simply . . . stopped." She shook her head. "It would have been difficult indeed to turn to music as a profession when I no longer had the gift of song that I always took for granted."

Gilbert rose to his feet, then crouched down beside the chair she was sitting in. Taking her hand, he brought her fingers to his lips. "Forgive me. I should have known that losing your parents would change you, even if I never thought there'd come a day when music left your life."

She smiled. "Apology accepted, although I should tell you that ever since I moved out of my cousins' house, music has begun swirling through my mind again, which is why I offered to teach it at Miss Snook's school."

"That's a relief."

"Indeed, but now it's your turn." She leaned forward, her eyes alight with curiosity. "What's something surprising I might not know about you?"

Gilbert took a second to consider the question, finding he really had nothing much of interest to disclose, which was somewhat disappointing but went far in proving that he *was* a man who believed in sticking to his well-thought-out schedule. "Astonishing as I'm sure you'll find this, nothing springs to mind that you'd find out of the ordinary, or anything that remotely constitutes a nasty surprise."

"Why am I *not* astonished to hear that?"

"Because you know me so well, which . . ."

She held up a hand, stopping him mid-sentence. "Do not even travel down the *this is further proof of why we should marry* road again."

"Perhaps I *was* about to surprise you and say something completely different."

"You weren't, and before you argue with that, allow me to suggest we change the subject to something we won't argue about."

"And I know just the subject to distract you." He gestured to a chess set he'd set up on a small table underneath a window while she'd been sleeping. "Care to join me in a bit of a friendly match?"

"Does friendly mean you're going to let me win?"

"If I let you win, will you have a change of heart about marrying me?"

"Not at all."

"Then prepare yourself for a less-than-friendly game."

"My favorite kind." With that, Temperance stood up, cracked her knuckles, sent him a saucy smile, and moved to the chess set.

The next few hours were spent battling over the pieces with Gilbert winning every game, and knowing better than to apologize for every win.

Curiously enough, there was something intimate about being enclosed in a Pullman car with Temperance, and while it was true they'd often spent time alone in their youth, there was something different about that circumstance now . . . something intriguing.

He couldn't seem to get enough of simply watching her, fascinated by the way she bit her lip when she was considering a move on the chessboard, or how she'd take to sulking for all of a few seconds after he'd taken control of the game time and time again.

Throwing up her hands in defeat when he captured her queen, Temperance reached for a piece of the apple he'd cut up for her, stilling when she glanced out the window. "I think we're almost to Grand Central Depot," she said, getting to her feet to move closer to the window.

He joined her at the window. "Indeed we are, which means we'll soon be able to hire a hansom cab and get you back to that school of yours — Miss Snook's School for the Education of the Feminine Mind, a mouthful if I've ever heard one."

"I think it has a nice ring to it, but I don't believe there'll be any need to hire a cab. Knowing Miss Henrietta, she'll have a carriage waiting for us." She smiled. "She probably began making plans to come fetch me from the train depot the second the telegram I sent her got delivered."

"Did you tell her you were with me?"

"I did. I thought that would alleviate some of her worry since she believes you're a gentleman of good moral fiber."

"I wasn't aware Miss Henrietta Huxley was familiar enough with me to hold that type of opinion."

"Miss Henrietta, as well as her sister, Miss Mabel, are incredibly well informed about everything that goes on in the city." Temperance returned her attention to the scene outside the window. "She and her sister spent years as recluses, but during that time, they became incredibly proficient in the art of observation, making them privy to the most interesting aspects of society and all that transpires within it."

"But I don't travel in society."

"Yet," Temperance countered. "Society has you in their greedy sights, Gilbert. And because you intend to continually increase your business holdings, you and I know that to do that successfully, you'll have no choice but to enter the hallowed circle of the New York Four Hundred."

Gilbert frowned. "Is that another reason why you rejected my offer of marriage? Because I might begin mingling in high society?"

"No, although that would be a valid reason. I simply hadn't thought of it quite yet." She turned and gave his arm a poke. "I am curious, though, about how your mother will react to you moving in society. I well remember her disdain for what she considered inexcusable snobbery."

"She's more opposed to the aristocratic societal nonsense she found in London over the society we have to contend with here in the states. I think her brief time as the Countess of Strafford gave her a more-than-distasteful view of the airs people adopted over in England to prove their superiority over the common man. She was thought of as an upstart young lady from America whose father used his fortune to secure his daughter a title while providing the Earl of

Strafford with enough money to get his estates back in fine form." Gilbert shook his head. "My mother loathed her time in England. And since my father was old enough to be her grandfather at the time she married him, I've always believed she was rather relieved when he died before I was born, giving her a way out of a life she despised."

"Do you still think about how your life would have turned out if your father had not died before you were born?"

Gilbert reached for her hand, taking hold of it exactly as he'd done too many times to count when he and Temperance used to discuss the circumstances of his birth. "I've stopped imagining my life as the son of an earl. I finally realized that my father, being over sixty before I was born, would not have been the father I used to dream he would have been to me. In all likelihood, I wouldn't have seen him much. But because my mother abandoned England not long after I was born and brought me to the states, much to my half brother's delight since I'm all but convinced he was embarrassed by my mother's marriage to his father, I was able to grow up relatively normal. Add in that my mother then married a salt-of-the-earth type of gentleman in Mr. William

Beckwith, and I have to believe my life became much improved over what it would have been if I'd been raised in England. I would have certainly always been known as the son of an important man, yet only a second son. And I would not have been expected to make anything of myself and would have probably turned into the worst type of reprobate."

Temperance laughed. "You don't have the temperament of a reprobate. If you'll recall, I've known you since we could barely walk, and even back then, you were always one to abide by every rule. Reprobates, if you'll recall, don't care for rules."

"You do have a bothersome way of ruining a perfectly lovely story."

"Thinking of you as a reprobate is not lovely, simply amusing, but since the train is now pulling directly into the depot, allow us to discontinue this conversation until later." She walked back to the table and pulled out his traveling bag. "I'll leave your satchel for you to fetch since I know you don't want me to get another look at your list."

"Since you don't seem keen to put stock in my list, by all means, look away."

She smiled. "I think it would be best if I allow you to retain your dignity, because you must know that my looking over a list of what I'll certainly consider questionable attributes you've given yourself will not benefit our friendship in the least. And —" she held up her hand when he opened his mouth — "to avoid an argument, allow me to deftly turn the conversation to what your plans are regarding Clementine, Wayne, and Fanny Flowerdew."

Resisting the urge to point out yet again how bothersome she could be, Gilbert walked over to the table, stuffed his list into his satchel, slung the strap over his shoulder, and shrugged. "I sent Fanny a return telegram while you were composing your telegram to Miss Henrietta, telling her I was taking the next train back to New York. Because of that, I imagine I'll mosey on over to their residence tomorrow to see what they have to say for themselves."

"Why would you extend Fanny the courtesy of allowing her to know you were returning to New York?"

"It was a strategic move on my part and has probably caused them to begin composing an elaborate tale, one filled to the gills with all manner of fabrications as they struggle to get their stories straight."

"I'm afraid I don't understand how allowing them time to get their stories straight can be a strategic move on your part."

Gilbert arched a brow. "I use strategies like that all the time in my business endeavors, especially when I feel as if everything isn't aboveboard. By giving them time to fabricate additional stories, I've allowed them to embrace a false sense of security. I didn't mention anything in my telegram about finding you, so they have no way of knowing I'm on to their lies. That will give me the advantage of surprise, one I'll use after they've had an opportunity to really dig themselves into holes by expanding on details they're probably even now inventing, but details I know to be false."

"I think you're underestimating my relatives. They're far more cunning than you imagine them to be, and they might have gone further than simply fabricating additional story points. You may very well find a man of the cloth lurking in the shadows of their drawing room, ready to step in and help you and Clementine say some vows when you're least expecting it."

"And I think you're underestimating me by believing I'd allow myself to be taken in by your relatives more than once. I'm well aware that I was played the fool, but I have no intention of experiencing that again. Frankly, I wouldn't be opposed to never speaking with your relatives again. But because I'm now aware of the abuse they sent your way, I'm afraid they've earned a bit of discomfort, and don't think for a minute you can talk me out of that."

"I wasn't planning on talking you out of that. If you'll recall, I spent hours enclosed in a coffin because of my relatives. I also might have been forced to marry you if Fanny's aunt hadn't been so discreet in running us to ground outside the Palmer House."

"You're still going to have to marry me."

"And you're going to have to stop bringing that up," she countered right as the squeal of the brakes sounded and the train slowed and came to a complete stop.

Taking his traveling bag from her, Gilbert gestured her toward the door, not bothering to continue with their argument because Temperance was looking stubborn again. Following her out of the Pullman car, he took her arm as he joined her on the platform, looking around to get his bearings.

Grand Central Depot was always a little overwhelming, what with the trains pulling into the closed building, the sound lending another level of chaos to all the many people jostling about. That no one had ever considered trying to direct the crowd in any sort of logical fashion always amazed Gilbert, but since now was hardly the moment to concern himself with the logistics of how to manage the crowds more effectively, he tightened his grip on Temperance's arm.

Steering her rather forcefully through the station while dodging steam coming from idling trains, and then dodging people who were obviously late for their departures, they finally reached the doors to the depot. Nodding to a man who was holding the door open for them, they moved to the sidewalk right before Temperance let out a laugh of delight.

"I knew she would be waiting for us. Miss Henrietta! Over here."

Before Gilbert could stop her, Temperance was off, waving at Miss Henrietta Huxley, who was smiling and waving back, her sister, Miss Mabel Huxley, waving as well. An older gentleman Gilbert was not acquainted with was already moving in Temperance's direction, and to Gilbert's surprise, that gentleman picked Temperance straight off her feet, swung her around, then set her back down. He immediately tugged the bottom of his jacket back into place, and inclined his head in a way that left Gilbert suspecting that the man might be the Huxley sisters' famed butler, Mr. Barclay, a man Temperance had mentioned often on their long journey, and a man she held in high esteem.

Taking a step toward the reunion unfolding in front of him, Gilbert suddenly froze on the spot when someone called out his name, someone who sounded remarkably like Miss Clementine Flowerdew.

He forced himself to turn in the direction of the voice, wincing as Clementine, her parents, Wayne and Fanny Flowerdew, and two other young ladies he'd met during his stay in Newport, Miss Ava Appleton and Miss Melissa Wells, came into view.

The entire group was waving madly at him, beaming bright smiles his way.

Returning his gaze to Clementine, he blinked as his gaze settled on the yellow of her gown, a color that had his lips curving. When he realized the Flowerdews and Clementine's friends were obviously expecting him to join them, and finding himself beyond curious as to what they could possibly say to him, Gilbert began striding their way, stopping directly in front of Clementine.

He was completely taken aback when she threw herself at him and wrapped her arms securely around his waist. She then proceeded to hold him tight for far longer than propriety allowed.

Temperance's warning immediately sprang to mind, the one she'd only recently uttered about not underestimating her relatives. Calling himself every type of fool for allowing the Flowerdews to know when he was returning, he practically had to pry Clementine off him. Opening his mouth, although he wasn't exactly certain what words he should allow to escape, he was denied any words at all when Clementine folded her hands demurely in front of her right before she launched into what was clearly a well-rehearsed bit of nonsense.

"I cannot thank you enough, Gilbert," she began, her use of his given name having Miss Appleton and Miss Wells exchanging significant looks. "That you'd drop everything to come to my aid and travel all the way to Chicago warms my heart no small amount. I'm simply sorry your trip was all for naught since I was able to free myself from the clutches of madmen, although by the time I made my escape and traveled back to my home, my mother had already received that ransom letter and had sent you off to rescue me."

It took every ounce of restraint Gilbert had at his disposal to resist breaking into applause over what was one of the most ridiculous stories he'd ever heard. "You managed to free yourself from your abductors?" he asked slowly.

Clementine's eyes widened right before she began batting her lashes. "I did, even though I was frightened for my very life during my escape." Another batting of lashes came his way before she raised a hand to her throat. "You cannot imagine the terror I felt as this criminal made off with me, plucking me straight off that street as I was simply traveling to the Family Dance Academy to learn a new quadrille."

She went from batting her lashes to fluttering them. "Did I mention that I've been asked to perform the Opera Bouffe Quadrille? It's quite the honor for me since that quadrille has been chosen to open the first Patriarch Ball of the year."

"How delightful" was all he could think to say.

"Oh, it is, and —" Clementine suddenly stopped speaking, her eyes narrowed on something over his shoulder. Her smile slid off her face before she seemed to force it back into place and return her attention to him.

"Is something the matter?' he asked.

"I thought I saw someone I wasn't expecting to see here, but I'm sure I was simply mistaken." The batting of lashes commenced again, until Fanny Flowerdew, Clementine's mother, let out a gasp, the reason for the gasp becoming all too apparent as Temperance sauntered up to join them.

Chapter Eight

Finding herself the object of such undivided attention, as well as finding herself pinned under the horrified stares of her relatives, Temperance found she had the most unusual desire to giggle.

She was not a giggler, and had never once been tempted to embrace that habit. But now, when confronted with the idea her Flowerdew cousins might soon be facing the comeuppance they so richly deserved, instead of feeling even a smidgen of satisfaction, she felt the urge to giggle, or perhaps, better yet, release a completely unladylike snort.

"I'm telling you, Ava, that *is* Temperance Flowerdew, evidently here to welcome Mr. Cavendish home as well, although . . . why do you imagine she's chosen to dress in a color everyone knows Clementine favors?"

Tearing her gaze from Clementine, who was now looking more horrified than ever as her attention settled on the yellow dress in question, one that certainly didn't fit Temperance since the bodice was too large and the hem too short, she found Miss Ava Appleton and Miss Melissa Wells looking her up and down.

The sheer speculation resting in the ladies' eyes was reason for concern, but since she certainly couldn't do anything about being perused by two of the biggest gossips within society, nor would she be able to stem any of the gossip they may choose to spread about their encounter with her, she settled for sending them a nod before she turned her gaze on Gilbert.

The urge to giggle or snort immediately returned when she noticed he was looking rather wild about the eyes. He certainly didn't seem to be in a state of mind where he'd be capable of lending her any support since he'd apparently been struck mute by the sheer unlikeliness of the scene unfolding around him.

Knowing it was going to be up to her to make the first move, Temperance returned her attention to her relatives, none of whom seemed remotely glad to see her.

"What a delightful surprise to find all of you at the train depot at exactly this particular moment in time," she chirped in a voice that was downright cheerful, the cheerfulness evidently responsible for the immediate cessation of whispering between Miss Appleton and Miss Wells.

"I'm anything but delighted to find you here, Temperance, and can't even begin to fathom why you'd follow us to the train station," Clementine all but hissed as her cheeks began to mottle.

"I didn't follow you. I just departed from a train."

"And we've missed you dreadfully while you were away in *Florida,*" Wayne suddenly said, speaking up as he stepped forward and sent her a smile that she assumed was meant to be one of fondness, but came across more on the lines of frightening since he seemed to be gritting his teeth while attempting to smile. He was also glaring at her, as if to dare her to contradict him, but she was unable to respond at all when Clementine suddenly plunked her hands on her hips.

"Why would she get to go off to Florida, and why wasn't I offered a trip to the ocean?"

"Not now, *dear,*" Wayne said between still gritted teeth, not even bothering to glance in his daughter's direction as he continued glaring Temperance's way.

Having seen that specific glare often over

the past three years, and not appreciating being glared at in the first place since she'd done absolutely nothing to deserve it, Temperance lifted her chin. "You know perfectly well I've not been to Florida, Wayne, nor, if you're about to spout another ridiculous idea, was I gallivanting about, enjoying a courtship with some gentleman who came straight from your disturbed imagination."

A tic began to throb on Wayne's temple. "Your impertinence does not show you in a favorable light."

"I'm sure it doesn't, just as I'm sure learning I was in Chicago is not going to have a favorable effect on whatever new schemes you, Fanny, and Clementine have decided to pursue."

Fanny began waving her hand in front of her face. "You were in Chicago?"

Temperance nodded. "I was, and you'll never believe who I encountered at the Palmer House."

Fanny immediately turned to Miss Appleton and Miss Wells. "If you ladies will excuse us for just the tiniest second, I'm afraid we have some family matters to discuss of a private nature."

Without allowing Miss Appleton or Miss Wells an opportunity to respond, even though they clearly weren't keen to be abandoned during such a juicy conversation, Fanny took hold of Temperance's arm and began pulling her down the sidewalk, not stopping until they reached a spot devoid of people.

Looking around, Temperance found Miss Henrietta, Miss Mabel, and Mr. Barclay, the Huxley's butler, stepping closer, but she shook her head ever so slightly, causing them to stop a discreet distance away. Since Miss Henrietta and her sister were well adept at reading lips, Temperance knew the sisters would be watching every word that slipped out of her relatives' mouths, and that they would be more than willing to step in if they thought Temperance was in over her head.

Once Wayne and Clementine joined them, minus Gilbert who'd been waylaid by Miss Appleton and Miss Wells, both of whom were clutching Gilbert's arms as they began peppering him with questions, Temperance reluctantly directed her attention to Wayne, who was now bristling with anger.

"Explain yourself," he demanded.

"I don't believe I'm the one who needs to do any explaining." Temperance crossed her arms over her chest. "If anything, I deserve an apology since I was snatched straight off the street, the victim of a case of mistaken identity, although" — she nodded to Clementine — "that was a riveting tale you told Gilbert about how you managed to escape from your abductors when you and I know you were never abducted in the first place."

Clementine's face blanched. "How do you know I told Gilbert that? You'd yet to join us when I imparted that information."

"Miss Henrietta has made it a point to become more than proficient with reading lips. She was watching you when you were speaking with Gilbert, then told me what you'd said."

With eyes turning as big as saucers, Clementine began looking around, stilling when Miss Henrietta sent her a cheeky wave. Shuddering, she looked back at Temperance as Wayne and Fanny turned their backs on Miss Henrietta, their obvious attempt at depriving her of further lipreading having Temperance forcing down the laughter that was bubbling up her throat.

"What is that busybody doing here?" Clementine asked.

"She came to give me a ride home after I sent her a telegram telling her I was alive and well and traveling back to New York after an unexpected journey to Chicago." Temperance pressed her lips together to keep from smiling when she saw Miss

Mabel strolling ever so casually past them, apparently taking up a new position to keep a closer eye on the situation.

"You should have not involved Miss Henrietta Huxley in our personal affairs," Wayne said as Fanny nodded in agreement.

"Well, *you* should not have come up with such a ridiculous plan to force Gilbert into a marriage with your daughter," Temperance countered before she smiled. "I should warn you that Miss Henrietta, after I went missing, took it upon herself to hire a Pinkerton detective to investigate what happened to me. There's no telling what that man may have discovered. But the Pinkerton men are known to be thorough in their investigations, so it wouldn't surprise me in the least to learn they've uncovered some of your secrets, especially secrets pertaining to an ill-conceived abduction attempt."

Wayne's eyes narrowed even as his face began to darken. "You listen here, girlie, if you think for one second I'm going to . . ." His voice trailed away to nothing when Fanny suddenly gripped his arm before she began smiling far too pleasantly at someone over Wayne's shoulder.

Temperance glanced that way and found Gilbert striding up to join them, his face set in an expression that could only be described as furious. Stopping directly beside her, he reached out, gave her arm a squeeze, then set his sights on Wayne, who took a step backward.

"Your days of abusing Temperance have come to an end, Wayne," he said, every word holding more than a hint of hostility.

"I'm surprised you'd be so gullible as to allow yourself to be taken in by my cousin," Wayne began. "She's clearly been feeding you some outlandish lies about me."

Gilbert's eyes flashed. "Temperance was never one to lie, although, clearly, that can't be said for everyone in your family."

"I'm sure I have no idea what you're implying."

Gilbert smiled. "I'm sure you do, but since I've just had a most illuminating conversation with Miss Appleton and Miss Wells, one that revolved around me disabusing them of the notion they needed to congratulate me on my upcoming nuptials to Clementine, I decided it was past time for me to set the record straight."

"You didn't tell Miss Appleton and Miss Wells we're not going to get married, did you?" Clementine all but whispered.

The fine hair on the nape of Temperance's neck stood to attention when Gilbert's smile widened, even though the temper in his eyes increased.

"I do hate to disappoint ladies, Miss Flowerdew, but I must admit that I did make it abundantly clear to Miss Appleton and Miss Wells that their felicitations as pertained to my matrimonial state were misplaced." He inclined his head. "You see, while I do have every intention of speaking vows in the not-too-distant future, I'm afraid they won't be spoken with you, but with the woman I've decided I simply cannot live without — your darling cousin, Temperance."

"I believe that went rather well," Gilbert said an hour later as he walked beside Temperance down the long marble hallway of Miss Snook's School for the Education of the Feminine Mind.

"How could that have gone well?" Temperance argued, slapping away the hand Gilbert was trying to wrap around her arm. "You allowed Miss Appleton and Miss Wells to believe you and I are getting married, while allowing my cousins to believe that nonsense as well."

Gilbert smiled. "You're simply irritated because you didn't want to accept the idea we'd have to get married after spending time alone in Chicago, but now realize I've been right about the matter all along."

"No one who came to meet us at the train station knew the particulars of what happened during our little foray into Chicago, and we should have kept it that way," Temperance muttered. "I cannot begin to tell you how annoyed I am with you for making such a muddle of things and have no idea why you would have allowed everyone to believe you and I are getting married."

"I must say I'm annoyed with the situation as well," Miss Henrietta said, walking briskly up to join them. "I was so looking forward to taking you in hand, Temperance, and now you've gone and ruined all of my fun." She smiled at Gilbert. "Do know, though, dear, that you were a part of my plan from the moment I laid eyes on you at Permilia and Asher's engagement celebration. I would, however, have appreciated being allowed to participate more fully in seeing that plan to fruition."

Gilbert stopped in his tracks. "I was part of your plan?"

"Indeed, but now that you and Temperance have apparently settled matters between you, I'll have to turn my attention elsewhere."

Temperance threw up her hands. "Gilbert and I have not settled any matters between us. I was taken as much by surprise as my cousins when he informed them we were to be married."

Miss Henrietta smoothed a stray strand of white hair away from her face. "I have no inkling as to why you'd be surprised that the two of you need to marry. You admitted you were waylaid by Mrs. Boggart Hobbes while you were in Chicago, a society matron known to be one of the strictest abiders of the proprieties New York has ever seen."

"And as I tried to explain on the carriage ride here," Temperance began, "before you, Miss Henrietta, decided to take another one of your hair-raising shortcuts that left me incapable of speech as we were in danger for our very lives, Mrs. Boggart Hobbes is not a threat. I highly doubt she would have said so much as a peep about recognizing me in Chicago because she knows Clementine wants Gilbert for herself."

Miss Henrietta lifted her chin. "My driving did not put anyone's life at risk." She turned and arched a brow at Mr. Barclay, who was following them down the hallway. "Were you in fear for your life?"

Mr. Barclay inclined his head. "I'm sure you know I always close my eyes and descend into prayer when you insist on taking the reins, Miss Henrietta. And on that note,

I do think I'll go see about getting some fresh tea, a wonderful tonic if there ever was one to soothe overwrought nerves, those nerves brought about by your superb handling of the carriage through side alleys that really ought to be avoided."

"He truly is a most remarkable gentleman," Temperance said as Mr. Barclay beat a hasty retreat while Miss Henrietta watched him with a fond smile on her face. "And should be given a fortune when he retires for simply putting up with you and Miss Mabel all these years."

Miss Henrietta waved that aside. "Mr. Barclay already possesses a respectable fortune, having taken his salary and invested it wisely over the years he's worked for Mabel and me. Why, the man could have retired years ago, but has chosen to remain in his position because he believes it keeps him young."

"He'd remain much younger if he simply refused to get into a buggy with you holding the reins."

"I wonder where my sister went?" Miss Henrietta asked, completely ignoring Temperance's last remark.

"I'm right here, Henrietta," Miss Mabel said, walking down the hallway while waving a piece of parchment in her hand. "I stopped to look at all the calling cards and letters on the tray in the entranceway that we neglected to sort through today, and good thing I did." She stopped directly next to her sister. "There's a note here from Miss Edwina Sinclair, stating that she and Agent McParland are thankful we allowed the Pinkerton Agency to know Temperance had been found alive and well. She also mentioned that Agent McParland has uncovered something Temperance might find interesting, so she and Agent McParland will be paying a visit here tomorrow at noon."

"Is Edwina still pursuing the idea of becoming a female Pinkerton detective?" Gilbert asked.

"Indeed," Miss Mabel said. "But why are we lingering in the hallway when we have such a delightful library only a few steps away from us, one I know has a cheery fire already lit in the fireplace and comfortable places for us to sit?" She smiled at Temperance. "I still have many questions to ask about your adventure, dear, and questions pertaining to the plans I know we'll need to begin making regarding yet another engagement celebration."

Before Temperance could argue with that, Miss Mabel and Miss Henrietta breezed forward, disappearing into the library.

"This is not going to be pleasant," Temperance muttered as Gilbert grinned back at her, his delight in evidently believing he'd gotten his way causing annoyance to slide over her once again. Sending him a scowl, she walked into the library, her annoyance disappearing in a split second when she was greeted by a gathering of young women who were students at Miss Snook's school, all of whom crowded around Temperance to welcome her home.

Not all the students who attended the school lived on the premises, but when Miss Henrietta had learned that many of the young women who'd chosen to better themselves by attending classes had been turned out from their positions as maids, factory workers, and nannies, she'd generously offered her old home as a place for those women to stay. She didn't charge them rent in exchange for a room, only the expectation that they'd excel in their studies and perhaps lend a hand around the mansion turned school since there was much to do to keep the place in a good state of repair.

That Miss Henrietta and Miss Mabel had given Miss Snook the use of their mansion to use as premises for a school spoke volumes about how the sisters had come to loathe the house their reprobate of a father had built for them. From what little Temperance knew about their father, he'd been a vile man — so vile in fact that he'd had more than one wife stashed about the city, each wife unaware of the others until Mr. Huxley had decided to bring everyone together, expecting them to live in houses right next to the mansion Miss Henrietta and Miss Mabel had called home.

The sisters had finally come to terms with the unpleasant secrets of their past. And after coming to those terms, they'd moved out of the mansion on Broadway and back to a house next to Gramercy Park where they'd spent happier times during their youth. But while Miss Mabel enjoyed living in that home, Miss Henrietta spent many a night in the school. She'd been delighted to take over the role of house mother, although she'd completely redecorated her personal suite of rooms, as well as tossed all memories of her father straight into the trash.

". . . and I personally made the sugar cakes," a young woman by the name of Bernice Small said as she brandished a platter of bite-sized cakes, all of which had been decorated with brightly colored icing. "I know how you enjoy my cakes."

With her heart turning warm at such an unexpected greeting, Temperance soon found herself sitting in a chair in front of a small table, a sheer mountain of treats placed in front of her to sample.

Not being a lady who ever refused a meal, especially not one of the decadent type, Temperance spent the next few minutes trying every treat she'd been given as Miss Henrietta introduced Gilbert to all the women.

Her irritation with him completely disappeared when he went out of his way to put the women at ease, taking time to kiss each woman's hand, even though the women seemed completely taken aback by the gesture.

After every woman had made Gilbert's acquaintance, they then took their leave, but not before sending Temperance smiles and winks of approval. She pretended she didn't notice, convinced it would not aid her situation in the least to acknowledge the idea that everyone seemed to find Gilbert more than charming.

Handing him a plate stacked with treats, Temperance picked up her plate again as Gilbert took a chair beside her, while Miss Henrietta and Miss Mabel situated themselves on a fainting couch.

"So," Miss Henrietta began after she'd nibbled her way around the edges of one of

Bernice's cakes. "When is the wedding?"

Temperance paused with a fork filled with cake halfway to her mouth. "Should I assume we're not talking about Gertrude's wedding to Harrison or Permilia's wedding to Asher?"

"You're trying my patience," Miss Henrietta said before leveling her gaze on Gilbert as she sent him a nod. "Perhaps it would expedite the conversation if *you* answer all my questions from this point forward."

Gilbert smiled. "I'm afraid Temperance and I haven't sorted out all the pesky details just yet, having only recently decided we should wed."

Setting aside her cake, Temperance sat forward. *"We* never decided to wed. If you'll recall, I said there was no *reason* to wed, while also pointing out that there's every likelihood we'll *murder* each other if any vows are spoken between us because we are not well suited for *marriage."*

"I think you suit admirably together," Miss Mabel said, smiling as Mr. Barclay entered the room carrying a silver tray that had a silver teapot on it. "Ah, lovely, fresh tea, and do say you'll join us in a cup, Mr. Barclay. We were just about to delve into the planning of yet another engagement celebration, and this time with our darling

Temperance as the future bride."

To Temperance's surprise and relief, Mr. Barclay set down the tray right before he leveled a stern eye on Miss Mabel. "It seems to me that Miss Temperance is not overly excited about this peculiar engagement situation with Mr. Cavendish. And since she has no family to look after her best interests except for us, allow me to point out that you two" — he nodded to Miss Mabel and then to Miss Henrietta — "are not helping her by badgering her into a marriage she clearly has no desire to enter." He lifted his chin. "Because of that, I'm hereby stating that I'm firmly on her side and will now take on the daunting role of being the voice of reason in this most disturbing situation."

Mr. Barclay walked over to a chair close to Temperance and sat down, evidently forgetting all about the tea he'd neglected to serve.

Gilbert, being a gentleman who noticed whenever something was amiss, rose to his feet, made short shrift of pouring out the tea, then handed the cups all around, smiling ever so slightly when he handed a cup to Mr. Barclay and was rewarded for his efforts with a scowl.

For the briefest of moments, silence settled over the library until Temperance sat forward.

"While I understand that Gilbert and I broke practically every rule of propriety there is, I'm not of the belief we need to get married since I know Mrs. Boggart Hobbes will not carry tales from Chicago to New York. However —" she narrowed her eyes at Gilbert — "because you told Miss Appleton and Miss Wells we are to marry, the situation has turned a little concerning. Which is why I'm going to ask everyone in this room to come up with a plan that will see us released from any matrimonial expectations."

"I think that ship has sailed," Miss Henrietta said. "You mark my words, Miss Appleton and Miss Wells are even now spreading the tale of your engagement, which will make it impossible for the two of you *not* to wed."

"You'll make a beautiful bride," Miss Mabel remarked. "Although I do believe it might be for the best if a formal announcement isn't made until after Gertrude's engagement celebration, which is to be held here in a little less than two weeks if anyone has forgotten. We wouldn't want to detract from her special day, so perhaps you should make the formal announcement a week after that celebration. That will give us plenty of time to plan another ball."

"We're not planning a ball, and . . ." Temperance stopped speaking when a perfectly reasonable solution to their dilemma popped to mind. She turned to Gilbert. "Where are your parents?"

"In India," he said, his eyes narrowing as if he'd already figured out where she was going with her question.

"And when are they are expected to return?"

"Not for a few months."

She sat back and folded her hands in her lap. "Well, there you have it — a perfectly reasonable explanation as to why we cannot announce an engagement. Gilbert's mother, Florence Beckwith, is a somewhat frightening woman. I'd hate to think of the animosity she'd hold toward me forevermore if I were to allow an engagement announcement to be made without her having prior knowledge that Gilbert and I were considering marriage. In order to save the perfectly friendly relationship I've always shared with Gilbert's mother, having known her practically from birth, we'll simply tell anyone who asks that we're waiting to formally announce our future plans until we obtain the blessing of Gilbert's beloved mother."

"That's a stretch and you know it," Gilbert said.

"It may be a stretch, but by the time your parents arrive back in the country, no one will even remember we were supposed to be engaged, thus saving us a trip down the altar and a life of regrets in the end."

Chapter Nine

"Are you quite certain we're talking about the same Temperance Flowerdew, a delightful friend of my Gertrude, but a young lady I've never thought of as being an overly stubborn sort?"

Pulling Blaze, his positively ancient horse, to a stop in the middle of a gravel path in Central Park, Gilbert shifted in the saddle, directing his attention to his very good friend, Mr. Harrison Sinclair. The sight of his friend brought an immediate grin to his face.

Harrison was a gentleman known for embracing a somewhat curious sense of style, and today was no exception. His jacket, while fitting his muscular frame to perfection, was crafted out of material that had large stripes of orange running down it, and he'd paired that jacket with green trousers that were tucked into knee-high riding boots that could stand a bit of a polishing. His hair, always kept a touch longer than was fashionable, was tied at the nape of his neck with a bit of blue ribbon, one Gilbert thought might have at one time been worn by Harrison's lovely fiancée, Miss Gertrude Cadwalader.

That Gertrude apparently took no issue with Harrison's preference for unusual fashions spoke volumes about her true character. And because she'd also made it known she enjoyed Harrison's peculiar sense of style, there was little likelihood Harrison would ever abandon his habit of pairing plaids, stripes, and mismatching colors, since he did enjoy indulging his soon-to-be wife.

"I don't know how Temperance has managed to fool everyone in the city about her stubborn nature, but believe me, she's downright contrary at times, and this, unfortunately, seems to be one of them," Gilbert said, forcing his attention away from the orange stripes, which were, oddly enough, slightly mesmerizing.

Harrison grinned as he urged Rupert, his beast of a stallion, back into motion. "Admit it, you're simply put out with her because she's disrupted whatever plan you'd begun assembling in that far-too-logical mind of yours."

Having no choice but to trail after Harrison if he wanted to continue with their conversation, although he really thought one of his best friends should be a little more sympathetic to his plight, Gilbert nudged Blaze forward. "She's deliberately ignoring the rules of decorum by refusing to marry me. They're called rules for a reason, and as such, she certainly shouldn't be treating them so willy-nilly."

"You just told me Temperance has agreed to continue on with allowing everyone to believe the two of you are engaged. She's simply not agreeable to actually marrying you in the end."

"Society will not forget about this farce of an engagement," Gilbert argued. "Why, I heard it from Tobias, a man I've recently hired on as my valet, that talk is already swirling about town regarding my engagement, and the social season hasn't even begun yet." He blew out a breath. "I shudder to think how much that talk will increase once all of society gathers at their nightly frivolities and ladies vie with each other to divulge the latest intrigues."

"How did your new valet hear about the talk swirling around the city?"

"You're losing focus, Harrison. We're talking about Temperance and her refusal to take our engagement seriously."

"Yes, but aren't you curious as to how Tobias came to hear of the gossip surrounding you?"

Gilbert rolled his eyes, then ducked his head when he noticed a low-hanging branch that he'd almost run into, an oversight he would have never experienced if his thoughts weren't being distracted by Temperance. "Tobias is a man with many talents, Harrison, one of them being the ability to fade into the background in any situation. That allows him to eavesdrop on the most delicate of conversations, a talent he apparently puts to use often."

"Don't tell me you've begun hiring men of questionable natures, because that'll find you dead in your bed some night for certain."

"Tobias doesn't have a questionable nature," Gilbert returned. "He simply used to be employed as an underbutler to my brother, but managed to annoy my brother's wife, thus finding himself without employment in England. He arrived on my doorstep a month or so ago, and because I gave him a position on the spot, he's now determined to repay me by going above and beyond the role of valet and putting his talent for eavesdropping to good use."

"Isn't the role of valet a step down for a man who was once an underbutler to an earl?"

"Since I already employ a butler and an underbutler, I couldn't very well give those gentlemen the boot in order to give Tobias those particular positions. But, again, we're becoming completely distracted from the issue at hand — that issue, if you've forgotten, being how I'm supposed to convince Temperance she wants nothing more than to marry me."

"I don't think, because of her adamant refusal of your offer, that Temperance wants to marry you," Harrison pointed out.

"Well, quite, but you experienced reluctance from Gertrude at first. I thought, mistakenly so it now seems, that you'd be able to offer me invaluable advice that would have Temperance changing her mind."

"The only reason Gertrude changed *her* mind was because she came to the realization I was the love of her life and she didn't want to live that life without me." Harrison pulled Rupert to a stop again. "Do you think you could possibly be the love of Temperance's life?"

"Do you think she'd continue refusing my offer of marriage if I *was*?"

Harrison grinned. "An excellent point, but tell me this. Is Temperance the love of your life?"

"I'm not a gentleman inclined to embrace those particular emotions."

Harrison's grin slid straight off his face. "Then that's the problem right there. Temperance is what I would consider a whimsical lady, prone to dreams of a world that's filled with, well, I'm not really sure, but I imagine that adorable puppies, fey creatures, and plenty of sweet cakes inhabit her dreams on a frequent basis. What you need to understand is that a lady prone to whimsy expects a gentleman to ply her with romantic phrases and gestures, so if you truly want to bring her around to your way of thinking, you're going to have to change your unromantic ways."

"You think she'd change her mind about marrying me if I got her a puppy?"

"How did you get that solution out of what I just said?"

"Because I can't very well get her some fey creatures since I'd have a difficult time of it trying to run some of those down, even if I knew exactly what type of creatures they might be. As for the cake, well, that seems too easy to obtain."

For a long moment, Harrison simply

looked at Gilbert, then he gave a sad shake of his head and urged his horse forward again, this time at a bit of a gallop.

"I suppose we should go after him, Blaze," Gilbert said, and with a toss of his head, Blaze was lurching into motion, catching up to Harrison a few minutes later, but only because Harrison had pulled his horse to a stop again.

"I do wish you'd remember that Blaze isn't as young as he used to be and gets his feelings hurt when he's shown up time and time again by Rupert," Gilbert said, pulling up alongside his friend. "And, add in the fact that I didn't prepare Blaze in advance for this jaunt to the park, only deciding to join you here after my appointment with a Mr. Ashwell was unexpectedly canceled today, he's more sluggish than ever." He gave his horse a pat, brushing aside a mane that was tangled more often than not because Blaze put up a fuss if anyone took longer than five minutes grooming him. "This poor old boy was eating some tasty oats when I went to get him saddled from the livery and refused to allow the groom to put a saddle on him until I promised him the treat of a few apples after our ride."

Harrison cocked a brow. "And you truly believe that Blaze understood that promise, and that he didn't simply give in because he was leery of the groom who was probably glaring back at him in annoyance, a direct result of having to hold a heavy saddle in his arms until Blaze turned cooperative?"

"I didn't consider that scenario."

"Well, you should have, but tell me this — why do you continuously choose to ride Blaze during our rides in Central Park when I know you have younger horses at your disposal?"

Gilbert gave Blaze another pat. "He's always been my favorite, more friend than means of transportation, and I wouldn't want to hurt his feelings by abandoning him to some obscure pasture simply because he's old."

Tilting his head, Harrison considered Gilbert. "That's actually rather encouraging to learn about you, especially with you recently claiming to be a gentleman in possession of limited emotional capacities."

"I never said I had limited emotional capacities."

"You claimed to not embrace the notion of love, yet you clearly love your horse, which means there's hope for you yet."

Gilbert's brows drew together. "If this is your idea of extending me sound gentlemanly advice, you're not very good at it."

"You don't want advice," Harrison countered. "You want me to agree with you that Temperance is being unreasonable. But the more you say about the matter, the more I'm convinced she has the right measure of things and that the two of you might not be meant to spend the rest of your lives together."

"She's always been a very dear friend to me."

"Do tell me you haven't been bringing that up often as a way to convince her to marry you, have you?"

"Why wouldn't I bring that up? It's the most compelling argument I have."

Steering Rupert off the gravel path, Harrison stopped underneath a tree that was beginning to turn a vibrant red. He swung out of the saddle, waited for Gilbert to join him, then together, they moved to the large trunk of the tree, both leaning their backs against it as the wind stirred fallen leaves around them.

"Because you seem to feel I'm faltering in giving you solid advice," Harrison said, pulling his attention away from leaves that were drifting to the ground. "Why don't we begin again, and this time, so I can better advise you, why don't we start with you explaining why you're so determined to marry her."

"I would think that's obvious. We broke almost every rule there is regarding proprieties, and because of that, we have no choice but to get married."

Harrison crossed his arms over his chest. "You do realize you have this very concerning habit of adhering to rules, keeping schedules, and generally living your life as if there's a list that needs to be followed, one where your hand might get slapped if you stray from it, don't you?"

Not knowing if he should be insulted or complimented, Gilbert frowned. "Adhering to rules allows me to avoid the chaos that can occur when rules are broken and lists aren't made." He held up his hand when Harrison opened his mouth. "And because I know your next question will be to inquire whether I've always been a stickler for rules, yes, although I do believe my preference for living a structured life solidified during my time at the Phillips Academy, a preparatory school I enjoyed attending. They demanded their students abide by the strictest of rules, and I've clung to that lesson well over the years."

"Perhaps you should consider abandoning that stance," Harrison said. "It doesn't seem to be aiding your case with Temperance, what with her being a lady who doesn't seem to enjoy the idea of too many rules and all."

"Permilia Griswold is a lady who doesn't enjoy rules either, and yet she and our friend, Asher, are soon to be wed. He, as you very well know, is quite like me in that he's a most practical sort, as well as a gentleman who appreciates embracing a life of structure."

Harrison's eyes crinkled at the corners. "Something he apparently learned at that school you both attended. However, I'm not certain if you're aware of this or not, but Asher decided he was turning rather boring, what with his preference for keeping to a tight schedule, and asked me to assist him in changing his attitude, wanting to become a man who could enjoy nails for breakfast and bullets for lunch."

"You encouraged Asher to eat nails for breakfast?"

Harrison grinned. "Well, no, but my point is that Asher, realizing he was falling in love with Permilia, but also realizing his dull attitude might not encourage her to return his affections, knew he needed to make a few changes in his life."

"I've never considered having to change the way I approach life to secure a wife. I certainly don't think I need to change with

Temperance since she knows everything about me, and yet has never led me to believe she finds me lacking."

"But she doesn't want to marry you, so there's obviously something holding her back from accepting your proposal. I believe that something is your lack of having even a single ounce of romance lurking in that too-sensible body of yours. That, my friend, needs to change if you want to claim her as your wife."

"Not likely."

"Then you need to accept defeat, embrace the idea Temperance has of allowing your faux engagement to simply run its course, and hope everyone will forget about it after a few months." Harrison smiled. "Considering that even I've heard talk about you being eyed by numerous young society ladies, I have to believe society will be more than open to a broken engagement and will forgive you as long as you throw yourself into the midst of their societal world."

"I can't break off my engagement to Temperance. She'll be seen as a scorned woman."

"I wasn't suggesting you allow society to think *you* ended the engagement. Temperance can do that, and save her reputation by . . . well, I'm not sure how that works, but she seems to be a clever lady. I bet with the help of Gertrude and Permilia, she'll devise a plan that will see both of you unengaged and unscathed in the process."

The thought of not being engaged, even though he didn't feel legitimately engaged in the first place, left Gilbert rather disheartened.

At some point, he'd started to enjoy the thought of being married to Temperance, knowing that even though she was his opposite in every sense of the word, life with her by his side would never be boring. There would undoubtedly be moments when their opposite ways might cause a touch of friction, but . . .

A blast of what sounded exactly like a gunshot rang out right as the bark on the tree he and Harrison were standing under exploded.

Dropping to the ground, Gilbert yanked the pistol he often carried with him when he was in the city from its holster, moving backward across the ground to find some cover behind the tree.

"Awfully bold of someone to try to rob us in broad daylight," Harrison said, a gun already in his hand as he joined Gilbert.

"One would have thought they'd demand our money first before shooting at us."

"Excellent point, which means it's probably not a robber."

"Most likely it's an associate of yours from the docks, one you've apparently annoyed."

Harrison released a snort. "You're obviously confusing me with someone else. I don't annoy people in general, especially associates."

"I distinctly recall that you were ambushed in this very park only a few months back, lending credence to the idea our attacker is more likely after you than me."

Harrison crawled a few inches to the right. "Asher was the intended victim that time, not me, and that has absolutely nothing to do with the situation we're currently in, although . . ."

Another shot rang out, and Blaze, not being an adventurous horse, nor caring for loud noises, let out a whinny right before he galloped away, moving faster than Gilbert had seen him move in years.

"So much for making an escape on horseback," he muttered right as he caught sight of a man darting between the trees. "See him?"

"There's another one five feet to the left," Harrison said and with a nod between them, they rolled from their hiding spots and began shooting.

Howls of pain implied at least one of their bullets had met its mark. Before they could investigate further, though, the sound of horses racing away suggested the shooters were already on the move, which seemed to also suggest that if a bullet had met its mark, it hadn't done much harm.

A second later, Harrison was astride Rupert and in pursuit, leaving Gilbert behind since Blaze was nowhere to be seen.

Keeping his pistol at the ready, he scanned the surrounding area, finding not a single threat left. He did, however, discover a shrub that was rustling somewhat suspiciously, and one that had what looked to be the hindquarters of a horse poking out of it. Walking toward the shrub, he shook his head when he found Blaze hiding behind it, trembling like mad from head to hoof.

"Sorry about this, old boy," he murmured, smoothing a hand down Blaze's side, which did absolutely nothing to alleviate the trembling. A second later, after the distinctive sound of another gunshot sounded in the distance, Blaze's trembling increased, as did Gilbert's concern for Harrison.

Telling Blaze he'd be back directly, not that he was afraid Blaze was going to wander off since he'd moved further into the safety of the shrub, Gilbert turned in the direction of the gunshot and broke into a run, traveling no more than twenty feet before Harrison rode into view.

"They got away?" he called as Harrison slowed Rupert to a walk.

"One of the men fired off a shot at me right on the main path, one that was filled with ladies taking their afternoon stroll. I stopped the chase because I didn't want any of those ladies to suffer an unintentional gunshot wound from criminals who clearly were desperate to get away."

Harrison pulled Rupert to a stop a foot from Gilbert. "I'm afraid I didn't get a good look at either shooter, although if I were to hazard a guess, I'd say they were men for hire."

"Who'd want to hire someone to shoot you?"

Harrison rolled his eyes. "I don't believe I was their intended target."

"Well I can't think of a single person who'd want to see *me* laid low."

"And while I would normally agree that you're not exactly the type to draw someone's ire, I can think of three people, all of whom have the last name of Flowerdew, who are unquestionably put out with you because you laid waste to their plans."

Gilbert nodded. "Undoubtedly true, but I

don't believe Wayne, Fanny, or Clementine would resort to attempted murder. That seems a bit of an overreaction to what is really no more than a case of disappointment, although I wouldn't put it past them to begin spreading nasty rumors about me."

Harrison swung down from Rupert. "I didn't say I thought it was set in stone that the Flowerdews were behind our recent ambush. I was simply pointing out that they do seem to be furious with you, and . . . they were the first people to spring to mind. Add in the pesky notion you neglected to accept their invitation to call on them earlier this morning to discuss the matter of you choosing Temperance over their fair Clementine, and I'm relatively certain they're beyond miffed by what they must see as an unforgivable slight."

"They should be counting their lucky stars that Temperance and I didn't have them arrested for kidnapping and fraud. As for them being miffed about me not calling on them to discuss matters further, I was amazed at their audacity for even issuing me such a ridiculous invitation in the first place."

Harrison gave Rupert a pat before returning his attention to Gilbert. "While it does seem unlikely the Flowerdews were responsible for our ambush, it's clear someone wishes to do one of us harm, unless we just experienced a case of mistaken identity. Because we are unable to prove that at the moment, I think we'll need to adopt a sense of caution for the time being, along with warning those nearest and dearest to us that dangerous times might very well have come to the city again."

A sense of dread began trickling through him. "A most excellent suggestion, which means I need to get to Temperance as quickly as possible because danger does seem to be dogging her steps these days."

Chapter Ten

Standing on her tiptoes, Temperance stretched over the scaffolding that allowed her to reach the ceiling in the third-floor ballroom, nailing a hook into the crease that connected the wall with the ceiling. She practically jumped out of her skin, though, when someone below her let out a scream.

With her heart pounding like mad, she dropped the hammer to the board that made up the floor of her scaffold, turned, steadied herself on the railing that wobbled ever so slightly beneath her touch, then peered over the side, finding Miss Jane Snook peering right back up at her.

Even though she'd taken up the position of full-time instructor of music and art at Miss Snook's School for the Education of the Feminine Mind a few months before, she rarely saw Miss Snook and certainly couldn't say she knew the woman well.

The only thing she did know about Miss

Snook was that the woman had started a school to improve the lives of unfortunate women forced to work as domestics or in the factories, using a boardinghouse Temperance assumed Miss Snook owned as her first location for the school. After Miss Henrietta and Miss Mabel decided to abandon their mansion on Broadway to take up residence in the home they preferred by Gramercy Park, they'd offered Miss Snook the use of their former home for her school, an offer she hadn't hesitated to accept.

Because space was no longer an issue, Miss Snook spent her time, when she wasn't teaching English classes at the school, scouring the city for potential students, which was why Temperance rarely encountered the woman.

"Miss Flowerdew," Miss Snook called. "You need to get down from there right this very minute. It's not safe for you to dangle so far from the ground. If that flimsy contraption you're standing on gives out, well, I hardly believe it would encourage women to enroll in this school if rumors start swirling around that we make a habit of killing off our instructors."

Unable to help herself, Temperance smiled because Miss Snook sounded exactly like the teacher she was, and she was even shaking a finger Temperance's way. As usual, the woman was dressed in a serviceable gray day gown, her white-blond hair pulled in a severe chignon at the nape of her neck and black spectacles perched on the bridge of her nose.

"I'm perfectly safe," Temperance called back as Miss Snook stopped shaking her finger and crossed her arms over her chest in a gesture that implied she wasn't in agreement. "Miss Cutler helped me build the scaffold, and if I need remind you, she spent years at her father's side, helping him with his carpentry work."

"Be that as it may, I have no idea why you have a need to nail something into the ceiling. I shudder to think what Miss Henrietta will say after she learns you've been ruining the plaster in the ballroom."

"I'm not ruining the plaster, merely putting in a few hooks that will allow me to drape lengths of orange and red silk across the ceiling, lending the ballroom a sunset appearance."

"Why, pray tell, would you want to do that?"

"For Gertrude's engagement ball, of course. And, just to alleviate your concern about Miss Henrietta, she knows what I'm up to and heartily approves since she wants

Gertrude's special night to be an occasion Gertrude and Harrison will never forget."

"Which is a result I want as well, but I still have no understanding why you need to risk you neck in creating a sunset to obtain that goal."

Temperance leaned over the railing, stilling when Miss Snook gasped. "When Gertrude first met Harrison, she was, curiously enough, dyed an interesting shade of orange, a color that reminded Harrison of a sunset. Orange has since become one of Harrison's favorite colors, so Gertrude wanted orange to be a large part of her special evening." Temperance gestured to the ceiling. "I was considering painting the ceiling, but my little adventure to Chicago took precious time out of my schedule, forcing me to come up with an alternative plan."

Miss Snook tugged a handkerchief from her sleeve and blotted her forehead. She tucked the handkerchief away, smoothed a hand over her hair, then returned her attention to Temperance. "Given your artistic gifts, I'm certain your creation will be lovely, but I'm uncomfortable with you putting yourself in such danger."

"I spent many an hour on scaffolding far less stable than this one when I was assisting a renowned painter in Paris with a ceiling scene he was painting in an old church. I'm fine, but perhaps it might be for the best if you were to remove yourself from the ballroom since I'm clearly making you uncomfortable."

"I can't leave you up there with no one to keep an eye on you."

"Mr. Barclay will return directly. He's only fetching the bolts of silk I need from Rutherford & Company, so there's no need to fret."

"I'd feel better if you got down from there until Mr. Barclay returns."

Knowing she needed to move the scaffolding a few feet anyway to secure another hook to the ceiling, and knowing Miss Snook could be a somewhat bossy sort, Temperance nodded. "Very well, I'm coming down." She reached for the gate Miss Cutler had included on the scaffolding that opened with the use of a hinge, her foot brushing against the hammer and sending it skittering across the scaffold floor. "Watch out," she called right before the hammer disappeared from sight.

A loud bang sounded a second later, but thankfully, when she looked down, she found Miss Snook unharmed, having darted out of the way.

"Are you —"

The rest of her question got lost when Gilbert suddenly dashed into the room, brandishing a pistol of all things. He skidded to a halt right in front of Miss Snook who, instead of running away from a pistol-wielding gentleman she'd never met before, was pushing her spectacles farther up her nose and lifting her chin.

"Who in the world are you?" she demanded in her sternest voice yet. "And what are you doing brandishing a gun in the middle of my school?"

"I thought I heard a gunshot," Gilbert returned.

"It was just a hammer," Temperance called. "I lost it over the edge of the scaffold."

Gilbert immediately looked up, took a single step toward the scaffold, then stopped. "Have you lost your mind? Get down from there."

Temperance frowned. "You obviously have me confused with someone else, since you have to remember I don't care to be ordered about."

"Don't make me come up there and get you."

She crossed her arms over her chest. "I'd like to see you try, because unless *I'm* confusing you with someone else, you've always had an aversion to heights, a condition I highly doubt has changed over the years."

"You don't believe I'm capable of climbing up there and fetching you down?"

She leaned over the railing. "The last time I saw you climb up higher than you were comfortable climbing, you tossed up your accounts all over the place."

"That was a really tall tree, and I distinctly recall suffering from a stomach ailment before I made the climb."

"You were not suffering from a stomach ailment."

"I beg to differ with you on that, and —"

"Children," Miss Snook interrupted, holding up her hand and cutting Gilbert off midsentence. "Do not make me separate the two of you into opposite corners, but know that I will resort to that if your nonsense continues." She inclined her head toward Gilbert. "May I assume you're the Mr. Gilbert Cavendish whom Miss Flowerdew has remarked upon a time or two?"

"Indeed I am, although I would hope Temperance would have remarked on me more than a time or two since word is soon to travel about the city we're engaged." Gilbert tucked his pistol away and stepped closer to Miss Snook. He reached out and took hold of her hand, but before he could put the expected kiss on it, Miss Snook yanked her hand away from him and pushed her spectacles back into place again.

"There's no need for charm, Mr. Cavendish," Miss Snook began. "I'm immune to it. As for you being engaged to Miss Flowerdew, from what I understand, that's only a ruse, brought about by your attempt to thwart Miss Clementine Flowerdew's desire to walk down the aisle with you."

Gilbert sent Temperance a scowl. "Our plan will never work if you keep telling everyone it's a ruse."

"I never said a word to Miss Snook about our situation."

Miss Snook waved that aside. "You didn't need to, dear. You're now living in a school filled to the brim with young women who were forced to become very adept at eavesdropping in order to anticipate the moods of their reprehensible employers at their previous positions. Surely you must know that nothing gets by them."

"Of course I know that, although I must say I'm a little taken aback they'd run to you with everything they overhear or observe," Temperance said.

"If you really think about that, Miss Flowerdew, you'll not be taken aback at all.

I have given these women new opportunities, and with that comes a certain level of gratitude." She turned to Gilbert. "I'll leave you to watch over Miss Flowerdew. Do try to get her to come down, won't you? She was about to do just that before you burst into the room and annoyed her by turning demanding."

Miss Snook headed for the door, but before she could exit, Harrison rushed into the room with *his* pistol drawn, practically knocking Miss Snook off her feet when he rushed right into her. Catching her before she could fall, he helped her find her balance.

"I do beg your pardon, Miss Snook," Harrison said. "I truly did not mean to barrel into you. My only excuse is that I heard a gunshot and thought someone was under attack in the ballroom. Clearly, there's no mad assailant running amok up here."

"While there is certainly madness afoot, Mr. Sinclair, it's not being perpetuated by an assailant, simply Miss Flowerdew and her unbeknownst to me stubborn nature."

"I told you Temperance possessed a stubborn nature, Harrison, and now you've heard it from someone other than me," Gilbert said as Miss Snook shoved her spectacles back into place rather forcefully before she sailed out of the ballroom without another word.

"I do believe Miss Snook is in what one might call an aggravated frame of mind," Harrison said, tucking his pistol away before he looked up, settled his sights on Temperance, and smiled. "Hello, Temperance. What a delightful spot you seem to have found up there."

"Don't encourage her," Gilbert said. "I'm trying to get her to come down, but she's turned stubborn and is refusing."

"What is she doing up there in the first place?" Harrison asked.

"It's none of your business what I'm doing up here, Harrison, because Gertrude doesn't want you to know about it, so stop asking questions," Temperance called.

"She's far more vocal than she used to be when I first made her acquaintance," Harrison said to Gilbert, quite as if Temperance couldn't hear him. "I must say I do find this new, talkative Temperance more interesting than the practically mute Temperance she used to be. You should take satisfaction in the idea she's reclaimed her voice because you reentered her life."

Temperance opened her mouth to argue that point, but snapped it shut again when she realized Harrison was right. She *had* found her voice after reuniting with Gilbert. And while she was still exasperated with the man, she couldn't deny that it was because of him she'd reclaimed her sense of self as well as her life, which . . .

Temperance sucked in a sharp breath when a troubling thought struck from out of nowhere.

She'd been floundering for years, had lost her identity, and it wasn't until she'd reunited with Gilbert that she'd found the incentive to regain the very essence of who she was. She'd begun hearing music again directly after spending an evening with him at a ball, and then not long after that, she'd found the inspiration to begin painting once more, something she'd not done since learning her parents had died. That she'd rediscovered her love for her most passionate pursuits directly after seeing Gilbert again could only mean one thing. . . .

He was a far more important part of her life than she'd realized.

"Does Temperance make it a habit of descending into what looks to be some type of trance?" Harrison asked, pulling Temperance back to the situation at hand.

Pushing aside thoughts that certainly needed further contemplation, but not while the object of those thoughts was peering up at her, Temperance summoned up a smile. "I'm not in a trance, Harrison, I just got distracted for a moment."

"Distracted thinking about what you're doing up on that scaffold?" Harrison called.

"I can't tell you what I'm doing up here because it's a surprise."

"A surprise for whom?"

"Never you mind about that, darling."

Turning her attention to the door, Temperance found Gertrude Cadwalader standing there in a lovely walking dress of burnt orange, her honey-golden hair swept up into a knot on top of her head. She was smiling at Harrison, which was no surprise, nor was it a surprise when Harrison strode to Gertrude's side, giving her a kiss on the cheek before taking her hand and tucking it into the crook of his arm.

"You could give me a hint," Harrison said.

Gertrude shook her head. "Not likely, and before you try to charm it out of me, answer me this — what are you doing here?"

"I'm afraid the explanation for that will need to wait until Temperance joins us on the ground," Harrison said. "It's a rather delicate matter, so we don't want to have to explain with raised voices that might be overheard."

"That's certainly not the answer I was

expecting," Gertrude said before she lifted her head and nodded to Temperance. "Shall we repair to the library to hear the gentlemen out?"

"I'll be right down."

Harrison smiled. "I think this is where I take my leave since . . . well, you're up rather high, wearing a skirt, and . . . no need to say more."

Temperance watched as Harrison and Gertrude strolled from the room before she swung open the gate, pausing for a second as she considered Gilbert.

"You might want to close your eyes because watching me climb down from here is certain to make you queasy."

"I can watch you climb down from there without becoming queasy," Gilbert shot back. "But I will turn around since it would hardly be gentlemanly of me to watch you climb from such a height while wearing a skirt, which Harrison just pointed out."

"I'm wearing a split skirt, one Permilia found for me when I told her I didn't believe Miss Snook would approve of me roaming around the school in the trousers I normally wear when I'm in the middle of an artistic project."

"Then I'll not turn around, proving once and for all that I'm perfectly capable of watching you descend from such a great height without fainting dead away or casting up my accounts."

"You're simply not turning around because you want to keep an eye on me and make certain I don't fall. But I don't need you to keep an eye on me."

"One would have thought you'd become less contrary with age, not more."

"I spent three years not being contrary at all. I'm simply trying to make up for lost time." Edging her way onto the rungs that were serving as a ladder, Temperance made short shrift of reaching the ground, bending over to untie the two lengths of ribbon she'd wrapped around each leg to keep the voluminous fabric of the split skirt out of her way. Shaking out that material, she straightened, finding Gilbert watching her closely.

"You don't approve?" she asked.

"We may have been apart for years, Temperance, but I remember you well enough to know the only answer to that question is . . . *Of course I approve.* That's a *wonderful* split skirt, and I do hope ladies will soon take to wearing them about town and perhaps even wearing them to *balls.*"

"You're annoying."

"Thank you."

Unable to help but return the grin he was

sending her, Temperance took his arm and walked across the ballroom.

"What surprise do you and Gertrude have in store for Harrison that requires you to risk that stubborn neck of yours?" Gilbert asked when they reached the door.

"I'm not risking my neck, nor is it stubborn, but because I know you'll continue pestering me until I answer your question, I'm going to try to create a sunset illusion over the ceiling."

Gilbert stopped walking, turned, and considered the ceiling. "How would you go about that?"

"I'll string thin strands of rope through hooks secured to the sides of the room, adding additional hooks to the middle of the ceiling so the silk I'll then drape over the ropes will create a puffy, cloudlike feel. I'm hoping that by adding some colored glass to the chandeliers, it'll look exactly like the sky looks when the sun is setting over the ocean."

Gilbert turned to her. "How do you know how to do that?"

"I don't know. I just saw it in my mind, and now I just have to hope it'll work."

"How do you see that in your mind?"

She smiled. "How do you see a column of figures and know the sum with barely any tallying on your part?"

"It's simply something I'm able to do without thinking."

"That's how I see my art."

Gilbert frowned. "Is it the same with your music? Can you see the notes in your head?"

"I hear the notes in my head, but I have no idea why I'm then able to play them on an instrument." She prodded him back into motion again. "I like to believe God gives everyone a special gift, although I've only recently reclaimed my artistic abilities, which I must admit, is all thanks to being reunited with you — which had me remembering who I truly am."

"Perhaps I do have my uses after all."

She smiled. "I could possibly agree with that if I didn't think doing so would turn you smug."

As they traveled down the three flights of stairs to the library, the conversation turned easy, reminding Temperance exactly how comfortable she'd always been in Gilbert's presence. They'd always been able to argue and annoy each other, and yet return to their easy friendship in a blink of an eye.

When they reached the hallway that led to the library, they made it all of two feet before what sounded like a scuffle erupted through the door that led to the kitchen, right before the sound of what truly did seem to be a gunshot rang out.

Before Temperance could react, Gilbert was pushing her behind him right as two figures burst out of the doorway, figures who turned out to be none other than Eugene and Mercy, her erstwhile kidnappers, followed by Mr. Barclay, who was, concerningly enough, holding a smoking pistol in his hand.

Chapter Eleven

Of anything Gilbert expected Temperance to do, darting past him and running toward what looked to be members of the criminal set was at the very bottom of his list of expectations.

Before he could do more than blink, though, the criminal who was rather small in stature and whose face was covered in whiskers was wrapping arms covered in a tattered shirt around Temperance. Curiously enough, instead of screaming or attempting to get away, Temperance bent her head and began whispering furiously into the criminal's ear.

As he tried to wrap his mind around that bit of peculiarity, his attention was suddenly drawn to the sight of Mr. Barclay, a gentleman well past his prime, diving through the air, landing on the back of the larger man, and, in a tumble of flailing arms and legs, plummeting toward the ground.

To Gilbert's relief, Mr. Barclay somehow managed to land on top of the man he'd just knocked over, where he continued to sprawl over the man's back even as the man he'd brought down began to struggle.

Glancing at Temperance, Gilbert found her still whispering into the bearded person's ear, clearly in no distress, which allowed him to turn his attention to assisting Mr. Barclay. He managed to take all of two steps toward the butler when Harrison and Gertrude suddenly burst out of the library, Harrison's gun already in hand. As Harrison barked out an order for the man to stop struggling, additional chaos entered the mix when another man dashed into view — none other than Agent Samuel McParland, a reputable Pinkerton detective.

"Don't let them shoot us, Miss Flowerdew," the criminal still holding fast to Temperance said in a remarkably high tone of voice, a voice that sounded feminine, if Gilbert wasn't much mistaken. "We ain't here to harm you, only to *warn* you."

Temperance, for some unknown reason, sent a pointed look to the pistol Gilbert was only now retrieving and scowled. "For heaven's sake, Gilbert, put that away. You're scaring Mercy half to death, and —" She twisted to look Mr. Barclay's way, a tricky feat if there ever was one since Mercy, apparently a woman, although a bearded one, was now wrapping her arms around Temperance's neck, practically strangling Temperance in the process. "While I'm more than impressed with your heroic actions, Mr. Barclay, Eugene does seem to be laboring for breath. It might be prudent to get off him before he loses all ability to breathe."

"Forgive me, Miss Temperance, but I'm afraid your far-too-trusting nature is allowing these criminals to dupe you," Mr. Barclay said, lifting his head but nothing else. "I discovered them sneaking in the back door after I returned from Rutherford & Company, which clearly suggests they're here for some nefarious purpose."

"We couldn't very well walk up to the front door and ask to see Miss Flowerdew," Mercy argued. "Me and Eugene worked our whole lives in service, and while we don't claim to understand all the rules, we do know that if you're of the serving class, you got to use the back door."

Mr. Barclay inclined his head and shifted around, earning a groan from the man named Eugene in the process. "That is certainly true, but one expects even servants to knock on a back door when paying a visit, and as you know, you did not knock even once. You tried to tiptoe in after me, proof you're up to something dastardly and, if you'll recall, the man underneath me pulled out a knife."

"Only because you pulled a pistol and then shot at me," Eugene argued.

"My dear man, I didn't shoot *at* you because if I had, you'd be dead. I shot at the wall, an action that was supposed to have you and your cohort running for your very lives — *out* of the house, not *into* it."

Mercy shook her head. "We came to warn Miss Flowerdew, and we couldn't very well do that if we'd run out of the house before we warned her."

"A likely story," Gilbert said, earning a narrowing of the eyes from Temperance. He narrowed his eyes right back at her. "I have no understanding why you seem to be so protective of these miscreants, Temperance, especially since I'm rapidly concluding they are trying to pull the wool over your eyes with this ridiculous idea that they're here to warn you. You mark my words, as soon as that wool is done doing what it's meant to do, they'll then go about the troubling business of trying to murder you."

"Mercy is not here to murder me."

"It certainly seemed to Harrison and me that murder was on her and her companion's mind when they ambushed us in the middle of Central Park."

"I don't recall you mentioning a thing about being ambushed in Central Park."

"I would have mentioned it by now if I had not discovered you facing a life-or-death situation in the ballroom when I first arrived. Although, now that I think about it, one would have thought you'd have been suspicious that I burst into the ballroom with my pistol drawn."

Temperance's brows drew together. "How could I have possible come to the conclusion something of a suspicious nature was occurring? I thought you were simply being you — overthinking a perfectly ordinary happenstance."

"Who in their right mind would believe dropping a hammer from such a height is an ordinary happenstance?" he shot back.

"Are you suggesting I'm not in my right mind?"

"*Not* that I believe entering this riveting conversation is going to benefit me in the least," Harrison interrupted as he helped Mr. Barclay to his feet, dusting the man off while keeping his pistol trained on Eugene. "But now might not be the best time to pursue this rather unusual courtship ritual the two of you seem to be engaged in."

"We're *not* courting," Temperance said, turning her temper on Harrison. "And do give it a rest with the pistols. Mercy and Eugene aren't here to harm me. They say they're here to warn me."

Gilbert took a single step toward her, thankful at least that Mercy was slowly relaxing her hold on Temperance, although why the woman was wearing whiskers was more than confusing. He stopped moving, though, when a thought sprang to mind. "Didn't you tell me that you were abducted by two members of the criminal persuasion who went by the names Mercy and Eugene?"

"I told you it was a mistake to let our real names slip. We should've stuck with Vivian and Thurman," Eugene said from his position on the floor.

"Miss Flowerdew done heard us using our real names, Eugene," Mercy said with a roll of her eyes before she nodded to Gilbert. "But you got the wrong idea about us, mister. We weren't anywhere near Central Park today, and I know for fact we never tried to kill you." She lifted her chin. "Me and Eugene ain't no killers."

Gilbert considered her for a brief moment. "I will admit that you do not resemble the men who ambushed me today because both of those men were larger than you. Nevertheless, if I'm understanding the situation correctly, you are guilty of kidnapping, even if you're not guilty of attacking me today."

"Which means they belong in jail," Agent McParland said, stepping forward with a pair of handcuffs already in his hand.

Gilbert braced himself when Temperance immediately began looking stubborn right before she shrugged out of Mercy's hold, but only to take hold of Mercy's hand.

"They don't belong in jail because it wasn't a real abduction, but a plot conceived by my relatives to force Gilbert into a marriage with Clementine."

"But we *thought* it was an abduction," Mercy added.

Temperance gave Mercy's hand a pat. "That's not helping your case, Mercy, but may I suggest we continue this discussion in the library where we can sit and enjoy some tea? That will lend the atmosphere a more civilized air. Although everyone needs to put away their pistols because I won't be able to enjoy my tea with the threat of someone getting accidentally shot hanging over the room."

"I wouldn't mind a cup of tea," Mercy said, smacking her lips.

"And some cake might be lovely, if there's any lyin' about," Eugene added.

Temperance caught Gilbert's eye. "I hardly think these two would ask for tea and cake if they were here to murder me."

"Did it ever occur to you that they may be trying to get you to lower your defenses, and then, when you're at your most vulnerable, they'll make their move?"

"Since they admitted to me on the long ride to Chicago that they're not criminals by choice, having been forced to take on the job of abducting me because they were desperate for funds, I don't believe they're capable of planning out anything resembling an intricate plot."

"Now, there ain't no reason to go insultin' us," Eugene said, getting to his feet and shaking his head. "Me and Mercy might not make the best kidnappers around, but I bet we could fashion us a good plot if we tried real hard."

"As I said to Mercy, you're not helping your case," Temperance said before she began tugging Mercy toward the library.

"You won't let them haul us away to jail, will you, Miss Flowerdew?" Mercy asked.

"Of course not."

Grabbing hold of Eugene's arm as she walked past him, Temperance pulled him along with her and Mercy into the library, followed closely by Agent McParland and Gertrude.

"I'm beginning to believe you might have a most excellent point regarding Temperance's stubborn nature," Harrison said as he walked beside Gilbert into the library. "Although I don't recall you mentioning much about her temper."

"I've apparently forgotten that part of her charm, which does have me questioning why I still seem keen to convince her to marry me."

"I'm not marrying you, and I don't have a temper," Temperance called from where she'd already taken a seat on a small settee, sandwiched between Mercy and Eugene, a sight that left Gilbert shaking his head.

"Wouldn't it be a more practical move to find a seat where you're not sitting between criminals I've yet to be convinced are *not* here to murder you?"

"It'd be hard to murder anyone right now since I dropped my knife when that man tried to shoot me," Eugene said with a nod to Mr. Barclay, who paused in the act of lowering himself into a chair and released a huff.

"I didn't try to shoot you, merely scare you."

"And I would say you were successful with that," Temperance said with a small smile before she frowned. "But where are your spectacles, Mr. Barclay? I distinctly recall you telling me you're far more accurate with your aim when you're wearing them."

"I'm afraid they're still residing in my jacket pocket," Mr. Barclay returned. "I didn't have time to pull them out and put them on since I was taken by surprise by these two."

Mercy's mouth dropped open. "Are you tellin' me you can't see without spectacles, but took a shot at us anyways?"

Mr. Barclay waved that aside. "I can see somewhat well without my spectacles, but my shot is always truer when I'm wearing them."

Snapping her mouth shut, Mercy folded her arms over her chest while Temperance reached out and placed a hand on Mercy's knee.

"Rest assured, you were never in danger of Mr. Barclay shooting you. He stated he aimed for the wall, and I can attest that he's a remarkably fine shot even without his spectacles, his proficiency with a pistol improving greatly ever since he began shooting lessons with Mr. Harrison Sinclair." Temperance nodded Harrison's way. "It's well known throughout the city that Harrison is an expert marksman."

"Which is why it's fortunate you encountered me instead of Mr. Sinclair," Mr. Barclay added, settling back in his chair. "He's also known throughout the city as a very dangerous gentleman and might not have shown you the same courtesy I did of merely trying to scare you instead of shoot you." He nodded to Temperance. "I do hope I may count on you to explain to Miss Snook why there's now a lovely hole in the wall of her school. She's a bit frightening, and I am an elderly, feeble sort."

Temperance's eyes crinkled at the corners. "You're also evidently a great weaver of tales. But you did race to my rescue, so I'll explain the hole to Miss Snook, though there's always the possibility we can repair it before she takes notice."

"Takes notice of what?"

Turning toward the door, Gilbert found Miss Snook standing in the doorway, hands on her hips, her glasses perched on the very edge of her nose.

"I thought you were teaching a class," Temperance said somewhat weakly.

"It's rather difficult to teach a class when a gunshot distracted all of my students. I was forced to abandon the lesson to come investigate the matter." Miss Snook looked over the rim of her glasses at Mercy and Eugene. "I see we have more unexpected guests."

Eugene surprised Gilbert when he rose to his feet and bowed Miss Snook's way. "Beggin' your pardon, ma'am. We didn't mean to make a ruckus. I'm Eugene Miner, and that there" — he nodded to Mercy — "is my sister, Miss Mercy Miner."

"I'm Miss Snook, proprietress of this school," Miss Snook tilted her head. "May I assume you're here to enroll in the school, but through some manner of misunderstanding, were taken for shifty sorts?"

Eugene scratched his head. "We sure was taken for shifty sorts, ma'am, but getting back to that school business you mentioned, I thought this here school was a school for the women."

"It is, but we aren't so rigid with our enrollment that we're not open to exceptions."

Eugene stopped scratching his head. "Huh, that's odd, but we ain't here to enroll in your school."

Miss Snook's gaze lingered on Mercy, who'd uncrossed her arms and was now sitting forward on the settee. "Because I don't care to pry unless that prying is encouraged,

I won't ask any other questions of you two, but do know that enrollment in my school is an option for you in the future." She turned and nodded to Agent McParland, who'd risen to his feet as well. "And you would be?"

"I'm Agent Samuel McParland, Miss Snook. Detective with the Pinkerton Agency."

Miss Snook stiffened just the slightest bit. "How lovely. And now, since no one seems to be bleeding all over the library floor, I think it may be for the best if I return to class and leave all of you to return to whatever it was I interrupted."

Turning smartly on her heel, Miss Snook quit the library.

"Was it something I said?" Agent McParland asked as he retook his seat.

"Miss Snook can be somewhat abrupt, Agent McParland," Temperance said. "Do not take it personally." She smiled. "Now then, where were we?"

"I think you were about ready to order some tea and cake," Mercy said.

"Forgive me, Mercy, I forgot about the tea and cakes." Temperance nodded to Gertrude, who didn't hesitate to stand and walk out of the room, obviously on her way to order refreshments from the kitchen.

"Thank you, Miss Flowerdew," Mercy said, rubbing her stomach. "Me and Eugene are a little hungry. We used up all of our money to get back to New York and haven't had a meal for what feels like months."

Harrison shook his head and headed after Gertrude, evidently on his way to order something more substantial than tea and cake.

"Good heavens, the bolts of fabric I retrieved from Rutherford & Company are lying piggly-wiggly about in the kitchen, and Mr. Sinclair is not supposed to see them," Mr. Barclay exclaimed, practically jumping out of his chair before he bolted out of the library.

"I wonder if he realizes Harrison isn't a gentleman prone to noticing things like bolts of fabric," Gilbert said to no one in particular, earning a nod in response from Agent McParland before that gentleman cleared his throat, drawing everyone's attention.

"While we wait for tea, may I suggest we get down to business, specifically, what the two of you need to warn Miss Flowerdew about, or better yet, the circumstances that caused you to abduct her in the first place." Agent McParland settled his undivided attention on Mercy and Eugene.

Mercy tugged on her beard. "We weren't supposed to abduct this Miss Flowerdew, but the other Miss Flowerdew, a mistake we made on account of getting some wrong information from sources we know on the streets."

"Having sources on the street implies you've been involved with criminal acts for some time now," Agent McParland said.

Releasing a snort, Mercy shook her head. "It don't imply nothing of the sort. Me and Eugene have been employed in service for years and years, but were released from our last position with a measly two dollars and no references. We was getting hungry, had no place to live, and that's why we took on the job to abduct Miss Flowerdew. And, just so we're clear, our sources were other people of the serving sort who had been let go from the last house we worked at." She looked to Temperance. "One of the maids I used to work with pointed you out to me the day before we snatched you up, telling me you always started your day at a little bakery down Broadway. I thought it would be easier to snatch you right after you left the bakery then to wait until you were going to your dance class because me and Eugene couldn't find out where that dance academy was, not since we done forgot the name of the place."

"You never did explain why Mrs. Baldwin released you from service," Temperance said.

Eugene let out a grunt. "We didn't do nothing wrong to get dismissed from our positions. Mrs. Baldwin decided it wasn't helping her rise up the social ladder to keep on staff that didn't speak English so good. She got rid of the lot of us and hired her on some servants who speak some fancy language."

"French," Mercy added. "But the people she hired on don't really speak French. They just learned enough words to make her believe they did."

Temperance's eyes flashed. "And she didn't bother to give her former staff references?"

Mercy tugged on her beard again. "She thought giving us references would look poorly on her, since society might not be impressed that she'd hired on uneducated people to begin with. Society folks don't want people who can't read and write good to work in their new fancy houses these days, not caring that it don't take no reading for me to clean out a bedchamber, or for Eugene to muck out a stall."

Pursing her lips, Temperance soothed a hand down Mercy's arm. "Someone needs to have a little chat with Mrs. Baldwin about her abysmal lack of compassion."

"This Mrs. Baldwin is no different from many members of society," Gilbert said, walking across the library and sitting in a chair that was closer to Temperance, on the off chance Mercy and Eugene did have plans to harm her. "And forgive me for pointing this out, something that's certain to incur your displeasure, but even though Mrs. Baldwin unjustly turned Mercy and Eugene out, that is no excuse for them abducting you."

The look Temperance shot him was hot enough to scorch his face, but before she could let loose the tirade she clearly longed to direct his way, Mercy, thankfully, spoke up.

"Me and Eugene know we was wrong to accept the job to steal Miss Flowerdew. Our only excuse is that it didn't really sound like a crime, not after the man who hired us explained that Miss Flowerdew was not expected to make a fuss, and that we was to travel to Chicago in a Pullman car and stay at the swanky Palmer House."

"You traveled to Chicago in a Pullman car?" Agent McParland asked, looking up from a notepad he'd recently pulled out and balanced on his knees.

Mercy leaned forward, her gaze riveted on the notepad. "Why are you writing everything down?"

"I'm a Pinkerton detective. Taking notes goes with the territory."

Mercy shrank back against the settee. "Are you going to use what I say to put me behind bars?"

"If what you have to say is incriminating, yes."

"Then I ain't sayin' another word."

"He's not going to send you to jail," Temperance said before she quirked a brow Agent McParland's way. "Are you?"

"I can't make any guarantees, not when she and Eugene have admitted they abducted you, which is a crime, if that was in question." Agent McParland returned his attention to Mercy. "But I will say that if you cooperate, it'll go easier on you and your brother."

Mercy leaned over Temperance and nodded to Eugene. "What should we do?"

"We might as well come clean, Mercy. Our lives just keep gettin' worse and worse since we agreed to take on the job of abducting Miss Flowerdew. I have to think that Pastor Roy, if he was still alive, would say our lives ain't gonna get no better until we own up to the bad we've done and ask for some forgiveness."

"I was afraid you was gonna say that," Mercy said, sitting back before she released a sigh. "We don't know who hired us. Me and Eugene were having us a drink at a pub down by the Battery, and that's where this man approached us. He kept his hat pulled low over his face, but he bought us another drink and a loaf of bread, which we sure did appreciate since we was hungry. When we was done eating, he asked if we'd like to earn some money. After he explained what needed to be done, and because gettin' Miss Flowerdew out of town and to Chicago didn't sound like a *real* crime, we agreed to do it."

"We just got confused about which Miss Flowerdew we was supposed to take," Eugene added, sitting forward. "Who'd of thought there'd be more than one of them?"

"Didn't this man give you a description of the Miss Flowerdew he wanted you to take?" Agent McParland asked.

"He did, but even though the Miss Flowerdew we snatched wasn't wearing yellow like we'd been told she'd be wearing, we thought we had the right lady since that friend of mine told me she knew for sure that she" — Mercy nodded to Temperance — "was Miss Flowerdew." She blew out a breath. "We should have known we'd made a mistake when she didn't come quietly and we had to stuff her into a coffin to get her to Chicago."

Agent McParland set aside his notes and pinned Temperance under a steely eye. "You were stuffed into a coffin?"

Temperance shrugged. "It sounds much worse than it was. And because Eugene doused me with a sleeping potion and let me out of the coffin when I awoke, I wasn't overly traumatized."

Agent McParland seemed to swell on the spot. "They doused you with a sleeping potion and yet you still don't believe they belong in jail?"

"Ah, lovely, here's Gertrude and Harrison with the food and drink," Temperance said, completely neglecting to respond to Agent McParland as she got up from the settee. She nodded to Mercy and Eugene before she gestured to the carts Gertrude and Harrison were pushing, each cart filled with tea, cakes, and sandwiches. "You two go first."

As Mercy and Eugene hurried to the carts, Temperance returned her attention to Agent McParland. "While I appreciate your indignation on my account, Agent McParland, there was no harm done to me during my unexpected adventure. With that said, I expect you to discontinue threatening Mercy and Eugene with arrest because no one ever enjoyed a meal with a stay in jail hanging over their heads."

"Would you like some cake?" Gilbert asked Agent McParland, who was now looking quite as if he had no idea how to proceed, especially since the woman he was trying to seek justice for clearly didn't feel as if any justice needed to be served.

"I'd like Miss Flowerdew to stop arguing with my every word," Agent McParland began before he smiled. "But since that's unlikely to happen, a piece of cake would be most welcome."

The next ten minutes passed with little conversation as Gilbert, along with Agent McParland, enjoyed the cake some of the students at the school had made, while Mercy and Eugene sampled everything that had been brought from the kitchen.

When every last crumb had been devoured, and every spot of tea drunk, Mercy blotted her lips with the napkin Temperance handed her, shook the crumbs from her beard, then nodded. "I thank you for that, Miss Flowerdew," she began. "And now that I can think again since my belly isn't rumbling, I need to tell you why Eugene and I are really here. You're in danger."

Temperance set aside the cup she'd been holding. "Danger?"

Eugene leaned forward and nodded. "Talk on the street is that someone's been trying to hire on people to see one Miss Temperance Flowerdew good and dead."

Chapter Twelve

For the briefest of seconds, Temperance's mind went curiously blank, until a thought began to fester. It wasn't a pleasant thought, but one that exactly explained who would be at the top of the list of people wanting her dead. With anger churning through her veins, she shot to her feet.

"If all of you will excuse me, I have a matter of great urgency I need to address." She began stomping her way across the room.

"Not that I want to disrupt what is clearly a very dramatic exit, Temperance, but I must insist you delay your departure until you explain that matter of great urgency that no one in this room except you seems to understand."

Turning, she found that Gilbert had already risen from his chair and was watching her somewhat warily. Heaving a breath, she crossed her arms over her chest. "I would think it obvious what that matter is and where I'm off to next."

Gilbert shook his head. "I'm afraid it's not obvious, at least not to me."

She lifted her chin. "My cousins have evidently taken complete leave of their senses and have decided to put a price on my head, which will effectively have me out of their lives for good."

Striding to her side, Gilbert took hold of her arm. "And you've decided to what — saunter over to their home and confront them?"

"I'm far too angry to saunter, Gilbert. I'll borrow Miss Henrietta's buggy, which will allow me to arrive at Park Avenue in a far timelier fashion."

His hand tightened on her arm. "You cannot go rushing willy-nilly over to your cousins' on your own, particularly when there is the chance you're mistaken about the culprits behind this threat on your life. As Harrison and I only recently discussed, your cousins are evidently somewhat nasty people, but I'm not sure they're the type to stoop to murder."

Temperance shrugged her way out of his hold. "I'm not mistaken, Gilbert. Wayne, Fanny, and Clementine are the only people I know who'd want me dead. Truth be told, I'm now feeling all sorts of a fool for not having implicated them in my abduction in the first place. I simply thought it would be detrimental to the Flowerdew name, of which I unfortunately share, to allow all of society to learn about the ridiculous plot they concocted to force you into marriage with Clementine. Now, however, they've stepped over a line, and they need to be held accountable for their madness once and for all."

"Are you absolutely certain your relatives were responsible for your disappearance, although . . ." Agent McParland rose to his feet and frowned. "Am I to understand *you* really weren't supposed to be the target of that abduction?"

Temperance blinked. "Goodness, do forgive me, Agent McParland. I fear with all the confusion the arrival of Mercy and Eugene created, and learning Gilbert and Harrison had been ambushed in Central Park, I neglected to realize you're still in the dark about numerous matters."

She walked back across the room. "I've also forgotten the reason you wanted to pay me a call today was to discuss some interesting information you uncovered in the last few days while you were searching for me at Miss Henrietta's request." She plopped down on a dainty chair. "Perhaps it would be for the best for me to delay my trip to confront my Flowerdew cousins while you fill me in. I have the sneaking suspicion your information might have something to do with the unseemly business of my cousins wanting me dead."

"It very well could," Agent McParland said, retaking his seat. "But before I delve into that, if you could bring me up-to-date about what really happened to you, that may fill in some of the questions I have regarding your relatives."

Nodding, Temperance began recounting everything that had happened to her, beginning with Eugene tossing her into the carriage. Twenty minutes later, she finished with "And Wayne, Fanny, and Clementine left the train depot in a cloud of indignation, proclaiming to Miss Appleton and Miss Wells that I was delusional. They also stated most emphatically that Gilbert wasn't a gentleman they'd now consider a good match for their darling Clementine. He'd apparently ruined their good opinion through his careless disregard of Clementine's tender feelings, which they evidently didn't believe him capable of because Gilbert is, after all, related to an earl." She wrinkled her nose. "I think they may have changed their opinion about him again, though, because they sent Gilbert a note asking him to call on them this morning."

Agent McParland turned to Gilbert. "You're related to an earl?"

"The Earl of Strafford is my half brother, but I don't believe that has anything to do with someone wanting to murder Temperance."

"True." Agent McParland smiled. "I was simply curious. I've never met anyone related to a real aristocrat before, but you seem normal enough." He bent to look through his notes. "Clearly, this is a case that's destined to become more fascinating by the second. I'm looking forward to tracking down the culprits who ambushed you and Harrison today in Central Park."

"There won't be much tracking involved, Agent McParland," Temperance said. "Not when it's highly likely Wayne's responsible for that nasty bit of skullduggery."

Gilbert frowned. "As I mentioned to Harrison earlier, having me murdered seems a bit of an overreaction and does come with the very real consequence of spending a life in jail, if one gets caught."

Temperance sat forward. "But you embarrassed my cousins. To them, that is unforgivable, especially since there were witnesses."

"It still seems to be an overreaction."

"As does the idea they'd hire someone to murder me simply because they believe I've stolen a gentleman Clementine desires, but I'm convinced that's what they've done."

"Perhaps that's not the real reason they want you dead," Agent McParland said as he flipped through his notepad, scanning the pages. He stilled when he was about halfway through his notes, silently mouthed the words he'd written, then lifted his head. "When Miss Henrietta contacted me about your disappearance, I didn't know where to start, but did know that disappearances are normally perpetuated by someone known to the victim."

Temperance's brows drew together. "Wayne didn't mention anything at the train depot about you paying him a visit, or even let on he knew I'd gone missing."

"That's because I never paid him a visit." Agent McParland tapped a finger against his chin. "It's hardly productive to allow a suspect to learn they're being investigated. Which is why I began looking into Wayne Flowerdew's life without allowing him to know I was looking."

He looked back at his notes again. "What struck me as odd is that I could not find a credible source of employment for Wayne. I also found it curious that even though he apparently has no reliable income, he was able to move his family to Park Avenue and into a rather fine brownstone."

"Wayne moved everyone to the city not long after he came and fetched me from Paris," Temperance said. "He and Fanny wanted Clementine to make her debut in New York high society instead of in the small town they were living in at the time."

Agent McParland turned his full attention to Temperance. "And all of you moved to New York not long after you returned from Paris?"

"We did, but if you're going where I think you are with your line of questioning, do know that there was no money left from my father's estate for Wayne to use to purchase the brownstone."

"And you know this . . . how?" Agent McParland pressed.

"I met with my father's attorney, Mr. John Howland, as soon as I landed in New York. He was given the unpleasant task of informing me that the entirety of my father's fortune had been lost due to a bad investment decision on my father's part before he died."

Agent McParland began jotting down some notes. "Would you happen to have this Mr. Howland's direction?"

"From what I remember, he has an office off Fourth Avenue, but I haven't spoken to the man since our meeting where he told me I was destitute and that my father had left instructions for Wayne to become my guardian."

Agent McParland frowned. "Mr. Howland's never bothered to look in on you to see how you were faring?"

Temperance smiled. "From what little I recall of him, he seemed to be a most nervous sort and was not at all comfortable divulging the sad state of my finances to me. It's been my experience that nervous men of business do tend to remove themselves from situations that may involve distraught young ladies, many of whom are known to dissolve into bouts of weeping."

"You dissolved into a bout of weeping when you met with your father's solicitor?" Gilbert asked, leaning forward.

She waved that aside. "Of course not, although I was rendered practically speechless after everything that was disclosed that day."

Agent McParland scribbled something else on his notepad. "I'm going to need you to provide me with an accounting of your father's assets."

"I never received an accounting of my

father's assets because I was told there was nothing left." She frowned. "I do recall Mr. Howland mentioning something to me about giving Wayne a ledger that might have had all the debts my father had incurred written in it, but Wayne never shared the contents of that ledger with me. And, to be honest, I never had the desire to see proof of my father's financial mistakes."

Agent McParland's lips thinned. "I see."

Temperance rose to her feet. "What does that mean, *I see*?"

Agent McParland hesitated, glanced to Gilbert who was looking grim and getting to his feet as well, then back to Temperance. "It means I believe, given the information I've already uncovered about your cousin, that there's a good chance you have been swindled. I'm just not certain how he went about it or how much swindling was involved."

Temperance pressed a hand against a temple that was beginning to throb, a direct result of the fury that was now rushing through her. "If what you say is true, Agent McParland, and I have been swindled in some manner and Wayne's learned someone's been poking around in his business, it would explain why he might want me dead." She lifted her chin and nodded, just once.

"Having said that, if you'll excuse me, I'm off to do what I should have done from the very beginning — demand the truth from my cousin. But someone will need to loan me the use of a pistol because I may have need of one."

While Gilbert had always been somewhat powerless to refuse Temperance, lending her a pistol was not a request he was comfortable accommodating. Taking a step backward when she began advancing his way looking far too determined, he crossed his arms over his chest and shook his head when she held out a hand.

"I'm not giving you my pistol, Temperance," he began, taking another step backward when she kept advancing. "You're a horrible shot, and you know as well as I do that you'll end up shooting yourself. That would allow Wayne to get his way in the end, if he *is* the one behind wanting you dead."

Gilbert was not reassured when Temperance rolled her eyes and kept her hand extended.

"Of course Wayne's behind it, as well as Clementine, if I'm not much mistaken. They've never cared for me and certainly never wanted me to join their family. If I discover they not only want me dead, but also stole whatever pittance might have been left of my father's money, well, I guarantee you my proficiency with a pistol will be most impressive."

Gilbert cleared his throat. "You're not going to shoot your relatives. You don't have the stomach for that nasty business."

"Watch me."

Gilbert shot a look to Agent McParland who, surprisingly enough, was smiling. "I could use a little help here."

Agent McParland's smile widened. "We can't blame Miss Flowerdew for wanting to extract a small amount of retribution. From what I can tell, she's earned it."

"That's not the type of help I was looking for, Agent McParland," Gilbert muttered before he caught Temperance's eye. "But because these types of situations are no place for a lady, I'll go with Agent McParland and confront your cousins. I'll even take notes so you won't feel left out."

Temperance's nose shot straight into the air. "I think not. I've been allowing others to direct my life for far too long, and it's past time I took matters back into my own hands. You're more than welcome to tag along with me and take notes if it'll make you feel useful, but I won't be left behind."

"Don't you need to teach a class or something?" Gilbert asked, wincing when he detected just a trace of desperation in his tone.

"I would be more than happy to take over your afternoon classes," Mr. Barclay said, stepping back into the room and nodding Temperance's way. "It's a little known fact, but I'm somewhat musical, so I do believe I can fill in for you in a pinch, while imparting some knowledge about the piano to your students in the process."

Temperance smiled. "You never told me you play the piano."

"I'm a gentleman of many talents," Mr. Barclay said, inclining his head before he frowned. "But my talents aside, I'm afraid I'm in full agreement with Mr. Cavendish in regard to lending you a pistol."

He held up a hand when Temperance opened her mouth, clearly intending to argue. "I've seen you attempt to shoot a pistol before, Miss Temperance, and you have no talent when it comes to hitting a target."

"You allowed Temperance to shoot a pistol?" Gilbert asked.

Mr. Barclay nodded before he glanced to Harrison, who was sitting beside Gertrude, both of them seemingly content to simply watch the events unfolding in front of them. "Mr. Sinclair has been working with me to perfect my abilities with a pistol since I do accompany Miss Temperance and her students throughout the city for their sketching and painting lessons. Because she occasionally choses somewhat questionable parts of the city to allow her students to experience art as it's supposed to be experienced, I felt I needed to improve my skills in order to protect everyone more effectively."

"Have you ever thought about suggesting a safer place to sketch?" Gilbert asked.

"This from a man I know was considering handing over his pistol to a lady for the briefest of seconds" was all Mr. Barclay said to that, earning a small smile from Gilbert in return.

"She is difficult to deny," he admitted, glancing at Temperance, who immediately held out her hand again. "But not *that* difficult," he added, his smile widening when she dropped her hand and began looking irritable.

"While I completely agree that Temperance should not be given a weapon, I do believe she cannot be denied a confrontation with her reprehensible relatives."

Turning his attention to the door, Gilbert

found Miss Henrietta marching into the room, smiling pleasantly at everyone before she stopped directly in front of him.

"I'm certain you're soon to be upset with me, dear," she began, "but I've been lurking right outside the door, eavesdropping if that was in question, and I'm convinced Temperance must be allowed to travel with you, Agent McParland, and Harrison. She needs to hear the truth, whatever that truth may be, directly out of Wayne Flowerdew's mouth, not secondhand."

Before Gilbert could get even the most basic of arguments past his lips, Miss Henrietta moved to stand in front of Eugene and Mercy, holding up a jacket she'd been holding.

"You," she said with a nod to Eugene, "will travel with them, posing as a driver, which will then allow you to identify Wayne Flowerdew as the man who hired you to abduct Temperance in the first place. While you" — she looked to Mercy — "will retire to the second floor, where you'll make use of a bathing chamber to rid yourself of those dreadful whiskers."

Mercy immediately looked mutinous. "I need these whiskers to disguise myself because I'm a wanted woman."

"You're not," Miss Henrietta countered.

"You're being dramatic, and even if you were a wanted woman, since you're going to begin learning how to operate a typewriter here at Miss Snook's school, you'll have no need to disguise yourself from this point forward."

"I ain't attending school."

Miss Henrietta didn't so much as bat an eye. "You will attend school, and you'll be gracious about it because it'll give you a future, something that you won't see if you continue taking on questionable work to feed you and your brother."

"What's Eugene going to do without me?"

"He's not going to be without you because he's going to come work for me as my personal driver." Miss Henrietta released a sigh. "It's been pointed out far too often of late that I frighten folks half to death when I take the reins and have even caused poor Mr. Barclay to descend into prayer when he rides with me." Miss Henrietta smiled at Eugene. "You'd be doing me a great service if you'd accept my offer, as well as a great service to the people of New York who've apparently been in fear for their lives when they see me tooling down the street."

"That's mighty kind of you, ma'am," Eugene said with an inclination of his head, even as Mercy began muttering under her breath, something that sounded like a protest, but not a very committed one.

"And since that's settled," Miss Henrietta said, "I believe it's time for Temperance to get on her way to have a little chat with her Flowerdew cousins."

"Aren't you afraid she's putting herself in danger?" Gilbert asked.

Miss Henrietta waved that straight aside. "Wayne Flowerdew, from what I can tell, is a coward. As a coward, he won't hurt Temperance if there's an audience, so do make sure to stick by her side throughout your visit."

With that, Miss Henrietta entwined her arm with Temperance's, and as Temperance shot him a smile of clear victory, the two ladies strolled out of the room.

"I'm not certain I understand how we lost this battle," Agent McParland said, moving toward the door with Eugene, who was already shrugging into the jacket Miss Henrietta had given him.

"Having grown up surrounded by women, I understand exactly how we lost," Harrison said, placing a kiss on Gertrude's forehead before he turned to Gilbert. "But before Gertrude gets it into her head that she needs to join us as well, another battle I'm certain to lose, what say we go and confront us some Flowerdews?"

Knowing Temperance would find a way to get to her cousins even if he refused to accommodate her, Gilbert headed for the door, praying Miss Henrietta was right that Wayne was merely a coward and not some criminal mastermind posing as a gentleman.

CHAPTER THIRTEEN

"Didn't you find it somewhat curious that Gertrude wasn't the least put out over not being invited to join us?" Temperance asked, peering out the window of the closed carriage Miss Henrietta had decided was a much safer option over the open buggy Temperance normally preferred using around town.

"Gertrude's a sensible sort," Gilbert said, drumming his fingers against the crushed velvet seat. "She realized it would only add an unneeded level of confusion if she accompanied us, an idea you, my less-than-sensible friend, seem all too willing to ignore."

Temperance pulled her attention from the scene whizzing by outside the window, the whizzing a direct result of Eugene's questionable driving abilities. "Miss Henrietta believes this venture will allow me to find closure with my cousins, something I apparently need." She stopped talking when the carriage rocked back and forth as it careened over numerous bumps in the road. "I'm beginning to get the distinct impression we should have asked Mercy to take on the role of driver. Eugene, I'm sad to say, seems to be even less proficient at the reins than Miss Henrietta."

Gilbert grabbed hold of the strap above his head, looking a little green. "I'm not going to argue with that, but only because I'm about to toss up my accounts, so I am now going to descend into silence until we reach Park Avenue."

Pressing her lips together to hold back a laugh, Temperance reached over and gave Gilbert's knee a pat, remembering all the many times they'd traveled together in their youth when Gilbert would turn green after being enclosed in a carriage for a great length of time, or if the ride was anything other than smooth.

Settling back against the seat, she smiled at her memories, realizing that even though they'd been apart for years, as friends often were when they turned from children into adults, she was just as comfortable with him now as she'd been back then. It was as if they'd not been apart, although . . . she did feel somewhat different with him at times, fluttery or something to that effect, as if butterflies had taken up residence in her body and —

"I think I'm going to be sick."

The next second, she was sitting all alone, Gilbert having yelled at Eugene to stop, but he didn't bother to wait for the carriage to do more than slow down before he flung himself through the door and disappeared from sight.

Scrambling after him as the carriage came to a rough halt, Temperance stuck her head out and found Gilbert lying in the middle of the street, Agent McParland and Harrison already blocking him from harm with their horses.

Jumping to the ground, Temperance lifted the hem of her skirt and charged in Gilbert's direction, not appreciating it in the least when he sat up and sent her a scowl.

"You shouldn't be out here" were the first words out of his mouth, words that sent her temper rising.

"You shouldn't be out here either, and you certainly shouldn't have flung yourself from a wildly careening carriage."

He gave a wave of a now muddy hand. "You've seen me bolt from moving carriages many times over the years, which you always seemed to appreciate since it spared you from . . . well, no one likes to be stuck in a carriage while someone is retching up their last meal."

She folded her arms over her chest. "Well, quite, but you were much younger then, and evidently more agile, since you always used to be able to land on your feet, unlike now when you could have been killed under the wheels of passing carriages."

To her surprise, Gilbert grinned and placed his hand over his chest. "Words to warm a man's heart."

Temperance frowned. "Honestly, Gilbert, it's not like you in the least to talk of such things. Did you suffer an injury to your head when you hit the street?"

His grin stayed firmly in place. "Not at all. I'm simply pleased to discover, even though you've vehemently refused my offer of marriage numerous times now, that you still hold me in great affection because you obviously don't want to see me dead. That right there is yet another reason you should stop being so stubborn and simply agree to marry me."

She threw up her hands. "I'll always hold you in affection, but how is it possible I've neglected to remember how you're never content to lose an argument? Clearly, you're more annoying than ever, which means I'm getting back in the carriage, and no, I'm not marrying you."

"Harsh words to speak to a poor gentleman who was only inches away from death."

"A situation that could have been avoided if you'd had the common sense to remain in the carriage and simply asked Eugene to slow down, or if you'd only stuck your head out the window to get a refreshing breath of air." She moved a step closer to him and thrust out a hand.

"And you're worried enough about me to offer a hand up, yet another reason to give me hope you'll change your mind in the end."

Temperance pulled back her hand, turned on her heel, and stomped back toward the carriage.

"Smooth," she heard Harrison say behind her, his words having the corners of her mouth lift.

"She adores me," Gilbert returned.

Forcing herself to keep walking and not turn around, Temperance accepted Eugene's offer of assistance to get into the carriage, taking a moment to get her skirts settled around her. To her surprise, Eugene joined her a moment later, sending her a sheepish smile that displayed a few missing teeth.

"Mr. Cavendish is taking over the reins, and since I can't fit up on the driver's seat with him, he told me to join you in here. He also gave me the task of protecting you if something goes *awry,* which I'm thinking means bad."

"I'm sure nothing will go awry, Eugene, although I am curious as to how you'll go about protecting me since I know full well you've been deprived of your knife."

Eugene leaned over and pulled up a pant leg, exposing a very hairy leg in the process, as well as a wicked-looking knife strapped to his calf. "I always have a spare on this leg, and" — he pulled up his other pant leg — "another one here, and" — he yanked down the pant leg, unbuttoned the buttons on the jacket Miss Henrietta had given him, then pulled up his shirt, exposing far more skin than Temperance had been expecting, along with yet another knife that seemed to be kept in place by a thin rope tied numerous times around Eugene's hairy stomach.

She resisted a shudder. "Yes, I see, although, that sight is something I'll never get out of my mind again," she said somewhat weakly, as Eugene gave his stomach a pat, pulled his shirt down, then rebuttoned his jacket.

"A person can't have enough knives, Miss

Flowerdew, and I never feel safe without one, or three, on my person."

"And you really know how to use those in a fight?"

Eugene nodded. "Learned out of necessity, I did, but I'd be pleased as punch to give you a few lessons on account of the fact that you do seem to find yourself in danger often."

"If you'll recall, you were the reason I was in danger the first time, but . . ." She considered him. "Perhaps it wouldn't be a bad idea to learn how to defend myself."

"You pick the time, miss, and I'll bring the knives." He gave his stomach another pat as the carriage rolled into motion, Gilbert obviously far more competent at the reins than Eugene had been since he didn't drive the carriage through a single hole as they trundled down the road.

"Is it safe to say Mr. Cavendish is one of them safe sorts, prefers keeping horses at a plod?" Eugene asked, gesturing to the window where nothing was whizzing by.

"Gilbert is a complicated gentleman, Eugene, one who shows caution in some areas, such as his driving, but then at other times, abandons that caution and surprises a person, such as when he decides to throw himself from moving carriages to prevent tossing up his accounts."

"He seems keen to marry you."

"That's simply because he's never been a gentleman to accept being thwarted, and he sees getting me to accept his marriage proposal as a challenge." She traced a finger along the window edge. "Gilbert's never been one to give in graciously."

"He also seems keen to keep you safe."

"Gilbert spent our childhood racing to my rescue. He's simply fallen back into that role, but I don't need him to rescue me this time. I enjoy the life I'm creating for myself, and I don't want to —" Temperance stopped talking, realizing she was saying far more than she'd intended, and to a man who'd only recently shut her in a coffin. Shaking herself, she summoned up a smile. "But enough about that. Let's talk about you. Are you going to accept Miss Henrietta's offer of becoming her personal driver?"

"You reckon Miss Henrietta really wants to hire me on as her driver and teach Mercy how to use one of them typewriters?"

"She wouldn't have made the offer if she wasn't comfortable hiring you. And given your interesting approach to driving a carriage, I have the most curious feeling you and Miss Henrietta are going to get along splendidly."

Eugene smiled, but sobered a second later. "I sure am sorry there's someone else out there who wants to harm you, Miss Flowerdew. It ain't right, not when you've turned out to be such a nice lady and all."

"I'm sure we'll get it sorted out in the end."

"Me and Mercy have been saying prayers for you, seeing as how we wronged you in the first place. We decided we needed to return back to the way we was before we started going down that road best left untraveled. We're hoping our prayers will bring something good into your life, as well as hoping God might someday be forgivin' us for taking on work we knew wasn't right."

Temperance smiled. "That's very kind of you, Eugene. I appreciate the prayers, and do know that I understand why you took on the job of snatching me. Desperate times make us different people, but now those times are behind you, and I'm quite certain God has taken note of that and has already forgiven you." She tilted her head. "And now that I think about it, I do believe I've been somewhat neglectful with my own prayers over the years, forgetting how important it is to give thanks, but also to spend the time remembering to pray for the needs of others. I'm afraid I may have allowed the problems of my life to overshadow the problems of those around me, so thank you for reminding me how simple it is to say a prayer when there's a need, and not only prayers to improve my lot in life."

Eugene smiled. "Life has a way of making us forgetful, Miss Flowerdew, but it also has a way of making us remember in the end. Me and Mercy weren't expectin' kindness from you, but you treated us properly even when we'd done snatched you, and that got us to thinkin' we needed to start livin' on the straight and narrow again."

Temperance returned his smile before she looked out the window, her nerves beginning to jingle when she noticed they were already on Park Avenue and moving ever closer to their destination. Drawing in a deep breath, she willed her nerves to settle, closed her eyes, and sent up a prayer, realizing as she did so that it had been a long time since she'd turned over a problem to God. While she certainly wasn't struck by an immediate solution regarding how she should navigate the disaster involving her relatives, her nerves did seem to settle and her thoughts cleared, a circumstance that would certainly come in handy once she confronted Wayne. Lifting her head as the carriage slowed to a stop, she squared her shoulders.

"You won't be in any danger, Miss Flowerdew," Eugene said. "We menfolk will keep you safe, don't you fear."

Following Eugene out of the carriage, Temperance found Gilbert already waiting for her, his arm extended and his expression determined. She walked to join him, took the offered arm, then waited as Agent McParland and Harrison got down from their horses and moved their way.

Turning toward the brownstone that had never felt like home, Temperance let her gaze drift over the building. It was an impressive home, three stories high, but it wasn't built on the lines of the fashionable mansions that were popping up along Fifth Avenue. Wayne had made the claim often that he preferred living in a brownstone, more in keeping with the established Knickerbocker set.

Temperance had never questioned that claim, but now, when faced with the possibility that Wayne had no job, which meant he had no income flowing into the family coffers, she couldn't help but wonder if there had been a small inheritance left from her father's fortune, one Wayne had managed to swindle from her, but . . .

Shaking herself from ideas that were

hardly helpful, and thoughts that were rather farfetched since she'd seen with her own eyes how horrified Wayne had been to learn she'd been left a pauper after her parents died, she lifted her chin right as Gilbert gave her arm a squeeze.

"Are you ready for this?" he asked.

"I don't know if one can be ready for something like this, but because Wayne is the only one with answers to the vast number of questions I have, there's no choice but to confront him."

"I can do it for you, Temperance. You don't have to do this if you find it distressing."

Her heart gave an unexpected lurch. Gilbert had always stepped in to deal with anything unpleasant for her, and she'd missed that support over the years. But she was no longer a child, which meant she could no longer expect her dear friend to navigate through the unpleasantness for her.

"I can do this."

Moving together, they walked to the front door of the brownstone, Temperance frowning when the door wasn't immediately opened for them. Knowing it was quite unlike Wayne to allow his butler to shirk what was a most important task, she considered the door for a moment, wondering if someone should step forward and make use of the knocker mounted on the wood.

Before she could make that suggestion, though, or do the task herself, Agent McParland stepped around her, rapped the brass door knocker several times, then stepped back.

To Temperance's concern, no one answered.

"Perhaps they've gone out," she finally said after a full minute passed and the door remained closed.

"And gave the entire staff the day off?" Gilbert asked.

"That would be a rather unusual circumstance."

Agent McParland stepped forward again and jiggled the doorknob. Finding it locked, he reached into his pocket, pulling out a thin piece of metal.

"You're going to break in?" Harrison asked, joining Agent McParland.

"As Temperance just said, it's unusual that no one is answering the door," Agent McParland returned. "And I'm not breaking in. I'm merely going to check on the welfare of Temperance's relatives since there is cause to believe it is in question."

Sticking the piece of metal into the lock, he maneuvered it around, stilling when Eugene edged forward and peered over Agent McParland's shoulder.

"That's a skill that could come in handy at times," Eugene said to no one in particular.

Temperance fought a smile. "Eugene . . ."

Eugene stepped back and winced. "Sorry. Don't know what I was thinkin."

A second later, the lock clicked, Agent McParland withdrew the metal, then nodded to Gilbert. "It might be best if you were to wait out here with Temperance. There's no telling what I may find."

Temperance opened her mouth, a protest on the tip of her tongue, until she remembered that Agent McParland was a professional, which meant she needed to allow him to do what he did best. Closing her mouth, she sent him a nod, earning a flash of a grin from Gilbert in return, who'd obviously known she'd been about to argue with the man before she came to her senses.

Ignoring the grin, even though the sight of it, for some curious reason, was making her pulse hitch up a notch, Temperance watched as Agent McParland slipped into the house, Harrison right behind him, leaving her on the stoop with Gilbert and Eugene.

The seconds ticked away, until . . . someone started screaming.

Chapter Fourteen

Gilbert's first instinct was to pick Temperance up and run as fast as he could away from the house. But before he could move so much as a single muscle, she was running — not away from the house, but into it, leaving him and Eugene behind.

"She's mighty fast for a girl," Eugene said, before he lurched into motion, running alongside Gilbert into the house.

Following what now seemed to be some type of shrieking — and high-pitched shrieking at that — Gilbert dashed down a hallway and through an open door, skidding to a halt at the sight that met his eyes.

Agent McParland was standing in the middle of what turned out to be a drawing room, hands raised even as he ducked to the right when Clementine, wearing a mobcap on her head and wielding a mop, swung the mop at Agent McParland's head. Wayne Flowerdew was holding a pistol in his hand, one that, thankfully, seemed out of bullets since he was fumbling around with additional bullets that were scattered on top of a desk. Fanny Flowerdew stood behind him, her eyes wide as she stared at Temperance, who was simply standing off to the right, frozen in place, as if she couldn't quite comprehend what was unfolding before her in the drawing room.

"Take that," Clementine screeched, poking the mop toward Agent McParland again, but stopping midpoke when she caught sight of Gilbert. Her mouth dropped open, she lowered the mop, snatched the cap off her head, and curiously enough, sent him a charming smile before she dipped into a curtsy.

"Well, isn't this a lovely . . ." Whatever else she'd been about to say seemed to get stuck in her throat when her gaze drifted from him and settled on Temperance. Fire seemed to flash right out of her eyes.

"Temperance," she all but spat, her single word having the immediate result of Wayne abandoning his desk, along with his pistol, as his head shot up and his expression turned hard.

"You!" he bellowed, striding around the desk, but stopped in his tracks when Gilbert stepped in front of Temperance and arched a brow at Wayne. "Oh, Mr. Cavendish. This is an unusual time to pay a call, and we're not in a position to entertain at the moment because . . ." He gestured around the room, drawing attention to the fact that it was in a state of disarray with open trunks lying about, and odds and ends strewn all over the place.

"Are you going somewhere?" Gilbert asked right as Temperance sidled past him and began roaming around the room, poking her head into one open trunk after another.

"Stop being nosey," Wayne snapped, and for a second, Gilbert thought he was speaking to him, until Wayne marched up to the trunk Temperance was peering into and slammed it shut.

Temperance straightened and, curiously enough, she smiled. "I was simply making certain you weren't trying to stash away anything that didn't belong to you." Her smile faded just a touch. "I would hate to find myself accused of theft somewhere down the road or have one of my friends framed for a crime they certainly didn't commit, a circumstance I'm sure you're aware happened to my dear friend, Gertrude Cadwalader."

Wayne raised a hand to his chest. "Your

friend was framed for theft?"

Temperance shot Gilbert a look. "And this right here is exactly why you should have lent me your pistol."

Gilbert's brows drew together. "And I would say this right here is exactly why I *didn't* lend you a pistol."

"And *I* would say," Wayne began, "that while I'm sure there's a reason all of you broke into my home, which, if there's any question, is against the law, we're not receiving callers today. Because of that, I must insist you take your leave because we're on a bit of a tight schedule."

"Why isn't someone manning the door?" Temperance asked, ignoring Wayne's request right as Harrison, whom Gilbert hadn't realized had been missing from sight, suddenly pushed himself up from behind a fainting couch, rubbing a hand over his head and holding a lamp that had a large hole in it. The sight of Harrison had Clementine releasing a gasp right before she set aside the mop and smoothed her hair into place.

"Mr. Sinclair," she all put purred as she smiled and fluttered her lashes. "I do beg your pardon. I certainly wouldn't have thrown that lamp if I'd recognized you." She fluttered her lashes again. "I thought you and that other man" — she jerked her head to Agent McParland — "were burglars here to rob us of our worldly possessions."

Harrison set aside the lamp and raked a hand through hair that was standing on end. "And here I thought you screamed something about 'filthy debt collectors' right before you smashed me over the head with a lamp and rendered me senseless for a few moments."

Clementine didn't so much as flinch as she gave an airy wave of her hand. "Burglars, filthy debt collectors, they're all the same when you think about it. Regardless, I do apologize for being so true with my aim."

"She's had a lot of practice," Temperance said, inserting herself into the conversation, "which is why I've gotten so adept at dodging flying objects since I grew weary of suffering bumps and bruises whenever Clementine became annoyed with me."

"I'm sure there's another lamp around here somewhere I could fling your way," Clementine said sweetly, although it looked to Gilbert as if a vein had started throbbing on her forehead.

Temperance sent her cousin a sweet smile in return, one Gilbert found absolutely terrifying, and then drifted over to a chair, pushed the pile of books stacked on it to the floor, then took a seat before directing her attention back to Wayne. "Where are the members of your staff, and why, if I'm not mistaken, are you leaving town?"

"It's . . . ah . . . Thursday. Fanny and I always give the staff the day off on Thursday."

"It's Tuesday, and you never give all the staff time off at the same time."

Wayne narrowed his eyes on her. "What's happened to you? You seem far more assertive than I've ever known you to be, and . . . talkative. You never used to talk."

Temperance shrugged. "I've come to the conclusion that the reserved, timid, and yes, practically mute attitude I embraced over the past few years was a direct result of the grief I was experiencing due to the loss of my parents." Her eyes began to spark with something dangerous as she kept her attention on Wayne. "That attitude was not helped by having to experience such abuse at the hands of your family. I've now abandoned that attitude and have vowed to never become a victim again."

"You were never a victim," Fanny said with a sniff. "And I take issue with the manner in which you're portraying us to everyone present in this room. It hardly lends them a good impression of the family."

Temperance shot a look at Fanny that had her cousin's wife retreating back into silence before she looked back to Wayne. "Because you did mention that I'm assertive now, allow me to put that into good use and move this conversation right along. There is a reason we've paid you a visit today, one that centers around this question." She leaned forward. "Why have you hired someone to murder me, and how are you going to go about the tricky business of canceling whatever price you've put on my head?"

Wayne blinked, Fanny sucked in a sharp breath, and Clementine smiled more broadly than ever as she hummed a cheery tune under her breath.

"On my word but that's a peculiar accusation," Wayne began. "I haven't settled a price on your head."

Temperance's lips thinned. "Word on the street is that someone wants me dead. You're the only person I know who would want to see the breath snuffed out of me, especially since it was because of me that your plans in regard to . . ." She tossed a nod Gilbert's way. "Well, all that, went awry."

Wayne shuddered ever so slightly as he glanced at Gilbert before he returned his attention to Temperance. "I may not care for you, but I don't want to see you dead."

Agent McParland cleared his throat, attracting everyone's attention. "But you were responsible for setting up the events that led to Temperance's abduction, weren't you?"

Wayne narrowed his eyes on Agent McParland. "I don't believe we've had the pleasure of an introduction."

Agent McParland inclined his head. "I'm Agent Samuel McParland, with the Pinkerton Agency."

"And you're here because my cousin has convinced you I want her dead?" Wayne asked slowly.

"That, and I have some questions regarding Temperance's abduction, a case of mistaken identity if I'm understanding the peculiarities of the case correctly." He smiled. "You do realize that organizing an abduction is a criminal offense, don't you?"

Wayne shook his head. "I'm sure I have no idea what you're accusing me of, Agent . . . McParland, did you say?"

Agent McParland didn't bother to reply as he turned and nodded to Eugene, who was standing in the doorway, shuffling around on his overly large feet. "Are you able to identify this man as the man who approached you and your sister with a plan to abduct Miss Flowerdew?"

Eugene, to Gilbert's surprise, shook his head. "I'm afraid that's not the man, Agent McParland. The man I met had a different voice, rougher, not refined, and he was taller, with not much meat on him."

"See?" Wayne said with a nod to Agent McParland. "I told you."

Temperance released what sounded exactly like a snort. "Please. You would never mingle with the criminal class or travel into the worst parts of town to find those criminals in the first place. You hired someone to do your dirty work — the same person, if I'm not mistaken, you then hired to handle my murder."

"I don't have the funds to hire anyone, let alone waste those funds on you," Wayne said, then snapped his mouth shut as if he'd not meant to disclose such troubling news.

Temperance rose to her feet. "That's why there aren't any servants and why Clementine thought Agent McParland and Harrison were debt collectors, isn't it?"

Instead of answering her, Wayne turned on his heel, moved to a chair piled high with books, shoved some of those books to the floor, then sat down on the rest of them and directed his attention out the floor-to-ceiling window.

Silence settled over the drawing room until Agent McParland fished a notepad out of his pocket, walked to a chair directly beside Wayne, sat down, and began riffling through the pages. Stopping on a page, he lifted his head. "Should I assume that you've gone through the funds I believe you got from Temperance's estate?"

Wayne turned his head and frowned at Agent McParland. "There were no funds to be had after Temperance's father died." He nodded to Temperance. "You know that."

"I know what I was told," she countered. "But I'm now questioning the truth of it because Agent McParland discovered an interesting tidbit regarding your lack of employment. That got me to wondering how you could afford this brownstone, a purchase you made soon after I came to live with you."

Wayne waved that aside. "My lack of employment is no secret, Temperance." He gestured to Fanny. "Fanny's father settled a large dowry on her."

"Over twenty years ago," Temperance said. "And while I don't recall much about you growing up, I do recall my father mentioning to my mother once how you were a man known to enjoy a lifestyle that far exceeded your means."

"Since your father lost his many millions in a poor investment opportunity, I don't believe you should put much stock in anything he said pertaining to my ability to handle funds."

Temperance looked to Gilbert. "It is odd, isn't it, that my father would make my cousin my guardian when he evidently questioned his ability to manage money."

"It is," Gilbert agreed. "Although I would have to imagine your father never thought he'd meet such an untimely end or that an investment mistake would render him penniless." He looked to Wayne. "But speaking of that, I wonder how it came to be that Temperance was left absolutely nothing, especially when the house her parents owned in Connecticut was a very fine establishment. The sale of that house should have given Temperance some type of inheritance."

Wayne shifted on the chair. "Mr. Howland, the attorney who managed Temperance's father's estate, showed me stacks and stacks of bills he settled from the money made through the sale of that house."

"Where did the money come from to fetch me home from Paris?" Temperance asked.

To Gilbert's surprise, Fanny suddenly flung herself on top of a pile of books stacked on a fainting couch and released a dramatic breath. "You may as well disclose all, dear. From what I can tell, Temperance and this Pinkerton man seem to believe you're some type of thief. If we ever want to see our daughter well-settled, we certainly can't have talk of that nature spreading about town. Why, my aunt will cut us off without a dime if that nasty business begins making the rounds, and then where will we be?"

"Your aunt has already given us an ultimatum, Fanny," Wayne replied. "One that required us getting Clementine good and engaged before the fall season begins in earnest. Clearly, we've not been successful with that, so there's every reason to believe she'll not allow us to stay long in her home, throwing us into the streets with all our worldly possessions scattered about for everyone to see and realize our dire straits."

"Father," Clementine all but screeched. "Have a care with what you say. Mr. Cavendish is not yet officially engaged to Temperance, so . . ." She glided across the drawing room, stopping directly in front of Gilbert. "There's still time for you to change your mind and offer for me, Mr. Cavendish, instead of my cousin."

Gilbert had no idea how to respond to

that bit of nonsense, having never in his entire life been confronted with a lady he thought might have just proposed to him. Thankfully, he was spared a response when Temperance marched across the room.

"You're embarrassing yourself, Clementine," she said as she took hold of Clementine's arm and practically dragged her away from Gilbert. "I would never allow Gilbert to marry you, he's much too dear to me. But getting back to what Fanny thinks should be disclosed . . ." She pushed Clementine into a chair, then nodded to Wayne. "I'm listening, and in case it was in question, the topic was where you got the money to fetch me home from Paris."

For a long moment, Wayne didn't say a word, but then his shoulders sagged another inch, and he looked rather resigned. "Mr. Howland gave me the money to see you back to the states, as well as a few thousand dollars, which I thought was to compensate for my troubles." He shook his head. "I had no idea that was all the money left from your father's fortune, because if I had, I wouldn't have used it to secure this house, or even agreed to take you under my roof in the first place."

"You used that money to buy this house?" Temperance asked.

"It wasn't enough to buy the house, just rent it until more funds became available." Wayne blew out a breath. "Imagine my horror when upon our return from Paris, I learned there was no additional money *and* I was stuck with you until you turned twenty-five."

"But what did you tell this Mr. Howland?" Gilbert pressed. "Was he not horrified to discover you'd used up all of Temperance's inheritance on a house that wasn't for her?"

Wayne frowned. "She got to live here, so it was somewhat meant for her. And yes, Mr. Howland was horrified when I disclosed what I'd done, but felt it best not to disclose that to Temperance because there was no way to retrieve the money I'd already spent."

"I might have to set up an appointment with this Mr. Howland," Agent McParland said, looking up from the notes he'd been taking. "It seems less than ethical for a man of affairs to withhold such pertinent information from a client." He settled his attention on Wayne. "Where can I find him?"

For some reason, all the color seemed to leak right out of Wayne's face. "I don't believe there's any reason to speak with Mr. Howland. It was my error, not his, and he probably doesn't even recall the particulars of Temperance's case since it was years ago."

"Wonder what Wayne's hiding," Harrison said quietly, coming up to stand beside Gilbert.

"I'm not sure," Gilbert returned as Eugene walked up to join them as well.

"He don't seem like the sort to know how to go about hiring criminals," Eugene said out of the corner of his mouth. "Ask him about that abduction again."

Gilbert smiled. "Excellent idea, Eugene. Thank you."

As Eugene beamed a smile back at him, exposing missing teeth in the process, Gilbert caught Wayne's eye, noticing as he did so that Wayne was now an interesting shade of green.

"Who hired the people responsible for Temperance's abduction?" he asked.

"I never said I was responsible for that," Wayne shot back.

"Of course you were responsible," Temperance said, rolling her eyes. "Why else would there have been a yellow gown waiting in the room reserved for a Mr. Smith and wife at the Palmer House?"

Agent McParland cleared his throat, drawing Wayne's attention. "As I tell most everyone of the questionable sort, it'll go easier on you if you cooperate."

Wayne rose to his feet and moved to the

window, looking out. "I've done nothing illegal, so there's no reason to threaten me, Agent McParland. Might I have arranged for my daughter to be abducted? I suppose there's no harm in owning up to that, but it was done merely as an amusing incident, and Clementine was fully aware of what was planned."

"Father, I knew nothing of the sort," Clementine all but sputtered, her sputters coming to an abrupt end when Wayne turned from the window and held up his hand.

"Be quiet, Clementine," he said before he looked out the window again. "And since I know you're determined to find out how I went about making arrangements for that *amusing* incident, I sought out Mr. Howland. He's a rather savvy sort, and I knew he'd be able to arrange all the particulars of the *amusing* abduction because, as an attorney, he knows all sorts of people in the city."

"You had the money to hire Mr. Howland to hire on criminals who were then supposed to follow through on the abduction?" Temperance asked.

"Mr. Howland didn't charge me, and he didn't plan out the abduction, simply arranged for the less-than-proficient members of what I thought were the criminal set to see Clementine safely to Chicago."

"Where she'd then be rescued by Gilbert and seen by Aunt Minnie, or rather, Mrs. Boggart Hobbes, who'd then encourage Gilbert to marry Clementine to save her reputation?" Temperance asked a little too sweetly.

Gilbert wasn't certain, but he thought Wayne muttered "That was the plan" before he leaned closer to the glass, his attention firmly settled on something outside the window.

"Where did you get the funds to put this plan into motion?" Agent McParland asked.

"I sold one of my diamond necklaces," Fanny said, speaking up. "And a bracelet that I still miss most dreadfully, but I thought it would be worth it in the end if Clementine ended up with . . ." She shot a look to Gilbert, winced, then pressed her lips together and didn't say another word.

"And what did you have to sell to settle a price on Temperance's head?" Agent McParland pressed.

Wayne tore his attention from whatever he'd been looking at outside. "I don't know how I'm going to convince you of this, Agent McParland, but I never put a price on —"

The sound of breaking glass drowned out the rest of his words as Wayne suddenly stumbled away from the window, clutching his arm before he slumped to the ground. The sound of gunfire split the air, and glass from every window began to shatter.

Rushing to Temperance's side, Gilbert picked her up and dove behind a settee as the sound of additional shots being fired reverberated in his ears and mayhem descended on the drawing room.

Chapter Fifteen

The solid weight of Gilbert's body over hers made breathing next to impossible. But when Temperance realized the body protecting her from the bullets still raining into the drawing room wasn't moving, all thoughts of breathing disappeared as panic pulsed through her veins.

"Gilbert," she yelled, her voice muffled against his chest. "Gilbert, answer me," she yelled again as tears stung her eyes and her throat closed with terror.

When he didn't respond, or stir so much as a single inch, she tried to push him off her, her attempts futile because her arms were pinned underneath him.

"They're getting away," someone shouted, allowing her to realize that the assault had stopped and the only sound she could hear now was that of crunching glass as someone walked across the floor.

"Stay down," she heard Harrison call out

from the other side of the room.

Wiggling to see if she could inch her way from underneath Gilbert, she stilled when she felt a rumble, and then . . .

"Don't even think about moving," Gilbert rasped, the sound of his voice the most beautiful thing she'd ever heard.

With a groan, he lifted himself up on an elbow, brushed aside a strand of hair that was covering her eyes, then peered into her face, taking a second to capture one of the tears trailing down her cheek.

"Are you hurt?" he asked.

"I'm fine, but . . . I thought you were dead."

Gilbert's eyes twinkled. "Clearly I'm not, which means the good Lord above must still have plans for me." He winced. "I did knock the wind out of myself when I landed, but I must have knocked the wind out of you as well, since I used you for a cushion." With that, he rolled off her as they were joined by Agent McParland.

"Are either of you hurt?" Agent McParland asked, squatting down next to them.

"We're fine, just a bit stunned," Gilbert said, pushing himself to a sitting position and helping Temperance do the same. "Everyone else?"

"I've been shot," Wayne howled, drawing

Temperance's attention. Curiously enough, he was not still by the window, but by the door leading to the hallway. Standing over him as he laid on the floor was Eugene, who'd evidently had the presence of mind to get Wayne out of direct danger when bullets began to fly.

"You ain't dying, sir," Eugene said, bending down to hand Wayne a handkerchief that was less than pristine. "I already looked at your arm, and the bullet went clean through, not even hitting the bone."

Those words had Wayne releasing a feeble moan right before he fainted dead away.

"My poor darling," Fanny cried, emerging from under the desk before she began crawling across the floor to Wayne's side. She took one look at the wound on his arm, shuddered, then lifted her head. "We must get him straight to a hospital."

"Indeed," Agent McParland said. "But you will need to wait until I make certain the danger is gone." He rose to his feet and nodded to Fanny. "Put pressure on the wound, although do know that since it's not bleeding overly much, your husband should be fine." He looked to Gilbert. "I'll be back as soon as I can."

"I'll come with you," Harrison said, shaking shards of glass out of hair that was no longer bound by the ribbon he'd been wearing.

"Wouldn't it be better if you stayed here to protect us, Mr. Sinclair?" Clementine asked, popping up from where she'd been hiding under a drop-leaf table. She immediately began assuming her damsel-in-distress pose, complete with the nibbling of a lip and the wringing of hands in a most dramatic fashion.

"I wish I could, Miss Flowerdew, but I can't very well leave Agent McParland to deal with numerous criminals on his own." Harrison gestured to Eugene. "No need to fret you'll be in danger. Eugene will protect you, as well as Gilbert." With that, he and Agent McParland strode from the room, their pistols at the ready.

"Like the man said, ain't no need to fret that someone will harm you," Eugene said, pushing open his jacket before he pulled up his shirt, exposing his hairy stomach in the process. Retrieving his knife even as he ignored Clementine and Fanny gaping at him, he pulled his shirt back over his stomach and drew himself up to his full height, looking rather intimidating.

"Goodness," Fanny breathed before she bent over her husband, pulling a clean handkerchief out of the sleeve of her gown and pretending she didn't see the one Eugene had given Wayne. Pressing it over Wayne's arm, Fanny began whispering what seemed to be terms of endearment to her husband, something that gave Temperance pause.

She'd never thought about her cousins as being anything other than ghastly, but now, when faced with the idea that Fanny did seem to hold Wayne in deepest affection, she couldn't help but wonder if they were truly as terrible as she'd assumed.

"This should put an end to that nonsensical idea you had about my father hiring on someone to murder you," Clementine said as she picked her way across the debris scattered on the drawing room floor to join her mother, glaring at Temperance all the while.

"How do you reason that out?"

Clementine sank to her knees, reaching out to smoothe a hand over her father's forehead, another display of affection Temperance had not been expecting to witness.

"Someone just shot up our home," Clementine said. "And while it is true that none of us particularly enjoyed having you around, we don't want to see you dead. You've been a bother, there's no question about that, especially since you did steal the gentleman I wanted straight away from me."

She nodded to Gilbert, not bothering to flutter her lashes so much as once at him, then turned her gaze back on Temperance. "The event we just experienced seems to suggest someone has taken issue with anyone possessing the name Flowerdew, which should have you concluding that my parents and I are not the ones who put a price on your head."

"The question of the hour, though, is who has taken issue with the Flowerdew family," Gilbert said. He gestured to the room at large. "This was quite the planned-out attack, and one that has a hint of desperation to it because it was carried out in the middle of the day, not under cloak of darkness."

Temperance took a moment to look at the destruction surrounding her. Jagged pieces of glass held stubbornly to the side of the windows, while the heavy velvet drapes that framed those windows were pierced with holes and were sagging from their rods. The walls were marked with holes from the bullets, and the furniture had tufts of cotton sticking out of almost every piece. The settee she'd been sitting on was riddled with holes, proof that her life had been in jeopardy, spared only because . . .

Drawing in a sharp breath, she turned to Gilbert. "What were you thinking?"

Gilbert stopped brushing bits of what looked to be pieces of fabric from his jacket. "I'm afraid you have me at a disadvantage, Temperance. To what are you referring, and why, pray tell, do I get the distinct impression you're suddenly put out with me?"

She jerked a hand toward the settee. "You could have been killed coming to my assistance. There were bullets raining down on the room."

"Surely you don't believe I would have simply run for cover and allowed you to take one of those bullets, do you?"

"You could have been killed," she said again. "Did that not enter your head?"

Gilbert took hold of her hand and gave it a squeeze. "I didn't really consider the matter."

"But . . . why?" she whispered.

His brows drew together. "Why what?"

"Why would you not have considered the idea you were placing yourself in death's direct path by rescuing me?"

For a long moment, Gilbert simply stared at her, quite as if he found her to be some peculiar creature he'd never seen before. But then he shook his head and squeezed her hand again. "I don't know why you're surprised I reacted how I did when bullets were whizzing around the room. It's what we do, Temperance, it's what we've always done. We look out for one another." He raised her hand to his lips and pressed an unexpected kiss on it. "Would you not have done the same if I'd been sitting on that particular piece of furniture and we came under attack?"

"Of course, although I might have had a touch of difficulty picking you up, but . . ." The rest of her words died a rapid death when he sent her a quirk of a brow even as he smiled a bit smugly.

"You're very annoying" were the most eloquent words she seemed capable of getting out of her mouth.

His smile widened. "As are you, and not very appreciative either, since I did just save your life and you're cross with me for doing so." He shook his head. "I'm amazed you would question my judgment with saving you, because, again, I've saved you often in the past, something you've clearly forgotten."

"You saved me from numerous reprimands from our parents when I got us into too much mischief," she corrected. "That's not the same as saving my life."

"It's the same principle." His smile faded. "But I am sorry I frightened you, although I'm encouraged by the idea you'd mourn my death. Makes me think you may very well decide to marry me yet."

Temperance opened her mouth, an argument on the tip of her tongue, but swallowed that argument as she considered him for a long moment.

When she'd thought he *was* dead, it was one of the most horrible moments of her life, punching a hole in her heart.

Gilbert was her very dear friend, had always been exceedingly dear to her, and she loved him for that. But lately, if she were honest with herself, that love had begun to change.

It had begun to turn into something . . . more.

That thought caught her by complete surprise and had her pulling her hand out of his, even as she forced a smile.

Evidently, while she'd been reclaiming her sense of self, she'd apparently set aside all sense of practicality, not that she'd ever been a very practical sort to begin with, because . . . it would be beyond ridiculous to love Gilbert in anything other than a strictly friendly fashion.

He was a gentleman who approached life in a no-nonsense manner, and had never been one to embrace an overly affectionate attitude, becoming uncomfortable whenever he was confronted with situations of the emotional kind.

He would never be able to return affections of the romantic sort, which meant she'd be a fool to allow her emotions to go unchecked in regard to him, because . . .

A loud moan ripped her straight from her musings. Turning her head, she found Wayne stirring as Fanny doused his face with water she'd apparently found in the bottom of a half-broken vase.

"I don't think there's any need for a bath, Fanny," Wayne said, opening his eyes as Fanny let out a sigh of relief and Clementine stifled what might have been a sob.

Gilbert pushed himself to his feet. "While I'm beyond curious as to what you were thinking before Wayne came to, especially because you had a most peculiar look on your face, I know you well enough to realize it would be futile on my part to expect you to disclose what were obviously unsettling thoughts." He sent her a significant look. "I also know you get annoyed with me when I pester you about something you don't care to disclose, so to distract myself, shall we go and join your cousins on the other side of the room?"

Knowing he was quite correct and that she certainly wasn't going to disclose her troubling thoughts, Temperance took the hand Gilbert offered her and was soon pulled to her feet. Walking beside him over the glass-strewn floor, she stopped next to Eugene. She was relieved to discover that he seemed to be taking his task of protecting them to heart, since his knife was gripped firmly in his hand and his gaze kept darting every which way.

Sending him a smile, one he missed because he was now looking out into the hallway, Temperance looked to Wayne, finding him staring up at her. "Are you feeling any better?" she asked, earning a scowl in response.

"I don't know how I could feel better, Temperance," he returned. "I've been shot, admitted I'm facing financial ruin, have been evicted from this home because I've neglected to pay the rent for the past few months, and Fanny's Aunt Minnie is more than likely going to be opposed to us moving in with her since we didn't meet her deadline of securing Clementine a groom. That means we've nowhere to live, so no, I'm not feeling better."

"Don't forget there could be future attempts on our lives," Fanny said as she continued dabbing his forehead with the handkerchief.

"Indeed." He sighed. "I must say I cannot fathom who would want to shoot me. I'm a likeable sort, aren't I?"

Temperance was spared a response to that tricky question when Eugene suddenly stiffened as he looked out into the hallway, but then relaxed a moment before Agent McParland strode into the room.

"We didn't catch anyone," Agent McParland said, letting out a grunt of disgust as he came to a stop beside Gilbert.

"But only because someone let our horses go and it took precious time to run them to ground," Harrison added as he walked into the room and shook his head. "Rupert was five houses down, and Samuel's horse was found on the next block."

"Who is Samuel?" Clementine asked.

Harrison gestured to Agent McParland. "He's Samuel."

Clementine's brow puckered. "Isn't it rather odd to call a Pinkerton agent by his given name?"

"Since he's evidently considering asking my sister, Edwina, to marry him at some point in the future, something he only just mentioned as we walked back to the house," Harrison began, "I decided it was slightly ridiculous for me not to use his name since he's apparently going to be my brother-in-law someday."

Temperance smiled at Agent McParland. "I *adore* Edwina, and while it comes as no surprise the two of you are going to get married since she expressed that hope to me a few months ago, allow me to extend to you my best wishes for a wonderful life together."

Agent McParland returned Temperance's smile before he winced. "I haven't actually asked Edwina to marry me, so you might want to keep that quiet. We still have a few issues to resolve that are standing in our way, so . . . mum's the word for the time being."

"Why is it that every eligible gentleman I encounter of late seems to become less than eligible shortly after I make his acquaintance?" Clementine asked to the room at large as she immediately set about the task of looking disgruntled.

Agent McParland quirked a brow at Clementine. "I wasn't aware you were turning a romantic eye in my direction, Miss Flowerdew."

"I wasn't. I was simply making a point."

Agent McParland's eyes began to twinkle. "Yes, well, my marital intentions aside, I'm afraid it's become obvious someone wants to put an end to anyone closely associated with the Flowerdew name. That means all of you will need to be extremely careful from this point forward, as well as hire on a few guards to keep watch over you."

"We don't have the funds to hire on any guards," Fanny said rather weakly. "And my aunt has yet to return from Chicago, so . . . we'll be dead before the sun rises tomorrow."

Even though Temperance had been at odds with her cousins for a very long time, and even though they'd been less than hospitable to her over the past few years, they *were* blood. Because of that, and because she knew Fanny might just have the right measure of things and someone might try to murder them before the sun rose the next day, she opened her mouth, not allowing herself another second to reconsider what she was about to offer.

"You'll have to come back with me and stay at Miss Snook's School for the Education of the Feminine Mind until other arrangements can be made."

For a long moment no one said a single word, but then Clementine took one step toward her. "You're asking us" — she gestured to herself, her mother, then father — "to come stay with you at the Huxley sisters' old home?"

"I am."

"But you don't care for us."

"True, and you don't care for me either, but that's not really a viable reason to neglect to offer you shelter." She lifted her chin. "And since that settles the question as to where you'll be staying for the foreseeable future, what say we get Wayne off the floor and seen to by a physician?"

"I don't have the funds to seek out the services of a physician," Wayne admitted.

"I'll cover the cost," Gilbert said, stepping forward and bending down to take hold of Wayne's good arm. After getting him to his feet, he kept a steadying arm on him as he led him out of the drawing room.

Accepting the arm Eugene offered her, Temperance went with him down the hallway, pausing inside the main door while Agent McParland and Harrison checked to make certain the coast was clear.

Harrison arrived back at the door a few minutes later. "It looks safe enough." Moving over to where Gilbert was keeping a firm hand on Wayne, who was swaying on his feet, Harrison helped Gilbert get him through the door, followed by Clementine and Fanny. Walking after them, and with Eugene drawing himself up to his full height while brandishing his knife, Temperance waited for her cousins to get settled in the carriage, then released her hold on Eugene when Gilbert offered her his hand. After helping her into the carriage, he stuck his head in and surprised her when he lifted her hand to his lips and kissed it.

"I'm going to drive, so there's no need to fear the ride back will cause Wayne additional harm, and we're going to have Eugene take up position on the back of the carriage." He reached behind him, pulled out a spare pistol and handed it to Eugene, who looked as if Christmas had come early.

"You do know how to use that, don't you?" Gilbert asked.

"I'll figure it out."

With those less-than-reassuring words, and after sending her a bit of a wince, Gilbert shut the door to the carriage, leaving her alone with her cousins.

"I do not want you to get the wrong idea after I tell you something," Clementine suddenly said. "Such as come to the conclusion you think I might want to become your friend."

"After everything you and I have gone through, Clementine, it would be difficult to come to that conclusion at this particular point in time," Temperance returned.

Clementine inclined her head. "Indeed,

but you have shown my parents and me an unexpected kindness, and because of that, I'm going to tell you something that is not easy for me to say." She caught Temperance's eye. "You should marry Gilbert Cavendish."

Temperance's mouth grew slack. "What?"

The corners of Clementine's lips twitched. "You should marry him, Temperance.

"He's obviously a bit deranged, because he seems to hold you in great affection. But he's also obviously a bit of a romantic, and if I'd been in your shoes and had him whisk me straight from the jaws of death, I would have become a puddle of mush at his feet and told him I'd marry him just as soon as we could reach the nearest church."

"While I do believe you've just rendered me the greatest surprise of this unusual day," Temperance began, "I can't marry Gilbert. We'd kill each other if we got married because we're simply too different."

Clementine's lips lifted into a genuine smile. "You may be different, but in my humble opinion, Mr. Cavendish doesn't look at you as if he wants to kill you. He looks at you as if he'd like to kiss you."

Having no idea how to respond to that bit of nonsense, or how to deal with a Clementine who wasn't being horrid to her, Temperance turned her attention to the scene outside the window, wondering how it had happened that her entire world suddenly seemed to have turned topsy-turvy.

Chapter Sixteen

One week later

Gilbert was regrettably coming to the conclusion that Temperance had, for some unknown reason, begun to adopt a most peculiar attitude toward him, which was becoming more and more apparent with every visit he paid her at Miss Snook's school.

She'd always been a touch peculiar, especially if she happened to be in what she'd always called her muse frame of mind. But during the week since they'd experienced mayhem at the Flowerdew residence, she'd not proclaimed herself following any particular muse, which meant the peculiarity she was embracing had something to do with him.

She was overly polite whenever they were in the same room, and . . . she'd taken to watching him whenever he came to call.

It wasn't a warm and affectionate type of

watching, but more on the lines of apprehensive, although why Temperance was apprehensive around him, he certainly had no idea.

Running a hand through hair he only then realized was standing on end, a concerning circumstance given his rescheduled appointment with Mr. Ashwell from England that was to take place soon, Gilbert pushed back from his desk. Rising to his feet, he began walking toward the small retiring room located on the other side of his office, pausing when a quiet knock sounded on the door. The door opened a second later, revealing his secretary, Mrs. Martin.

"Forgive me for disturbing you, Mr. Cavendish," she began.

"You're not disturbing me at all, Mrs. Martin. Although, if you're here to tell me Mr. Ashwell has arrived early for our two o'clock appointment, I will need you to delay our meeting for a few minutes. I have yet to pull out the files pertaining to his interest in exporting furniture from England, so perhaps you could offer the man a cup of coffee or tea until I'm better prepared."

Mrs. Martin slid her spectacles down her nose, peering at him in concern over the rim. "It's almost three, Mr. Cavendish, and

I assumed that since Mr. Ashwell is nearly an hour late, he canceled his meeting with you today."

"Is it *really* almost three?" Gilbert asked, pulling out his pocket watch and glancing at the time before he returned the watch and frowned. "How curious."

"As is the idea you neglected to inform me that Mr. Ashwell was late and hadn't canceled his meeting."

Gilbert fought a sigh. Ever since he'd gone off to Chicago on his erstwhile rescue mission, his ability to stick to his trusty schedule had gone horribly awry. He'd not been concerned about his lack of a strict schedule while he'd been in Chicago, or over the day or two after he'd returned, since there'd been much to see settled. However, during the week since the attack at the Flowerdew house, he'd been trying to return to his former way of life, but he simply could not adhere to his diligently penned-out scheduling system — one he'd used for years, and one that had never failed him until now.

Realizing that Mrs. Martin was waiting for some type of reply, he summoned up a smile. "It would seem as if Mr. Ashwell is no longer keen to export his furniture from England, but do make a reminder of this, Mrs. Martin, and refuse to extend him another appointment with me if he happens to send a note around."

"Certainly, Mr. Cavendish." She looked at him expectantly.

Gilbert's smile faded. "Was there something else?"

Mrs. Martin pushed her spectacles back up her nose. "You do recall that I normally only disturb you if a matter of importance has arisen, don't you?"

He refused another urge to sigh. Given his lack of attention to his schedule, and lack of keeping Mrs. Martin's schedule synchronized with his, it was little wonder the woman was continuing to watch him rather warily.

"Quite right," he finally said when Mrs. Martin tipped her glasses down her nose again, revealing narrowed eyes in the process. "A matter of importance . . . and . . . dare I hope that this matter of importance isn't one of, shall we say, a disturbing nature?"

"That depends on whether you gave approval for five young women to descend on this office, all of whom are supposed to immerse themselves in typing out real letters of business."

Gilbert's brows drew together. "I don't recall giving approval for five young women to descend on us, and surely I would have told you to write such an unusual occurrence in our schedule book if I had." He tilted his head. "Did they say why they were supposed to type out real letters of business?"

"They told me a woman by the name of Miss Snook believes that getting business experience will help them secure proper typing positions once they graduate from that somewhat scandalous school located on Broadway . . . a school for the education of the feminine mind, if I'm remembering correctly."

Gilbert raked a hand through his hair. "I do recall Miss Henrietta Huxley broaching something about typing. But I didn't realize when I muttered a response that might have implied I thought real experience was a good idea that she'd take that as my agreement to take on a few of her students."

"Would you like me to send them away?"

Gilbert's eyes widened. "Perish that thought. Miss Henrietta is a most frightening sort, and not one I care to offend. We'll need to find something for these young women to type. Although, do we have that many spare typewriters?"

"The women arrived with their own typewriters, Mr. Cavendish."

Gilbert frowned. "Aren't typewriters somewhat heavy?"

"They are, but these women brought their typewriters in a wagon."

"Miss Henrietta does seem to think of everything."

"I'll take your word for that, having never met a Miss Henrietta. However, we're getting woefully off subject."

Nodding, Gilbert opened his mouth but found he had no words at his disposal since he'd completely forgotten what the original subject was that he was apparently supposed to be addressing.

Mrs. Martin released the tiniest of sighs. "May I suggest we put the women to work typing up the handwritten invoices we've been meaning to send out?"

Pretending not to notice the increased level of concern lurking in Mrs. Martin's eyes, Gilbert smiled. "A most excellent suggestion, Mrs. Martin. Remind me to compensate you well after we sit down for your yearly review because I truly do not know what I would do without you."

"You missed my yearly review. It was supposed to be yesterday."

"Surely not?"

"I'm afraid so."

"I must have neglected to write that in my

appointment ledger," he said, walking back to his desk where he flipped through his ledger, stopping on the appointment page for the day before. Running his finger down the page, he stopped on the appointment that clearly proved he'd not forgotten to write down his meeting with Mrs. Martin, but had somehow managed to overlook it.

"And this is exactly what happens when a gentleman strays from his normal routine," Gilbert said under his breath as he scanned the rest of the page, noticing he'd also missed an appointment with his tailor.

Lifting his head, he caught Mrs. Martin's eye. "I do apologize, Mrs. Martin. I have no excuse for missing our meeting, but allow me to reschedule your review right this very second. Do know I will not miss it again." He regarded his ledger again, flipping the pages forward, his frown deepening. "How odd. I seem to have all of tomorrow afternoon free."

"Because it's Mr. Harrison Sinclair's engagement celebration, and you wanted to have a proper amount of time to get ready, as well as extra time to arrive at the celebration in case Miss Flowerdew needed your assistance."

"The engagement celebration is tomorrow?"

Mrs. Martin removed her spectacles, wiped them on a handkerchief she pulled from her sleeve, then shook her head as she returned her attention to him. "Perhaps I should cancel all of your morning appointments tomorrow as well so you'll have time to visit your physician."

"I don't need to visit my physician. There's nothing wrong with me."

A single quirk of her brow was her only response to that before she slipped her spectacles back up her nose, turned on a sensible heel, and walked for the door, turning once she reached it. "Did you want me to organize the women from the school, or would you care to come welcome them and help me decide where we should put them?"

"I forgot all about the women."

"Which, again, is why you should seek out the counsel of your physician." With that, Mrs. Martin walked through the door, and knowing there was nothing left to do but go after her since he'd never actually answered her question, he followed, stopping once he reached the outer office. He smiled when he saw five women, all whom were sitting stiff as pokers on the comfortable chairs he kept for visitors. That they were clearly not comfortable in their surroundings, there was little doubt, which had him moving to greet them, hoping to put them at ease.

"Ladies," he began, drawing their attention. "I must say I'm delighted to see all of you here today, especially when your typing services are so desperately needed."

"That's too bad," one of the women exclaimed as she rose to her feet. "We ain't what anyone would call good at this typing yet, but we'll try to not disappoint you too much, Mr. Cavendish."

Gilbert considered the young woman looking at him expectantly, then grinned. "Mercy, I didn't recognize you at first without your whiskers."

Mercy grinned right before she dipped into a slightly clumsy curtsy. "Miss Henrietta and Miss Snook sure have taken me in hand, Mr. Cavendish." She shook her head somewhat sadly. "But I ain't supposed to answer to Mercy no more. I'm Miss Miner, and . . . I ain't supposed to say *ain't* either, but I can't remember what to say in place of that."

"*I'm not* would be a good suggestion," Mrs. Martin said briskly, stepping forward. "But since Mr. Cavendish is a very busy gentleman, we mustn't keep him. If all of you will follow me, I'll take you to . . ." She turned to Gilbert. "Shall I have them set up their typewriters in the spare storage room?"

"I don't believe Miss Henrietta would approve of that," Gilbert said. "The conference room might be a better choice."

Mercy beamed a smile at him. "A conference room sounds much better than a storage room, Mr. Cavendish. And I bet after I tell Temperance how considerate you're being with us, she'll give you a firm date for that wedding of yours once and for all."

Gilbert swallowed a groan when Mrs. Martin's eyes began flashing and she crossed her arms over her chest, looking more than a little put out with him.

Knowing he had absolutely no excuse for not mentioning to her that she might hear something about engagement plans regarding him and Temperance, even though he knew it was not a real engagement, he cleared his throat but couldn't seem to come up with a single explanation, no matter how hard he tried.

Lifting her chin, Mrs. Martin sent him an unexpected sniff before she turned to the students from Miss Snook's school. "Ladies, if you'll follow me, I'll get you right to work." Marching her way toward a back hallway, she turned and pinned him beneath a stern gaze. "You have no other appointments today, so perhaps you should take the rest of the day off, enjoy some fresh air, and hope your ability to maintain an organized life returns to you."

With that, Mrs. Martin strode from the room, Mercy and the other students following her.

Not particularly wanting to suffer what would surely be a lecture if he didn't take Mrs. Martin's suggestion, Gilbert headed for the front door, finding Tobias, his recently hired valet, standing guard on the front stoop.

"You do realize that there are Pinkerton detectives discreetly watching out for me, don't you — detectives I was forced to hire after Miss Henrietta said she'd do it for me if I refused?" he asked as Tobias fell into step beside him and then matched him stride for stride after they reached the sidewalk and began walking down Wall Street.

"That Miss Henrietta certainly seems to be an assertive sort, Lord Cavendish. But even with those detectives out there, I'll not be shirking my duty to you. Those detectives can't travel directly beside you without drawing attention, something I can do since everyone knows a man of business is often accompanied by his valet."

Gilbert arched a brow. "It's simply Mr. Cavendish, Tobias, not lord, and I don't know any American gentleman who travels around with his valet by his side."

"You're not fully an American, Mr. Cavendish, on account of your father being an aristocrat," Tobias pointed out. "As for the valet business, I imagine it'll soon be all the trend for gentlemen to travel with their valets once talk begins swirling around that you've embraced what is evidently a new and fashionable trend."

"You're not going to leave my side until the culprits who attacked me, Temperance, and the rest of the Flowerdew family are captured, are you?"

"I'm afraid not, sir. It would be an insufficient way to show you my appreciation for taking me on after your sister-in-law, or rather half-sister-in-law, released me from service, spread the rumor I was lacking in any type of skill, and made it next to impossible for me to obtain employment anywhere in London."

"Alice does seem to be a rather difficult sort."

Tobias's pace slowed. "Difficult does not do justice in describing Lady Strafford. I do believe your half brother, Lord Strafford, has come to the conclusion her youth and, forgive me because these are his words, not mine, impressive childbearing hips were not worth the price he's now paying in order to secure the earldom a much-desired heir."

"She's very beautiful" was all Gilbert could think to add to what was nothing less than the truth about Alice.

"Quite, although because she's well aware of that beauty, it diminishes it somewhat, and then there's her brother."

Gilbert frowned. "I thought Andrew was off on a grand tour of the Orient?"

"He returned to London only a week before Lady Strafford released me from service." Tobias shook his head. "He's a good deal more unlikable than his sister, and I do believe Lord Strafford is about at his wits' end with Lady Strafford and her petulant brother."

"All the more reason for me to limit my visits to London, as well as to that monstrosity of a castle that's home to the Strafford seat." Gilbert raised a hand and gestured to a hansom cab. "But tell me this, Tobias, do you miss England, or are you beginning to acclimate yourself to America?"

"It's different here, but I don't dislike it," Tobias began before he smiled. "Oddly enough, I keep thinking I'm seeing people I used to know back in London, but I suppose that's common when a person picks up and abandons everything they've ever known. One believes a stranger's face is familiar, when it's really nothing of the sort. But, on a different note, is there a reason we're taking a hansom cab instead of one of your carriages or simply taking horses from the livery?"

"I didn't have time to send a note to the livery to have a carriage readied," Gilbert said as the hansom cab drew to a stop beside them. "And, since Blaze has yet to recover from our adventure in Central Park last week, shaking like a leaf every time I show my face in his stall, I want to spare him the additional trauma he'd suffer if he saw me riding past him on another horse, which would certainly hurt his tender horse feelings."

"You're a complicated gentleman, Mr. Cavendish," Tobias said as Gilbert gave the hansom driver directions to Broadway, or more specifically, Miss Snook's School for the Education of the Feminine Mind.

Ignoring the telling look Tobias sent him after hearing their destination, Gilbert climbed into the cab, Tobias right behind him. To provide a distraction from the questions he knew Tobias longed to broach about Miss Snook's school and why Gilbert wanted to travel there *again,* Gilbert turned the conversation to England. Tobias, thankfully, was only too willing to speak about the land of his birth.

Before he knew it, the cab was slowing to a stop, and after paying the driver, Gilbert, with Tobias by his side, made his way past the wrought-iron fence that kept Miss Snook's school separated from the crowds traveling down the sidewalk. He was not surprised to discover two burly men, who were obviously Pinkerton agents, standing guard on either side of the front door, with other Pinkerton agents, if he wasn't much mistaken, strolling casually up and down the sidewalk beside the school.

What he was surprised to find was the door being opened by a man who was not Mr. Barclay, but who quickly reassured Gilbert nothing was amiss. That man was simply standing in for Mr. Barclay because he was currently participating in a lesson being held in the back courtyard.

Inquiring as to what type of lesson was specifically going on in the back courtyard, he was surprised when the man merely shook his head before gesturing Gilbert and Tobias into the house.

Tobias waited until the door was firmly closed before he nodded to the man who'd taken up his position again right beside the door. "You're supposed to ask us who we are and whom we're here to see."

"I'm only one of the pastry cooks," the man explained. "And because I was pressed into service at the last moment, I've been assured by Miss Snook that as long as I answer the door and don't allow any members of the questionable sort in, I'm doing a fine job." He frowned. "You're not members of the questionable sort, are you?"

"It's a touch late to ask that now," Tobias said, and without another word, he turned and headed down the hallway, Gilbert smiling at his side.

"And here I was coming to the belief you weren't actually missing your position as an underbutler," Gilbert said, right as an older woman rounded the corner in front of him, her arms filled with what looked to be numerous pieces of brightly colored cloth.

"Mrs. Davenport," he said, striding to intercept her. "Allow me to help you."

Mrs. Davenport, a society matron who, until recently, had been Gertrude Cadwalader's employer, and a woman with a curious history of being fond of helping herself to items that did not belong to her, which thankfully had been resolved once she'd come to terms with her troubling past, stopped walking and smiled at him.

"Ah, Gilbert, my dear boy," she began

before she frowned. "But . . . you don't mind if I call you Gilbert, do you, even though we've yet to become well acquainted?"

Gilbert took the hand she suddenly thrust his way, even though a good portion of the arm attached to that hand was covered with fabric. Bringing it to his lips, he placed a kiss on her knuckles, and smiled. "I would be honored for you to address me as Gilbert. But what are you doing back in the city? I was led to believe you were off on holiday with your daughter and her family who've come to the states for an extended visit."

"My daughter has recently returned to England, and even though she invited me to return to England with her, I couldn't very well miss the engagement celebration of my darling Gertrude." Mrs. Davenport began piling what turned out to be gowns into his arms. "If you could nip upstairs with these and leave them in the pink dressing room on the second floor, I'd much appreciate it. But do promise not to tell anyone you've seen these."

"Because . . . ?" Gilbert pressed when Mrs. Davenport didn't bother to explain, instead turning her attention to Tobias, who was standing straight as a pin behind him, adopting what Gilbert always thought of as his British butler attitude, not moving so much as a single muscle when Mrs. Davenport began inspecting the cut of his jacket.

"What a fine hand someone used on this seam," Mrs. Davenport said, lifting up Tobias's arm and moving close to give it a gander. "Was it made here in the city?"

"I brought it with me from England," Tobias said.

"Ah, you're British, how delightful."

"Tobias is certainly delightful, Mrs. Davenport, but getting back to why I'm not supposed to mention I've seen these gowns?" Gilbert asked.

Mrs. Davenport released Tobias's arm. "Forgive me. I can't seem to resist inspecting a properly sewn garment these days. As for those gowns, Gertrude wanted the ladies attending her celebration to wear bright colors instead of the expected pastels and ivories. Being unable to deny her such a small request, especially after the trouble I caused her over the many years she worked for me, I, along with some of the other students of design here at the school, created gowns for almost every lady to wear. But it's a surprise for dear Harrison, as are the decorations Temperance has been creating in the ballroom this past week."

"I won't breathe a word of the gowns to anyone," Gilbert said. "But speaking of Temperance, would you happen to know where she is?"

"She's in the back courtyard with Mr. Barclay and Eugene." Mrs. Davenport leaned closer to him. "Don't tell Temperance I said this, since everyone does seem to believe I'm a most progressive sort and it might damage that reputation, but I'm not completely certain it's wise for a lady to learn how to wield a knife. Knives seem to be such crude weapons and not suited to the delicate hands of a lady. I also imagine they require a person to possess a strong stomach because, well, slashing an attacker with a knife would cause a great deal of blood to be spilled, which is not something I would care to witness."

Gilbert turned and dumped all the gowns Mrs. Davenport had recently unloaded on him into Tobias's already outstretched arms. Turning on his heel, he headed toward the back courtyard, wondering for what felt like the hundredth time that week how his always predictable life had turned into anything but predictable.

Walking through the back door, he faltered for the briefest of seconds when he saw Temperance staggering around, telling stains of red marking her white blouse. Horror coursed through him when she suddenly collapsed to the ground, that horror prompting him to rush forward, drawing the pistol he was never without these days as he ran.

Chapter Seventeen

Grinning as the unexpected thought struck that taking to the stage might be her next great adventure, given the enjoyment she was experiencing over the dramatic scene she'd just enacted, Temperance pushed up from the ground. Her grin slipped right off her face, though, when she saw Gilbert charging across the courtyard with his ever-handy pistol held at the ready. Unfortunately, that pistol was aimed directly at Eugene, who was frozen in place, holding one of the paperboard knives she'd created that was, regrettably, dripping with what looked exactly like blood.

"Don't shoot him, Gilbert," she yelled, jumping to her feet and holding up a hand to stop Miss Edwina Sinclair, Pinkerton detective-in-the-making, who'd abandoned the painting she'd been working on and was aiming *her* pistol at Gilbert's back. "Don't shoot *him,* Edwina," she yelled. "It's Gilbert."

Time seemed to slow as Edwina lowered her weapon. Gilbert stopped running, lowered his pistol, then turned around, his gaze immediately settling on her, or rather, the red-stained shirt she was wearing over her gown.

"Explain" was all he said as he shoved his pistol out of sight.

She summoned up a smile. "I think the scene speaks for itself."

"I'm afraid it doesn't, so try again."

She kept her smile firmly in place. "While I realize you're not one to embrace an active imagination, Gilbert, surely you must see that I'm simply in the middle of a lesson regarding how best to fend off an attacker wielding a knife. I'm also attempting to learn how to use a knife as well."

"You have Pinkerton agents guarding you who will be more than happy to fend off any attackers who might come at you with knives."

"And speaking of those Pinkerton agents," Edwina said, stepping forward as she tucked her pistol discreetly back into the pocket of an apron she was wearing. "I can hardly be expected to keep my true reason for accompanying Temperance everywhere a secret if you spring on us unexpectedly with your gun drawn. You're lucky I didn't shoot you, Gilbert, which would have put a rapid end to my desire to become a full-fledged Pinkerton agent, a situation that would have left me cross with you forever."

Gilbert shook himself ever so slightly, quite as if he'd forgotten there was someone else in the courtyard, then smiled at Edwina. Walking over to where she was standing, he took her hand in his and lifted it to his lips, even though Edwina seemed to be trying to pull her hand away from him.

"You're not supposed to kiss the hand of a detective, Gilbert," she all but hissed.

"But since, if I'm surmising correctly, you're supposed to be undercover, it would look peculiar if I didn't kiss your hand since you're the sister of my very good friend Harrison," Gilbert countered, holding Edwina's hand, if Temperance wasn't mistaken, longer than necessary, probably because he knew it was annoying Edwina.

Temperance's lips began to curve, until she remembered that she really couldn't afford to allow herself to be charmed by him, although why Gilbert annoying Edwina was charming in the first place, she had no idea, other than to think it was because he'd always done things to annoy her back in the days of their childhood when . . .

"You're still pursuing the mad idea of becoming a Pinkerton detective then?" Gilbert asked, which earned him a swat on the arm from Edwina's other hand before she tugged the hand he was still holding away from him.

Edwina's eyes narrowed and her beautiful face suddenly looked somewhat dangerous. "That almost seems to suggest you thought I'd abandon my quest to become an agent, as if it were a whim that I would soon tire of."

Gilbert didn't even wince over having so much animosity directed his way. "You *did* abandon your desire to enter society rather suddenly."

"That was different."

"I think not," Gilbert argued. "And far be it from me to point out the obvious, but participating in society events, even with the intrigues I've learned swirl through those events like water, would be far less dangerous for you to negotiate through than pursuing a position as a Pinkerton man, er . . . lady."

Edwina's nose shot straight up into the air. "My brother believes I'll make a fine Pinkerton."

Gilbert inclined his head. "Yes, well, Harrison has always been a bit of an odd sort. And I'm sure that even though he's voicing his support with your choice, he's hoping you'll simply end up marrying Agent Samuel McParland, have ten children with him, and forget all about your interest in tracking down criminals."

"Samuel believes I'll make an exceptional detective."

"That's because he's fallen head over heels in love with you and believes encouraging you with this peculiar pursuit will win you over in the end."

Edwina waved that straight away. "He won me over before I even decided I wanted to become a detective." She turned to Temperance. "I've forgotten how Gilbert tends to adopt a rather stodgy nature upon occasion, which does have me wondering how the two of you ever became such fast friends."

"We balance each other, Edwina," Gilbert said before Temperance had a chance to answer. "Temperance has always enjoyed leading an adventurous life, while I prefer stability. But when we're together, I make certain she doesn't land into too much mischief while she makes certain I don't turn stodgy more often than occasionally."

For the briefest of seconds, Temperance

found herself unable to breathe.

She'd been trying to convince herself ever since Gilbert had informed her they'd have to wed that they would not suit on account of them being direct opposites. But that's exactly why they *would* suit.

She was often far too carefree, and he was often too much of a stickler for the rules, but when they were together it was exactly as Gilbert stated — they balanced each other.

Why had she never realized that? And what in the world was she to do with that epiphany now that she'd realized she was growing overly fond of him, yet knew he would never return her affection in the way she desired?

"Ah, Mr. Cavendish, here to join in on the fun, are you?"

Temperance blinked out of her thoughts as Mr. Barclay walked across the courtyard, holding pristine white shirts in his hand.

"Do not say you actually believe it's a good idea to teach Temperance how to handle herself in a knife fight," Gilbert said as Mr. Barclay smiled and shook his head, handing him one of the shirts.

"She wanted me to take her out to practice shooting a pistol, Mr. Cavendish. But I've seen Miss Temperance's skill, or lack thereof, with a pistol, and believe me, teaching her how to handle a knife, especially since we're not using real knives, was a far safer choice."

Temperance wrinkled her nose. "I'm not that bad a shot, Mr. Barclay."

"My dear child, you're horrible with a pistol."

"I hit the target you urged me to aim for down on the beach that one time," she argued.

Mr. Barclay gave a sad shake of his head. "No, you didn't. You were supposed to be aiming for the large boulder beside the ocean, not the ocean." He smiled. "It would be downright impossible to miss that large of a target."

Gilbert, to Temperance's annoyance, began smiling as well. "Shall we tell Mr. Barclay about the time I tried to teach you how to shoot, but when you were about to pull the trigger, you panicked and dropped the gun?" His smile turned into a grin. "Only the good Lord above knows how you didn't end up shooting yourself when the pistol fired after it hit the ground. And don't even get me started on the long walk back to your parents' cottage we were forced to take since you scared off our horses."

Temperance scratched her nose. "They

weren't horses, they were ponies, and if I recall correctly, we were sent to bed without our supper since we weren't supposed to be in possession of a pistol in the first place because we were children."

Gilbert's grin turned rather sly. "You, my darling, may have gone to bed without your supper, but I had one of the downstairs maids at my cottage bring me up a picnic that left me stuffed to the gills."

Her mouth dropped open. "You never told me you did that."

"I'm not *always* a stickler for the rules, Temperance, especially when adhering to those rules means I'll suffer an empty stomach."

"Since you're not a stickler for the rules," Mr. Barclay said, nodding to the shirt he'd handed Gilbert. "What say you put that on and have a go of it with Eugene?"

Gilbert held up the shirt. "I'm afraid I don't understand the point of the shirts, or why you've apparently dipped those less-than-dangerous knives into red paint."

"It's so we can tell when we land a strike," Temperance said. "And the red paint was my idea because I thought it lent the lesson a dash of dramatic authenticity."

He looked at her red-splattered shirt, then at Mr. Barclay's shirt, which was splattered as well. "May I assume the two of you haven't perfected the art of wielding a knife?"

Mr. Barclay inclined his head. "I'm not as young as I used to be, and Miss Temperance is still a little too exuberant in her method."

Gilbert turned to Eugene, who was still standing in the same spot, his gaze fixed squarely on Edwina, something his gaze had been doing often since he'd laid eyes on Harrison's unusually beautiful sister. Quirking a brow, Gilbert gestured to the one streak of red on Eugene's shirt and nodded to Mr. Barclay. "May I assume you got in one strike?"

"I'm afraid that strike was at the hands of Miss Temperance," Mr. Barclay said as Eugene turned almost as red as the paint on his shirt and began taking an interest in the clouds passing overhead.

Temperance swallowed a laugh, unwilling to embarrass Eugene further by explaining that the only reason she'd bested him that one time was because he'd been distracted by Edwina, who'd somehow managed to knock over her easel. He'd immediately forgotten he was in the midst of a lesson with Temperance and hurried to help Edwina set her easel to rights. Temperance cleared her throat. "Perhaps I'm more accomplished than you think."

Gilbert glanced to Eugene, then to Edwina, who was ambling over to her easel, then back to Eugene who was once again watching Edwina as she ambled. He then turned a grin Temperance's way, one she couldn't help but return. "You're more than welcome to continue believing that, but I'm not certain that was truly the case."

She stuck her tongue out at him. "I'd like to see you do better. Eugene's incredibly fast."

To her surprise, Gilbert shook out the white shirt, pulled it over his head, then held out his hand. "I'll need one of those knives."

Turning on her heel and praying Gilbert hadn't seen her mouth drop open, Temperance headed across the courtyard, stopping beside the pile of paperboard knives she'd made. Plucking one from the top, she turned, finding Gilbert standing directly behind her.

Her breath suddenly became lodged in her throat, and her pulse began galloping through her veins, even as she realized that Gilbert seemed to be much larger than she'd ever noticed before, and his closeness was making her somewhat nervous.

Telling herself she was being beyond ridiculous because it wasn't as if she'd never been close to Gilbert before, although she certainly had never experienced her pulse reacting so erratically just because she was near him, Temperance forced a smile and met his gaze — a mistake if there was one because his gaze held a distinct glint in it, one that seemed downright dangerous.

She'd never once thought of Gilbert as a dangerous gentleman, even though she knew he was considered an expert marksman, enjoyed the sport of boxing, and . . .

"Did you really make these knives?" Gilbert asked, recalling her back to the present moment, where she was standing still as a statue while the knife she'd picked up was dangling limply from her hand.

Managing a nod even as a concerning tingle swept up her arm when he reached out and took the knife from her, his fingers grazing the top of her hand, she swallowed past a throat that was remarkably dry. "I made the paperboard from small bits of wet paper I strained through a screen, and . . ." She stopped rambling and drew in a much needed breath of air, but instead of steadying nerves that seemed rather jingly, she suddenly got a whiff of something that made her lose all track of what she'd been going to say next.

It was a scent that held a distinct trace of

lime, mixed with sandalwood if she wasn't mistaken, but there was something else mingling with those scents, something intriguing, and something she knew she needed to push right out of her mind.

Clearing a throat that was still dry, she shook herself ever so slightly and ignored that Gilbert was watching her closely. "I'm sure you remember how I can go on about my art, so in order to spare you from going glassy-eyed with boredom, I'll leave the rest of my papermaking process for another time — perhaps when you're suffering from ennui and need something that will put you straight to sleep."

"You could never bore me, Temperance," he said, reaching out to tuck a stray piece of her hair behind her ear.

It was a gesture he'd performed many times over the years, but now, to her concern, it seemed remarkably intimate and sent additional tingles over her. Heat crawled up her neck, but thankfully, Gilbert didn't notice since he was turning and moving across the courtyard, palming the knife she'd given him as if he'd been handling knives for years.

Knowing she was gawking at a man she'd known for practically her entire life, Temperance tore her gaze away from him and walked over to join Edwina. She stepped around the easel her friend was using, in the desperate hope she could distract herself with the painting Edwina had been working on.

What she found on the canvas had her at a complete loss for words.

"What do you think?" Edwina asked, dabbing at the canvas with a brush that was holding entirely too much paint.

"It's ah . . . quite the most interesting rendition of a tree I've ever seen," Temperance said somewhat weakly.

Edwina stopped her dabbing. "It's not a tree. I'm painting a picture of Eugene."

Temperance leaned forward and squinted at the canvas. "Are you really?"

Setting aside her paintbrush, Edwina let out a laugh. "I'm complete rubbish at this, Temperance, but I do thank you for trying to be diplomatic about this mess of a portrait."

"People are one of the most difficult subjects to paint."

Edwina eyed the painting for a second before she bit her lip. "Perhaps I should have started off with a tree."

"You can always try a tree next time, Miss Edwina," Mr. Barclay said, joining them before he glanced at the painting, shuddered just a touch, then nodded to where Eugene and Gilbert were squaring off in the middle of the courtyard. "Any guesses on who might draw first paint?"

Edwina smiled. "Eugene's fast, there's no question about that, but I've seen Gilbert fight before with Harrison. I'm going to say Gilbert will best Eugene, and he'll do it quickly too, going for the unexpected strike."

"You've seen Gilbert fight before?" Temperance asked.

Nodding, Edwina stepped away from her easel. "He's been friends with Harrison for years. He met him through Asher Rutherford when Gilbert needed a boat and Asher directed him to Sinclair Shipping. Since I was always around when he visited, and I, being the annoying little sister I am, always tagged after Harrison and Gilbert, I think of Gilbert as an adopted brother." She smiled. "And he, I do believe, treats me as a sister since he seems to have no problem with speaking his opinions to me or irritating me whenever he feels I'm wrong."

"He's always been like a brother to me as well," Temperance said, pretending she didn't see the rolling of the eyes Edwina exchanged with Mr. Barclay.

Turning her attention back to Gilbert and

Eugene, she felt her knees turn a little weak when Gilbert flashed her a smile, which was something she'd read about but never experienced, even as he continued circling around Eugene, right before he lunged.

Their sparring was over a moment later with Eugene clapping Gilbert on the back, a large slash of red staining the front of his shirt, while Gilbert's shirt remained white as white could be.

"I had a feelin' you was going to be tricky," Eugene said.

"I had an advantage since I haven't spent time out here teaching Temperance and Mr. Barclay how to fight. You're probably fatigued," Gilbert returned, earning a smile from Eugene in the process.

"That's a right gentlemanly thing to say, sir, but now, if you'll excuse me, I do need to be checkin' in with Miss Henrietta. She mentioned somethin' about wanting to go visit the tearoom at Rutherford & Company, and because she was kind enough to offer me a position, I don't want to keep her waitin'."

As Eugene made for the house, Gilbert surprised Temperance once again when he waved her forward. "You want to try to go up against me?"

"I thought you'd decided I didn't need to

learn how to fend off an attacker with a knife."

"It wouldn't hurt to teach you how to defend yourself a little more effectively, and besides . . ." He grinned. "It'll be amusing."

Unable to resist his grin, while hoping she'd somehow manage to dribble at least a bit of paint on him even if she missed her mark, Temperance exchanged her splattered shirt for a fresh one. After pulling the new shirt over her gown, she hurried over to the pile of knives and chose the longest one of the bunch. After dipping it in the paint, she moved to stand a few feet away from Gilbert, nodding when she was ready.

His eyes got that dangerous glint in them right before he started toward her, and the very sight of that glint had her spinning on her heel and running, not toward him, but away from him as fast as she could.

"That's an unexpected move," she heard Mr. Barclay say as she dashed past him.

"She must be trying to take him by surprise," Edwina added.

Unfortunately, Gilbert was faster than ever, and before she could do more than let out a whoosh of air, she found herself picked straight up, swung around, then set on her feet. The next second, she felt him trail his paper knife all the way down her arm, leaving it covered in red.

Without bothering to consider what the repercussions might be, she slapped the broad side of her paper knife smack-dab against his shirt, then patted his cheek with a hand now splattered with paint.

"And so it begins" was all he said before he bolted away from her, ran to the bucket of paint, picked it up, and headed directly her way again.

Sprinting across the courtyard, she let out a less-than-ladylike shriek when she was suddenly doused with the entire contents of the paint bucket. Not one to admit defeat easily, she changed directions, dashed up to Edwina's easel, grabbed the paint pallet from the stand, then turned, faltering for the merest of seconds when she realized Gilbert was only a foot away from her, grinning from ear to ear and looking quite pleased with himself.

Knowing the piddling bit of paint on the pallet was not going to do much damage, Temperance did the only thing she could think of — she charged his way, then threw herself at him, smearing him with the paint completely covering her.

Slipping on cobblestones that were slick from the paint, she tumbled to the ground, but brought him down with her when she refused to release his arm.

Dissolving into laughter and feeling more amused than she'd felt in a very long time, Temperance drew in a ragged breath of air, turning her head to find Gilbert grinning back at her.

"I would say I'm the clear winner in our skirmish," he said.

"As much as this pains me to say, I do believe you may be —"

"On my word, what in the world is going on back here?"

Any sense of amusement disappeared as Temperance pushed paint-covered hair out of her eyes and peered up at the shadowy figure that had materialized directly above her.

To her concern, peering down at her was none other than Mrs. Boggart Hobbes, Fanny's Aunt Minnie, and the lady who'd discovered Temperance and Gilbert together in Chicago. Unfortunately, given the scowl on her face, Mrs. Boggart Hobbes did not appear to be in an understanding frame of mind.

Chapter Eighteen

While Gilbert floundered for something to say, Temperance, faced with a scowling society matron looming over them, sat up, swiped a hand across a face covered in paint, smearing that paint in the process, then released a chuckle, then another, right before she began to laugh.

The sound of her laughter caused a curious sensation to settle in his heart, one he'd never felt before, but one that warmed him all the way to his paint-covered boots.

She'd experienced more than her fair share of hardship over the years since her parents had died, but seeing her laugh gave unmistakable credence to the idea she'd been strong enough to survive that hardship, had persevered even with the daunting circumstances she'd faced, and . . . she'd become even more captivating than she'd been in their youth.

Her ability to turn the most ordinary of

situations into the extraordinary was a gift not many people possessed, and he wanted nothing more than to be given the pleasure of experiencing every extraordinary situation she was certain to encounter by her side.

As that unexpected idea began burrowing deeper and deeper into his very soul, Gilbert felt his lips curve, until he realized that Mrs. Boggart Hobbes was in the midst of a tirade, one he'd completely missed. Glancing at Temperance, he found her releasing a last chuckle as she wiped her eyes with her sleeve, smearing the paint once again over her face and leaving her looking somewhat deranged.

Realizing he'd forgotten his manners since he was still on the ground and Mrs. Boggart Hobbes was now shaking a finger *his* way, muttering something about the rules of etiquette, which seemed rather odd given the circumstances, Gilbert rose to his feet. Extending a hand to a now hiccupping Temperance, he pulled her up next to him, tucked a chunk of dark hair drenched with paint behind her ear, then found himself held immobile when she lifted her gaze to his.

Her green eyes were twinkling with amusement, and they looked greener than usual, what with the contrast they made set in a face painted red. A river of red was trailing down her face and dripping from her jawline onto a shirt that was saturated with paint and was more than likely ruining the gown underneath it.

Temperance didn't seem concerned about her condition at all as she cleared her throat, reached out, and took hold of his hand, quite like she'd done every time they'd found themselves caught in a bout of mischief in their youth. She then turned her attention to the society matron who was scowling back at her.

"Mrs. Boggart Hobbes," Temperance began, lifting her chin. "This is an unexpected surprise."

Mrs. Boggart Hobbes lifted her chin as well. "I seem to recall you saying almost the exact same words to me when I discovered you in Chicago." Her chin lifted another inch. "You then led me to believe that there was nothing untoward about you being in the company of Mr. Cavendish, some ridiculous excuse about you being abducted and taken to Chicago against your will. But now, seeing the untoward manner in which the two of you were frolicking about this courtyard, it would seem you were less than truthful with me."

"Gilbert and I weren't frolicking," Temperance argued as her eyes continued to twinkle. She leaned forward, that action causing Mrs. Boggart Hobbes to take a large step backward, clearly to avoid having paint dripped on her. "We were engaged in a mock knife fight, but I fear I became a little overly exuberant in my attempt to win, and, well" — she gestured to her paint-covered body — "Gilbert couldn't be expected to ignore an opportunity to retaliate."

Mrs. Boggart Hobbes released a sniff before she turned to Gilbert. "I'm disappointed in you, Mr. Cavendish." She waved to Clementine, who was standing a few feet away from them, with Wayne and Fanny on either side of her, all of the Flowerdews looking quite like deer caught in the lantern light as they gaped his way. "My darling Clementine led me to believe you were a gentleman above reproach. Sadly, even if you do possess the honorary title of Lord Cavendish and your father was an earl, I'm afraid you've taken after your mother's side of the family."

Gilbert stiffened as any sense of amusement he'd been experiencing disappeared. "Do not say another disparaging word about my mother. She is a lady through and through, and I will not tolerate any nonsense to the contrary."

Mrs. Boggart Hobbes drew herself up. "Your grandparents bought your mother her title along with her first husband, believing having a countess in the family would turn them respectable. But instead, she ruined any chance her family may have had at entering society when she abandoned England after your father died, turning her nose up at the honor she'd been given of joining the aristocracy. She then went and married a man in trade, one who would never be accepted into society, given his coarse and merchant ways. Because of that, you were brought up in a common environment instead of in the elite world of British nobility." She nodded. "That, Mr. Cavendish, is exactly why I blame your mother for your faults — faults that have now convinced me my darling Clementine is far too refined for the likes of you."

Gilbert opened his mouth, but then closed it again, deciding against pointing out that he'd never wanted to pursue a relationship with Clementine in the first place. Sending Mrs. Boggart Hobbes an inclination of his head, he turned to Temperance, whose eyes were flashing in a manner he knew was not going to bode well for Mrs. Boggart Hobbes. Before he could suggest they repair into the house to stave off an argument that was certain to be of epic proportions, Temperance stepped forward.

"Gilbert's mother, Florence, or rather Mrs. William Beckwith, since you seem so keen to maintain an attitude of formality at this most unusual moment," Temperance began in a voice that had turned icy, "is a remarkable woman. The courage it must have taken for her to leave England after the death of her husband is commendable, especially since she did so to protect Gilbert from a life of snobbery she'd discovered she couldn't abide."

Mrs. Boggart Hobbes drew herself up. "She removed her son from a life of privilege and status, depriving him of his true position in the world."

Temperance arched a paint-encrusted brow. "Gilbert has created his own position in life, and he's hardly suffered a life of depravation."

"He was born to live amongst the aristocracy, and Florence's disdain for mingling with members of that aristocracy removed him from his position of superiority over common folk."

Gilbert braced himself as Temperance seemed to swell on the spot.

"This notion everyone in high society

seems to hold that they have superiority over those of a lesser status or wealth is ridiculous," Temperance all but spat. "In all honesty, I'm beginning to believe that my time spent as a poor relation to Wayne and Fanny was God's way of allowing me to see that none of us are superior to one another. I've been given the opportunity to know ladies who've been relegated to the wall-flower section because of lack of funds, pedigree, or many other nonsensical reasons, but those ladies have proven time and time again that they're no less worthy than anyone else. Quite frankly, they possess more moral fiber than most of society's esteemed members."

Mrs. Boggart Hobbes's second jowl began to quiver. "My family has never behaved in a manner that is anything less than moral."

"Your darling Fanny, along with Clementine and Wayne, concocted a less-than-moral plan to have Clementine abducted — a plan that was ill-conceived from the beginning, but a plan that was put into play in the hopes of trapping Gilbert into marriage."

With her nose flaring ever so slightly, Mrs. Boggart Hobbes shook a finger Temperance's way. "That's preposterous, and I will not allow you to slander the good names of my Fanny and Clementine."

Temperance didn't pay the least little mind to the finger shaking. "Clementine also arranged to have a painting stolen from Mr. Harrison Sinclair's yacht, and if it's escaped your notice, that's known as theft — hardly a moral act."

"I have to imagine you stole that painting, Temperance," Mrs. Boggart Hobbes returned. "With the intention of framing Clementine because you've always been jealous of her."

"I *returned* the painting after I discovered it lurking up by my attic room, and I certainly wouldn't have done that if I'd been responsible for the theft in the first place."

"You lived in the attic?" Gilbert asked as Mrs. Boggart Hobbes began turning red in the face.

"I did," Temperance said, not taking her eyes from Mrs. Boggart Hobbes. "It wasn't pleasant, but . . . speaking of that room." She drew in a breath, released it, and then, oddly enough, she smiled, a sight that was less than reassuring since the paint had begun drying on her face and the smile set it to cracking.

"Since we're on the subject of moral character — were you aware that Wayne used what should have been my inheritance to move his family to this city? And," she continued before Mrs. Boggart Hobbes could respond, "when he learned there was no more money coming from my father's estate, he forced me to assume a role of servitude, never disclosing it was my money that allowed him to move to the brownstone on Park Avenue in the first place. Again, in most circles, that would be considered theft, so I'll thank you very much to discontinue your argument about the superiority of your family."

"Wayne is your blood, not mine. And that proves that you, girl, came from inferior stock, especially since that father of yours didn't end up providing for you after he died."

"While I won't dignify your comments about my father or family with a response because it's beneath me to roll about in the mud with you, do know that Fanny, your darling niece, had to be aware of the idea Wayne had gone through most of her dowry. That suggests she also knew he'd gotten the money to move them to New York by unsavory means since he's evidently never held a position of steady employment."

For the briefest of moments, silence settled around the courtyard as Mrs. Boggart Hobbes considered Fanny, Wayne, and

Clementine. She then sent Temperance the briefest of nods. "I will send funds around to repay you whatever it was Wayne took, although I will deduct what I feel is a fair amount for your room and board over the years you lived with them."

Temperance crossed her arms over her chest. "I worked for that room and board, and again, I was only given the attic. It didn't even have a fireplace in it, which made for some rather chilly mornings."

"Very well, I'll take that into consideration." Mrs. Boggart Hobbes swiveled on her heel and gestured to Clementine and her parents. "Come along. It's time we repaired to my house."

"You want us to come live with you?" Clementine asked, having been unusually quiet throughout the entire argument between her Aunt Minnie and Temperance.

"Why do you think I called today at this ridiculous school?"

Clementine frowned. "I assumed you wanted to check on our welfare after receiving the note my mother sent to you explaining how'd we'd been forced to abandon Park Avenue because someone tried to murder us."

"A circumstance I'm certain can be blamed on your association with Temperance and Mr. Cavendish," Mrs. Boggart Hobbes said with a dismissive wave of hand in Temperance and Gilbert's direction.

"I'm not certain how you've come to that conclusion," Temperance said. "My life was only put in danger after I was snatched from the streets and taken to Chicago, a circumstance, if you've forgotten, that was not of my making."

Mrs. Boggart Hobbes ignored Temperance as she moved to entwine her arm with Clementine's. "I'll hire guards to keep you safe, darling, but do know that from this point forward, *I* will be managing your future. *I* will choose a suitable gentleman for you, as well as settle a nice dowry on you to ascertain we attract numerous gentlemen for me to consider. I have to imagine that we'll have you married off in no time."

"You're going to settle a dowry on Clementine?" Wayne asked.

"I am, as well as put you on a very strict allowance, but one that will let you maintain the image I expect our family to uphold from this point forward."

Mrs. Boggart Hobbes directed her attention to Gilbert. "As for you, Mr. Cavendish, I'm going to make a personal appeal to Mrs. Astor, imploring her to ban you from society forever, no matter that you possess that honorary title." She smiled ever so slightly at Temperance. "I do hope you won't be too distressed, dear, after you marry the man, which we know you'll end up doing, and discover all of society's doors are —"

"Good heavens, am I to understand you and Temperance have finally fulfilled my lifelong desire to see the two of you wed — and to each other?"

As the voice that had just spoken those words washed over Gilbert, he found himself momentarily confused — until Temperance bolted into motion, dashing across the courtyard toward his mother, who was holding her arms wide-open, evidently unconcerned that Temperance was covered in paint.

An unexpected ache settled in Gilbert's heart as he watched Temperance being drawn into his mother's embrace, an act he'd witnessed far too many times to count, but an act that finally brought home the truth regarding exactly how much Temperance had suffered from the moment her parents died.

She'd never been one to cry, but now, reunited with a woman she'd always enjoyed a close relationship with, she was certainly crying, the sight of her tears leaving him with an unusually strong urge to protect her. He wanted to shelter Temperance from all the troubles of life, especially the ones that had tried to stomp her spirit straight out of her, and yet he had not been successful in the end.

Her spirit, something he'd always appreciated, was alive and almost well again, and he vowed to make certain it would never be injured again, not even if . . .

"Shall I offer you my congratulations now, or save them until I can offer them to you and Temperance together?"

Gilbert tore his gaze from Temperance, finding his stepfather, William Beckwith, approaching him.

"Father," he said, stepping forward with his hand extended, although he drew it back after he saw it was covered in paint.

"We've been parted for months, son. I think a hug is more in order than a handshake," William said, and before Gilbert could protest, he found himself being giving an exuberant hug, one that left his stepfather smeared with red paint.

Stepping back, William smiled. "Nice to see you and Temperance haven't abandoned your habit of pursuing unusual pastimes."

"She wanted to learn how to wield a knife."

William's smile widened as he shook a

head full of hair that was once black but was now streaked with gray. "Who would have ever known that learning to use a knife, although I can't imagine why Temperance would get it into her head to learn such a curious skill, came with a great deal of . . . is that paint?"

"She decided it would add a sense of authenticity to the lesson if we dipped the knives in paint so we could tell when a strike met its mark."

"Did she then decide it would make it even more authentic if the two of you dipped yourselves into that paint?"

"We might have gotten a little distracted from the original plan."

"I do hope you're not trying to convince your stepfather that Temperance is fully to blame for the condition we've found the two of you in."

Holding open her arms as she came to a stop beside her husband, Gilbert's mother, Florence, beamed a smile at him, evidently unconcerned that the traveling dress she was wearing, one that looked to be expensive, was almost completely ruined.

Knowing he couldn't very well deprive a mother he hadn't seen for months a hug, even though doing so would ruin her gown for good, Gilbert pulled her close. He held on to her for a long moment as he heard Temperance greet his stepfather, but when he heard Temperance release a ragged breath, he kissed his mother on the forehead and stepped back.

His heart gave another lurch as his stepfather enfolded Temperance into a strong hug and didn't let her go, smoothing a hand over her paint-drenched hair as he murmured quiet words to her.

"I still do not understand why Temperance's parents changed their minds about your stepfather and me becoming Temperance's guardians in case of their deaths," his mother said quietly by his side.

Gilbert frowned. "You were originally supposed to be Temperance's guardians?"

Florence nodded. "We were, and Grace and Anthony Flowerdew were to look after you if anything happened to us."

"I'm sure my half brother, Charles, was relieved to learn I wasn't to be foisted off on him if you made an untimely departure from this earth." His smile faded. "Why do you think Temperance's parents changed their minds?"

"I suppose they decided, what with your stepfather and I choosing to spend our time traveling throughout India and the Far East, that they wanted someone more readily available if the unthinkable happened, which it did."

"But I barely knew Wayne," Temperance suddenly said, stepping out of William's embrace even though she immediately took hold of his hand, as if she needed to stay connected to him.

Florence raised a hand to her throat. "Perhaps Grace knew that you'd become distressed seeing me, her very best friend, every day in the event she died."

Temperance wrinkled her nose, causing dried paint to flake off her face. "My mother knew how much I adored you, knew I was comfortable coming to you whenever I needed a voice of reason, since she freely admitted that was not her forte."

Stepping forward, Florence pulled Temperance away from William and took both of Temperance's hands into her own. "But you never answered any of my letters."

"You wrote me letters?"

Florence exchanged a quick glance with her husband before returning her attention to Temperance. "I did. Dozens of them."

"I'll be right back" was all Temperance said before she withdrew from his mother's hold, turned on her heel, and stalked over to where Wayne, Fanny, Clementine, and Mrs. Boggart Hobbes were watching the reunion with blatant curiosity. However, as soon as Wayne seemed to realize Temperance was singling him out, he immediately headed for the door of the school.

"Stop right there, Wayne," Temperance practically bellowed. "You've got a bit of explaining to do."

"It's unbecoming for a young lady to shout in such a common way," Mrs. Boggart Hobbes said in a voice that some might consider a shout as well.

Temperance didn't break her stride, nor did she address Mrs. Boggart Hobbes's remark. Catching up with Wayne before he could disappear into the house, she took hold of his arm, and marched him back across the courtyard. Stopping once she reached Gilbert's side, she kept a firm grip of Wayne's arm even as she nodded to him, then to Florence.

"Would you care to tell Gilbert's mother why you neglected to give me any of the letters she wrote me?"

"I don't believe I've ever had the pleasure of receiving an introduction to Gilbert's mother," Wayne said in a clear effort to buy himself some time. "And do have a care with your grip, Temperance. I was only recently shot in that arm, and it's still rather tender."

Temperance disregarded his request, keeping her hand wrapped around the arm in question. "We mustn't neglect the pleasantries at such an unusual time, so allow me to introduce you to Gilbert's parents." She tugged him forward, stopping directly in front of Florence and William. "Wayne, this is Mr. William Beckwith and his wife, Florence Beckwith. William and Florence, this is my cousin, twice removed, Mr. Wayne Flowerdew."

"Pleasure to meet you," Wayne said.

"That remains to be seen," Florence said, pursing her lips. "Why is it, do you suppose, that you and I have never had the pleasure of an introduction before, especially since Grace and Anthony were my closest friends, and Anthony was your cousin?"

"Anthony and I didn't share what anyone would consider a close relationship. We only saw each other at the occasional family gatherings."

"And yet he left you the care of his only daughter," Florence pointed out.

"I was surprised as anyone to discover that."

"Hmm" was all Florence said to that. "May I assume you didn't bother to pass along the letters I wrote to Temperance because you didn't want to take the chance of anyone meddling in what must have turned out to be a lucrative arrangement for you?"

Wayne reached up and pulled on his neckcloth. "Now wait just a minute, Mrs. Beckwith, I didn't do any such nonsense. I've already admitted that I helped myself to a few thousand dollars I was given when I was asked to fetch Temperance back from Paris and deliver the news about her parents. But I didn't know that was the only money she had left in the world, and by the time I found that out, well, the money had already been spent. As for any letters you may have sent, I assure you, I never received them. I find it distressing that you would make the claim you mailed them to me and I never passed them along."

"I didn't mail them to you. I mailed them to one of Anthony's attorneys, a man by the name of Mr. Howland. He's the man who tracked me down in India to deliver the news about Temperance's parents." Florence's brows drew together. "I assumed he'd pass the letters on to you, and then you'd get them to Temperance." She paused. "He never mentioned a word about Temperance not being left any money, though, and he led me to believe that while you'd been named her guardian, she was taking an extended tour of the continents to honor the memory of her parents by following in their footsteps and living a life of adventure."

"What?" Temperance breathed as she let go of Wayne's arm and swayed a little on her feet.

Moving up next to her, Gilbert put a steadying arm around her, waited until she found her balance, then kept his arm around her for support as his mother exchanged another look with William, who was looking furious.

"May we assume, Temperance, that you did not take an extended tour through the continents?" William asked.

"There was no money to take a tour. Father lost his fortune due to a bad investment decision."

William shot a look to Wayne. "And you have proof of that?"

Wayne turned pale. "I was given a ledger filled with figures Mr. Howland said showed all the debts owed, but to tell you the truth, figures were never my strong point, so I didn't delve into the ledger very thoroughly."

William caught Gilbert's eye. "We need to pay this Mr. Howland a visit — the sooner the better. But, before we do that, we should probably move on to the reason we've returned from India earlier than expected."

"I'm not sure now is exactly the moment for that disclosure, dear," Florence said.

Gilbert frowned. "Do forgive me. I didn't even think to inquire why you're here, or even how you knew I'd be found at Miss Snook's school."

His mother's lips quirked. "We stopped by your office, where we, surprisingly enough, were met with a somewhat frazzled Mrs. Martin."

"I didn't tell Mrs. Martin I was coming here," Gilbert said.

"Mrs. Martin isn't the one who told us where to find you." Florence smiled. "That came from a lovely young woman by the name of Miss Mercy Miner. She came barreling out of the conference room after she heard us speaking with Mrs. Martin, and —"

"Told you I was here," Gilbert finished for her.

"No, first she dragged us into the conference room to watch her new skill with a typewriter, and after we'd apparently given her the proper amount of encouragement, she then disclosed that you were more than likely to be found here." Florence smiled. "I found her to be a most delightful sort, and . . ." She stopped talking and shook her head. "I fear I'm allowing myself to become distracted because I obviously don't know how to tell you this news."

Gilbert's stomach sank. "You're not ill, are you?"

His mother waved that aside. "Oh, no, I'm fit as a fiddle . . . unlike your half brother."

"I wasn't expecting you to disclose the information exactly like that," William said under his breath, earning a sigh from Florence in response.

"Quite, but . . ." She stopped talking and drew in a deep breath.

"May I assume Charles is ill?" Gilbert prompted.

Florence shook her head as she released the breath. "I'm afraid he's more than ill, dear. He went missing at sea while racing his yacht, and he's been declared dead, which means . . . you are now the new Earl of Strafford."

Chapter Nineteen

The next afternoon

Temperance fluffed the last length of draped silk, stretching over the scaffold to reach a pleat that was not fluffed to her satisfaction.

"It is a fortuitous circumstance that your darling Gilbert isn't present," a voice called up to her, the unexpected sound having her jump just the tiniest bit as she grabbed hold of the railing.

Peering down, she found Miss Henrietta peering up at her, shaking her head of white hair, apparently oblivious that she'd almost caused Temperance to plummet straight to the ground.

"You just scared me half to death," she called to Miss Henrietta. "It would hardly lend a festive air to Gertrude's engagement celebration if my poor, mangled body was found lying in the ballroom."

"I've always believed a good shock is wonderful for the system. Tends to get the blood moving at a fast clip."

"You believe no such thing, and I'll thank you to discontinue calling Gilbert my *darling.*"

"I know you're of the opinion you don't need to marry him, but since you've now been written about in all the newspapers in the city, I'm afraid you're going to need to change your opinion about that."

"What do you mean I've been written about in the papers?"

"Honestly, Miss Henrietta, I thought we agreed we wouldn't tell Temperance about the articles, which is why I asked Mr. Barclay to hide all the papers."

Turning her attention to the doorway, Temperance found Miss Permilia Griswold, one of her dearest friends, strolling into the ballroom, her red hair bundled up in rags, apparently done so by one of the hair stylists Miss Henrietta had hired to assist the ladies who'd decided to prepare for the ball at the school.

A smile tugged at Temperance's lips as her gaze traveled over Permilia. While Permilia was usually dressed in the first state of fashion, she was currently wearing a flowing wrapper, albeit one adorned with fashionable feathers, the shade of green exactly matching the paste covering Permilia's face.

That paste, if Temperance wasn't mistaken, was compliments of Mrs. Davenport, who seemed convinced one of her many missions in life was to smother feminine faces with whatever latest concoction she'd created to hold wrinkles at bay.

Tearing her attention from Permilia's green face, she leaned over the scaffold. "Why is everyone determined to hide all the newspapers from me?" she called.

Permilia tipped her head and settled her gaze on Temperance. "We didn't want to spoil your evening with what's been written, although it's quickly become apparent that not *everyone* was determined to keep the news from you."

"It's better she's prepared," Miss Henrietta argued. "That way no one can spring this unsettling news on her tonight, catching her unaware." With that, Miss Henrietta pulled out a paper she'd stashed in a pocket of her apron, waving it in Temperance's direction. "Perhaps you should climb down from there and read one of the articles, dear. It's not a bad write-up at all, although, again, I do believe you'll need to readjust your decision about marrying Gilbert. Once news of this sort makes the front page, well, I'm afraid your future has been decided for you."

"I made the front page?"

"Indeed."

"I'll be right down."

Taking a second to make certain each side of her split skirt was still tied securely around each leg so the material wouldn't get in her way, Temperance hurried down the ladder of the scaffolding, releasing her skirt from the ties once she reached the ground. Shaking out the fabric, she headed for Miss Henrietta, thrusting out a hand once she reached that lady's side.

"There's no need to scowl at *me,*" Miss Henrietta said, handing over the paper. "I didn't write the articles."

"Yes, but since the reporters who did aren't available, I'm taking my aggravation out on you."

Miss Henrietta smiled. "I do appreciate your blunt honesty and am just tickled to death you're no longer the mousy and timid young lady I first met."

"Considering all the trouble I've encountered since abandoning that attitude, I'm not certain I'm as tickled about the re-embracing of my true nature as you are."

Permilia moved closer to Temperance and smoothed a hand down her arm. "I appreciate you abandoning your timid attitude as well, Temperance. When I first met you, you rarely spoke, and somehow managed to hide the idea you're much more on the lines of an adventurous sort than the timid wallflower I found lurking in all the ballrooms."

"I can't argue with any of that since I did spend a lot of my time lurking at all the balls Clementine forced me to attend." Temperance smiled. "As soon as I reunited with Gilbert, though, I realized I'd lost my sense of self and decided it was past time to reclaim the somewhat adventurous soul I used to be before my parents died."

"It's telling, you making such a decision because of reuniting with Gilbert," Miss Henrietta said with a knowing nod of her head.

"I'm sure you're right," Temperance agreed, which had Miss Henrietta blinking. "But even though I've realized he's more important to me than I cared to admit, his becoming the Earl of Strafford changes everything."

Miss Henrietta nodded again. "Well, of course it changes everything. You're going to become a countess, and there are not many young ladies who'll ever be able to become that."

"But I don't want to become a countess."

"Every lady wants to become a countess, or a princess," Miss Henrietta argued.

Temperance smiled. "I'm sure I did want to become a princess at one time, even mentioned to Gilbert a short while back that I always dreamed of a fairy tale whenever I considered marrying. But . . ."

"Why is there always a but?" Miss Henrietta asked Permilia, who simply smiled and shook her head.

"There's a but in my case because the reality of taking on the role of countess is not one I think I'd enjoy," Temperance began. "I don't care to spend the rest of my days having to abide by the strict rules I'm sure a countess is expected to observe from the moment she wakes up in the morning until she goes to bed at night."

"I imagine spending the rest of your life with Gilbert would be more than enough compensation for having to follow a few rules here and there," Miss Henrietta said.

"This from a lady who freely admits she spies on everyone, speaks her mind even when she knows that it is certain to raise more than a few eyebrows, and . . . well, I could go on and on, but I do believe there are a few newspapers I need to peruse." With that, Temperance shook open the paper, scanned the front page, and felt her mouth drop open.

She lifted her head. "Why would Gilbert

inheriting a title be considered front-page news?"

Permilia smiled. "Because society places a great deal of importance on titles. And now that society can claim an earl as one of their members, even though Gilbert has barely attended any society events, all the papers knew they'd sell out of their editions today by splashing the news about his title on the front page." Her smile dimmed. "Did you not read the part where it mentions you yet?"

"I'm afraid I got distracted." She looked back at the article and began to read it out loud. " *'Mr. Gilbert Cavendish, considered one of the most eligible gentlemen in New York, has now taken over the role of The Most Eligible Gentleman. Reliable sources have told us he's recently inherited an earldom, making him the new Lord Strafford. Those sources also told us he's now in possession of an impressive castle in the country, a townhome in London, and stables filled with prime horseflesh.'* " She frowned. "I wonder who these reliable sources are?"

Permilia winced. "If you continue reading, I believe that'll become obvious."

Returning to the article, Temperance skimmed over a few sentences, drawing in a sharp breath a second later.

"What part are you reading, dear?" Miss Henrietta asked, moving closer.

" 'According to our most reliable source,' " Temperance read out loud, *" 'Lord Strafford may not remain as The Most Eligible Gentleman for long because he's soon to announce his engagement to Miss Temperance Flowerdew, cousin of the beautiful Miss Clementine Flowerdew, who . . .' "*

She thrust the paper back at Miss Henrietta. "I do think I need to nip out for just an hour or so because this time Clementine has gone too far." She headed for the door, finding her way blocked by Miss Henrietta, who'd charged after her, moving surprisingly fast for a woman of her age.

"You cannot go have a little chat with Clementine. If you've forgotten, there's a price on your head. And while the Pinkerton detectives are diligently trying to solve the question of who put that price on your head, they've been unsuccessful thus far, which means you're not going anywhere."

"Besides," Permilia added, coming up to join them, "you'll have plenty of time to speak with Clementine this evening because Gertrude invited her to the ball." She wiped her chin with a handkerchief because the green concoction on her face seemed to be sliding ever so slowly down her face.

"Why would she have done that?"

Miss Henrietta smiled. "Because Gertrude is a kind soul and didn't want to exclude Clementine from the festivities, especially since your cousin did step in over the past week and assist us with getting this ballroom ready for tonight's celebration." Miss Henrietta let out a sigh. "I do wish Clementine's dreadful aunt, Mrs. Boggart Hobbes, had not whisked the poor girl away from us. It's my belief that Clementine has potential to be so much more than the insipid young lady she portrays to the world, that unfortunate circumstance a direct result of being raised by parents with lofty social aspirations."

Temperance frowned. "How, pray tell, did you come to that conclusion? Clementine clearly sold me out to the papers, which doesn't exactly lend credence to the notion she has the potential to abandon her nasty disposition."

"I believe she contacted the papers as a peculiar way of trying to make matters right with you," Miss Henrietta said, holding up her hand when Temperance opened her mouth to argue. "And while I understand your reluctance to see the good in her, given the manner in which she treated you over the years, I've recently realized that God puts us in certain situations that allow us to see our faults. In Clementine's case, she found herself benefiting from your kindness of offering her family a place to stay, and that, my dear, must have caused her to look at life a little differently."

"I suppose that's possible, although . . ." Temperance stopped speaking when Eugene walked into the room, carrying an arrangement of flowers.

"Another delivery has been made, Miss Temperance," he began. "They're unloading more down in the kitchen and wanted me to find out where the rest of the arrangements are supposed to be placed."

"You may put that one on any table that doesn't have flowers," Temperance said. "And I'll go right now and see what else has been delivered." She nodded to the scaffold. "Would it be possible for you to take that down for me, Eugene? I've finished with it for the day."

As Eugene assured her he'd get it down in a jiffy, Temperance made her way out of the ballroom, Permilia by her side, while Miss Henrietta disappeared down another hallway, saying she needed to check on Miss Snook, who'd come down with a nasty cold and was keeping herself well away from everyone.

"You're not really going to refuse to marry Gilbert because he's an earl now, are you?" Permilia asked as they reached the staircase.

"You seem to be forgetting that Gilbert and I are only pretending we're engaged, which means it really makes no difference to me if he's an earl or not, since I wasn't planning on marrying him in the first place."

Permilia arched a single brow and stopped walking. "And clearly you're forgetting that I've been privy to watching you when you're with Gilbert, and it's obvious you hold him in high esteem."

"True, but we're simply not well suited for marriage. Add in the fact that I'd rather have a tooth pulled than assume the role of countess, and . . . it'll be best all around if Gilbert and I figure out a way to gracefully extract ourselves from our pretend engagement, even if all those articles in the papers are going to make that somewhat tricky."

"But aren't you the least little bit curious as to what it would be like to live in a castle?"

Temperance began to head down the steps. "Living in a castle is not a valid reason to marry someone. And because Gilbert has made himself scarce since learning he inherited a title, I've come to the conclusion that he realizes he's going to need a wife who is up for the challenge of taking on the daunting role of countess, something he knows perfectly well I'd not be very proficient at."

Permilia caught up with her after she reached the landing. "I think you'd make a lovely countess."

"That is kind of you to say, but no, I wouldn't."

Considering her for a long moment, Permilia released the merest hint of a sigh. "Oh, very well, I'll stop harping."

"You weren't harping."

"I was, but because I don't want to annoy you further, allow me to deftly turn the conversation to a matter I've yet to share with you, even if that matter does pertain to . . . castles."

"Oh dear."

Permilia laughed. "It's not what you think. I was simply going to tell you some news that I recently received, news about my father who is in the process of purchasing his very own castle over in Scotland."

"Is that why your father has yet to return to New York, and why you and Asher haven't set a date for your wedding?"

"It's one of the reasons we haven't set a date, although the store has been keeping us so busy that we simply haven't had the time to plan out a wedding."

"I'm sure you wouldn't need to plan a single thing, not with Miss Henrietta, Miss Mabel, and Mrs. Davenport always longing to organize our lives for us."

"Indeed, but now that I've learned my father and stepmother, Ida, will be returning to the states in the next month because my father is selling his business to Mr. Slater, Asher and I are considering a wedding close to Christmas."

"Isn't Mr. Slater the gentleman your stepsister, Lucy, set her cap for, but then changed her mind about after he'd sailed her, your father, and Ida over to London?"

Permilia grinned. "The very same. Father was feeling guilty about Lucy refusing Mr. Slater's suit. And after he and Ida traveled to Scotland, where my father felt an instant kinship with a clan of Scotsmen, probably because they convinced him, what with his red hair, that he must have Scottish ancestry, Father decided it was time to get rid of his mining ventures. Mr. Slater was only too willing to buy him out, which will make *his* mining ventures some of the largest in the country."

"And Ida, a woman known to be enamored with New York society, is willing to abandon her society life in this city to take up residence in Scotland?"

"Oddly enough, Ida has developed a love for Scotland and seems to have actually fallen in love with my father as well."

"How delightful."

"Quite," Permilia said. "And Lucy, after refusing an offer of marriage from a British viscount, has apparently fallen for a Scotsman and is to get married come spring, where she'll then take up residence in an ancient castle not far from the one my father's purchasing."

Temperance began walking down the second flight of stairs. "I'm sure you're much relieved that your father's marriage has turned around. I was afraid he and Ida would decide to live separate lives at some point, but now, he seems to have found his happily-ever-after as well."

"He has. And because he's feeling guilty about putting an ocean between us, although with us being friends with Harrison, we'll always have a yacht or two at our disposal to visit Scotland, Father is insisting on buying Asher and me a cottage in Newport." She smiled. "Since I adore Newport, and wouldn't mind bringing a small Rutherford & Company shop into some space at the Newport Casino, I've decided to be gracious and accept my father's gift."

Stepping from the stairs, Temperance exchanged smiles with Permilia. Agreeing to rejoin her friend after she dealt with what should be the last of the flower deliveries, Temperance headed off down a hallway.

She reached the backroom a short time later, finding two deliverymen wearing work aprons that were embroidered with a rose — a signature design that Charles Klunder, New York's renowned florist, used to advertise his business.

Giving the many flower arrangements that were littering the tables and floor a quick glance, she lifted her head. "These are meant for the dining room, so if you'll follow me, I'll show you where to put them."

Leading the way to the large room on the first floor where the guests that evening were to be served a sumptuous twelve-course meal, Temperance moved through the tables, turning to gesture the men forward when she found some tables that had no flowers on them.

Her hand froze midgesture, though, when one of the men dropped a flower arrangement to the ground, breaking the vase in the process, right as he pulled a pistol from his apron pocket and aimed it her way.

Her only thought was to avoid a bullet, so she snatched up a sharp knife meant to cut the meat during course number five and threw it at the man. She let out an incredibly loud shriek when a far sharper knife than she'd just thrown whizzed past her ear, and she dropped to the floor in search of cover.

A howl of rage suggested she might have, curiously enough, met her mark with her knife, but before she could give herself a pat on the back, a shot rang out, glass shattered, and the sound of footsteps pounding her way had her scrambling across the floor on all fours.

As additional shots rang out, terror rose in her throat, but then she heard Gilbert yelling over the mayhem, and she knew without a doubt that today was not going to be the day she died.

Chapter Twenty

Rage pounded through Gilbert's veins as he set his sights on the two men randomly firing their pistols through the dining room, trying to hit Temperance, who was obviously on the ground somewhere.

He had no idea if she'd been hit but knew the only way to get to her was by dealing with the men trying to kill her. Pulling out his pistol, he took deliberate aim at one of the men, pulled the trigger, then felt a flash of satisfaction when that man staggered backward, dropped his pistol, and plunged to the ground. Aiming for the other man, he fired off a shot, missed, then crouched behind a table and began exchanging bullets across the dining room.

As the vase shattered on the table he was crouching behind, Gilbert stuck his hand in his pocket, pulling out more bullets. Before he could reload his pistol though, the bullets that had been whizzing his way suddenly stopped. A second later, amidst a bout of swearing, Gilbert realized the man's pistol was jammed, and knowing it was now or never, he sprang into motion.

Racing around the tables that separated him from the attacker, he got to within two feet of the man and launched himself through the air, taking the man to the floor a second later.

In a rumble of grunts, curses, and flailing limbs, Gilbert managed to pin the man to the ground, drawing back a fist and planting it against the man's jaw.

Unfortunately, the man turned out to be a hardy sort, and the next second, Gilbert was rolling across a floor covered in shattered glass with Temperance's attacker rolling with him.

A turned-over chair stopped their momentum just as a torrent of water poured over their heads, and a crystal vase was brought down on the attacker's head. The man's eyes rolled up into his head as his body went limp.

Shaking wet hair out of his eyes, Gilbert rolled to the right, looked up, and found Temperance standing over him, holding a crystal vase and looking completely furious.

Before he could get so much as a single word out of his mouth, she raised the vase over her head again, but paused when a voice rang out.

"Temperance, don't hit him again. He'll not be able to give us answers if he's not left with at least a semblance of wits about him."

Turning his head, Gilbert caught sight of Edwina Sinclair racing over the glass-strewn floor, her feet encased in what seemed to be gardening boots. She'd obviously been interrupted in the process of getting prepared for the ball that evening because she was wearing a velvet wrapper with feathers attached to the collar, and half her hair was wrapped up in rags, while the other half was streaming over her shoulder. Her face was covered in an unusual orange paste, but she didn't appear to be bothered by that as she lurched to a stop beside the unconscious man, bent over, then nudged him with her pistol. Straightening, she gave Temperance a nod of clear approval.

"Excellent job, Temperance. You've laid him low and saved Gilbert some additional bruises in the end, although . . ." Edwina looked back at him. "Your nose is bleeding, Gilbert, and I imagine you're going to sport two black eyes before long."

"Goodness, Gilbert, I didn't notice you were bleeding," Temperance said, whipping a napkin from a table before crouching down beside him and pressing it against his nose. "Don't squirm," she admonished when he realized his nose was throbbing somewhat painfully.

Helping him to a sitting position, she kept the napkin pressed firmly against his nose even as she brushed wet hair from his eyes. "I'm sorry about the water. The vase was the first thing I saw to use as a weapon."

"It was a good choice," he said, his voice muffled because of the napkin. "Although you should have yelled for help instead of taking on the job yourself. You could have been hurt coming to my rescue."

She smiled and patted his shoulder. "If you'll recall, it's what we do — we look out for one another." She turned her head as additional people began swarming into the dining room. "It does seem as if our rescuing each other is going to get a bit of a reprieve because it appears there's a good half-dozen Pinkerton agents on the scene now."

"I'm afraid *my* days of being a fledgling agent are certain to be numbered," Edwina said, a note of disgust in her voice. "I can't imagine many of the other agents would have been so negligent as to allow two full-blown criminals to slip into the very house they were supposed to be guarding." She blew out a breath. "I also can't imagine they'd be so negligent because they were enjoying a new skin regimen that's supposed to hold wrinkles at bay."

"I think you're being a little hard on yourself, Edwina, especially since, if you'll recall, you're not on duty," Temperance pointed out, peeking under the napkin still attached to Gilbert's nose before she pressed it right back again. "Still bleeding," she told him before she looked up at Edwina. "And, really, it's not as if we could have expected these men to sneak in here dressed in uniforms worn by our florist of choice today. Who goes to those lengths to do away with an ordinary woman whose death, in my humble opinion, won't benefit a single soul?"

"Someone who was given the job of killing you and is now scared to death they're going to be killed because they haven't been able to achieve any success with seeing you dead."

Looking past Edwina, who'd immediately begun beaming at the newcomer, although she did seem to be trying to hide that fact behind a raised hand since it wasn't every day a Pinkerton detective was seen beaming warmly at a fellow agent, Gilbert discovered

Agent Samuel McParland had joined them. He was already looking the unconscious man up and down before he shook his head.

"That's Richard the Snake, and I bet the other man is Bernie the Butcher, which means someone's put a very attractive price on your head, Temperance."

Temperance frowned. "Why would anyone of the criminal persuasion call themselves Richard the Snake? That's hardly discreet. He should have simply called himself The Snake, or Slithers, which is far scarier and lends a bit of mystery to his identity."

Agent McParland crouched down, opened one of Richard the Snake's eyes, then took his finger away. "Odd as this is going to seem, this man's name isn't Richard. It's Harvey, but before you ask me why he goes by Richard, I have no idea, nor can we ask him since I do believe he's going to be out for a while. What happened to him?"

"Temperance brought a crystal vase down on his head," Gilbert said.

"Nice." Agent McParland smiled at Temperance before he straightened. "That man alive?" he yelled to Eugene, who was standing next to the man Gilbert had shot, holding a silver knife in his hand that seemed to be dripping blood.

"He's fine, 'cept for the bullet hole in his

arm," Eugene said. "And the hole left by this fancy piece of dinnerware."

Agent McParland caught Gilbert's eye. "You stabbed him with a dinner knife?"

"That must have been Temperance, although I was responsible for shooting Bernie the, er . . . Butcher."

"Seems like he got carved up instead of doing the carving he's so fond of," Agent McParland said before he arched a brow Temperance's way. "Want to explain to me how it happened that you ended up alone with two members of the criminal class who seem intent on murdering you?"

Taking a moment to explain what had happened, Temperance ended with "Gilbert arrived on the scene, there was a fierce gun battle, he shot one of the men, and I helped by hitting that man with a vase."

Agent McParland's brows drew together. "I believe you neglected to address how you managed to stab the man with a dinner knife."

A trace of a smile flickered over Temperance's face. "I didn't stab him. I merely got lucky when I threw the knife his way. Imagine my surprise when I actually hit someone." She turned her smile on Gilbert. "If nothing else, that knife-wielding lesson taught me I'm ill-equipped to handle myself in a knife fight, which is why I threw it and ran."

The rage that had been lingering in his veins disappeared as something warm, and quite frankly, fuzzy, replaced it. Even though Temperance had always been an impulsive sort, she'd matured over the years they'd been apart — had even become a bit practical. That practicality, mixed in with the whimsicality she'd always embraced, made her downright irresistible and . . . made him long to kiss her.

As soon as that thought took hold, his gaze dropped to her lips, lingering on the small crescent-shaped indentation that was right next to the corner of her lip, brought about by her smile.

He wanted to kiss that spot, and then move on to kiss the fullness of lips that were a very enticing shade of pink, something he'd never noticed before, but something he certainly wasn't going to forget again.

Leaning forward, he stilled when Temperance suddenly whipped the napkin from his nose, replacing it with a soaking wet napkin someone had handed her. Just like that, he was swept back to reality and to a room filled to the gills with people, which certainly wasn't a setting that was appropriate for sharing a first kiss with Temperance, or even *thinking* about a first kiss with her.

"Forgive me, Gilbert, am I hurting you?" Temperance asked, her smile fading away.

"Not at all" were the only words he seemed capable of summoning up.

"Why are you scowling then?"

Gilbert was spared an immediate response when Agent McParland and a few other agents carted the two criminals from the dining room. Bernie the Butcher began causing such a ruckus that it took four agents to subdue him, which went far in proving the man was not a bargain criminal-for-hire, especially since he'd been shot and stabbed with a knife, yet was still able to fight.

After the agents left the room, trailed by Edwina, who was clomping after them in her garden boots, Gilbert accepted the hand Temperance held out to him, and with water dripping off him and shards of broken glass tinkling to the floor, he rose to his feet.

Temperance immediately began dusting him off with another napkin, right as the room swarmed with additional people, all of whom seemed to be in some state of dishabille. Before he could do more than gape at the ladies rushing his way in a flutter of wrappers that all sported brightly colored feathers, and all of whom had different colored paste on their faces, Gilbert was surrounded.

"Are either of you hurt?" Miss Henrietta demanded as she pulled Temperance into a hug, one she seemed in no hurry to end since she kept Temperance close as she peered at him through violet paste that lent her a somewhat terrifying appearance. "Why is your face all bloody?"

Gilbert grabbed another napkin, shook it free of glass, then took a swipe at his face. "One of the attackers punched me in the nose, but I'm fine." He smiled. "I'm sure the black eyes I've been told I'll soon sport will lend me the reputation of dashing gentleman of intrigue about town."

"Add that in with the news you're now the Earl of Strafford, and I'm afraid the ladies will be relentless in their pursuit," Permilia said, stepping up next to him. Shaking her head, she took the napkin from him. "Allow me. You're missing the worst of it."

Shooting a glance to Temperance to see how she was reacting to the reminder he'd inherited a somewhat lofty title, Gilbert found her still being fussed over by Miss Henrietta, who was now holding Temperance's hand and peppering her with questions.

"Do tell me," Permilia said quietly to Gilbert, "that you've been spending your time over the past day and a half composing one of your infamous lists that will assist you in presenting Temperance with a compelling argument as to why she'd be quite content to become a countess."

His lips curved. "Asher has obviously been carrying tales to you about my habit of creating lists. But yes, I have begun compiling a list."

"May I hope it's a detailed list — filled with very compelling ideas?"

Gilbert leaned closer. "I'm afraid it's not complete, which is one of the reasons I've made myself scarce over the past day."

Permilia frowned. "How complete is it?"

"I've only come up with one valid reason for her to want to become a countess — that reason being there's plenty of beautiful scenery in England I know she'd love to paint, although . . ."

"You made yourself scarce because you've been struggling to make a list?" Temperance asked, sidling up right beside him even as she sent him a look of exasperation.

Gilbert arched a brow. "Did it ever occur to you that Permilia and I were having what one might call a private conversation?"

She arched a brow right back at him. "You

should have sought out a private setting then, but getting back to you making yourself scarce — you do realize that I've been more than put out with you for not calling on me to discuss your new circumstances, don't you?"

"Since I knew you found the idea of me acquiring a title disconcerting, and since I've always known that you prefer to sort through troubling information well removed from the source of that trouble, I thought you'd appreciate me giving you uninterrupted time to reconcile yourself with the idea of becoming a countess."

"That was very considerate of him, dear," Miss Henrietta called from a few feet away.

Temperance immediately turned her back on Miss Henrietta and tugged him around as well, effectively stopping that woman from reading their lips.

"I would make an abysmal countess, as you very well know."

He ignored that. "I also knew you were out of sorts yesterday — or perhaps furious would be a better word — after learning your parents changed their plans about whom they wanted as your guardian in case anything happened to them. Discovering they'd chosen Wayne over my parents must have left you reeling, which, again, is why I thought it would be for the best to allow you time to digest everything that had been disclosed without having me around to distract you."

Something interesting flashed through Temperance's eyes before she took hold of his arm and, for some unknown reason, began pulling him toward the door.

"You're not throwing me out, are you?" was all he could think to ask.

She stopped in her tracks. "Don't be ridiculous. I only wish to continue this conversation elsewhere. If you've neglected to notice, we've got quite the audience, some of whom have been stealing closer and closer to us."

Turning, he found Miss Henrietta and Mrs. Davenport still advancing their way, both ladies stopping abruptly when they evidently realized they'd been spotted.

"Where are you two going?" Miss Henrietta asked, batting innocent lashes his way.

"I need to have a private chat with Gilbert," Temperance said.

She inclined her head. "The library would be a lovely spot for a chat, and . . . I'll have tea sent around immediately."

"Why are you looking so . . . pleased?" Temperance asked Miss Henrietta, right as Mrs. Davenport, her face covered in orange paste, sent Gilbert a smile as she sauntered ever so casually past him, dropping something into his pocket.

"I'm sure I'm not looking pleased, dear," Miss Henrietta returned. "It must be the violet-colored paste Mrs. Davenport convinced me to put on my face." She gave a little flutter of her hands. "Who knew it would affect my expressions, although . . . speaking of expressions, I am beyond curious as to what caused the expression you were just wearing. May I dare hope it was an epiphany on your part regarding . . ." She batted lashes Gilbert's way once again.

"Your talent with observation is certain to get you into trouble one day" was all Temperance said to that before she pulled Gilbert into motion and out of the room, moving down the hallway at a fast clip.

As he broke into a trot to keep pace with her, he stuck his hand in his pocket, swallowing a laugh when his fingers enclosed around the object Mrs. Davenport had slipped into his pocket. It was a ring.

Why she thought he might need a ring at this point in time was anyone's guess, unless she and Miss Henrietta had come to some type of conclusion about that epiphany Miss Henrietta had mentioned, one that very well might revolve around Temperance's feelings for . . .

"I've got your tea," Mr. Barclay said, following them into the library and causing Gilbert to grin over the idea that he and Temperance seemed to be in the process of being well and truly taken in hand by meddlers of the most impressive sort.

Taking a seat beside Temperance on a settee, he didn't bother to hide his grin as Mr. Barclay went about pouring the tea, delivering it with a great deal of aplomb, and then hurrying from the room, closing the door behind him, and breaking numerous rules of decorum in the process.

"Is it me, or have the members of the elderly set suddenly begun acting more peculiar than usual?" he asked, taking a sip of his tea while Temperance did the same.

"How did you know I was upset about my parents changing their minds about whom they chose to become my guardian?" she asked instead of answering his question.

"That's why you dragged me out of the dining room?"

"Just answer the question."

He set aside his tea. "It's not difficult to answer, Temperance. I just knew — the same way I knew you loathed being sent off to Miss Porter's School for Young Ladies all those years ago."

"You knew I loathed Miss Porter's?"

"Of course."

"I never told anyone that."

"You didn't have to tell me, Temperance. I always knew. I also knew you weren't delighted about going off on a tour of Europe to improve your artistic skills. I'm sure you only agreed to that tour because you didn't want to disappoint your parents or cause them to cancel one of their trips to some obscure part of the world."

"I had a lovely time in Europe."

"I'm sure you did, but I'm also certain you would have been just as content to stay on this side of the ocean and in the company of your parents."

"I couldn't expect them to stay with me. They always felt their travel around the world was a calling from God — a calling that required them to assist the poor souls in curious lands who'd never been exposed to God's word."

"And that was a noble calling to be sure, but it came with the price of leaving you behind — something you resent them for and something you feel guilty about."

For a long moment she considered him, then leaned forward. "I actually stopped playing musical instruments because I wanted to annoy them."

"You told me you stopped playing because people expected you to stick to playing classical pieces instead of allowing you to experiment with many different genres."

"Well, yes, but . . ." She sent him a smile that had guilt written all over it. "It was really all due to my parents arranging for me to stay with this musical genius who expected me to practice all hours of the day and night. I thought if I simply stopped playing, my parents would have no choice but to return home to deal with my obstinacy."

"And did that work?"

"It did. They cut their journey short and collected me from Boston, where I was staying."

She bit her lip. "I was wracked with guilt for months because they were so understanding about me giving up music. They decided I was exhausted from all the practice and took me on a three-month holiday to the beach. It was a lovely holiday, and yet, I knew I was keeping them from their calling, which is why I didn't put up much of a fuss when Mother suggested I attend Miss Porter's School for Young Ladies."

"You should have told your parents how you really felt, Temperance. They were wonderful people. I'm sure they simply believed they were giving you a future by enrolling you in a finishing school and then sending you off to Europe to pursue your painting."

"I couldn't very well tell them the truth because I knew if I did that, I'd be a huge disappointment to God."

Of anything he'd been expecting, Temperance believing she'd disappoint God if she'd revealed her true feelings to her parents had never crossed his mind.

Rising to his feet, he moved directly next to her, crouching down to take her hand as he met her gaze.

"You're going to need to explain that a little more sufficiently," he said.

She heaved a sigh. "I'm sure you must remember how you and I were dreadful at times when our families attended church together, frequently missing entire sermons while we scribbled notes back and forth to each other. But there were times when I did listen to the sermons, and many of those sermons returned to the idea of what a blessing God found it to be when His children were willing to grab hold of the calling He sent them."

"And because of those sermons," Gilbert continued for her when her eyes suddenly turned suspiciously bright and she wiped her nose with her sleeve, "you somehow came to the conclusion that if you stood in the way of your parents and their many mission trips, you would be disappointing God because He gave them the desire to travel the world and seek out people in need."

She gave a sniffle, accepted the handkerchief he pulled out of his pocket, and after she blew her nose, she lifted her head. "Exactly."

"Did you ever consider the idea that God gave *you* to your parents? Or did you ever think that maybe He was disappointed at times with your parents for not being there for you?"

"I didn't need them as much as the people they traveled to help. I had my father's fortune behind me to secure all the luxuries and necessities of life. It seemed petty to expect more."

"But you did want more — you wanted the attention of your parents." He squeezed her hand. "There's nothing wrong with wanting that type of attention, nor is there anything wrong with you being furious with your parents for leaving your welfare in the hands of Wayne and his horrid family instead of my parents."

Temperance blew her nose again and finally gave a small nod. "I am furious with my parents, but I shouldn't be because they're dead, and it's an insult to their memory."

"It's human to be angry with them, just as it's human for you to be angry with God as well."

A hint of a smile teased Temperance's lips. "I'm not going to deny that I've been angry with God over the past three years for allowing my parents to be taken from me. Being around Eugene and Mercy, though, has reminded me that my relationship with God needs to be repaired, and I do believe I'm ready to put the anger I've held for Him aside." The hint of a smile turned into a real one. "But now is hardly the time to delve further into that, what with the ball that's to be held soon in this very house."

"May I assume it's also not the time to delve into what the future might hold for the two of us?"

"I don't think the future holds much of anything except friendship for the two of us," she said before she leaned closer to him, her face only inches from his. "But know this, my friend. I do cherish your friendship and find it comforting that someone in this world knows me so well."

"But you don't cherish me enough to want to become my countess?"

She leaned even closer, surprising him when she pressed her lips for the briefest second against his, pulling back all too soon. "It's because I cherish you that I won't become your countess, although do know that if events had not unfolded as they recently have, I might have entertained the thought of marrying you. Now, though, with you having to accept your late brother's title, you're going to have to find a lady more suited to the life you're soon to live."

With that, she gave him one last feather-light kiss, rose to her feet, and glided from the room, leaving him behind.

Chapter Twenty-One

"Stop squirming," Mrs. Davenport said, letting out a huff of exasperation as she tried to adjust a bustle that, in Temperance's mind, was larger than it needed to be.

"Do you not believe the back of this gown would drape just as nicely without this monstrosity you've attached to my behind?" she asked, finally catching sight of her backside in the mirror and earning another huff from Mrs. Davenport in the process.

"Since I am currently a student of fashion, I do know what is all the rage this season, and that bustle you're wearing, my dear, is all the rage."

"At least she didn't create it from an old birdcage," Gertrude pointed out, stepping up beside Temperance, looking resplendent in a gown of bright orange, her honey-gold hair swept up on the crown of her head, with orange jewels Temperance thought might be topaz woven into the strands.

"I notice your bustle isn't nearly as large," Temperance couldn't help pointing out.

"That's because, if you've forgotten, Mrs. Davenport *did* attach a birdcage to *my* bottom a few months back, with disastrous results. Because of that, she and I have agreed she'll avoid attaching any type of bustle to me for the rest of my days."

"It was only half a birdcage." Mrs. Davenport stepped back from Temperance, looking her over with a critical eye. "You do wear gowns well, my dear, and I must say, you were quite right about choosing such a vivid shade of pink."

Temperance smoothed a hand down the silk of her gown. "It is a shame we ladies are normally required to wear subdued colors instead of more vibrant ones." She nodded to Gertrude. "It was brilliant on your part to ask all of us to abandon the pastels for the night. It'll make for a truly exceptional evening."

Gertrude smiled. "I can hardly wait to see how everything looks when the chandeliers are lit against the silken sky you created in the ballroom. And do not even get me started on how absolutely charming the centerpieces are — what with the ships you created and the miniature sandy beaches you used to showcase them."

"Don't forget that at the end of the night the guests will be absolutely delighted to learn they get to dig through that sand to find all sorts of treasures," Mrs. Davenport added, tucking a strand of her dyed black hair behind her ear. "Although it really wasn't an original idea on my part when I suggested the treasure hunt as a way for the guests to uncover their favors." She smiled. "One of my society friends told me she'd been given the pleasure of digging for treasure at a ball held in Newport two seasons ago."

"I don't imagine many of the guests present tonight attended that particular ball," Gertrude said. "Harrison and I didn't invite the entire New York Four Hundred." She gave a bit of a shudder. "That would have caused all sorts of havoc, and I think we've suffered enough havoc to last us a while."

"Indeed," Temperance said, shuddering as well before she smiled. "But speaking of the centerpieces, I do need to take one last look at the third-floor ballroom, and then I need to check on how the progress is going in the dining room."

"No need to check the dining room, Miss Temperance," Mercy said, striding into the room and looking completely unlike herself in a simple gown of deep blue, her dark hair braided around her head and her cheeks flushed an attractive shade of pink. "Me and the rest of the girls already have that room lookin' shipshape again. As for the ballroom, Eugene and some of the other men got them chandeliers all lit up, and oh my, but it does look a treat up there."

Temperance walked to join Mercy, who immediately gave Temperance a twirl, wobbling on heels she was evidently unused to. "What do you think?"

"You look absolutely lovely, Mercy. The blue suits you to perfection."

Mercy nodded. "It does, doesn't it?"

Temperance returned the nod. "I'm surprised you were able to get ready so quickly though. I have no idea how you and the other students were able to get the dining room put to rights before the first guests started arriving."

"You're forgettin' that me and many of Miss Snook's students spent years tidying up the big houses we worked in. We're good at tidying, so it was no great feat that we got the dining room put back together before the ball started. But getting back to how I'm lookin' . . ." Mercy twirled around again, wobbling only a touch before she dipped into a slightly awkward curtsy and grinned. "I ain't, I mean, I've never had me no fancy dress before, so I do thank you and the rest of the ladies for providing me with it." She nodded to Gertrude. "It sure was a kindness for you to invite us to your special night, Miss Gertrude. Do know that all of us here at the school wish you only the very best with your dashing, and oh-so-scrump . . . ti . . . ous Mr. Harrison Sinclair."

"Don't let Harrison hear you calling him scrumptious," Edwina said, looking up from a stack of paperwork she was reading in a chair beside the fireplace. "He's smug enough as it is, what with him soon to be married to the love of his life."

Mercy nodded. "Mum's the word, Miss Edwina, although I've witnessed you being a little smug as well, especially when that *charming* Agent McParland is paying you attention."

Edwina sent Mercy a wink. "Guilty as charged."

Mercy sent her a wink right back before she nodded to the papers Edwina had been looking through. "Seems an odd time to be catching up on your readin'."

"I'm afraid with all the nastiness that happened this afternoon, I was unable to complete the task I was asked to do by Samuel, or, ah, Agent McParland I suppose I should say since this is a business matter." She held up one of the papers. "All of these pages contain the notes of numerous agents, many of whom have horrible handwriting. It's my job to look through their notes and see if I can find any sort of pattern that may shed some light on who might be behind trying to do in Temperance and her family."

Temperance walked across the room, stopping directly in front of Edwina. "Have you found anything yet?"

Pursing her lips, Edwina looked down, riffled through a few of the pages, then pulled out a sheet from the pile. Running her finger down a page of scribbled notes, she stopped and lifted her head. "It's not anything definitive, but this page of notes was written out by two agents who tried to secure an appointment with Mr. John Howland, your father's old attorney."

"They didn't succeed?" Temperance asked as Mrs. Davenport, apparently not done with her fussing, began tugging the back of Temperance's skirt, almost pulling Temperance off her feet in the process.

"He's apparently left town," Edwina said right as Temperance regained her balance.

Pulling her skirt away from Mrs. Davenport, who was now in the process of trying to fluff it up, something it certainly didn't need since the bustle attached to her was doing a fine job of that, Temperance frowned. "I'm no Pinkerton, but that seems suspicious."

"Agreed, and it's even more suspicious that when these two agents questioned Mr. Howland's secretary, she didn't know when Mr. Howland was expected to return, nor where he'd gone."

"Gilbert's secretary always knows where he is on any given day. I would assume Mr. Howland would expect no less from his secretary, which makes one wonder if he does have something to do with the skullduggery that's been swarming around me of late."

"Have you ever noticed how often you bring Gilbert into the conversation?" Edwina asked, completely neglecting to address what Temperance thought had been a very telling point about Mr. Howland. "And has anyone mentioned that you get this dreamy expression in your eyes when you do mention Gilbert, which again, you do often?"

"I don't get a dreamy expression in my eyes" was all she could think to say to that.

Mrs. Davenport let out a snort. "You do, dear, but it would be hard for you to see that expression, unless you just happened to be by a mirror when you bring Gilbert's name up in conversation."

"I think you should marry the man," Edwina added.

Before Temperance could reply to that, Mrs. Davenport began nodding in a vigorous fashion. "No truer words have ever been said, but Temperance is clearly still hesitant about the matter. Otherwise, well, I daresay she'd be wearing that lovely ring I gave Gilbert." She reached out and gave Temperance's skirt another tug, one that was a little more forceful than was strictly necessary.

After finding her balance yet again, Temperance quirked a brow. "You gave Gilbert a ring — as in an engagement ring?"

"What other type of ring would you expect me to give the man I've decided is perfect for you in every way?" Mrs. Davenport countered. "I've been carrying the ring around with me for days, and I finally decided that it was time to pass it on to Gilbert after he saved you from the jaws of death yet again." She gave a sad shake of her head. "I really thought the two of you would be well and truly engaged by now, but apparently you turned him down once more. He was looking quite perplexed when he took his leave earlier, as if he didn't know what to do after suffering another rejection at your hands."

"I'm certain he was only looking that way because I kissed him . . . twice," Temperance said, her words causing silence to descend on the room.

Miss Henrietta, who was sitting at a vanity table having her hair curled, turned to her. "You exchanged kisses with Gilbert and yet you're still determined *not* to marry him?"

"I wouldn't say I *exchanged* kisses with Gilbert because I didn't actually allow him time to return the kisses I gave him. In all honesty, I'm not certain what I gave him can be considered true kisses since they weren't of the lingering sort, but more along the lines of brief shows of true affection."

Miss Henrietta narrowed her eyes. "And this *true* affection you apparently hold for the man is not the type of affection that would normally end with a walk down the aisle?"

Temperance narrowed her eyes right back. "It is not, although I did tell him that if he wasn't destined to spend his life as the Earl of Strafford, I might have entertained the thought of considering a marriage proposal from him at some point in time."

"It's little wonder the poor man looked

perplexed," Edwina said, setting aside her paperwork. "And I must admit I am as well. How in the world did you reason out that even though you hold Gilbert in true affection, you can't marry him because he's found himself in possession of a lofty title, as well as a castle or two? He also has a rather nice fortune that will allow him to maintain his castles in style."

"Living life amongst the aristocracy is not something I believe I'd be good at, although living in a castle would be nice, even if I've heard they can be somewhat chilly during the winter."

"Again, Gilbert has enough money to see those castles updated with more modern heating methods, and it's not as if you'd have to mingle with other aristocrats all the time. You'd be out in the middle of nowhere for a good part of the year," Mrs. Davenport pointed out.

Temperance nodded. "Which is an excellent point, but from what I recall of British lords, they're required to sit in the House of Lords for certain months of the year, requiring them to repair to London. Unfortunately, I also recall that while Parliament is in session, that's when London's high season takes place, and that right there is why I can't marry Gilbert."

Edwina rose to her feet and shook out the folds of her dressing gown. "Surely you don't believe Gilbert will give up pursuing you so easily, do you? Ever since I've known him, he's always been a determined sort. Pair that with the notion you disclosed your affection by kissing him — twice from what you said — and I have to imagine he's even now pulling together a plan that will have you changing your mind." She smiled. "That plan will certainly consist of lists, charts, and perhaps even a graph or two, detailing the many reasons why it would be in your best interest to marry him."

"He'll be doing no such planning," Temperance argued. "Gilbert is a very practical sort, analytical as well, which means that after reflecting on our situation, he'll determine I'm right and accept that it would be a disaster for us to marry. I do not have any desire to take on the role of countess and would do a dreadful job of it, even if I did have a smidgen of interest in that role."

"You told me you attended one of the most elite finishing schools in America," Edwina argued. "And I've never noticed you putting a foot out of line when it comes to behaving with the utmost decorum in any polite setting."

"Just because I *know* how to behave

properly doesn't mean I care to behave *all* the time. I've discovered I enjoy having the luxury of independence, as well as the luxury of not always having to put my best foot forward. Why, if I clung to proper behavior all the time, I wouldn't be able to travel to Five Points to paint or have Mr. Barclay escort me to the ocean for target practice or have Eugene teach me how to defend myself in a knife brawl in the back courtyard. I'd have to give all that up, as well as give up spending time with all my friends here in New York. And even though I care for Gilbert, I'm afraid we'd grow to resent each other. *I* would resent the loss of my freedom, and *he* would resent the morose woman I'm certain to become because of it."

"But you'd have Gilbert, and you could exchange kisses with him whenever you wanted."

Temperance smiled. "Which would be lovely, but again, I'm not always a pleasant person when I'm unhappy, and I'm afraid Gilbert would eventually not even want to kiss me after a while. But . . ." Her smile widened. "In case any of you are concerned that I injured his manly pride by not allowing him an opportunity to give me the ring Mrs. Davenport apparently slipped him, I think by kissing him, and twice, he understands that I hold him in great affection but can't marry him in this present state."

Edwina exchanged a look with Mrs. Davenport. "Is it just me or does it seem like Temperance is trying to convince herself she's unwilling to marry Gilbert?"

"A most excellent observation, Edwina, and one I've made as well," Mrs. Davenport said before she fished a sparkling necklace filled with diamonds and pink stones out of her pocket. Draping the stones around Temperance's neck, she took a second to secure the clasp and took a step backward, nodding as she perused the jewels.

"Ah, perfect." Mrs. Davenport held up her hand when Temperance opened her mouth. "Do not even think about refusing to wear that piece. It's gorgeous against your pale skin, completes the outfit, and I have scads of jewelry I never wear, so you may consider that a gift from me, and no arguing. Now, go finish getting your hair styled while I help Edwina dress."

"While I'm delighted you've found your true calling in life, what with your love of fashion and design — and not the questionable type of fashion, Mrs. Davenport," Temperance said as she marched her way over to sit down beside Miss Henrietta, "I'm not certain I'm quite as delighted about this bossy nature you've acquired over the past few months."

"I've always been bossy, dear, and I fear I'll only get bossier the more competent I get with my designs."

"You've created a monster by taking Mrs. Davenport in hand," Temperance said under her breath to Miss Henrietta as Mrs. Davenport threw herself into getting Edwina into a brilliant red gown that not many people could wear.

"She is having a wonderful time of it, isn't she?" Miss Henrietta asked, gesturing for one of the hairdressers to step forward. "A sophisticated knot on top of Miss Flowerdew's hair should work well, but not too severe. And I'd like to see wisps of curls cascading from that knot, if you please."

"She's not the only one enjoying a bossy nature," Temperance said before the hairstylist began attacking Temperance's hair with a vengeance, making it next to impossible to speak since she knew if she opened her mouth shrieks of pain might escape.

Twenty minutes later, she was pronounced done. And not wanting Miss Henrietta, Mrs. Davenport, or Miss Mabel, who'd just dashed in the room, running late and looking frantic, to decide there was something else needing to be done to her appearance, she excused herself from the room, telling everyone she needed to check the ballroom one last time to make certain everything was perfect for Gertrude's special night.

Promising to meet in the main hallway in an hour to join the receiving line, even though she wasn't going to linger there, what with the rumors swirling around regarding her and Gilbert, she walked out of the room, Edwina walking by her side.

"The red suits you," she told her friend as they reached the staircase and made their way to the third floor.

Edwina's cheeks turned a delightful shade of pink. "I was a little hesitant at first to wear this color, but I have to admit I love it, and I do hope Samuel will love it as well."

"I imagine you in that dress is not going to be a sight he'll ever forget."

Edwina's eyes sparkled. "I'm looking forward to seeing him in formal wear." She released a bit of a sigh. "He is a lovely gentleman, but I'm beginning to become concerned that he'll never ask me to marry him. I'm worried that my desire to become one of the few Pinkerton ladies has caused him to change his mind about me, believing a relationship with me sets a bad precedent with his fellow detectives."

Reaching the third floor, Temperance stepped toward the door leading into the ballroom, pausing for a moment as a thought struck. "Would you abandon your quest to become an agent if that turns out to be why he hasn't asked you to marry him yet?"

Edwina bit her lip. "That's a tricky question, but yes, I would abandon my desire to become an agent. I like to think of myself as being progressive, but I love Samuel, and I want to enjoy my life with him by my side. If that means I must give up the Pinkerton dream, I don't believe I'll live to regret that, not when the alternative — a life without Samuel — seems unimaginable."

"You really *do* love Samuel, don't you?"

Edwina nodded. "He makes me laugh, makes me feel beautiful even when I know I'm not looking my best, and, best of all, he listens to what I have to say and values my opinion."

"He's very fortunate to have won your affections."

"True, but now I just need him to realize that and get on with matters."

Exchanging grins, Temperance moved into the ballroom, stopping to take in the sight of the billowing silken sky she'd created, the gleaming marble floor, and the small tables that edged the dance floor, all of which were draped in linen the color of the sea. Set in the middle of those tables were the centerpieces she'd made — ships created from a plaster mold she'd sculpted herself, resting on top of beds of sand and seashells that she and Mr. Barclay had collected on one of their many trips to the seaside.

Servers hired for the night, and screened by the Pinkerton Agency, were double-checking each table, and members of the orchestra Miss Henrietta had hired were beginning to set up their instruments.

A gleaming baby grand piano sat off to the side, the sight of it causing Temperance to smile as she remembered why she'd asked Mr. Barclay to have the piano brought into the ballroom from the music room.

She'd wanted to do something fun for her fellow wallflower's special evening. And even though she'd not played in front of anyone for eons, except for the simple pieces she'd shared with students at Miss Snook's school, she was comfortable with playing in front of her friends, knowing they would not have any expectations of how well she played, or —

The sound of feet pounding down the hallway had her turning for the door right as Edwina stuck out her leg and pulled a pistol from her garter. A second later, Gilbert burst into the ballroom with his pistol drawn, caught sight of her, then skidded to a stop.

"Temperance, oh, thank the good Lord you're fine," he said right as she noticed that he was looking anything other than fine.

His hair was sticking out all over the place, his formal black jacket was missing a sleeve, and his trousers seemed to be covered with mud. He also had what looked to be fresh blood on his already bruised face, but before she could ask a single question, Tobias, Gilbert's valet, rushed into the room, his pistol drawn and looking quite as disheveled as Gilbert.

"Is she hurt, Mr. Cavendish?" Tobias yelled, skidding to a stop when he seemed to notice Edwina was aiming her pistol directly at his heart. He held up his hands. "No need to shoot me, miss. I'm with him."

While Edwina lowered her pistol but didn't slip it back into her garter, Temperance moved to Gilbert's side.

"What happened?" she demanded.

Gilbert, instead of answering her, took a moment to look her up and down. A second later, he smiled.

"You look ravishing."

Temperance decided right then and there

that ravishing was going to be her favorite word from that moment forward.

She shook herself straight back to the situation at hand. "Thank you, and I'd say the same about you, although . . ." She gestured to his person. "What happened?" she asked again.

Gilbert shook his head. "Tobias and I were ambushed, which means . . . someone still wants us dead."

Chapter Twenty-Two

"What do you mean, someone ambushed you?" Temperance asked right before she began inspecting him, her eyes widening when she turned her attention to his arm, the one that was no longer covered with a sleeve. "Your arm is bleeding."

Gilbert glanced at his arm and shrugged. "It's merely a scratch, one I believe I got as I was being dragged from the carriage."

"You were *dragged* from the carriage?"

"We were taken by surprise, hence the reason I said we were ambushed."

"Two men appeared from out of nowhere," Tobias said. "One of them pulled our driver straight from his seat, scaring the horses half to death, which caused them to careen wildly down the street."

"I opened the door, hoping to get a shot off," Gilbert continued. "But before I could do that, I was grabbed by one of the ruffians, pulled from the carriage, and soon found myself lying in the very middle of a muddy street, trying to dodge the bullets that were whizzing by."

Tobias raked a hand through hair that was no longer covered with a hat. "And while Mr. Cavendish was doing that, I managed to jump from the carriage. Unfortunately, I landed hard, but thankfully the two Pinkerton detectives who were following us raced up on the scene as I was getting to my feet, and before anyone got good and dead, it was over."

"But what happened to your face?" Temperance asked, pulling a handkerchief from the bodice of her gown, which she immediately used to dab at something that was dribbling down his cheek, something he was afraid might be blood.

"Oh, that was my fault," Tobias admitted, wincing ever so slightly. "I'm afraid I was a bit woozy from my fall, and after I staggered to my feet, I bumped right into Mr. Cavendish, knocking him to the road again. Unfortunately, he went face first into the mud."

Gilbert couldn't help but notice that Temperance's lips were beginning to curve, something she certainly seemed to try to hide since she turned her head and settled her attention on Edwina, who was walking toward the door.

"I'm going to speak with the Pinkerton men who are stationed outside the house," Edwina said over her shoulder. "I won't be long."

As Edwina quit the ballroom, Temperance turned around again, her lips no longer curving, although her eyes were definitely twinkling.

Gilbert found himself absolutely mesmerized with her.

The color of her gown suited her to perfection, drawing attention to her creamy skin, which seemed to be dusted with something sparkly, lending her an air of mystery.

It was as if she'd somehow managed to capture the very essence of her being — a mix of fairy-tale creature, eccentric artist, and alluring woman — all bundled into one irresistible package.

There was little question that Temperance had become a lady entirely comfortable in her own skin, embracing her love of whimsy, while adopting an air of sophistication he never realized she possessed.

He found himself enchanted with her and wanted nothing more than to lean forward and kiss her, but not a fluttery type of kiss like she'd given him, but more on the —

Fingers snapping directly in front of his eyes pulled him out of his daydream and right back to reality, one that had Temperance not looking at *him,* but at *Tobias.*

"How hard did he hit the ground when you staggered into him?"

Tobias shot him a glance that was far too knowing, quite as if the man knew exactly why his employer seemed to be in a dazed and confused state of mind, before he adopted a rather mournful expression. "I'm afraid he took quite the tumble, Miss Flowerdew, and will probably suffer some confusion for the foreseeable future."

Gilbert smiled, but pressed his lips firmly together when Temperance turned his way again, and resisted the urge to give Tobias a rousing round of applause for his superior acting abilities and quick thinking. "I do feel a little light-headed," he finally said, realizing Temperance seemed to be waiting for some type of response from him.

"You should have mentioned that sooner. Sit down right this minute and I'll see if I can't find someone to bring you up a soothing cup of tea."

"Or a nice brandy," Gilbert countered as Temperance took him by the arm, marched him at a rather fast clip over to the nearest chair, and practically pushed him down into it.

"Since you just admitted you're lightheaded, brandy is the last thing you need, and . . . you're perspiring." She bent over to peer into his face, her closeness providing him with a whiff of the most compelling perfume he'd ever smelled in his life.

"Of course I'm perspiring," he said when he realized he'd gone mute for a few seconds and she was now prying open one of his eyes to peer into it. "I recently ran up three flights of incredibly steep steps." He blinked when she withdrew her finger. "But speaking of those steep steps, and because rushing up all those steps does seem to be becoming a habit, how do you think Miss Henrietta would feel about installing an elevator?"

Temperance straightened. "She adores you, so I'm certain she'd be more than receptive to installing an elevator if you broach the subject with her. Although, one has to hope there will come a time in the not-too-distant future where people will cease trying to do us in." She held up a finger right in front of his eyes. "Watch my finger."

Gilbert knew better than to argue with her, especially since she looked far too determined. However, the more she swished her finger in front of his face, the more whiffs of her intoxicating perfume he got, which made him somewhat distractible and . . .

"We'll need to send for the physician," she proclaimed, withdrawing her hand.

He shook his head, more to clear it than to protest, but Temperance evidently took it as a protest since she leaned forward and shook her finger in his face, sending additional whiffs of perfume his way and distracting him all over again.

"You're obviously suffering from a concussion, so we'll send for a physician, and I'll thank you to discontinue your arguing with me. If you've forgotten, guests are soon to descend on this house for a night of frivolity. I'd hate for you to faint dead away while dancing the Go-As-You-Please Quadrille simply because you're stubborn, which would put a distinct damper on that frivolity I just mentioned."

"I do hope I misheard you, Temperance, and that you wouldn't be so cruel as to schedule a dance you know perfectly well my darling Permilia is incapable of dancing."

Blowing out a sigh of relief, Gilbert turned and found Asher Rutherford, his very dear friend and Permilia's fiancé, striding across the room, looking very dapper indeed. Tonight, Asher was dressed in a well-cut formal black dinner jacket, his every hair in place, and the outlandish violet neckcloth he was wearing tied in an intricate knot. A diamond stickpin winked in the lights from the chandeliers.

"Asher, don't you look dashing," Temperance said, straightening as Asher reached them and immediately took her gloved hand and kissed it. "And no need to fret about the Go-As-You-Please Quadrille. Gertrude and I are going to introduce a new rendition of that particular dance, one I do believe you'll enjoy far more than the first time you danced that quadrille with Permilia."

"Does this new rendition require that the guests remain in their seats?" Asher asked hopefully.

"Not quite, but again, you'll enjoy the changes we've made, and you'll be relieved to learn Gertrude decided against having a Ticklish Water Polka included this evening."

"Only because she was almost mowed over by Permilia the last time Gertrude took to the dance floor at *my* engagement celebration and someone" — he shot a look to Gilbert who managed to send him a weak smile in return — "completely neglected to remember that Permilia once maimed a gentleman while trying to perform that polka. That someone *also* apparently thought I'd be pleased as punch to have the polka offered on my special night instead of the Go-As-You-Please."

"Isn't it splendid how the violet in Asher's neckcloth will exactly match the violet gown Permilia has chosen to wear tonight?" Gilbert asked Temperance, not abashed in the least to change the topic so abruptly. Unfortunately, his method of distraction had Temperance leaning down and peering into his eyes again.

"He's concussed for certain. I've never known Gilbert to take notice of a neckcloth matching a lady's gown before. It's unprecedented behavior and a clear cause for concern."

Asher leaned forward and peered into Gilbert's face as well. "He looks fine to me, Temperance, if you discount the two black eyes, blood smeared all over his face, and the abysmal state of his clothing." He straightened and smiled. "But that can be expected when one tangles with criminals on more than one occasion in a single day."

"You've heard about the ambush?"

"Indeed, Gilbert told me all about it after

I offered him a ride when I spotted him and Tobias limping down the road, their carriage apparently not fit to be driven since it's missing a wheel."

"Your carriage is missing a wheel?" Temperance asked.

Gilbert nodded. "Broke off when the horses bolted down an alley, but the horses are fine, if that was your next question."

"What about the men who attacked you?" Temperance pressed.

"They were apprehended by the Pinkerton agents and taken off to jail," Tobias said, stepping forward. "Unfortunately, once they were captured, they refused to say much, except to demand they be allowed to speak with an attorney." He shook his head. "The Pinkertons are convinced these men are professional killers because of how they attacked us. But it's odd that professional killers would sport British accents, implying they'd come all the way from England to try to kill us. Not that I've been in this country long, but I'm sure there must be assassins in America looking for work."

Temperance's eyes turned distant, and then she drew in a sharp breath and settled her attention on him. "What if these particular assassins were hired not to kill *Mr. Gilbert Cavendish* but to kill the new *Earl of*

Strafford?"

For the briefest of moments, Gilbert considered that idea, wondering if he *was* a bit concussed because he'd been so focused on the idea that someone wanted Temperance dead, he'd never once considered he might be the main target.

"But that's brilliant, Temperance," Edwina said, striding back into the room. "And now that your theory has been broached, I must say it makes a great deal of sense. From what I remember, Gilbert's brother supposedly died in a yacht accident, but if that wasn't the case . . ." She turned to Gilbert. "I'll send a note off to Samuel, explaining this latest development that demands investigating at once. While I'm doing that, make sure you don't leave Temperance's side, and . . . watch your back." Turning, Edwina glided out of the room, the train of her brilliant red gown whispering against the marble.

"I have a feeling Agent McParland is going to have a time of it tonight keeping the admirers at bay," Asher said, nodding to where Edwina had just disappeared from sight.

Temperance rolled her eyes. "Edwina won't pay any mind to admirers. She's determined to marry Samuel and has eyes only for him. If you ask me, I imagine her selection of that delectable gown she's wearing was a calculated choice, intended to speed matters up with the man."

"And that right there," Gilbert began, "is why I'm thankful my mother never had any other children, especially daughters. They seem to turn scary as they age."

Temperance reached out and poked his arm. "I do believe you just insulted me since you've remarked time and time again over the years that I'm like the sister you never had."

Gilbert poked her right back. "I was wrong about that idea because I don't believe I'd have asked you to marry me if I thought of you in a sisterly fashion, nor do I believe you think of me in a brotherly way because you did, well . . . kiss me."

Narrowing her eyes on him, and turning a delightful shade of pink, Temperance opened her mouth, and then, to his surprise, she closed it as if she had no words to say. Fortunately, Asher, who always had plenty to say, especially when awkward pauses descended on a crowd, cleared his throat.

"It is regrettable that Edwina still seems determine to pursue a position with the Pinkertons," Asher said, releasing a dramatic sigh. "I would love if she'd agree to become the face of Rutherford & Company. She recently turned down that particular offer *again,* all due to the pesky notion that she'll hardly be taken seriously if she allows her beautiful face to be used in all the fashion catalogs."

"That, and she could hardly expect to go undercover if everyone sees her face all over the city," Temperance said.

"Which was exactly the point Edwina's twin sister, Adelaide, made when I approached *her* about the position after Edwina turned me down." Asher released another sigh. "Although . . ." He suddenly got a very calculating look in his eyes right before he began considering Gilbert far too intensely.

Gilbert immediately shook his head. "Do not even think about it."

"Think about what?" Temperance asked.

Asher turned a charming smile on Temperance. "I wonder if you could convince our dear friend here" — he nodded to Gilbert — "to agree to become the face of my store."

Temperance's brows drew together. "The face he's *currently* sporting, or his normal one, the one that doesn't come with two black eyes and blood covering it?"

Asher looked Gilbert over again, tapping

a finger against his chin. "He's dangerous looking right now, and that could work to our advantage. Pair the danger with his new title and" — he threw out his arm, making an arch with it — "picture this . . . Gilbert standing . . . or perhaps sitting on a horse, but not his pathetic horse, Blaze, in front of an entrance to a castle. He's wearing clothing from my store, looking dangerous and . . . in script below the picture we could write . . . *Rutherford & Company — the store favored by the Earl of Strafford.*"

"Put that right out of your head," Gilbert muttered as Temperance sent him a cheeky grin.

"It would definitely draw business to Asher's store."

"At my expense."

"You could be a face of the store as well, Temperance," Asher continued, his eyes practically brimming with excitement. "We could do something about an elusive countess, mysterious, beautiful, and . . . you could be the face for the new perfume Permilia is in the process of having developed."

Temperance, to Gilbert's surprise, turned her grin on Asher. "Tempting, but no. I'm content to live without my face being used. Besides, it would be false advertising since Gilbert and I will eventually let it be known to the public that we've discovered we don't suit, which means I'll *never* be a countess."

"You *never* thought you'd be rid of your Flowerdew relatives or given an opportunity to teach in this school, so *never* isn't always a *never,*" Asher countered before he nodded to Gilbert. "But before I get myself embroiled in a situation that will more than likely have one or both of you cross with me, and since this is supposed to be a night of celebration, we need to get you put to rights, as well as Tobias," he added with a nod to Tobias.

"I'm not sure how we're going to go about that," Gilbert said. "If it has escaped your notice, I'm missing a sleeve and covered with mud."

"Which is why I already took the liberty of sending a request for new clothing off to my store for both of you. It'll be delivered here directly, so all that remains to be done in the meantime is for both of you to go off and find a bathing chamber."

Gilbert reached up and untied the neckcloth he just then realized seemed to be strangling him, the silk of it apparently beginning to shrink after being doused with water from one of the puddles he'd rolled around in. He drew it off and held it up.

"Any chance you have another one of

these to spare for me, and . . ." He glanced to Tobias and found his valet's neckcloth was looking the worse for wear as well. "One for Tobias."

"Of course. I brought an entire box of neckcloths with me in the carriage."

Stepping closer to Gilbert, Temperance considered the necktie he was holding. "Not that I want to point out the obvious, Gilbert, but orange mixed with green is a somewhat bold choice for you."

Gilbert stuffed his ruined neckcloth into a pocket. "Asher and I decided that to embrace the spirt of the evening, it would be amusing if we offered the gentlemen outlandish neckcloths to wear, in striking colors no less, to compliment the bright gowns of the ladies."

"You and Asher decided to equip all of the gentleman with unusual neckwear?"

"Simply because we're gentlemen who prefer to embrace a more sensible approach to life doesn't mean we can't be unpredictable at times."

Asher nodded. "Indeed, and while it is true that Gilbert and I enjoy a more structured, organized, and in Gilbert's case, scheduled way of life, we're perfectly capable of adopting a sense of fun and adventure. I can personally attest that since Permilia barreled her way into my heart, I've adopted a more carefree attitude, one that still requires structure every now and again, but balanced by a new appreciation for chaos."

He gestured to Gilbert before smiling at Temperance. "And one can tell by simply looking at poor Gilbert that he's beginning to experience his own type of chaos — chaos that began practically from the moment he reunited with you."

"I'm not embracing a life of chaos," Gilbert argued. "Unlike you, I'm still very fond of keeping to my schedule, and the only reason I'm looking a little out of sorts is because I was ambushed."

"You missed three appointments with me this week alone, one of which concerned actual business about an import opportunity I broached with you a month ago."

"You must be mistaken. I never miss appointments."

Asher smiled, sent a discreet nod Temperance's way, as if she explained everything, then shrugged. "While it is true that you never *used* to miss appointments, according to your secretary, Mrs. Martin, your schedule is a complete disaster, rendered that way because you've missed appointments that she's now trying to reschedule."

Asher gave a sad shake of his head. "The poor lady even went so far as to encourage *me* to encourage *you* to set up an appointment with your physician, and the sooner the better."

"Which is exactly what I suggested when I noticed he was having a difficult time focusing just a short time ago," Temperance said, plunking her hands on her hips and sending him a look that clearly said *I told you so.*

"I think he's fine now, Miss Flowerdew," Tobias said, speaking up and saving Gilbert from trying to explain his lack of focus had all been due to his fascination with her perfume. "But if you'll excuse us, we really must repair to a retiring room to set ourselves to rights."

"Shall I see if I have a neckcloth for Gilbert that will match that enchanting gown you're wearing, Temperance?" Asher asked, and just like that, Temperance seemed to completely forget about him as she sent a scowl Asher's way.

"The very last thing Gilbert and I need is to allow the gossips more fodder to share over tea tomorrow. If we're seen at the ball wearing matching colors, everyone will assume the articles in all the papers are true. And before you know it, Gilbert and I will have no avenue to escape the mayhem those articles have certainly caused around town. I'll then find myself sailing across the ocean and taking on a role I have no desire to take on." She glanced his way. "No offense."

"None taken. I understand why you don't want to become a countess, and I only wish I had the option of turning down my new title of earl as well."

Temperance narrowed her eyes. "Don't you want to accept the legacy of your father's family?"

"I wasn't raised to become an aristocrat, which will become glaringly obvious once I land in England. I don't believe the nobility will go so far as to shun me, not with the title and large fortune I have at my disposal. But even knowing that, I would be lying if I said I'm happy about assuming a title I never wanted in the first place."

As Gilbert got up from his chair, Temperance moved closer to him, reaching out to touch his check.

"Forgive me, Gilbert. I never gave your feelings about becoming an earl any true consideration."

"Does that mean you're now feeling sorry for me . . . which will also have you reconsidering your refusal to become my countess since you certainly wouldn't want your dear friend to face down the British aristocracy alone?"

For the merest of moments, Temperance didn't say a single word, but then her lips quirked into the smallest of grins even as she shook her head. "You really are suffering from a concussed state if you think you can convince me that taking pity on you is reason enough for me to take on the daunting role of countess."

"But is it reason enough to think about taking on that role if I tell you I'll be beyond forlorn to travel over to England without you by my side?"

Biting her lip, Temperance gazed at him with something curious in her eyes before she finally blew out a breath. "Honestly, Gilbert, when you put it that way, well . . . hmm . . ." Turning on her heel, she headed for the door, leaving him with a bit of unexpected hope when he was somewhat certain he heard her mumble "I suppose I'll need to give this matter more thought," before she walked out of sight.

Chapter Twenty-Three

"You do realize you cannot hide out in my suite of rooms for the entire evening, don't you?"

Temperance finished pouring a cup of tea for Miss Snook and straightened, trying to hide a smile as she looked at the woman buried beneath a mountain of blankets. Considering she'd seen Miss Snook stash a novel underneath one of those blankets, plus a plate of cookies if she wasn't much mistaken, she was rapidly coming to the conclusion there was absolutely nothing wrong with the woman, even though Miss Snook was claiming to be wracked with a ferocious fever and pounding head.

"*You* seem to be fine with the idea of hiding out," she said, handing Miss Snook the cup.

"That's because I'm desperately ill and have no wish to pass along my illness to the swarms of guests who are even now taking over my school." Miss Snook took a sip of her tea. "But since you do need to return soon because Gertrude is your dear friend and you can't abandon her on her special night, tell me why you're lingering in my room, and do not give me that nonsense about wanting to check in on me again. In case you've neglected to realize this, we've not had much of an opportunity to become well acquainted since you began teaching at this school. In my humble opinion, what with the ball about to commence, now seems like a very peculiar time for you to decide to remedy that."

"You're far too astute for your own good."

"Thank you," Miss Snook said primly.

"I know you're not ill."

"That would be difficult to prove, and you're trying to distract me."

Temperance heaved a sigh. "Alva Vanderbilt is here, along with Caroline Astor, and they both set their sights on me after they ambled through the receiving line, and . . . coward that I apparently am, I fled."

Miss Snook inclined her head. "I might have done the same thing, but I was under the belief Gertrude wasn't inviting the crème de la crème of society."

"Gertrude felt that since she'd been invited to the elaborate Vanderbilt ball this past March, it would be less than gracious of her to exclude Alva Vanderbilt. And since Alva is now on speaking terms with Caroline Astor, and Mrs. Astor is the queen of society, she needed to be invited as well. I'm sorry to say that with all the mayhem in my life as of late, I completely neglected to remember those two ladies were coming. I was unprepared to handle them and the questions they were certain to ask about Gilbert."

"Perhaps you *should* hide here all night."

Temperance nodded. "That would be lovely. I could read out loud to you from the book you were perusing before I disturbed you."

"I'm perfectly capable of reading to myself, although I do thank you for offering. But you can't miss the ball."

"I know, and I'm only intending on hiding out until most of the guests make it through the receiving line. One of the Pinkerton agents actually sought me out before I fled and suggested I remove myself from the vicinity of that line because the crowd of gawkers was growing concerning on the sidewalk outside the school. Not wanting to make myself an easy target if someone in that crowd is one of the people trying to see me dead, I agreed it would be a prudent choice to make myself scarce, so here I am." She tilted her head. "And while I know you're claiming to be desperately ill, you're looking rather fit to me, so tell me this — why don't you really want to attend the ball?"

"Why don't you really want to marry Gilbert Cavendish?"

"I see you're plowing full steam ahead with the getting-acquainted-with-me opportunity, but . . . I asked first, so . . ."

Miss Snook pulled one of the blankets up to her chin, glared at Temperance, and then wrinkled her nose when she seemed to realize she wasn't cowing Temperance in the least.

"That was my most intimidating look," she muttered.

"I lived with Wayne, Fanny, and Clementine Flowerdew for years. I'm quite accustomed to being glared at and it doesn't bother me at all."

"How annoying."

"Quite, but . . . ?"

For a moment, Temperance didn't believe Miss Snook was going to say anything, but then, she lowered the blanket, thrust a hand underneath it, pulled out her plate of cookies, and offered one to Temperance.

Never one to refuse an offer of a treat,

Temperance took one, nodded her thanks, and began to nibble it as Miss Snook suddenly looked rather disgruntled.

"I don't care for so many Pinkerton agents roaming about the place tonight."

Temperance choked on the cookie, coughing and wheezing for a good few seconds as she tried to catch her breath. Dashing a hand across eyes that were now watering, she drew in a needed gulp of air and lowered her voice. "Good heavens, Miss Snook, do not tell me that you're wanted by the law."

"Clearly that vivid of imagination of yours is getting away with you, Miss Flowerdew. Do I look like a woman who is wanted by the law?"

"That's difficult to say since you could be a master of disguise, hence the success you've enjoyed thus far of eluding capture."

"I'm not wanted by the law, nor am I a master of disguise. I simply suffer from an unfortunate childhood. That childhood is what compelled me to provide better lives for women not born to the manor, but born on the mean streets of this city, those who were destined to earn a paltry wage working in those manor houses because they don't have the skills necessary to obtain better wages and less dangerous work environments."

Temperance took a seat in the chair directly beside Miss Snook's bed. "If you suffered from an unfortunate childhood, how in the world did you manage to obtain the education needed to open up your school?"

Settling back against the pillows, Miss Snook began rubbing her temple. "That is exactly the information I don't want the Pinkerton agents to uncover. But since I'm certain that unusual mind of yours will be conjuring up all sorts of dastardly scenarios, allow me to simply say that my mother, a woman born in the meanest part of the city, worked as a scullery maid. Unfortunately, she was a very beautiful scullery maid and caught the interest of the wealthy gentleman whose house she worked in, and I was the result of that interest. That gentleman paid for my education even though he never publicly acknowledged my existence."

"Forgive me, Miss Snook. I should not have pried into your personal affairs."

Miss Snook waved the apology aside. "There's no need to apologize, Miss Flowerdew. If you'll recall, I did open the door for personal inquires when I asked why you don't want to marry Gilbert Cavendish."

"I suppose you did, but still. You're entitled to keep your secrets."

"Secrets have a way of coming out, and the secret of my past does make for a sordid tale." Miss Snook caught Temperance's eye. "There's no need to feel sorry for me though. I've recently come to terms with my past, thanks to the help of Reverend Benjamin Perry, a wonderful gentleman Gertrude introduced me to not so long ago. He advised me to accept that the circumstances of my birth are not a shame I need to continue carrying with me for the rest of my days, advice I've decided to heed. But because I am a woman alone, and I'm a woman who is pursuing a quest many in the city do not share since I encourage domestics to leave their places of employment, I must be mindful of my reputation. That reputation, as you very well know, would be ruined if word spread about my illegitimate status."

"I'll never say a word."

"I know you won't, and now . . . it's your turn. Why are you reluctant to marry Gilbert Cavendish, a gentleman, in my humble opinion, who seems to hold you in great affection?"

She swallowed the first explanation she wanted to give — the one that dealt with the idea they wouldn't suit because they were opposites — and she swallowed the next explanation — the one revolving around the notion she didn't care to become a countess. Temperance took a moment to truly consider the question. The conclusion she finally came to caught her by surprise and left her reeling.

Clearing a throat that was somewhat dry, she settled back on the chair. "My reluctance, I've just this moment realized, stems from a fear I've apparently been keeping well buried — that if I agree to marry Gilbert, a gentleman I might hold more than simple affection for, he won't return my affection in the manner I want him to, which will make me resent him. Gilbert is one of my very dearest friends, but if I marry him and then turn resentful, we'll no longer be friends. I'm not willing to lose his friendship."

"You've never seemed like a resentful type to me."

"I also never thought I was a selfish type, but I'm sorry to say I was mistaken about that," Temperance admitted. "I didn't even consider that Gilbert was reluctant to accept the title of earl and all the responsibilities that go along with it. All I was concerned about was pursuing my own happiness, wanting to stay here in New York because I've become comfortable here and finally feel as if I've found my place in the world."

Miss Snook considered her for a long moment. "Reverend Perry recently told me that our choices in life are colored by events that happened in our past. There's no way to avoid that, and what you need to understand, Temperance, is that you've survived degradation and neglect at the hands of your relatives and have come out stronger for that experience. Reverend Perry believes God gives us these difficult times to allow us an opportunity to grow. You've certainly grown, risen above that neglect, and seized life in a new and exciting way, finding yourself in the process if I'm not mistaken.

"You also seem to have learned what makes you happy, and there's no shame in that, nor does it make you selfish. God, I've come to believe, wants us to live lives of happiness. And while I'm certain you do feel guilty about not wanting to abandon your newfound happiness in New York to move across the ocean, you need to consider all your options.

"Will you still be happy here once Gilbert moves away? Are you, perhaps, projecting how miserable you'll be as a countess because you're unwilling to take the chance of loving Gilbert when there is a possibility he doesn't return that love? And is it possible for you to set aside your fears, agree to marry Gilbert, and discover you've been wrong about everything and will actually find your very own happily-ever-after?"

Temperance blinked in surprise. "We seem to have *really* traveled past the barely acquainted stage and plowed directly into let-us-now-solve-all-Temperance's-problems, haven't we?"

Miss Snook smiled. "Indeed we have, so . . . now that I've posed some most thought-provoking questions, it's time for you to reach deep into your very soul and find some answers."

Before she had an opportunity to further consider anything Miss Snook had said, a knock sounded on the outer door of Miss Snook's suite of rooms.

Temperance got to her feet. "I believe this is where I leave you to enjoy your questionable sickbed since it's undoubtedly someone looking for me on the other side of that door."

"I'll look forward to picking up where we left off sometime in the near future," Miss Snook called after Temperance as she moved through the door of the bedchamber and into the sitting room Miss Snook kept neat as a pin.

Uncertain she was keen to continue a conversation that had left her unsettled, she walked over to the door and opened it, finding Gilbert on the other side. He was looking very handsome indeed, even with the bluish-black bruises under his eyes. Her gaze dropped, as did her jaw, when she got a look at his fresh neckcloth, intricately tied, but sporting a large amount of . . . pink.

"You should know better than to issue me a challenge" were the first words out of Gilbert's mouth before he sent her a far-too-superior smile.

"How did you take me telling you to avoid any pink in your neckcloth as a challenge?"

"How did *you* take me telling you it wasn't a good idea to take an old rowboat you patched with mud into the middle of a very deep pond as a challenge?" he countered.

She refused to smile. "That was an obvious challenge because I needed to prove to you that my patching with mud would work."

"We sank and had to be rescued by your father."

She gave an airy wave of her hand. "That's beside the point, and you cannot use that as a reasonable comparison. I wasn't *challenging* you about the pink, I was *telling* you not to wear it."

"Which I took as a challenge because it's what we do — that and look out for one another." He smiled. "And that is exactly why I've come to fetch you. Mrs. Vanderbilt and Mrs. Astor have been trying to run me to ground, and those ladies frighten me half to death. I need you to run interference for me." He leaned forward toward the open door. "You certain you're too ill to join the festivities, Miss Snook?" he called.

A cough that was far too dramatic to be considered real was Miss Snook's first response. "I'm still feeling incredibly peaky, Mr. Cavendish, so you and Miss Flowerdew will need to enjoy the evening for me."

Pulling the door closed after Temperance stepped into the hallway, Gilbert shook his head. "She's not truly ill, is she?"

"No, and don't think I haven't thought about assuming an illness as well. It's only my deep affection for Gertrude that's forcing me to attend this ball tonight."

"You adore balls."

She opened her mouth to argue, but then smiled instead. "Oh, you're right, I do. And I want to see Harrison's reaction to the ballroom, so we'd best get up to the third floor."

"The receiving line is almost at an end,"

Gilbert said, taking her arm as they began strolling down the hallway. "Gertrude is brimming with excitement, and I don't believe I've ever seen Harrison looking so happy."

"How lovely."

Nodding to the Pinkerton detective who'd followed her when she'd gone to visit Miss Snook, Temperance reached the stairs, and together, she and Gilbert climbed them.

"Perhaps an elevator *would* be a welcome addition to this place," she said, feeling a bit winded after reaching the third floor.

"At least we didn't have to race up the stairs this time, nor did we have anyone chasing us." Gilbert slowed his pace, giving her an opportunity to catch her breath. He then stopped completely after they moved into the ballroom. "What an incredible talent you have, Temperance. I'm afraid I didn't appreciate what you'd done with the ballroom a short time ago, but it's amazing. You've captured the look of the sky when you're sailing the seas, and Harrison will adore it, especially since you created this for him and Gertrude."

A trace of heat settled on her cheeks. "I wasn't certain the plan I made to create the effect for the sky would work, but thank goodness it did." She nodded to the red, orange, yellow, and midnight-blue swirls of fabric that were draped over the entirety of the ballroom ceiling. "My venture to Chicago set me behind schedule, but thankfully Eugene was more than helpful with getting all that fabric secured, and he helped attach all the glittery stars to the windows and drapes."

"He's a good man, that Eugene, although he made a horrible criminal."

Pulling Gilbert farther into the room, Temperance took a few minutes to make certain everything was in place as servers began entering the room, holding silver trays filled with glasses of champagne and delectable treats that had been made by the women at the school who'd once worked in the kitchens of some of the most noted society members of the day.

As guests streamed into the ballroom, Temperance soon found herself garnering more than her fair share of attention.

"What are we going to tell everyone?" she whispered as a group of young ladies, with her cousin Clementine leading the pack, headed their way.

"We'll tell them that no formal announcement can be made because I'm in mourning for my brother, and it would be untoward to announce such pleasant news under such troubling conditions."

"That's brilliant," Temperance exclaimed. "Why didn't you think of it sooner? And . . . you should be wearing a black armband."

"Thank you for the brilliant part, and I didn't think of it before because I've been a little preoccupied with trying to dodge death."

"I bet Asher has something black you could use for an armband in one of his well-supplied pockets, so off you go. I'll meet up with you later."

"Asher and I are opening the ball with a speech," Gilbert told her, giving her hand a squeeze before he turned to scan the crowd.

"And I have something to do after that speech, but I'll find you after that."

Gilbert frowned, but before he could question her further, his gaze settled on an approaching Clementine and company. Sending them an inclination of his head, he tossed a look of apology to Temperance right before he bolted away.

"Coward," she muttered under her breath as Clementine reached her.

"Here she is, my darling, darling, cousin," Clementine gushed, taking Temperance so aback that she didn't have a second to prepare herself when her cousin, the same lady who'd only recently loathed the very sight of her, pulled her into an honest-to-goodness hug.

When her cousin did not immediately release her, and even gave her a small squeeze, Temperance couldn't help but wonder if perhaps the time had come when she and Clementine wouldn't hold quite so much animosity toward each other, an idea that was curiously appealing.

"You're looking lovely, Clementine," Temperance said after her cousin released her.

Clementine, surprisingly enough, grinned and leaned closer, lowering her voice. "I had to change in Aunt Minnie's kitchen after she and my parents thought I'd left for the ball." She stepped back and gestured to her golden gown. "Aunt Minnie believes bold colors are untoward, but I think they're lovely."

"Your aunt and parents decided not to attend this evening?"

"My parents are far too embarrassed by everything that has happened of late to show their faces here. And Aunt Minnie didn't want to attend because she feared she'd spend half the night answering questions regarding why my parents weren't in attendance."

"Perfectly understandable, and odd as this

is undoubtedly going to sound, I'm glad you came."

Clementine smiled. "Of course you're glad I came. You've probably been wanting to thank me for getting the newspapers to print all that delightful business about you and Gilbert."

"I'm not sure thanking you is exactly what I had in mind. Bodily harm was one of my first inclinations, although you'll be relieved to learn that does seem to have passed."

Clementine glanced to the ladies who'd followed her, all of whom were watching them with unbridled curiosity.

"I leaked that information so you wouldn't find yourself vying for Gilbert's attention, something I thought you would have realized as soon as you read the articles," Clementine whispered.

"How would I have realized that? It's a completely nonsensical notion."

"It's not, but this is hardly the time to quibble about such a trifling matter. I've promised my friends an introduction to you."

"I've known those ladies for years. In fact" — Temperance turned her gaze on the ladies in question and nodded — "Miss Potter once thrust an umbrella at me, demanding I hold it over her head for her while she searched for something in her reticule, unwilling to allow the sun to beat on her head for even the briefest of seconds."

"Well, don't remind her of that," Clementine said. "She'll be mortified."

"And I wasn't mortified by having to hold an umbrella over her head, something she neglected to thank me for after she found what she was looking for?"

"Ladies, do come and greet my cousin" was Clementine's response, proving she was still a bit of a nuisance, but a more friendly nuisance who could possibly turn into something more.

Thankfully, Temperance was spared a lengthy visit with Clementine's friends when a loud bell rang, brandished by Mr. Barclay, who'd abandoned his duties at the front door to Tobias for the evening and was now trying to get everyone's attention. As soon as the guests quieted down, he gestured Asher and Gilbert forward. Once Gertrude and Harrison were standing directly in front of the orchestra, Asher delivered one of the most heartfelt congratulatory speeches Temperance had ever heard, with Gilbert adding his own sentiments after Asher was done. Taking a glass of champagne from a server, Temperance raised her glass and toasted the happy couple, taking a sip as she felt her heart warm.

Standing beside Gertrude were Harrison's parents, Edwina, and Edwina and Harrison's other two sisters, Margaret and Adelaide. Miss Henrietta and Miss Mabel were also standing in the front of the room, and beside them was Mrs. Davenport, wiping her eyes and beaming at Gertrude — her affection for her former employee visible for everyone to see.

"They *will* be happy, won't they?"

Turning, Temperance found Permilia standing beside her, wiping a tear of her own away.

"I do believe they will, as will you and Asher." Temperance smiled. "I'm sure the very idea that wallflowers have somehow managed to get away from their walls and secure two of the most eligible gentlemen is befuddling society ladies all over the city."

"You know you could join the wallflower group that has stolen those eligible men right from underneath the noses of so many hopeful society ladies, don't you?"

"I could indeed, but now is not the time for that discussion." Temperance nodded to where the orchestra members were beginning to take their places. "That's my cue, so if you'll excuse me, I've a bit of a surprise."

Leaving Permilia looking rather confused, Temperance moved through the crowd, hoping her surprise was not going to be a complete disaster, but knowing that even if it was, her friends wouldn't mind at all.

Chapter Twenty-Four

As Temperance walked past him, flashing him a nervous grin, Gilbert had no idea what she was about until she moved up to a piano and dipped into a curtsy.

The entire ballroom went silent as she straightened, smiled, then drew in a deep breath.

"She's going to play," his mother whispered, appearing right beside him. "I haven't heard her play in years."

"Nor have I," he whispered back as Temperance began to speak.

"For those of you unfamiliar with who I am, I'm Miss Temperance Flowerdew."

Titters ran through the crowd, ones that Temperance waved aside. "Yes, I know, I've been in the papers of late. I'm not up here to talk about that, but I hope you'll humor me for a moment because I have something very important to say."

She paused for a brief second, and if

Gilbert wasn't much mistaken, her eyes were sparkling with unshed tears.

"Over the past few years," Temperance began, "I've been quite lonely, having lost my parents unexpectedly, as well as losing the only life I'd ever known. All that changed, however, when two extraordinary ladies decided they wanted to become my friends, even though I must admit I wondered why in the world such magnificent ladies would want to be friends with me."

Gilbert glanced to Gertrude and Permilia, who were both beginning to wipe their eyes with the handkerchiefs Asher was handing them.

"Because of that friendship though," Temperance continued, "I was able to set aside my loneliness and discover a new sense of happiness, one I never thought to feel again, and it's all due to Miss Permilia Griswold and Miss Gertrude Cadwalader." She brushed aside a tear. "You two ladies are dearer to me than I can ever explain, and I'm simply delighted you've both found gentlemen worthy of your love, and gentlemen I know want nothing more than to ensure your happiness."

She turned and walked to the piano bench, turning back to smile at Permilia and Gertrude. "I know it's not enough to ever repay your kindness, but I thought we could open the ball with a waltz, one I wrote to honor our friendship and celebrate the love you've found with your very special gentlemen."

With that, she sat down on the bench, placed her fingers over the keys, and waited as Harrison and Gertrude took to the floor, followed by Asher and Permilia, who didn't seem capable of refusing Gertrude's waving of a hand to join them.

Beaming at her friends who were beaming right back at her, Temperance closed her eyes for the briefest of moments, and then she began to play.

As Temperance's fingers flew over the keys and the sound of the waltz she'd written for her friends filled the room, Gilbert couldn't take his eyes off her.

Her talent was incomparable, and even though he'd heard her play before, there was something different about her abilities now, something mesmerizing.

Every note she played held a distinct measure of joy, and in a split second, as if God had leaned down from heaven and whispered into his ear, Gilbert understood exactly why she was reluctant to abandon her life in the city to accompany him to England.

She was alive now, beautifully so, and her happiness was a tangible thing, spreading from her very being and captivating everyone in the room.

Taking a quick glance around, he found more than one lady dabbing at her eyes, while Miss Henrietta, Miss Mabel, and Mrs. Davenport seemed to be weeping into their handkerchiefs. Even Alva Vanderbilt and Mrs. Astor, accompanied by Mr. Ward McAllister, the social arbiter of the day, seemed to be moved by the music. Those ladies were nodding their heads to the rhythm of the waltz, while Mr. McAllister was smiling, a rare event indeed from what Gilbert knew of the man.

"She is such a special young lady," his mother whispered, fishing out a handkerchief from the sleeve of a brilliantly blue ballgown. "I cannot believe I didn't find her and demand she come live with your stepfather and me."

"You had no way of knowing she'd been left in dire straits, Mother," Gilbert said as Temperance finished playing. "But do know that I have every intention of finding out from her father's attorney why we weren't informed of her plight, even if I have to hunt that man down myself."

Joining in as the guests broke into enthusiastic applause, Gilbert smiled at his mother, then returned his attention to Temperance, who'd risen from the piano bench and was already being embraced by Gertrude. Permilia soon took Gertrude's place, followed by Harrison and Asher, each gentleman taking her ungloved hand and kissing it.

Telling his mother he'd return directly, he began making his way to Temperance, his journey interrupted by curious guests intent on learning why he was sporting two black eyes and longing to learn if the news of his engagement to Miss Flowerdew was true. Unwilling to answer any of their questions, he settled for simply inclining his head time and time again, which might have allowed the guests to believe he and Temperance were truly engaged, something he was certain Temperance would take him to task for at some point in the evening.

When he finally broke away from three ladies who'd been trying to learn the particulars about how he proposed to Temperance, he increased his pace, dodged two gentlemen he pretended he didn't see gesturing for him to join them, and didn't stop walking until he reached Temperance's side. When she turned from Harrison and sent him a grin, he felt quite as if the marble floor beneath his feet had tilted, leaving him completely unbalanced.

"That went better than I expected," she admitted, her grin causing a small dimple to pop out on her cheek. "I wasn't certain playing an original piece would go over very well, and did you catch the part in the third stanza when I mistakenly hit a C note instead of a D?"

"It sounded like sheer perfection to me, and I imagine no one noticed the mistake."

She reached out and gave his arm a squeeze, the touch of her hand on his arm doing nothing to improve his sense of balance or lack thereof. "I well recall that you're somewhat tone deaf, but in this particular instance, I'm going to forget that and hope you're right about no one noticing."

Harrison stepped up to them and gave Gilbert a hearty clap on the back even as he sent him a significant look, as if he knew Gilbert was experiencing a most curious and unexpected moment. He then turned a charming smile on Temperance. "I'm certain no one heard a note out of place, Temperance, and how could they?" He waved a hand around. "If they weren't completely absorbed in the music, they would have been spending their time all agog at the decorations Gertrude told me you were responsible for." He leaned forward. "Tonight I see the splendor of this room, and I have you to thank for the feast my eyes are enjoying."

Temperance's face turned pink. "I'm so glad you're enjoying the decorations, Harrison." She smiled. "Your appreciation goes far in soothing what I'm certain was annoyance over the many lectures I received when various people found me on a scaffold that I kept trying to tell everyone was completely safe."

"Safe or not, I'm certain you won't need to make use of that scaffolding again," Gilbert added, earning a narrowing of the eyes from Temperance, until she caught sight of the black armband circling his upper arm.

She grinned and poked the armband that was, in actuality, a spare sock from one of Asher's always well-stocked pockets. "I knew Asher would have something you could use."

Asher stepped up to join them. "I do seem to get requests for the most peculiar items at times."

"Has it ever struck you how peculiar it is to us when you always seem to have just the right item available when we make those requests?" Gilbert asked as his mother slipped between him and Temperance.

"There's nothing peculiar about a gentleman making it a point to always be prepared for whatever odd circumstance life may fling his way," Asher said, whipping out a spare handkerchief and holding it at the ready while Gilbert's mother pulled Temperance into a hug.

"That was inspiring, my darling girl," his mother said, stepping away from Temperance and taking the handkerchief from Asher a second later. She dashed it over eyes that were a little misty. "I've missed hearing you play the piano, as well as missed simply having you around."

"I've missed you as well," Temperance returned. "I've been meaning to pay you a call all week. My intentions were put on hold, though, after Miss Henrietta turned somewhat bossy, insisting I stay inside the schoolgrounds until the madness of late comes to an end."

His mother bit her lip. "I meant to call on you as well, dear, but then decided you might not care for me to descend on you unannounced since our initial reunion did not go as planned. I know I caused you more than a touch of distress. I believe my dismay at learning you'd been left at the mercy of an uncaring cousin had me speaking of matters that should have been left for a later date — especially regarding your father's attorney and how he'd misled me about your well-being."

Temperance's forehead furrowed. "While I admit that the subject of my father's attorney is distressing, I was not troubled by that. Quite frankly, I've been coming to the conclusion that Mr. Howland might very well have something to do with the recent skullduggery Gilbert and I have been experiencing." She shook her head. "If you'd not allowed me to know of Mr. Howland's suspicious behavior, especially regarding how he clearly went out of his way to make certain you couldn't contact me, I wouldn't have considered him as a suspect, so I'm grateful to you, not distressed."

"But I blurted all of that out instead of approaching it more delicately."

Temperance smiled. "If you'll recall, Mrs. Beckwith, I've never been one who needs to be treated delicately, but . . ." Her smile widened as she glanced at something over his mother's shoulder. "We're becoming far too maudlin, and this is a ball, an event that's supposed to be filled with frivolity — and speaking of frivolity — Gertrude appears to be trying to get my attention, so if everyone will excuse me, I'm off to help reveal our next surprise."

To Gilbert's surprise, Temperance, instead of immediately hurrying off to join Gertrude, who'd moved to stand in front of the orchestra, stopped by his side and leaned close to him, her closeness lending him another whiff of her intriguing perfume.

"Because everyone in attendance tonight, except for our closest friends, seems to believe we're slightly engaged, even though I've been diligently spreading the rumor we can't make any announcements because you're in mourning for your brother, you may partner me in this next surprise, so . . . stay available."

With that, and leaving him with his senses spinning due to the perfume, Temperance moved to join Gertrude, who immediately waved to the crowd as the members of the orchestra picked up their instruments.

"I'd like to officially welcome everyone here tonight," Gertrude began. "Harrison and I are so honored you could join us this evening. And because we wanted it to be an evening filled with laughter, and bright colors of course, since my dear Harrison does have a great liking for bright colors . . ." She grinned at Harrison, who was wearing the most lurid orange neckcloth Gilbert had ever seen, as well as a black dinner jacket that had bright stripes of orange woven into the black fabric. Harrison returned the grin, and for a second, Gertrude was distracted, until Temperance gave her a less-than-discreet tap on the shoulder.

"Ah yes, where was I?" Gertrude asked, turning a delightful shade of pink.

"You were about to announce the rules for our first quadrille," Temperance said, earning gasps of anticipation from some of the ladies in response.

"Quite right, the quadrille." She gestured to Permilia, who seemed to be trying to edge her way out of the spotlight, but she wasn't fast enough. "As some of you know, Miss Griswold made a slight error when she was at the lovely Mrs. Vanderbilt's ball, believing the Go-As-You-Please Quadrille meant you could go anywhere you please."

Gilbert watched Mrs. Vanderbilt nod even as she sent a fond smile Permilia's way.

"And because of that, and because we have invited all the students who go to Miss Snook's School for the Education of the Feminine Mind to join us as guests this evening, and we haven't had enough time to devote to dancing lessons as of yet . . . although . . . speaking of those students has reminded me of something." Gertrude stopped talking and turned a somewhat determined eye on the guests in attendance, ones who were not all members of the society set, but most of whom were involved with successful businesses. "Many of those young women will soon be qualified to accept different positions in areas of business, especially typing, so make certain to seek out Miss Henrietta Huxley and allow her to know of any positions you have available that may be filled by our students once they graduate."

"And do know that I have access to the guest list," Miss Henrietta called out. "I know what business every gentleman here owns, and if you don't want to find me knocking on your office door, you'll seek me out and promise employment to our students after they complete their lessons."

Gilbert turned to his mother and grinned. "She's shameless."

"And more than a little frightening, which is why I imagine those young women she sent to your office will soon find themselves permanently employed."

"Too right they will," Gilbert agreed as Gertrude turned to Temperance.

"Where was I?" Gertrude asked Temperance.

"The quadrille," Temperance reminded her.

Gertrude nodded. "Right, the quadrille. So, here are the new rules for the Go-As-You-Please Quadrille. In honor of our dear friend Permilia, there will be no rules, no required dance steps, and all of you may dance as you please and where you please."

As everyone made a beeline for the ballroom floor, Gilbert strode to Temperance's side, smiling when she took his hand, the music began, and complete and utter mayhem took over the ballroom.

Guests were moving every which way, but everyone was laughing, and even though there were no rules, something that should have bothered him but didn't, he found himself swept up into the spirit of the dance, enjoying Temperance steering him rather forcefully about the room.

When the music ended, laughter and applause erupted, and another dance began, one he asked Edwina to partner him in.

"Where's your Agent McParland?" he asked as he spun her around.

"He's running late, but he sent a note promising he'll be here at some point," she said, completely oblivious to more than a few gentlemen they danced past tossing smiles her way.

"Still have your heart set on marrying the man?"

"Of course. Still have your heart set on convincing Temperance she'll make an admirable countess?"

He returned the smile. "While I would love to say yes, I'm no longer certain Temperance is meant to be my countess. She's obviously very content here in New York, and I don't believe I want to be the reason she loses that contentment."

"Then perhaps you need to discover a way that will allow you to stay here with her."

After thanking him for the dance when the music ended, Edwina moved off to join Harrison, and arm in arm, brother and sister took to the floor.

Making his way over to Miss Henrietta, he bowed over her hand, and even though she gave a bit of a feeble protest, he led her to the very middle of the assembled dancers, and they were soon gliding away.

Two dances later, he walked with Mrs. Vanderbilt over to Mr. McAllister, regretting that decision almost immediately when Mr. McAllister began peppering him with questions, wanting to know every little detail of how Gilbert's face had become so battered.

By the time he was finished being interrogated by Mr. McAllister, Mr. Barclay was announcing it was time for dinner, so after excusing himself, he headed across the room again, meeting up with Temperance in the middle of the ballroom.

"Thank goodness dinner is about to be served," Temperance exclaimed, taking his arm. "I'm famished."

"Are we going to enjoy an adventurous dinner to go along with the theme of the evening?" he asked, joining the swarm of guests who were making their way out of the ballroom and toward the first floor where dinner was to be served.

"I'm certain you *will* find some of the dishes adventurous."

Enjoying the sparkle of amusement in her eyes, as well as enjoying the evening far more than he'd enjoyed an evening in a very long time, Gilbert walked with Temperance into the dining room once they reached the first floor, a room that was filled with servers all bustling about with silver trays in their arms.

"Where shall we sit?" he asked.

"We're at Gertrude and Harrison's table, of course, but before we join them, I need to check on the students from the school. This is their first formal dinner, and I'm certain they're overwhelmed." She smiled.

"Gertrude's been diligent with their table manners, but sitting down to dine in the middle of a classroom is completely different from dining in the middle of a grand ball."

As she led him over to the tables where the students were sitting, Temperance stopped directly beside Mercy. Mercy immediately pointed out how they'd placed their linen napkins exactly so, and that they'd counted the silverware and were somewhat confident they'd manage to make it through the courses without too many mishaps.

"We're just tickled to pieces, Miss Temperance, to have been included tonight," Mercy began, her eyes bright with excitement. "I ain't, I mean, I've never been invited to sit down at a fancy meal like this before, although I have cleaned up the mess that's been left after these types of meals have finished many times."

"And we also had great fun doing that special quadrille," said Bernice, whom Gilbert remembered made the most scrumptious cakes. "We didn't have very many gentlemen partners, but it sure was nice of you, Mr. Cavendish, to join all of us in that polka."

"And I bet he's got some bruises on his

shins for his kindness," Mercy finished with a grin.

After telling the women to enjoy their meal, he walked with Temperance to their table. The first course of oysters on the half shell was immediately served, followed by two soups, one a consommé and the other a bisque. Footmen dressed in vivid orange livery whisked the oysters and soup away a short time later, a warmed plate was set down in front of everyone, then the fish course was served, a delicious bass in a rich cream sauce.

Comfortable conversation flowed freely, and looking around the table at his friends, Gilbert suddenly understood exactly why Temperance was reluctant to abandon the life she'd carved out for herself.

It was a blessing to find true friends in life, and here he was surrounded by exactly that. There were no differences of opinions, or trying to impress anyone with the successes any of them had achieved. There was only laugher, many stories, and a feeling of comradery.

As the next course was served, that one being the meat course that consisted of a filet of beef in a champagne sauce, he was suddenly struck by what Edwina had said to him — that he should consider ways to stay in New York.

Quite frankly, he didn't want to abandon his life in New York, nor did he want to live his life as an earl.

The problem, though, was that he was not a gentleman to shirk a responsibility, but . . . perhaps there was someone out there who'd welcome the opportunity to inherit a title, some distant relative he'd never met, but one whose life could be changed for the better if . . .

"Is something the matter?" Temperance whispered, leaning close to him.

He smiled. "Not at all. I'm simply trying to puzzle something out, something that could very well solve the dilemma of . . . well, no need to get into that right now. I haven't figured out all the particulars." He returned to slicing up his beef, trying to suppress a grin when he felt Temperance begin to bristle with annoyance.

"Puzzle what out? What particulars?" she pressed, a hint of impatience in her voice.

"If I'm successful with my puzzling, I'll tell you, but until then, mum's the word."

"Does this have something to do with how you're going to go about convincing me to become your countess?"

"Not at all."

"Surely you're not going to leave the

conversation there, are you? You must recall that I don't appreciate being kept in the dark."

"I'm afraid you'll have to linger in the dark for now, because, yes, I'm leaving the conversation exactly there." He sent her a smile, one she returned with a scowl. Finding the scowl utterly charming, he returned to the excellent piece of beef he'd been served, feeling, surprisingly enough, as if his future was suddenly going to be more promising than expected.

Chapter Twenty-Five

The next afternoon

Temperance had never considered herself a violent type, but she was rapidly concluding that if Gilbert didn't expand on whatever it was he was apparently still trying to puzzle out, she might reconsider her position on that subject.

It was maddening not knowing what he was thinking, and add in the pesky idea he'd not bothered to try to badger her into becoming his countess even one little time since the dinner the night before at the ball, and . . . well . . . she found herself completely unsettled.

She'd actually been giving a lot of thought to the idea of becoming a countess, or rather, *his* countess. And even knowing she'd have to give up the life she was just now coming to love, the thought of continuing that life without Gilbert was more than depressing.

"Come see my progress with painting the ocean," Gilbert called.

She set down her paintbrush and took a second to tuck a strand of hair that was flying every which way due to the stiff ocean breeze behind her ear.

Stomping her way through sand that was cool on her bare feet toward where Gilbert had set up his easel, she felt a bit of her annoyance slide away.

There was something wonderful about being whisked off unexpectedly to the seaside, although she was certainly confused why Gilbert would have arranged a surprise trip for her in the first place, given that he seemed to have changed his mind about marrying her.

It could have *almost* been considered a romantic gesture, something she'd not believed him capable of, except that they were surrounded by guards. Those guards were dressed for a day at the beach, wearing casual trousers and striped short-sleeved shirts and adopting carefree attitudes. As they ambled around, they hoped to be taken for gentlemen out for a day of sun, even though their real purpose was to protect her and Gilbert if someone of the criminal sort had plans to launch another attack.

It was comforting to know that the Pinkerton agents were now focusing their attention on trying to track down Mr. Howland, her father's attorney. He was at the top of their list of suspects who might be behind the attacks. But since there had been no success tracking him down, the man having disappeared into thin air, she'd not balked when Gilbert had insisted she travel in the company of Pinkerton agents, knowing the last thing she wanted to do was make herself an easy target for someone with murder on their mind.

Firmly pushing aside all thoughts of murder because that subject was somewhat depressing, Temperance stepped up behind Gilbert. Squinting, she considered his painting, biting her lip to hold back a smile when she realized it was completely awful.

"Well?" he asked.

She cleared her throat. "I like how you've added a sailboat. It really brings some life into the piece."

He turned back to his painting. "I didn't paint a sailboat. Where do you see that?"

She pointed to a swirl of yellow paint.

"Oh." He grinned. "That's not a boat. I had too much paint on my brush so I just dabbed it off right there."

"You also have a dab of paint on the sleeve of your jacket."

Gilbert inspected his sleeve, then shrugged. "I imagine most painters get paint on them occasionally."

"Aren't you going to wipe it off?"

Gilbert leaned closer to his painting, added a dash of green right next to the yellow, and nodded. "There, now it looks like a whale."

"But you have paint on your sleeve," she repeated again.

"So you said. What do you think about puppies?"

"You want to add a puppy to your ocean scene?"

He laughed. "No. Puppies might be out of my league to paint. I was simply wondering how you feel about puppies."

"Who doesn't care for puppies?"

"That's what Harrison said, but what about fey creatures?"

Temperance reached out and took hold of his arm, causing him to abandon his dabbing. "What is wrong with you?"

"I'm not certain I understand the question."

She planted her feet more firmly in the sand. "You have never — and I repeat, never — allowed something like a smear of paint to remain on your person after it's been pointed out to you. You've also never brought up the word *puppies* in any of our conversations during the entire time I've known you, and do not even get me started on the fey creature remark, because . . . I don't actually know what creatures would be considered fey."

"I didn't immediately wipe off the paint when you and I got into a bit of a paint tussle."

"That's because we were interrupted by Mrs. Boggart Hobbes."

"Well, quite, but to address your puppy remark, I used to talk about your dog all the time when we were children."

"Muffy died when I was five, so how often could we have spoken about her?"

"Ah, so the idea of puppies apparently bothers you. We'll move on to the fey creatures. According to the discussion I recently had with Harrison, we're of the belief that fey creatures encompass fairies, mermaids, and perhaps even dragons."

"I'm not certain where you expect me to go with this conversation."

He nodded. "It is an odd conversation to be sure, especially when, now that I think on it, dragons might not fall into the fey category."

"Not that I want to point out the obvious, but you even broaching the subject of dragons is odd."

Gilbert grinned. "I suppose it is. Tell me this then, what do you think of romantic gestures? Or better yet, when Harrison threw down his jacket over a puddle of water to impress Gertrude, did you find that romantic, or did you, like me, find it to be a most impractical move that ruined a perfectly fine jacket in the process?"

Feeling as if she'd suddenly stepped into an incredibly curious world, one where fey creatures and romace seemed to rule the day, and feeling quite convinced that Gilbert's brawls of the day before had injured his brain, Temperance's brows drew together. "Harrison's gesture was romantic, not because he ruined his jacket, but because he was willing to go to such extremes to win Gertrude's heart."

Gilbert considered that for a long moment before he frowned. "Ladies enjoy when gentlemen go to extremes?"

"I imagine it depends on what extremes they embrace to impress their ladies."

Abandoning his paintbrush, Gilbert flashed a smile before he retrieved a pistol from his pocket. "What say you and I go enjoy some target practice?"

Before she could inquire as to whether he *was* suffering an injury to his head, what with the abrupt change of topics, a loud clearing of a throat distracted her.

"I do not believe handing Miss Temperance a pistol in the frame of mind she's currently in is exactly what I would call a wise decision."

Turning, Temperance frowned at Mr. Barclay, who was standing behind his own easel, his paintbrush pointing her way. "What frame of mind do you believe I'm in?"

Mr. Barclay smiled. "An irritable one."

"And here I thought her irritability would be dispelled as soon as we got her out of Miss Snook's school and out into this beautiful fall day," Gilbert said.

"You brought me here because you were under the impression I was irritable?"

"You've been required to stay in the school for an extended period of time for safety reasons," Gilbert said. "Of course you're irritable, which is why I arranged for this outing." He shook his head. "Clearly, though, painting by the seaside is not improving your disposition, nor is the mention of fey creatures, hence the reason I suggested target practice."

Any irritability she'd still been holding for the man disappeared in a flash, replaced by something that left her distinctly weak at the knees. That Gilbert understood her so well, knew she thrived when she was allowed her freedom, left her realizing once and for all that she no longer merely held affection for the man. She loved him . . . desperately.

It was a realization that did nothing to help the state of her weak knees, but it was one she could no longer ignore.

"What shall we try to get you to shoot today?"

"She's very adept at hitting the ocean," Mr. Barclay suggested as he went back to his painting, eyeing his work critically. "But before she does that, and again, I'm not sure that is a grand plan on your part, Mr. Cavendish, I do need someone to look at my work and tell me what they believe I'm trying to paint."

Walking with Gilbert over to Mr. Barclay's easel, Temperance blinked and leaned closer to the canvas. "Good heavens, Mr. Barclay, it would seem you have numerous hidden talents because that's clearly a woman walking right beside the surf."

Mr. Barclay beamed. "I was hoping you wouldn't say it looked like a tree, as you did with Miss Edwina, or" — he turned his smile on Gilbert — "a boat." He gestured with his paintbrush to a figure in the distance, one who was bending over and picking up shells. "I was going to paint her sitting beside the beach, but I decided a standing figure is much easier to paint than a sitting one."

"I imagine you would have been perfectly capable of painting a sitting figure," Temperance said, returning her attention to the woman on the beach. "However, since it has just occurred to me that your muse might be a little surprised to suddenly find herself on a beach where people are shooting off a pistol, I think I should mosey her way and ask her if she objects to our target practice."

"I'll come with you," Gilbert said before he kicked off his shoes, stripped his socks from his feet, and tucked his pistol back into his pocket. "Ready?"

Temperance glanced at Gilbert's bare feet. "Who are you and what have you done with my friend?"

Taking hold of her hand, Gilbert pulled her into motion across the sand. "I'm still the same Gilbert you've always known."

"You're not wearing shoes."

"True, but since you just saw me take them off, I'm not certain why you're pointing that out."

"You always wear shoes."

"I enjoyed many a day at the beach with you throughout the years without shoes. They're not exactly sensible when one is trying to negotiate through sand."

Relief was immediate. "Oh, thank goodness. It was a sensible decision, you removing your shoes. For a minute there . . ."

"I also enjoy how squishy the sand feels pushing up between my toes."

Temperance stopped walking. "That's it. We're going to make an unexpected detour to visit your physician on our way back from the beach. Your behavior is downright peculiar today, and you're beginning to frighten me." She held up her hand when he opened his mouth. "And now that I think about it, how is it even possible that you managed to arrange so much time to take me to the seaside? Didn't you have appointments scheduled for this afternoon?"

"I suppose I did, but I sent a note around to Mrs. Martin, requesting she cancel them."

"You never cancel appointments."

"True, but if makes you feel better, I did have a perfectly normal meeting with my attorney earlier this morning."

Temperance smiled. "That's a relief. It's reassuring to hear you kept at least one appointment today."

Gilbert pulled her back into motion. "It wasn't a scheduled appointment. I dropped in on the man unannounced." He grinned. "You should have seen his face when I interrupted his breakfast."

"You went to your attorney's house?"

"I didn't feel like waiting until he arrived at his office."

"You never make unscheduled visits, nor have I ever known you to travel to a business associate's house."

"I had a matter of urgency to discuss with the man. And considering I've paid him a small fortune over the years to handle some of my affairs, he was perfectly affable about welcoming me into his home and to his breakfast table, where we enjoyed a lovely meal of eggs and ham while we discussed what I needed to discuss."

"And that something would be . . . ?"

"I can't tell you yet, not until I work out all the details." He grinned again. "But you'll be pleased to learn I didn't bother to make a graph, simply made a halfhearted attempt at a list, and decided to allow my attorney to proceed forward in whatever way he believes is best."

Before Temperance could voice her concern again, Gilbert pointed to a seagull that was flying right over the surf, a beautiful sight for certain, but not one that could hold her attention since Gilbert was behaving in a very un-Gilbert-like fashion.

"I don't believe I ever thanked you for putting my mother's mind at ease," he said, drawing her to a stop.

"There's no reason to thank me, Gilbert. Your mother was worried for no reason."

Gilbert shook his head. "She was very concerned she'd upset you by disclosing that she and my stepfather were originally supposed to be your guardians until your parents changed their minds. She still blames herself for not checking on you over the years, relying instead on the word of your father's attorney that you were grieving and wanted to be left alone."

Temperance gave his hand a squeeze. "None of what happened to me was your mother's fault. And horrible as this is going to sound, I recently realized, after speaking with your mother, that I never truly grieved for my parents. I never even held a memorial for them, an event I have to imagine your parents would have wanted to attend."

Bringing her hand to his lips, he pressed a quick kiss on it. "It would have been difficult for you to hold a memorial for them, especially since you had no funds, nor would there have been many people to attend a memorial in New York. From what I recall, your parents did not have many friends in the city, and since your house had been sold in Connecticut, well, the logistics of a service would have been tricky. It also would have been next to impossible to track my parents down. If you've forgotten, they were traveling through India at the time of your parents' deaths."

"My parents would have been disappointed that I didn't even bother to try."

"Your parents would be proud that you managed to survive a dreadful experience with your cousins and came out stronger for it."

Temperance shook her head. "I'm not as strong as you believe. Otherwise I wouldn't still be furious with my parents for abandoning me, or for leaving my welfare to a cousin who certainly didn't hold any affection for me."

He kissed her hand again. "You have every right to be angry. I've always thought anger is something that helps you through the many different phases of grief. You claimed you didn't grieve for your parents, but that isn't true. You're still grieving for them, and when you move past the anger you're continuing to hold, you'll find peace." He reached up and tucked a strand of her flyaway hair behind her ear. "And to help you find that peace, what do you think about holding a memorial service for your parents now? We could have it in Grace Church, Reverend Perry could officiate, and all of your friends could attend and help you remember the wonderful times with your parents, while also being around you as you finally say a proper good-bye to them."

Tears stung her eyes, and she managed to nod before Gilbert pulled her close, soothing a hand over the back of her hair.

Easing away from her far sooner than she liked, Gilbert tilted her chin up and caught her eye. "Shall we hurry and intercept the woman collecting shells? Hopefully she'll not be opposed to us doing some target practice because I imagine taking shots at the ocean will improve your spirits tremendously."

She smiled. "I can hit something smaller than the ocean."

Returning her smile, Gilbert pulled her toward the water, laughing with her as the foam washed over their feet, the chilly water doing wonders to wash away the last vestiges of sadness that had descended over her while she'd been speaking of her parents.

Enjoying the feel of the surf tugging

against her legs, she splashed her way closer to the woman, noticing that the woman was now rummaging through a bag that obviously held the treasures she'd found that day.

Not caring to startle her, Temperance stopped a few feet away, smiling when the memory flashed to mind of how often she and Gilbert had spent afternoons doing the very same thing, searching for shells and dragging their treasures home with them when the sun began to set.

Opening her mouth when the woman began to straighten, Temperance's words of greeting lodged in her throat when the lady turned her way, holding not a seashell in her hand, but a pistol.

Chapter Twenty-Six

For the briefest of seconds, Gilbert thought his eyes were deceiving him, until Temperance's grip on his hand turned painful and he realized the woman who'd been collecting shells *was* pointing a gun at Temperance.

Not wanting to take the chance of the pistol going off if he charged the woman or pulled his own gun, Gilbert lifted his gaze from the pistol to the woman's face, realizing in a split second that he was not facing a woman, but a man disguised as a woman, complete with wig and gown.

"Mr. Howland!" Temperance exclaimed in a voice that was brimming with disbelief. "Good heavens, sir, lower your weapon. If it has escaped your notice, there are Pinkerton agents even now swarming toward us, which means you'll soon find yourself good and dead if you continue pointing that gun at me."

"I'm not certain now is the exact moment to turn demanding, Temperance," Gilbert said out of the corner of his mouth, earning a nod of agreement from the man Temperance had just called Mr. Howland, her father's reprehensible attorney, if he wasn't mistaken.

"Excellent advice, Mr. Cavendish," Mr. Howland returned as he kept his pistol trained on Temperance. "Although I would have been spared this unpleasant interlude if Miss Flowerdew would have succumbed to any number of attempts I . . . well, just allow me to simply say that she's caused me a great deal of bother, along with a large amount of money."

Temperance lifted her chin. "So sorry to be such a bother, Mr. Howland, but you must realize that it was foolish in the extreme to come after me yourself. Although I must say your decision to disguise yourself as a woman was somewhat ingenious since you were able to get near me even with all the Pinkertons about."

"Those agents have been annoyingly thorough with their questions regarding me and anyone associated with me," Mr. Howland said, his gaze sliding to the right where Gilbert then noticed Agent Samuel McParland running toward them, his pistol drawn and his expression dangerous. “I had no choice but to assume a different identity, along with a different gender to throw them off my trail.”

“Efforts that now seem somewhat wasted since you’ve revealed yourself not only to me, but to the Pinkertons as well,” Temperance said right as Agent McParland splashed through the surf, stopping a few feet away from them when Mr. Howland cocked the pistol that was still aimed at Temperance.

“Lower your weapon,” Agent McParland ordered, seemingly unperturbed that he was facing a gentleman dressed as a woman. “You’re completely surrounded, and if it was in question, there’s no avenue of escape for you now.”

Mr. Howland didn’t so much as blink. “I’m not an idiot, sir. I’m well aware I’m surrounded, knew I would be the moment I decided to confront Miss Flowerdew.”

“And you still confronted her and have yet to lower your weapon,” Agent McParland pointed out.

“Miss Flowerdew and I have matters to discuss, and until we finish, I’m not lowering my weapon.”

Gilbert took a single step forward, stilling when he noticed Mr. Howland’s hand beginning to tremble. "You can discuss those matters with Temperance without threatening her, sir. Your pistol is making everyone nervous, and it's not wise to make Pinkerton agents nervous. They tend to turn deadly in those types of situations."

Mr. Howland ignored him, turning his full attention to Temperance. "This day would never have come to pass if you'd not rediscovered your spine, but had remained humbled under the thumb of that ridiculous cousin of yours." He dashed the hand not holding the pistol over a perspiring forehead, tilting his wig. "You also wouldn't find yourself in this nasty situation if you hadn't steered the Pinkerton men after me in the first place. I don't care to be chased down like a fox on a hunt."

"I didn't ask the Pinkertons to hunt you down, Mr. Howland," Temperance said. "They were only hired after it became clear someone wanted Gilbert and me dead. I'm afraid the Pinkertons, being competent sorts, discovered that someone might very well be you."

"Your life wouldn't have been in jeopardy if detectives hadn't begun showing up at my office, asking pesky questions about my dealings with your family." He swiped at his forehead again. "My secretary told me those questions implied that I'd not been honest in my dealings with you."

Temperance narrowed her eyes. "You haven't been honest."

"You have no proof of that, and I take great offense that my secretary now believes she has cause to question my integrity."

Gilbert frowned. "Did you not tell my mother, Mrs. William Beckwith, that Temperance had elected to continue on with a tour of the continents after her parents died?"

"That was a long time ago. It's difficult to say with any certainty."

"But you didn't bother to forward any of the letters my mother wrote to Temperance, did you? And when she inquired about why Temperance was not writing back to her, you then told my mother you'd heard from Temperance, but that she did not wish to correspond with my mother for some ridiculous reason."

"I was sparing the poor child additional grief by keeping her from having to deal with people who'd been close friends of her parents."

"But why did you lie about it?" Temperance asked. "I'm afraid I simply do not understand the reasoning behind what appears to be a great deal of subterfuge."

Mr. Howland, oddly enough, nodded. "I'm not surprised you'd be confused. You never seemed to me to be possessed of more than a modicum of intelligence, which is exactly why I was shocked when Pinkerton agents began snooping into my business. I never expected you to have the gumption to question the business dealings I had with your father."

When Temperance seemed to be at a loss for what to say to that, Gilbert stepped in. "I fear you did, indeed, underestimate Temperance. She may embrace a love of the arts, which has apparently allowed you to believe she's lacking in intelligence, but behind her air of whimsicality lies a mind that is far superior to most men I know."

Temperance, even with a gun being pointed her way, flashed him a smile, one that quickly faded when Mr. Howland began waving that pistol around.

"I don't think I'd go that far, Mr. Cavendish, although I will acknowledge that she's been incredibly difficult to . . . silence."

"And you've been incredibly diligent in your quest to have *both* of us silenced," Gilbert countered.

Mr. Howland gave another wave of the pistol. "I didn't try to have you killed, Mr. Cavendish, although since I've become aware of how involved you are in Miss Flowerdew's life, I probably should have considered that. If there *were* attempts on your life, those were simply because you were apparently in Miss Flowerdew's company."

Before he could argue, Temperance lifted her chin.

"I still don't understand what I did to you that would have you hiring on members of the criminal set to see me dead."

Mr. Howland considered her question for a long moment. "You were born to a man I grew to loathe — a man who was capable of amassing an enormous fortune, not through strenuous labor or by working from dawn to dusk, but simply through his uncanny talent for knowing what investments were going to increase his fortune. It was unfair, the lack of effort he put into making money, and I grew tired of watching him succeed time after time after time."

Trepidation slithered down Gilbert's spine. "What did you do?"

"I used the gifts I was given to improve my own lot in life — those gifts being a very ordinary face, an ability to convince people I am above reproach, and . . . an unsurpassable talent for forgery."

Temperance glanced Gilbert's way, her

eyes filled with gathering storm clouds. Knowing it would not bode well for the situation if she lost her temper, he cleared his throat, wanting to pull out as much information as he could from Mr. Howland before the Pinkerton detectives made their move — one that would hopefully not find anyone dead.

"So you used the misfortune of Mr. and Mrs. Flowerdew's death to help yourself to what should have been Temperance's inheritance, didn't you?" was the first thing that popped into his mind to say.

"My dear man, do you honestly believe I would have waited for Anthony Flowerdew to meet his demise on one of the many, many journeys he was so fond of making?" Mr. Howland let out a bark of laughter before Gilbert could reply. "It was maddening, watching Anthony go sailing off on one whim after another while I was stuck toiling behind a desk, pushing paperwork day after day." His lips twisted. "I finally came up with a brilliant plan that would give me the funds I deserved while putting an end to the annoyance I experienced every single time I encountered Anthony or received a hastily scribbled letter telling me to invest in one lucrative deal after another for him."

Temperance had gone remarkably still

beside him, but even knowing that what Mr. Howland had left to say was going to be downright horrific, Gilbert could not let Mr. Howland stop his tale. He knew Temperance was going to find the truth painful, but he also knew she needed to hear all of it in order to move on with her life.

"It was easy, if you want to know the truth of it," Mr. Howland continued. "I contacted a few of my more questionable associates, asked if they wanted some work. They did, and so I arranged for them to get on as crewmembers on a ship bound for South America."

He shook his head, along with the pistol, turning Gilbert's blood to ice.

"It was a painfully long wait for that ship to return, but the wait was well worth it once I learned my men, Bernie the Butcher and Richard the Snake, two men I understand are now residing in jail, had been successful, and my problem of Anthony Flowerdew and his far too beautiful wife, Grace — a lady, by the way, who seemed immune to my charm — were gone forever."

"You murdered my parents?" Temperance all but hissed as she tried to move forward, forcing Gilbert to tighten his hold on her hand.

"Have you not been listening to what I've

said?" Mr. Howland hissed right back at her. "*I* didn't murder them. Bernie the Butcher probably did, although I will admit Bernie and Richard the Snake were a little vague about the details, probably wanted to spare me the gory mess of it." He swiped a hand over a forehead that was perspiring more than ever. "But that was only part of my problem — the next revolved around you, Miss Flowerdew. It was a puzzle, what to do with you. I mean, there you were, over in Paris, a spoiled and frivolous girl, one destined to become one of the great American heiresses."

Temperance began bristling with temper, forcing Gilbert to dig his feet into the sand to hold her back.

"You *did* steal my inheritance, didn't you?"

"It was no easy feat, if that makes you feel any better," Mr. Howland said. "I had to forge papers that gave me executive power over your father's investments deals in his stead while he was away — a brilliant forgery, if I do say so myself, because I was then able to pull his position out of certain stocks, then repurchase those very same stocks under my name, not his."

"That *was* brilliant," Gilbert said, deciding to appeal to Mr. Howland's ego to keep the man from remembering he was holding a deadly weapon in his hand, especially since Mr. Howland was clearly becoming more agitated by the second.

"It was, but what was even more brilliant was the plan I formulated to deal with Temperance." He began inspecting his pistol. "You see, I'd met Anthony's good friend, your stepfather, Mr. William Beckwith, and knew him to be a very astute gentleman. I could not afford to allow him the opportunity of looking over Anthony's books because William would have known Anthony would never invest his entire fortune in one railroad stock. Luckily for me, William and your mother, Florence, departed for India not long after I came up with my plan."

Mr. Howland's eyes suddenly flashed with what almost seemed to Gilbert to be a trace of madness. "As luck would also have it, I'd been privy to a conversation Anthony had with Grace when they invited me to join them for dinner at Delmonico's one evening years ago. During that conversation, Anthony remarked that his cousin, Wayne Flowerdew, was a man known to live above his means without the motivation to earn his own fortune. That conversation was what determined my next step — forging Anthony's will to give guardianship of you, my dear Miss Flowerdew, to Wayne, instead of to whom your parents wanted — Mr. and Mrs. Beckwith."

Temperance stiffened, drew in a deep breath, then blew it out in a rush. "It must have bothered you to give Wayne a few thousand dollars of your ill-gotten fortune to whet his appetite for more and agree to fetch me from Paris."

"A few thousand dollars was a paltry sum compared to the entirety of your father's worth. And it worked like a charm. Wayne sailed off for Paris and fetched you back. As expected, you, the spoiled and pampered princess of my nemesis, crumpled the moment you learned you were left in this world without your parents and without the money you were so accustomed to having at your fingertips."

He heaved a sigh. "I was so disappointed when Wayne made the poor decision to move to New York, using the paltry amount of money he'd gotten to rent that place on Park Avenue. However, because I soon learned he'd turned you into nothing more than a poor relation, and something of a servant if I'm not mistaken, I forgave him that error in judgment, never imagining that you'd somehow find a backbone, which has led us to this very moment."

Temperance's face began to darken. "I didn't do a single thing to warrant the attacks you've recently directed my way. I had no idea you'd stolen my inheritance. It disgusts me that I never considered the matter, but because of that ignorance, I don't understand why you decided I needed to die, or why you'd want Gilbert dead as well."

"As I mentioned before, I don't want Mr. Cavendish dead. But as for you and those simpleton cousins of yours, I knew drastic measures were going to be needed after Wayne approached me to find him some men to perpetuate some ridiculous farce of an abduction. He threatened me, if you can believe it, told me he'd tell you about that money I gave him, as well as tell you that I agreed to never allow you to know about that money, which would have certainly sent you seeking an audience with me, one I wanted to avoid at all costs." He swiped his forehead again. "I've never been fond of confrontations."

"That's why you went through the bother of assisting Wayne with that ridiculous abduction scenario?" Gilbert asked. "You're not fond of confrontations?"

Mr. Howland inclined his head. "Partially, although the thought did spring to mind that I should simply do away with him, until I had another thought that centered around the idea that suspicions could be raised if another person I was associated with went . . . missing." He heaved a sigh. "Unfortunately, after the abduction was unsuccessful, I got to thinking that Wayne, being the coward he is, might very well turn on me if he was ever questioned about the abduction, so . . . I decided he'd simply have to go, along with his insipid wife and shrew of a daughter. Since I was going to be hiring on assassins, I figured I might as well have them turn their attention to Temperance as well."

Temperance frowned. "Didn't your wife ever question where your newfound wealth came from?"

"Of course, which is why I said that you can draw suspicion if too many people you are acquainted with go missing."

"You were responsible for your wife going missing?" Temperance all but whispered.

Waving that aside, Mr. Howland pushed back the wig that had fallen almost to his eyes due to his excessive perspiring. "She was always a sickly woman, so she would have died sooner or later, and it's not as if she went missing long. Her body was found slumped over a bench in a park, her death ruled to be from natural causes."

Temperance's eyes flashed. "From the sounds of it, her death was anything but natural."

"I'll tell you what's not natural," Mr. Howland began. "Being tortured by the continued breath that seems impossible to steal from your body." A trace of spittle trailed from his lips to his chin. "Because you refuse to die, Miss Flowerdew, thoughts of you plague me endlessly, those thoughts driving me to distraction."

"I'm certain thoughts of murder *would* drive you to distraction."

Mr. Howland, to Gilbert's surprise, shook his head. "It's not the murder that's distracting me now, Miss Flowerdew, it's the guilt."

For a second, Temperance gawked at the man, until her lips thinned. "I'm supposed to believe you feel guilty for trying to murder me, murdering my parents, *and* for stealing my father's fortune?"

"It's the only explanation I could come up with to explain why you've taken over my thoughts." Mr. Howland's shoulders sagged. "I've also come up with a way to remedy that unfortunate state of affairs, which is to . . ."

"Kill me?" Temperance finished for him.

He inclined his head as a small smile

played around his lips. "It's tempting, but I decided what would rid me of these thoughts would be to disclose all the wrongs I've done you. That will allow me to empty my mind of anything concerning the Flowerdew family. I've left papers detailing where I invested all your father's money, as well as my duplicity in taking that money. You'll find I didn't lose much of your father's fortune, so you may once again embrace a life of frivolity and lack of purpose. I'm hopeful that by telling you all this, I'll find a small measure of peace when I move to the great beyond. Do know that I have regrets about what I've done, but since I don't care to turn maudlin, I'll simply bid you good day, and . . ."

He raised the pistol to his temple, and without thinking, Gilbert released Temperance's hand and lunged, tackling Mr. Howland into the sudsy surf right as the pistol fired.

Chapter Twenty-Seven

The sight of Gilbert flailing about in the surf sent relief flowing over her, which quickly turned to disbelief when Mr. Howland staggered to his feet and dashed straight into the ocean. Lifting up the hem of her skirt, Temperance ran in after him, fighting through the waves the deeper she traveled into the sea.

"Leave me alone!" Mr. Howland bellowed before he dove under a wave, disappearing from sight.

Diving after him, even though her skirt immediately began tangling around her legs, Temperance began swimming, pulled to an abrupt stop when someone grabbed her around the waist. Breaking the surface, she shoved hair out of her face right as Gilbert hauled her up against a firmly muscled chest.

"Have you lost your mind?" he demanded.

"My mind is in fine working order, but I

can't say the same for Mr. Howland's. We need to tow him back to shore before he drowns."

"If you'll look over there, Agent McParland is already doing that."

Peering around Gilbert, she saw Agent McParland tugging a thrashing Mr. Howland toward shore while several of the other agents rushed through the water to assist him. "I forgot we had Pinkerton men here."

"Clearly."

She frowned. "Should I assume you're cross with me for going after him?"

"I'm more aggravated than cross. You're not exactly dressed for a dip in the sea, and you could have drowned if you'd gotten out too far."

"And that would have aggravated you?"

"It would have devastated me."

Warmth spread through her, even though the water they were in could only be described as frigid. "I think that's the nicest thing you've ever said to me."

He raked a hand through his hair, leaving it standing on end. "You will promise me here and now that you will never place yourself in such peril again."

"One would hope that with Mr. Howland soon to be out of our lives, neither of us will face such perilous times again."

He narrowed his eyes. "Your promise, Temperance."

She narrowed her eyes right back at him. "It's not as if I deliberately set out to place myself in peril. But since you're obviously going to be stubborn about this, and my teeth are beginning to chatter . . . I promise I'll never follow a murderer into the ocean again while dressed in what used to be a lovely walking gown but will now have to be assigned to the ragbag."

"You're going to be the death of me," he said right before a wave sent them tumbling through the water.

Sputtering to the surface a moment later, Gilbert hauled her right up next to him again. And even though it was hardly the time or the place, she had no control over knees that felt remarkably like jelly, the cause of that pesky feeling obviously a direct result of being pressed against his firmly muscled chest once more. Sweeping her straight up into his arms, he began heading to shore, their progress slowed time and time again when waves would lift him off his feet and carry them forward. To her surprise, he did not set her down when they reached the shallow surf, but kept her in his arms, splashing his way toward the beach.

"Would you like me to take Miss Temperance?" Eugene called, having abandoned his post guarding the carriage and now standing in the shallow water beside Mr. Barclay, who was missing his hat and looking paler than usual.

"I've got her," Gilbert called back, sloshing toward the two men who fell into step beside him as he walked out of the water.

"You took a good few years off my life, Miss Temperance," Mr. Barclay said, reaching out to touch her shoulder while Gilbert turned and began moving toward their carriage.

Temperance smiled. "I apologize for that, Mr. Barclay, and do know that Gilbert has already made me promise to never run into the ocean after a murderer again."

Mr. Barclay looked at Gilbert. "I would have thought you'd make her promise to never get into dangerous situations again."

"I tried, but Temperance, being Temperance, twisted the promise to one she knows she won't break."

"A lady with Miss Temperance's spirit will always find herself in some type of exciting situation," Eugene said, sending Temperance a hint of a grin. He gestured to the knife he was brandishing. "Even though you proved yourself to be horrible with wielding a knife, 'cept of course when you hit Richard the Snake, and you're not much better with a pistol, we may need to continue on with your defense lessons to better prepare you the next time you encounter someone of the murderous sort."

Temperance returned the grin as Gilbert released a snort.

"Let us pray Temperance's days of encountering murderous sorts are now firmly behind her, although continuing on with teaching her how to defend herself in a fight might not be a horrible idea," Gilbert said, striding over the sand.

"And it's amusing to boot," Eugene said, his grin widening.

Before Temperance could respond, they reached their carriage. Gilbert settled her on the seat, then set about the business of getting her snugly wrapped in the blanket that Mr. Barclay handed him.

"I'll be right back," Gilbert said, giving the blanket a last tuck. "I need to speak with Agent McParland, and then we'll get on our way to Miss Snook's school."

"Where I believe a nice plate of cakes and a few cups of hot chocolate are going to be in order," Mr. Barclay added, settling himself on the seat across from her and accepting the blanket Gilbert had pulled from under the seat with a nod of appreciation.

"He really is a most excellent gentleman," Mr. Barclay said after Gilbert strode away.

"He is indeed."

Mr. Barclay sat forward. "Because of that, you and I are going to have to put our heads together to figure out how best to convince him you've changed your mind about becoming his countess."

"I don't recall mentioning to you that I'd changed my mind about that."

Mr. Barclay inclined his head. "You didn't need to, dear. Having lived with Miss Henrietta and Miss Mabel all these many years, and having recently been available to many of the young women attending Miss Snook's school, I've become somewhat of an expert with understanding women and their many emotions." He smiled. "Because of that expertise, I'm more than aware of the fact that you hold Mr. Cavendish in the highest esteem, and since I hold you in the highest esteem as well, although not in the same way you hold Mr. Cavendish, I'm going to see to it that you acquire the love of your life, and I'll hear no argument about that from you, if you please."

Three hours later, Temperance was finally rid of the chill from her unexpected dip into the sea, Miss Henrietta having taken her firmly in hand the moment her foot stepped into Miss Snook's school. She'd been practically tossed into a steaming hot tub, plied with hot chocolate while in that tub, then rubbed down with thick towels that had been warmed on a rack near the fire. She'd then been dressed in her warmest gown, had woolen stockings pulled up her legs by one of Miss Snook's students, even though she'd tried to protest, saying she was perfectly capable of donning stockings all by herself. After she'd been fully clothed, she'd been led to a chair where Mrs. Davenport had insisted on toweling her hair dry before styling it. Thankfully, the styling had not been one of an intricate nature, and after Mrs. Davenport proclaimed she was done, Temperance had finally been released from her room. Pink-cheeked and with her hair arranged in a casual knot on top of her head, she had Miss Henrietta and Mrs. Davenport escort her to the library, quite as if her adventure might have caused her to forget the way.

Glancing around the library where everyone had gathered to hear every snippet of news she had to tell about her dangerous day at the beach, she couldn't help but smile as she looked at each person assembled there.

Miss Henrietta was sitting stiff as a poker in a chair next to the settee Temperance was now sitting on, with Mrs. Davenport in a chair right beside her. Mrs. Davenport was currently bent over a bustle she was creating, one that was incredibly large, but actually looked like a bustle one might find in a store.

Florence, Gilbert's mother, was sitting beside Temperance on the settee, holding Temperance's hand and doing her best to avoid Temperance's question of why she was at the school, or why she kept exchanging grins with Miss Henrietta and Mrs. Davenport. That pesky business was leaving Temperance with the distinct impression the ladies had gathered to do a touch of meddling but had been interrupted when she, Gilbert, Mr. Barclay, and Eugene arrived dripping wet at the school and promising to disclose all after everyone found dry clothing.

Any disclosures had been put on hold, though, after Miss Henrietta realized her sister, Miss Mabel, was not at the school but at Rutherford & Company. She'd immediately sent off a note to the store to call her sister home, insisting all tales about the latest adventure wait until Mabel arrived, since Mabel would be most put out if she missed even a smidgen of the story.

"Ah, Gilbert, there you are, dear, and looking much dryer than the last time I saw you," Florence said, letting go of Temperance's hand and rising to her feet as Gilbert strode into the room. She met him in the middle of the library, turning her cheek to accept the kiss Gilbert gave her.

"Mr. Barclay lent me some clothing he found in his wardrobe," Gilbert said with a rueful smile. "I'm afraid he's a good deal thinner than I am, so I'm sure to be holding my breath for the foreseeable future in the hope I don't split a seam."

Mrs. Davenport looked up from her bustle. "I've gotten very adept at fixing seams, my dear, so if you do split one, let me know."

Gilbert grinned. "While I appreciate the offer, Mrs. Davenport, I'm fairly sure if I do split a seam, what I'm wearing might be beyond repair. In that event, I'll simply send off a note to my house, asking someone to fetch me my own trousers."

He turned his grin on Temperance. "You're looking much better, and I see you've been supplied with the chocolate and cakes Mr. Barclay kept promising you on the ride here."

"The chocolate is delicious, but speaking of Mr. Barclay, where is he?" Temperance asked, her curiosity humming over what Mr. Barclay might have talked about with Gilbert when the two men went off to his room together.

"He had an errand to run," Gilbert said, walking over to join her on the settee. Taking her hand in his, he placed a quick kiss on it. "You really are looking much better, and I'm relieved to see some color back in your cheeks. You were incredibly pale after we got out of the ocean."

"October isn't exactly the time of year one should go for a swim."

"Which brings us back to that promise I wanted you to give me," he said, giving her hand a squeeze.

"What promise was that, dear?" Florence asked, settling into a chair directly across from them.

"He wants me to promise I'll abandon perilous situations from this point forward," Temperance said before Gilbert could answer.

Florence nodded. "Which I hope you will promise him. Even though we've been told relatively little about what happened today, the thought of you and Gilbert being confronted by a murderer gives me heart palpitations. I would be much relieved to know you never intend to put yourself in such danger again."

"Everyone does realize that I didn't *intentionally* place myself in a perilous situation today, don't they?" Temperance asked. "I certainly couldn't have known that Mr. Howland would take to disguising himself as a woman to avoid detection and decide the time was finally ripe for him to reveal himself to me down at the beach."

"A most excellent point," Florence said with a smile. "But it isn't exactly reassuring, because most people never encounter a disguised murderer. However, I suppose I can take a small amount of comfort in knowing that Gilbert was there with you and hope that he'll always be around if disaster comes knocking on your door."

Gilbert settled back against the settee. "I wouldn't take too much comfort in that, Mother. I'm not always able to intercede on Temperance's behalf, especially when she does the unexpected, such as throw herself into the ocean after Mr. Howland, who'd managed to get away from me."

"I thought everyone would have waited for me to rush home before divulging any part of what I'm going to assume is a most riveting tale."

Looking up, Temperance found Miss Mabel marching her way across the library, her eyes bright with excitement. Following her was none other than Edwina Sinclair, her color high and her eyes filled with what almost looked to be a large dose of disgust. Flinging herself onto a fainting couch right next to where Miss Mabel had taken a seat, Edwina let out a most unladylike snort.

"Do tell me that Miss Henrietta's note was wrong and that you weren't confronted by a madman dressed as a woman who held you at gunpoint" were the first words out of Edwina's mouth.

"Are you going to be overly distraught if I admit Miss Henrietta has the right measure of what happened to Gilbert and me today?" Temperance countered.

Edwina released a sigh. "I wouldn't say I'm overly distraught — more on the lines of resigned."

Temperance frowned. "Resigned about what?"

"That I'm not cut out for the role of Pinkerton agent." She crossed her arms over her chest. "I'm constantly missing all the most dramatic moments, and this time I missed capturing the culprit because I was perusing the hat section over at Rutherford & Company."

"Were you on duty?" Temperance asked.

"Well, no, but I don't imagine there's ever

been another fledgling agent who can make the claim they missed out on an important capture because they couldn't decide whether or not to purchase the navy hat trimmed with cream or the pink hat adorned with charming clusters of flowers."

Temperance fought a grin. "Which one did you purchase?"

"I couldn't decide between the two, so I bought both." She smiled. "I then accepted Asher's invitation to join him for a cup of tea in Rutherford & Company's tearoom, which effectively had me missing all the excitement this afternoon offered."

Mrs. Davenport looked up from the bustle she was still assembling. "I have to imagine that tea with Asher was quite interesting and could also help explain why you're doubting if you're meant to pursue a profession with the Pinkerton agency."

Before Edwina could respond, Mercy suddenly came charging into the room, pulling a wagon filled with typewriters she apparently forgot to leave by the front door. Stopping in the very center of the library, she nodded to Miss Henrietta.

"Did I miss much? Eugene was annoyingly closemouthed with many details. But that could have been because he was trying to make it back here after picking up me and the rest of the girls from Mr. Cavendish's office in a timely fashion, one that had him taking all sorts of shortcuts through the city, which made for a hair-raising ride home."

"Temperance and Gilbert have yet to disclose more than a few snippets here and there, Mercy, so you've not missed much," Miss Henrietta said as Mercy parked the wagon filled with typewriters by a chair, then sat down, her eyes alight with curiosity.

"All we know for certain is that Mr. Howland, the attorney who handled Temperance's inheritance, dressed himself in disguise and confronted Temperance on the beach," Mrs. Davenport said.

"Where he was then apprehended and will spend the rest of his life behind bars or confined to an asylum."

Everyone turned their attention to the door as Agent Samuel McParland strode into the room, his attention settling, unsurprisingly, on Edwina. Not stopping until he was standing directly in front of her, he inclined his head. "I wasn't expecting to find you here. I thought you were off shopping today."

Edwina's cheeks turned a little pink. "I *was* off shopping, but I learned of what transpired when Miss Henrietta sent a note to Miss Mabel, and then Miss Mabel shared the contents of that note with me." She rose to her feet. "And while I know this might distress you, what with you being my most enthusiastic champion when it comes to my quest to become a Pinkerton, I must tell you that, what with my tendency to miss occasions that can only be described as significant to the one case I was assigned, I'm not cut out for this type of work."

To Temperance's surprise, instead of looking even remotely distressed about that, Agent McParland released a hearty laugh. "Well, thank the good Lord for that."

Edwina immediately looked grumpy. "I wasn't expecting amusement on your part, *Agent McParland,* which leaves me with no conclusion but to believe you found me to be a most dreadful agent-in-the-making and are now relieved that I'll no longer be a burden to you and the agency."

Agent McParland leaned forward and took hold of Edwina's hand, one she immediately began trying to tug free. "You were never a burden, nor were you the *worst* agent-in-the-making we've ever trained."

"I don't believe you meant to phrase that exactly that way," Gilbert muttered, which had Agent McParland nodding in agreement before he raised Edwina's hand to his lips.

"Gilbert is quite right about that, but my only excuse for being so clumsy with my words is that you've now done away with the only barrier that was standing between us, which means, I need to go speak with your father, so if you'll excuse me . . ." He released Edwina's hand and made for the door, stopping in his tracks when Mrs. Davenport suddenly abandoned her bustle and her chair and dashed to block his path.

"You can't simply leave now," Mrs. Davenport said. "We have all sorts of questions — such as why you need to speak with Edwina's father, and . . . why aren't you concerned that she's willing to abandon her desire to become a Pinkerton, and . . ."

Mrs. Davenport stopped speaking when Agent McParland held up his hand. "I'm not concerned about Edwina abandoning her desire to become a Pinkerton because I encountered Asher outside his store on my way here. He, apparently under the belief I'd already spoken with Edwina, apologized for stealing Edwina away from the Pinkerton family, saying something to the effect that she'd finally, and with surprising enthusiasm, agreed to become the face of Rutherford & Company. I then concluded that meant she was abandoning her desire to become a Pinkerton since she can't very well have her face all over the city and expect to remain inconspicuous, something a Pinkerton strives to maintain."

Edwina was on her feet and across the library in a flash. "Why did you laugh when I told you I wasn't meant to become an agent if you'd already been told my change of plans?"

Agent McParland smiled. "I thought Asher might have been pulling a jest on me, so to hear the words come out of your mouth evidently brought on laughter of the relieved kind."

"Because . . . ?" Edwina prompted.

"I don't have to worry about other agents thinking I'm showing you favoritism or be concerned that . . . well, can't say more just yet, not until I speak with your father and make it all nice and proper."

A second later, Edwina was pulling Agent McParland toward the door, clearly eager for the man to get on with matters and seek out her father as soon as possible. Her efforts, however, came to a halt when Miss Henrietta cleared her throat in a telling fashion.

"While I, for one, am certainly delighted by this latest lovely event, that being a resolution to a budding romance all of us have been watching with bated breath, I must insist that before you go, Agent McParland, you at least take a short moment to fill us in on what happened today."

Even though Edwina heaved a sigh that could have been heard in the house across the street, she did turn with Agent McParland and walk with him to a fainting couch. Sitting beside him, Temperance swore she heard Edwina say something about hurrying up with the explanation. After sending her a smile, Agent McParland launched rather rapidly into an account of everything that had transpired throughout the afternoon.

"So after we determined that the man was suffering from some form of mental anguish," Agent McParland concluded ten minutes later, "we had him transported to The New York Lunatic Asylum on Blackwell Island. His condition will be assessed by the good doctors there, and if it's ever deemed he's truly competent again, he'll be transferred to jail, where he'll spend the rest of his days behind bars."

"Because he admitted to hiring on someone to murder Temperance and Gilbert?" Miss Henrietta asked.

Agent McParland frowned. "He readily

admitted to hiring someone to kill Temperance, her parents, and her cousins, but he's holding fast to his claim that he never wanted Gilbert dead."

"Why would he do that?" Florence pressed, sending her son a look filled with concern.

Shrugging, Agent McParland accepted a plate of cakes that Mercy handed to him. "I would love to think his mental anguish has caused him to forget some of his misdeeds, but . . . there is always the chance someone else out there wishes to see Gilbert come to a nasty end."

Florence's brows drew together. "Gilbert has always been a more-than-pleasant sort. I don't know of anyone who'd want to see him harmed."

"Perhaps it's not Gilbert someone wants to see harmed," Edwina said, leaning forward, "but the Earl of Strafford, a notion I do believe was broached at some point in time when we didn't know who was behind any of the threats."

Silence settled over the library until Agent McParland got to his feet. "I regretfully must admit I'd forgotten about that idea, although because you remembered, my dear Edwina, you should take comfort that, no matter your fondness for shopping and proclivity to miss the most eventful aspects of cases, you would have eventually made a fine Pinkerton." He smiled when she stuck her tongue out at him. "I do hope no one will mind if I don't immediately set off to pursue that idea since I clearly have matters of a more personal and pressing nature to attend to today."

No one voiced an argument to that, especially when Edwina took to glaring around the room, her glaring more than enough reason to encourage Agent McParland to get on his way. As the man made his way for the door, another man entered the library, one Temperance was delighted to see, Reverend Benjamin Perry.

As Reverend Perry beamed a smile all around, he was joined by a very pleased-looking Mr. Barclay.

For the briefest of moments, Temperance wondered if Mr. Barclay may have overstepped his role in helping her secure Gilbert's affections and brought Reverend Perry around to convince Gilbert some vows needed to be spoken, until Reverend Perry took a seat and launched into the true reason behind his visit.

"I understand from Mr. Barclay, Temperance, who was sent to call on me at Gilbert's request, that you're interested in holding a memorial for your parents."

Warmth flowed through her. Turning to Gilbert, she smiled. "You remembered I wanted to hold a memorial for my parents?"

Gilbert returned the smile. "Of course I remembered." He leaned closer and lowered his voice. "Although I've yet to understand why Mr. Barclay was so enthusiastic about informing Reverend Perry of your decision, or why he patted me on the arm and said my understanding you so well was a step of progress in the right direction. I've found myself wondering whether the man has decided to join all the matchmakers we seem to have roaming around us these days." He gave a quick gesture of a hand to the room at large.

Not caring to disclose that she knew for fact Mr. Barclay had turned an eye toward matchmaking, Temperance settled for a smile and a shrug before she returned her attention to Reverend Perry. "It was very kind of you, Reverend Perry, to travel here to discuss the memorial for my parents. I believe a simple affair would be fine, attended by my closest friends."

Reverend Perry nodded. "That's what Mr. Barclay thought you'd want, which is why I decided to call on you now. There's an opening on the schedule at the church tomorrow, and while I understand that is short notice, it's the only time available for the foreseeable future, unless you'd like to wait for a month or more."

"Tomorrow would be fine."

"Wonderful," Reverend Perry returned. "I'll simply need to know a bit about your parents and what you'd like me to say, and then I'll get right to work on an appropriate memorial."

"I'd be more than willing to lend some insight into Grace and Anthony Flowerdew," Gilbert's mother said with a smile. "They were two of my closest friends."

Gilbert, to Temperance's surprise, rose to his feet. "Since the next hour or so will be spent planning the memorial, I'm going to excuse myself for a bit. There's every chance that Mr. Howland was lying about not hiring on someone to try to kill me, but if he wasn't, there might be something to the notion that someone wants the Earl of Strafford dead. I think it may be wise to have my attorney send off another transatlantic telegram to the Strafford solicitor, asking his opinion on the matter."

"What do you mean, another transatlantic telegram?" Temperance asked slowly.

"Did I say another?"

"You did."

To her frustration, he didn't bother to explain. Instead, he turned on his heel and headed for the door, pausing once he reached it. "I won't be long since telegrams can't be too lengthy, although I'm sure the Strafford solicitor will be rather shocked to receive a telegram inquiring whether he knows if someone wants me dead, or . . ." Gilbert's brows drew together. "I should probably inquire whether anyone thought to investigate the death of my brother, which may actually turn out to have been under suspicious circumstances."

Sending her a last nod, he quit the room.

"I do hope he's successful in finding some answers," Miss Henrietta said, sitting forward. "It would be lovely if we could put all these nasty murder attempts behind us once and for all."

"Which will leave us all sorts of time to plan a few weddings," Mrs. Davenport added, sending Temperance a wink.

Settling back against the settee, Temperance wrinkled her nose. "If it has escaped the notice of everyone in this room, Gilbert has not broached the subject of marriage with me lately."

Miss Henrietta waved that straight aside. "He's been a bit preoccupied with trying to keep you alive. But you mark my words, once he's certain no one is still out there wishing you harm, he'll begin pursuing the topic of marriage again, and if I'm not mistaken, pursuing it with a vengeance."

"How do you know that?"

Miss Henrietta nodded to Reverend Perry. "As I'm sure the good Reverend Perry will agree, sometimes, my dear Temperance, a person simply needs to have faith."

Chapter Twenty-Eight

The next day

"And Gilbert never mentioned anything about you traveling to England with him and assuming the role of Lady Strafford, even after your life was placed in such peril yesterday?" Permilia asked, leaning across Gertrude to settle her gaze on Temperance as their carriage trundled down the road.

"Not a peep," Temperance admitted. "Although he did take my hand often yesterday as we went about one adventure after another, which I have to imagine is a promising sign."

Permilia nodded her head, which was covered by an enormous black hat, complete with a veil that she'd pushed out of the way. "It's more than promising. I've never taken Gilbert as the sort to want to hold a lady's hand, so that he did so — and often — yes, that's promising indeed."

"And," Gertrude added, shoving aside the

netting on her black hat, which wasn't nearly as large as Permilia's, "what you need to remember is this — gentlemen do not think as ladies think. Why, look at the misunderstandings Permilia and I both suffered before we finally realized Asher and Harrison loved us. They simply didn't know how to disclose their feelings in ways we could understand."

Permilia grinned. "Asher was of the belief he needed to turn into a more roguish sort to win my love, even going so far as to ask Harrison to teach him how to look dangerous."

"Harrison, loveable charmer that he is, did his very best to convince everyone he did not have time for a lady in his life. But then, when he decided he might enjoy having me around for the rest of his days, went to ridiculous lengths to woo me, although in a way I came to believe proved he'd lost his wits."

"But Gilbert hasn't done any of that, although he did broach a most curious topic regarding puppies and fey creatures, but I don't believe that counts."

Permilia rolled her eyes. "Of course it does, as does the fact that he's rescued you from the jaws of death more times than I care to remember."

"He's also abandoned his strict rule of sticking to his schedule," Gertrude added. "As well as missing appointments, numerous ones from what Harrison told me. That right there tells me the man is in love." She grinned. "Men can't seem to help making cakes of themselves when they finally realize they're in love. I believe it's because they've convinced themselves it's not manly to embrace that emotion, which leads to all sorts of shenanigans until they realize love is exactly what God wants all of us to embrace, and not merely the feminine set."

Before Temperance could badger her friends with additional questions concerning why they felt Gilbert's rescuing her or abandoning his schedule implied he was a man in the throes of what almost sounded like a romantic frame of mind, the carriage slowed to a stop in front of Grace Church. A moment later, Eugene opened the door. He'd insisted on driving her because he said he wasn't going to chance having some unknown madmen appear on the scene, even though Temperance was quite convinced attempts on her life were a thing of the past with Mr. Howland locked away.

Permilia looked at Temperance, a frown on her beautiful face. "Are you certain you're not overwhelmed by how quickly this memorial service has been pulled together?"

"It's past time I honored my parents by giving them a proper ceremony. And now that I'm no longer angry with them, I'm finally able to accept that they're no longer here, nor will I see them again until it's my time to move on from this world." Temperance sent her a small smile, then turned and took the hand Eugene was extending her way.

"You'll feel much better, Miss Temperance," he began, "after you've finally said your good-byes to your parents."

"I'm sure I will," she returned. "But before we go inside, I must thank you for providing us with such a smooth ride to the church. You didn't run over so much as a single hole in the road."

"Miss Henrietta gave me strict instructions to go easy on you." He leaned closer to her. "She's worried about you today, as is everyone."

"I'll be fine, although it is lovely to be surrounded by so many people who evidently care about me."

"Of course everyone cares about you," Eugene said roughly, helping her out of the carriage. "You're a good sort, even if you do seem to court trouble more than any lady I've ever known."

Exchanging a grin with him, she waited as Eugene went back and helped Permilia and Gertrude from the carriage. Linking arms, they walked into the church and down the long aisle, greeted as soon as they reached the front pews by Harrison, Asher, and Gilbert.

Taking the arm Gilbert held out for her, she walked with him to the very center of the first row of pews, nodding to the rest of her friends who'd already gathered in the church.

Miss Henrietta was looking regal in her black widow's weeds, and Miss Mabel, wearing an almost identical outfit, looked just as regal as she sat next to her sister. Next to Miss Mabel was Mrs. Davenport, sporting a black fitted gown she'd made herself, and sitting next to Mrs. Davenport was . . . Clementine. Her cousin nodded at Temperance, mouthed *My parents aren't here,* and smiled ever so slightly.

"Who would have ever thought my cousin would try her hand at being civil?" she whispered to Gilbert as he helped her into her chosen spot, then took the seat right next to her.

They were then joined by Asher, Permilia, Harrison, and Gertrude, and a second later, Edwina and Agent McParland took seats right behind them. Harrison's parents and his two other sisters, Adelaide and Margaret, settled into seats behind them as well.

"Ah, there's my mother and stepfather," Gilbert said, rising to his feet. "Would you like my mother to sit beside you?"

Tears stung her eyes. "As she was my mother's dearest friend, that would be lovely. Thank you."

Florence was soon sitting on one side of her with Gilbert on the other, and Temperance felt as if she'd finally found the sense of family she'd been missing for so long. She bowed her head and said a simple prayer of thanks.

It had been far too long since she'd felt any sense of true peace while she'd been in a church, but today, surrounded by friends who'd become so much more to her, peace came easily.

Looking up, she turned her attention to the front of the chapel, enjoying the hymn the choir had begun to sing.

After the hymn, Reverend Perry stepped forward and began the service with a prayer, one that spoke of hope, faith, and love. He then began his eulogy, including stories of Anthony and Grace Flowerdew that could have only come from Florence.

Glancing to Gilbert's mother, she found

Florence wiping her eyes with a handkerchief, and Temperance finally understood that she'd not been the only one to suffer from the loss of her parents. They'd had friends, good friends, who obviously missed them and mourned for them. Now she was finally mourning the loss of her parents as well, the way she should have three years before.

As Reverend Perry finished, he gave her a nod, and Temperance rose to her feet and moved to the front of the chapel, not saying a word as she accepted the violin Reverend Perry handed her.

Turning to face her friends, she drew in a breath. "My mother loved to listen to me play the violin, even though it was not an instrument society thought was appropriate for girls or women to play. Today, though, is all about my parents, so I thought it would be nice to dedicate a special song to them, played on my mother's favorite instrument. This is a piece from Beethoven — Violin Sonata No. 9, also known as Kreutzer Sonata. I won't play the piece in its entirety because it's quite long, so I've chosen the third movement because my mother found it inspiring."

Positioning the violin under her chin, she closed her eyes, then waited for the music to begin to form in her mind. Opening her eyes, she lifted her gaze to the ceiling. "This is for you, Mama."

Pulling the bow across the strings, she lost herself in the music, playing every note as if her mother could hear her, telling her mother and father with song exactly how sorry she was that she'd been angry with them for so long.

That anger had stolen the wonderful times she'd shared with her parents, the memories of those times only now beginning to flood back into her thoughts.

Her mother had been the one to encourage her to always abandon her shoes when she was in the sand — and not because it was practical but because sand felt marvelous on a girl's feet.

Her father had been the one to hand her a paintbrush for the very first time and had taken her to the ocean to paint her first ocean scene, proclaiming himself unsurprised when she'd painted an ocean that looked like an ocean, complete with the sun's reflection on the water and clouds that looked like they were drifting through the sky.

They'd been so proud of her, and . . . they'd wanted her to share her gifts with the world because she'd been given such special gifts.

She'd never realized they'd only wanted the world to experience the music she was capable of producing, but instead she'd resented them for pushing her in front of audiences.

She could only hope that her parents were watching her and that they knew this was her way of saying she was sorry.

As she played the last note, and with her cheeks wet with tears, she lowered the violin right before Gilbert reached her side and pulled her into his arms.

"Your parents would have loved that," he said, easing her just a bit away from him to look into her eyes. "And they would be so proud of the lady you've become."

"Of course we're proud of her, but I'm afraid this memorial service may be a touch premature because we're alive and well, although it did take us forever to get out of that jungle."

For a moment, Temperance thought she'd imagined that voice, until she stepped out of Gilbert's embrace, lifted her head, and found her mother and father, looking almost the same as they'd looked the last time she'd seen them, except thinner, standing in the aisle a few pews away, beaming smiles at her.

Before she could move so much as a single muscle, everything in front of her eyes began to spin, and then as her legs gave out, she began to fall.

Chapter Twenty-Nine

As the minutes ticked away and Temperance did not come around, even with Mrs. Davenport waving smelling salts she'd pulled from her reticule under Temperance's nose, Gilbert was finding it difficult to hold his panic at bay.

Temperance was not the type of lady to faint. She'd never, to his knowledge, fainted before, not even when faced with an abduction, more than a few attempts on her life, or allowing Miss Henrietta to drive her at breakneck speeds through the streets of New York City.

"Gilbert, come sit with her," Grace Flowerdew said, rising from her daughter's side and motioning Gilbert forward. "I need to rewet this rag."

Taking Grace's seat beside Temperance, he smoothed a hand over her forehead, willing her to open her eyes.

"You do realize you're dipping that in the

baptismal water, don't you?" he heard Miss Henrietta say.

"If that doesn't bring her around," Mrs. Davenport said, speaking up, "I don't know what will. I've never had my special smelling salt concoction fail me before, but she didn't so much as twitch when I held it under her nose."

"You used your *own* recipe for smelling salts on me?"

Relief flowed freely when Temperance's eyes fluttered opened, and she settled her green gaze on him and smiled.

It was a lovely smile, one that suggested she was glad to find him with her, and it left him reeling as he realized he could never abandon Temperance — not even if it meant he had to go to unusual lengths to figure out how to abdicate his role as the Earl of Strafford.

"I must have picked up a fever from that dip we took in the ocean yesterday, because I had the most peculiar hallucination," she whispered. "I thought my parents strolled down the aisle right after I finished playing the violin. It was a lovely hallucination, even though I'm incredibly sad that's all it was."

"You're not suffering from a fever," he said as a single tear rolled down her cheek. Catching it with a finger, he leaned forward, placed a kiss on her forehead, then placed his mouth right next to her ear. "Your parents really *are* here."

"You must be suffering from a fever as well. People don't come back from the dead."

"We were never dead," Grace said, hurrying up to rejoin them, the rag she was clutching dripping water on the floor.

As Gilbert moved aside, Grace took his spot and plunked the rag right over Temperance's face, then stilled, as if she didn't quite know what she was doing or what she should do next.

"I'm having a difficult time breathing," Temperance rasped.

Whipping the rag right off again, Grace tossed it aside before she gathered Temperance into her arms, holding her as if she'd never let go.

"My darling, darling girl. I'm so sorry we left you for so long."

"I don't understand," Temperance whispered. "How can you be here?"

"It was not without difficulty," her father said, moving to join his wife and daughter. "We were abandoned in the wilds of South America and left there to die."

"We were so gullible," Grace continued. "Did not have the slightest idea the two men who accompanied us off the ship, claiming they wanted to see some ruins, had murder on their minds."

"We figured that out rather quickly, though, when they held us at knifepoint after we got out of view of the ship and tied us up," Anthony said. "The only reason they didn't go through with the murder was because Richard the Snake seemed to have slight misgivings about murdering two people who'd spent a great deal of their time while onboard the ship assisting all the members of the crew and passengers who'd eaten a bad batch of fish." He shuddered. "That was not a pleasant experience for anyone involved."

"His misgivings didn't go so far, though, as to abandon *all* attempts to do us in," Grace added with a roll of her eyes. "They did leave us there to die, tying us up and stuffing rags in our mouths to muffle our yells before they ran out of the jungle, screaming there were wild savages on the loose, intent on killing everyone onboard the ship."

Anthony took a step closer to Temperance. "It was such a farfetched notion that Grace and I were certain someone would come and investigate, but no one did. By the time we were able to escape our bindings, the ship was gone and we'd been abandoned in a jungle in South America."

"That was three years ago," Temperance pointed out right before her father took her mother's place, gathered his daughter up into his arms, and hugged her tight.

"Do you have any idea how difficult it is to navigate through a jungle with no supplies, no money, and nothing to bargain with?" Anthony asked, pulling a little away from Temperance, but only to smooth her hair out of her face.

Gilbert tilted his head. "How did you do it?"

"We ran across some indigenous people, none of whom could understand us, nor could we understand them. However, they were a peaceful people and took us in, fed us, and allowed us to stay with them. We were there for at least a year, and by the time a tribe of nomads came through the area who were willing to allow us to travel with them, we could speak a little of their language, and they could understand some of ours."

"They were fascinated by the idea we only serve one God, and some of them even asked us to teach them more about our faith," Grace said. "That kept our hope alive, and we came to believe that our encountering these people might have been God's plan all along, although we would have preferred not being away from you for so long, Temperance."

"We finally reached a remote port as we traveled with the nomads, and we begged passage in exchange for work from a captain who took pity on us. We traveled north, reaching another port, and then we searched for a way to travel onward, taking on unusual jobs along the way to survive," Anthony said.

Grace smiled. "We reached Florida two weeks ago and sought out friends of ours who were amazed to discover us on their doorsteps." She frowned. "We sent off a telegram to you, even knowing that wasn't exactly the way we wanted to inform you we weren't dead. But then the thought struck that there was a good chance you wouldn't have wanted to live in the family house in Connecticut by yourself, not when it was so large."

"That's why we decided to seek out Mr. Howland, my solicitor, when the ship we were on stopped here in New York, hoping he'd know where to find you," Anthony said. "Unfortunately, when we arrived at his office, we were told by his secretary that Mr. Howland was not available, and then she mentioned something about The New York Lunatic Asylum, but wouldn't expand on that when I pressed her. She did, however, tell us we could find you at Miss Snook's School for the Education of the Feminine Mind. We were then told by the man who opened the door at that school, after he questioned us rather relentlessly regarding why we wanted to find you, that you were here at Grace Church."

Temperance blew out a breath. "Mr. Howland's secretary probably didn't know how to explain to you that the man who'd been her employer wasn't the man he portrayed himself to be, but was a man who couldn't be trusted."

As Temperance launched into the story of John Howland and everything he'd put her through, Gilbert walked over to join Reverend Perry, who was watching Temperance with a smile on his face.

"Is this where you tell me God moves in mysterious ways, or something to that effect?" Gilbert asked.

Reverend Perry's eyes twinkled. "I have no idea what God was thinking with this one, Gilbert. But it's not my place to question. I simply accept the results, and what we're witnessing now, my dear friend, are wonderful results."

"Temperance has gotten her family back."

"Indeed, although she's surrounded herself with people who've become her family, just not of the blood-related type." He nodded to Temperance. "Have you decided what you're going to do about her?"

"I have."

"But you're not going to tell me, are you?"

"I think I should tell her first."

"Do know that I'll need a bit of notice in order to officiate at your wedding. We seem to be having quite the demand for weddings held here at the church these days." With that, Reverend Perry excused himself, walking over to Temperance to take hold of her hand. He said a brief word of prayer, made his excuses to them, then turned to where everyone was gathered in one section of the pews, all of them seemingly unwilling to leave Temperance until they were certain she was all right.

"Could I interest any of you in a nice cup of tea, or perhaps coffee?"

"I'll help you make it," Miss Mabel said, and with Miss Henrietta and Mrs. Davenport following her, she walked out of the sanctuary and through a door past the pulpit.

"I need to introduce you to my friends," Temperance said, pushing herself up from the pew she'd been sitting on, wobbling on her feet for a second.

"You need to sit down," Grace said, turning to Gilbert and nodding. "Come sit with her again, Gilbert. Anthony and I will introduce ourselves to her friends." She took Anthony's arm and moved away.

"Since I'm not actually a friend," Clementine began, walking over to Temperance, "and since I admitted to cousin Anthony while you were in your senseless state that you and I suffered from a less-than-amiable relationship over the years, I think I'll be taking my leave." Clementine shook her head. "Your father is certain to inquire further about my family, and after he learns the details of your stay with us, well, I'm not sure I'm quite ready to deal with that just yet."

"You'll do no such thing, Clementine," Temperance said. "It's past time you and I mend our bridges for good, so come sit down by Gilbert and me."

Gilbert waited until Clementine took her seat, then sat down, content to simply watch his friends as they went about greeting Anthony and Grace. Temperance and Clementine began to talk about how Clementine's life was unfolding under the watchful eye of Mrs. Boggart Hobbes, the obvious disgruntlement in Clementine's tone suggesting she was not finding life with her Aunt Minnie very pleasant.

"Temperance, darling," Grace suddenly called. "Your friend Permilia has just asked me where your father and I are intending to live. I've just realized we have no home since Mr. Howland apparently sold our house in Connecticut."

"I told her she should move to New York because this is where you live," Permilia said.

Temperance shot Gilbert a look, seemed to be waiting for him to say something, then released the smallest of sighs. "You *should* buy a house in New York, Mother, although I do need to tell you that I adore living at Miss Snook's School for the Education of the Feminine Mind. I hope you won't be too disappointed if I decide to continue living and teaching there."

Harrison, with Asher by his side, suddenly strode down the aisle, stopping directly in front of Gilbert. "If you'll excuse us for a moment, Temperance, Asher and I need to have a word with our friend."

Before he could protest, Gilbert found himself hauled to his feet and tugged across the front of the church.

"Why are you hesitating?" Harrison asked,

lowering his voice to a whisper and stopping directly underneath a stained-glass window. "This is a prime opportunity to declare your intentions once and for all. But whatever you do, do not mess it up."

Gilbert glanced around the church, then shook his head. "Absolutely not. I've planned out a special moment for Temperance, and this" — he gestured around — "is not it. Besides, I don't have my romantic gesture with me now, one I put quite a bit of thought into."

"Don't be an idiot," Asher said, moving right up next to Gilbert as he crossed his arms over his chest. "If you don't act now, I fear you may lose any chance of winning Temperance's hand in marriage once and for all." He sent Gilbert a rather pitying look. "Is it really worth losing the love of your life simply because you're unwilling to stray from whatever plan you've created, one I'm sure comes with many lists and graphs?"

"I did not make a graph, although I might have made up a list," Gilbert admitted. "But if both of you believe I'm making a muddle of everything by not speaking up right this very moment, fine, I'll give it a go." He narrowed his eyes on his friends. "But it'll be on your heads if this goes badly."

"It'll be fine," Harrison assured him.

"Just tell her you love her," Asher added.

Gilbert frowned and glanced at all the people assembled in the chapel. "I'm not certain I'm comfortable declaring my love for her in front of everyone. I was hoping to do that in a more intimate setting, one where it would only be the two of us."

"She'll view your declaration of love in front of everyone as a grand romantic gesture," Asher said before he gave Gilbert a bit of a push in Temperance's direction. "Best to get it over with quickly, though. It'll be easier that way."

"Quickly was not a part of my plan either," Gilbert muttered, but because everyone was now watching him since he'd been pushed in a slightly forceful manner and was headed in Temperance's direction, he squared his shoulders and continued forward.

Stopping in front of where she was still sitting on a pew, he summoned up a smile, ignored that Clementine seemed to be giving him an encouraging nod, and leaned over to take Temperance's hand.

"Before you decide you're going to remain living at Miss Snook's school forever, I have a few matters I'd like to broach."

"You're going to ask me to become your countess again?" Temperance asked, her eyes alight with something that almost seemed like anticipation.

"Well, no."

Murmurs sounded around the chapel as Temperance yanked her hand back, right as Gilbert realized he'd already made a blunder of matters, which just went to prove he was less than effective with spur-of-the-moment decisions.

He cleared his throat and tried again.

"That didn't come out the way I intended," he began. "And in all honesty, I had begun to compose a special speech regarding what I want to say to you, Temperance. However, I wasn't planning on using that speech today, which is why my notes for what I wanted to say to you are at my house, in the top drawer of my desk, and . . ."

"We don't need a detailed description of where you've left your notes, dear," he heard his mother call. "Just embrace the spontaneity of the moment. You'll do fine."

Gilbert quirked a brow in the direction of his mother. "You've never been spontaneous in your life."

His mother, annoyingly enough, smiled. "I fled from England, abandoned my title of Dowager Countess, and hopped on a ship with you as an infant in the dead of night in order to make a most spectacular escape from what I thought was a life of boredom and far too many rules. That, my dear, was certainly a spontaneous act if there ever was one."

"I don't believe pointing out to Temperance how boring you found your life as a countess is exactly going to convince her she'd enjoy it."

"Ah, so you are going to ask her to become you countess?" Miss Henrietta called.

Gilbert paused, realizing that he wasn't intending to do anything of the sort, but had become completely rattled and had forgotten his plan.

He looked back at Temperance, who was scowling back at him, an entire storm now brewing in her eyes. The sight of those eyes, and the storm clouds that were often present in them, had him smiling, an obvious mistake considering she took one look at him, jumped to her feet, and began stomping her way through the church toward the door.

"Perhaps we shouldn't have pushed you to declare yourself," Asher said, moving beside him. "This has got to be the worst declaration of affections I've ever seen."

"That's helpful," Gilbert muttered before he began striding after Temperance. "Temperance, wait," he called, not encouraged when she increased her stomping.

"May I suggest breaking into a run?" Mrs. Davenport all but yelled. "She's remarkably fast when she sets her mind to it, and it does seem as if her mind is set to get away from you."

Breaking into a sprint because he thought Mrs. Davenport had just made a most excellent point, he swallowed an unexpected laugh when Temperance increased her pace, a remarkable feat considering she'd only recently suffered a fainting spell.

"You're being incredibly annoying," he called, his words having her stopping her in her tracks, spinning around, and marching back to him.

"I'm annoying?" she demanded once she stopped a few feet from him. "You're the one who kept insisting we have to get married."

"And you kept insisting we'd kill each other within weeks of exchanging vows."

"I don't believe you're going in the right direction with your responses," his mother called from behind him.

He pretended he hadn't heard her.

Temperance drew in a breath, let it out in one *whoosh,* then nodded, just once. "I did say exactly that, and because I am currently feeling a distinct urge to strangle you, I doubt I'm far off the mark." With that, she turned on her heel and practically sprinted down the aisle again, disappearing through the door of the church a few seconds later.

"Go after her," someone called.

Realizing he was out of his depth, he turned around. "And what should I do if I catch up with her?"

"Kiss her," Permilia and Gertrude called together.

"I suppose that couldn't hurt." He turned, strode down the aisle, and headed out the door.

Stopping for a second when he reached the sidewalk, he looked to the left, finding only two gentlemen walking toward him with another gentleman walking behind them. Turning to the right, he smiled when he saw Temperance's black hat bobbing rapidly away.

Gilbert broke into a run, passed a Pinkerton man who'd already begun to follow her, and *almost* caught up with Temperance until she significantly increased her pace, lending credence to Mrs. Davenport's observation regarding how fast Temperance could move.

"You're going to end up fainting again if you keep this up," he managed to yell, ignoring the fact that he sounded somewhat winded.

She put more distance between them.

"That corset you're wearing wasn't meant to allow strenuous activities" was all he could think to yell next.

She stopped and spun around so quickly that he was forced to dodge to the right to avoid plowing into her.

"What do you know about corsets?"

Dragging in a much-needed breath of air, and amazed that Temperance was barely out of breath, he summoned up a smile, one that did absolutely nothing to dispel the temper in her eyes. "Asher's one of my best friends and owns an entire department store. He's incredibly knowledgeable with matters pertaining to unmentionables, and we gentlemen do occasionally drift into talk about all those mysterious feminine garments."

"You, Asher, and I presume, Harrison, sit around talking about unmentionables?"

He nodded. "We also talk about romantic gestures."

"You've apparently not picked up many pointers about those."

"Apparently not, but you know me, Temperance. You know I'm lacking when it comes to matters of the emotional sort. That right there is what has me confused about why you're so irritated with me for stumbling earlier."

She crossed her arms over her chest. "If I had any idea why you were stumbling about, perhaps I wouldn't be so irritated. As it stands now, all I know is that you apparently have no interest in me becoming Lady Strafford, which does seem to suggest, since you're Lord Strafford, that you've decided I've been right all this time and that we would not suit."

"If you're so certain we won't suit, why are you so put out about me not wanting you to become Lady Strafford?"

"So you *don't* want me to become Lady Strafford, do you?"

"Only because I've taken steps to investigate how I can go about abdicating my title and repudiating my inheritance. But since I've yet to receive a reply to the transatlantic telegram cable my attorney and I sent off the other day, I was hesitant to broach the subject until I had real news to report. However, I have great hopes my late brother's attorney will be able to sort matters out to my satisfaction. And if that comes to pass, I'll no longer be Lord Strafford, which means you'll no longer have to worry about becoming a countess because that won't be an issue."

Temperance simply stared at him for the longest of seconds until she cleared her throat, a hint of a smile lifting her lips the tiniest touch. "I imagine you weren't intending on telling me that in quite such a thunderous tone of voice, were you, and . . . with a touch of temper in it, if I'm not mistaken."

Gilbert raked a hand through his hair as his lips began to curve. "In all honesty, I was intending on telling you everything during a lovely fall picnic I was planning to take you on, one that would have included a lovely round of target practice where you'd be practicing with your very own gun."

"You bought me a pistol?"

"Well, no, not yet. That's on my list of things I was supposed to do tomorrow, along with finalizing plans to buy a puppy and finding someone to make a dragon costume."

Temperance blinked. "You were going to dress up as a dragon, present me with my very own pistol and a puppy, and then disclose that you were trying to abdicate your title as Earl of Strafford."

"*I* wasn't going to dress up as a dragon. I wanted to dress the puppy up as a dragon."

"Should I ask why?"

"I'm sure the reason why is certain to sound somewhat ridiculous." He took one step closer to her. "You see, Harrison pointed out to me that you were a whimsical sort who apparently would think fondly of puppies and dragons, or more specifically, fey creatures as I do believe I brought up not that long ago. I'm afraid I never got around to explaining why I was bringing up such a curious topic."

"I thought you were suffering from a blow to your head."

He smiled. "Yes, I know. However, the romantic gestures Asher and Harrison used to impress Permilia and Gertrude were so outlandish they made those two fine gentlemen seem as if they'd lost their minds too. But because matters worked out well for them in the end, and they secured the ladies they wanted to spend the rest of their lives with, I thought it couldn't hurt to give a go at my own version of a romantic gesture."

"And that's why you brought up fey creatures, puppies, and target practice while we were at the beach?"

"I thought for certain I was on to something with the target practice, but then, well, I got distracted when Mr. Howland showed up, and . . . I never got to complete a single romantic gesture." He caught her eye. "I'm beginning to think romantic gestures, or any type of romance, are not going to be my strong suit."

Temperance moved a little closer to him. "I'm afraid I must disagree with that assessment. Trying to make arrangements to provide me with a puppy — if I'm following what you intended to do — and then dressing that puppy up as a dragon — although I'm still not certain why you and Harrison decided I'm a dragon type of lady — is a spectacular gesture, and one I certainly think qualifies as romantic."

"You're a dragon type because you had a castle your father's butler built you when you were a child. And while this explanation is only coming to me now, I'm sure when you played in that castle, besides having me rescue you all the time, you occasionally dreamed a dragon would show up."

"I suppose I did, which definitely makes your puppy dressed as a dragon a romantic gesture of impressive proportions."

Gilbert inclined his head. "Thank you, although I do want to point out that I did announce to you that I'm trying to give up an earldom, along with several *real* castles, a London townhome, and a country estate in Wales. It's curious, don't you think, that you would consider the puppy dressed as a dragon as a romantic gesture of impressive proportions over my decision to abdicate my title and my attempt to relinquish my late brother's estates to some relative I'm not sure actually exists just yet."

Temperance moved another few inches toward him. "Giving up your title, as well as your inheritance, is far too grand to be considered a romantic gesture. It's more on the lines of professing a deep and abiding —"

Before Temperance could finish, a man suddenly stepped directly up to them, standing far too close for comfort. As Gilbert instinctively reached for his pistol, his hand stilled when the man surprised him by presenting him with a bow.

"I'm delighted to hear you say that, Gilbert, because that proves to me without a shadow of a doubt that you are *not* the person responsible for trying to murder me."

Feeling quite as if he'd entered the pages of a mystery novel, Gilbert squinted and settled his attention on the man who'd just spoken in a clipped British accent — a gentleman who was supposed to be quite dead. His brother, Charles — the true Earl of Strafford.

Chapter Thirty

As Gilbert and the gentleman who'd just joined them stood in the middle of the sidewalk staring at each other, Temperance cleared her throat, but was stopped from speaking when they were suddenly surrounded by Pinkerton agents.

"Is there a problem here?" a burly agent with his cap tipped back on his head asked, his hand on the butt of a pistol that was visible beneath his open jacket.

"I'm not a problem," the man drawled with a lift of a chin that looked remarkably like Gilbert's. "I'm his brother, the Earl of Strafford, so step back, if you please."

"What about those two men?" the agent asked, not moving an inch as he nodded to two other men who were standing behind Gilbert's brother, a man who apparently wasn't as dead as expected.

"That's Lord Grantley and Lord Abinger, and I'll thank you to stop looking us over as if we're common criminals," Lord Strafford said before he dismissed the Pinkerton man with a flick of a wrist and returned his attention to Gilbert. "I imagine you're surprised to see me."

"A bit," Gilbert admitted. "Although since we've just encountered two people who were also presumed dead but are very much alive, I'm not as surprised as one would expect given the unusual day I'm having so far."

"Who else came back from the dead?" Lord Strafford asked.

Gilbert nodded to Temperance. "Her parents, Mr. and Mrs. Anthony Flowerdew, were presumed murdered by savages down in South America three years ago. I'm happy to report that was not the case since they recently showed up, during their memorial service no less, and turned that service into a more joyous occasion."

"Flowerdew, Flowerdew," Lord Strafford said, tapping a finger against his chin. "Why is that name so familiar?"

"Temperance and I have been friends since infancy," Gilbert said. "I'm sure I must have mentioned her during the few visits you and I enjoyed."

Lord Strafford eyed Temperance up and down, then nodded, quite as if he were bestowing his approval on her. "I do recall you mentioning Miss Flowerdew a time or two. However . . ." He stepped toward Temperance and presented her with a bow. "My brother has apparently misplaced his manners, a fault I'm sure he acquired through living in a less-than-civilized world all these years. Charles Cavendish, Earl of Strafford, at your service."

Temperance dipped into a curtsy she'd practiced for years while she attended finishing school, which earned a quirk of a brow from the earl in response. Straightening, she smiled, then shot Gilbert a look that had him moving forward.

"This is Miss Temperance Flowerdew, Charles."

Inclining her head, Temperance smiled. "You must not find fault with Gilbert misplacing his manners, Lord Strafford. I fear the shock of finding you alive has most likely rendered him a little scattered. You are his brother, after all, and I imagine his emotions are going every which way at the moment, trying to reconcile with the idea you're not dead."

"We Cavendish gentlemen are not prone to wearing our emotions on our sleeves," Charles drawled. "Nor are we prone to experiencing emotions of the affectionate sort often." He nodded to his brother. "I imagine you barely grieved my death."

Gilbert frowned. "That's not true. I was very troubled when I heard the news you'd suffered a boating accident. And" — he continued even as Charles opened his mouth — "if you hadn't interrupted my conversation with Temperance, you would have heard me tell her next that I was going to travel to England to pay my respects to you. You are my brother, albeit a half one, and I do hold you in high esteem."

"I always thought you loathed me and were envious that I inherited the title and all of Father's estates."

"Which does explain how you concluded I wanted to see you murdered."

Before Charles could expand on why he'd thought that, Miss Henrietta suddenly moved into view, waving cheerfully in their direction, followed by everyone else.

"Do tell us he kissed you, Temperance."

Mrs. Davenport waved next. "And that he gave you the ring I gave him to give you."

"Did he get down on one knee?" Clementine called.

"On my word, that man beside Gilbert looks exactly like Charles Cavendish, my late husband's son. What an uncanny resemblance," Florence said as she began walking closer, stopping in her tracks a second later. "Good heavens, it is you, Charles, but . . . how extraordinary. It's not every day one gets to witness three people return from the grave."

"That does seem to be the consensus," Charles said before he presented Florence with a bow. "You're looking well, Florence."

"As are you, Charles, quite a bit more alive than I was expecting, but let us not continue this discussion out on the sidewalk. Reverend Perry just gently reminded us that Grace Church does have a service shortly, so . . . shall we repair to Gilbert's house?"

Charles's brows drew together as he glanced at the crowd now assembled only feet away from him. "I do not believe I'll be comfortable disclosing the unfortunate events I've experienced of late with so many people listening."

"We'll return to the school," Miss Henrietta said before she sidled up to Temperance. "I'll take your parents back there, get them settled in one of the few bedchambers we still have available, and" — she gave Temperance's arm a squeeze — "I'll start to fill them in on everything you've been up to since they've been gone. That will allow them time to adjust to the idea their darling girl ended up as a poor relation."

Even though Temperance was reluctant to be parted from her parents for any length of time, she realized Miss Henrietta made a most excellent point. Her parents were not going to enjoy hearing about the trials their daughter had suffered, but if she wasn't there when they heard the gory details, they'd be better able to process everything.

"Clementine," Miss Henrietta continued, "has, surprisingly enough, decided she wants to disclose all the unpleasant details of your time with her family to your parents. I'm of the opinion we should let her."

Temperance raised a hand to her throat. "I have no idea what's gotten into her. Divulging those unpleasant details will not endear her to my parents since her behavior toward me over the time I lived with her does not show her in a favorable light."

"But it's a light she needs to accept if she's ever going to reach the potential I know she's capable of — becoming a decent lady, not an awful one." With that, Miss Henrietta patted Temperance's cheek and moved away, organizing everyone into carriages in no time at all.

"Don't forget the ring," Mrs. Davenport called as her carriage bolted past, driven, concerningly enough, by a smiling Miss

Henrietta. Mr. Barclay sat beside her with his eyes closed, obviously mouthing one of his silent prayers.

Shaking her head at that somewhat amusing sight, she took the arm Gilbert was extending her and smiled. "It's a very peculiar day, although oddly enough, I'm finding I can't help but wonder what curious event is waiting for us next."

"I'm sure whatever my brother has to disclose is going to be of a curious nature. And, well, there's always the curious state of the house I'm residing in on Fifth Avenue. It's not remotely finished yet, but I am interested to hear what you think about the progress that's been made so far." He led her over to where Eugene was holding open the door to Gilbert's carriage.

Leaning closer to her, Eugene lowered his voice. "I'm coming with you, Miss Temperance." He shot a look to Gilbert's brother, who was climbing into a black carriage, his two friends immediately after him. "He seems to be a shifty sort, but ain't no need to fret." He tapped his stomach. "I'm armed and on high alert."

"Since that shifty sort is my brother, I'm going to urge you to keep your knives hidden since I don't believe Charles will take kindly to being held at knifepoint," Gilbert said, helping Temperance into the carriage and then following her.

Eugene sent Temperance a look that clearly suggested he thought there was little hope he wouldn't be pulling out his knife at some point, then shut the door, leaving Temperance all alone with Gilbert. The carriage rocked as Eugene took his place beside Gilbert's driver, and a second later, they were off.

"It's rather odd that I've never been invited to see your house before. I only know that it's located somewhere on Fifth Avenue," Temperance said, her pulse picking up when Gilbert took hold of her hand and brought it almost absently to his lips.

Giving her fingers a quick kiss, he smiled. "Beside the fact that such an invitation would break about a hundred rules of propriety since I've been living in that house as a bachelor, I haven't invited you over because the house is barely habitable. Construction is occurring in almost every room except the library, and there are numerous scaffolds scattered about." He sent her a rather significant look. "Since we've been experiencing enough dangerous situations of late, the last thing I wanted to do was put you in the path of temptation, knowing how much you seem to enjoy perilous heights."

Realizing it was not going to benefit her in the least to argue with that statement considering it was nothing less than the truth, Temperance settled for sending Gilbert a smile, spending the time it took to travel the length of Broadway discussing the startling events that had just transpired.

"I get the distinct feeling your parents are not going to travel as much as they have in the past," Gilbert remarked as they drove past Miss Snook's School for the Education of the Feminine Mind, waving through the window to Miss Henrietta, who'd already pulled her carriage right up in front of the school. Her parents bounded out of the open carriage a second later, looking remarkably windblown but not looking at all concerned that they'd probably experienced an unforgettable ride down Broadway.

"I imagine your parents will stay in the city for the foreseeable future as well," Temperance said, turning back to Gilbert after they turned off Broadway and Miss Snook's school disappeared from sight. "They always enjoyed such a great friendship with my parents, which I imagine they're eager to resume."

"Our parents' relationship reminds me of the ones we share with our friends, something I came to realize I wasn't prepared to abandon."

"That wasn't the only reason, though, was it, that you were investigating ways to abdicate your title — a problem that has been miraculously solved with the return of your brother to the living?"

"Of course not, but I'm not going to get into my main reason until we get everything straightened away. Then you and I will find a nice quiet place, and then . . . well, you'll simply have to wait and see."

"You're being annoying again."

"Oh look, we're on Fifth Avenue, and almost to my house."

As the carriage began to slow a short time later, Temperance's annoyance disappeared when the carriage stopped in front of a house that was obviously still under construction, but clearly fashioned along the same lines as the mansion Mrs. Vanderbilt had created a few blocks away.

With anticipation humming through her, she was out on the sidewalk a moment after Eugene opened the door, her gaze running over a structure that could only be described as whimsical. Turning to Gilbert, she grinned.

"This isn't anything I would have expected you to build."

Gilbert returned the grin. "I know, but after consulting with Mr. Richard Hunt, the architect Alva Vanderbilt used for her lovely mansion, I felt a distinct urge to use a most unconventional design, one I've come to believe I chose, even if subconsciously, with you in mind."

Even the mere act of breathing turned difficult. But before Temperance could summon up a single word in response to what truly was a most telling statement, Gilbert stepped directly up next to her, put his hands on either side of her face, and then . . . he kissed her.

It wasn't a kiss remotely similar to the one, or perhaps two, she'd given him, but a real kiss, filled with tenderness, strength, and something more, something intriguing.

"And this is yet another example of what happens when a person is raised in a country that is barely civilized. If you'd been raised properly in England, Gilbert, you'd understand that we British frown on kissing in public, finding it quite beyond the pale."

"I see your brother shares your ability to be annoying," Temperance muttered as Gilbert eased away from her and grinned.

"I'm afraid so, and on that note, before he turns more contrary than ever, let us remove ourselves into the house, and . . . look, my parents have arrived."

Pretending she didn't notice that Florence and William were beaming at her, which suggested they'd just witnessed their son kissing her, Temperance took hold of Gilbert's arm, pleased when knees that had gone distinctly weak steadied. Walking with him up the sidewalk that led to the front door, they were followed by his brother and his two friends, with Florence and William bringing up the rear.

"Have you not been able to find yourself a decent butler yet?" Charles asked when the front door remained closed after they reached it.

"I have a very competent butler, as well as a proficient underbutler. And my valet, Tobias, as you might recall, was an excellent underbutler in your house before that wife of yours tossed him out on the streets." Gilbert frowned. "But speaking of Lady Strafford, should I assume she's aware that you're not dead?"

Charles gave a flick of a lace-covered wrist. "I haven't gotten around to telling her I'm alive just yet. But don't look so alarmed. I'm sure I'll get around to returning home in the next few weeks, where I'll then enjoy a most charming reunion with my shrew of a wife."

"Why do you expect it to be a charming reunion if you consider your wife to be a shrew?" Temperance couldn't resist asking.

For a second, she didn't think Charles was going to respond, but then he shrugged. "Even though I'm quite certain Alice has been enjoying the idea that I, her much older and greatly detested husband, is supposedly dead, I know she doesn't relish the idea of taking on the role of Dowager Countess. She's also probably dreading the day Gilbert shows up in England to take over the role of Earl of Strafford, which will see her position within London society diminished. That being said, when I do eventually show up alive and quite well, I have to imagine she'll smile prettily at me, welcome me back amongst the living, and then we'll go our separate ways again five minutes after we've been reunited."

"While that is a most touching scene you've just painted for us, Lord Strafford," began Lord Grantley, or at least Temperance thought that was his name, "if you haven't noticed, the wind has become somewhat brisk. I would hate to take a chill and suffer from a cold once we finally get on our way back to our beloved England."

"When I was in England, it was raining all the time and far chillier than it is here,"

Temperance pointed out, earning a look that suggested Lord Grantley found her vastly unpleasant, right before he turned his head from her as if she were now beneath his notice.

"And that right there is why I balked at becoming a countess," she said cheerfully as Gilbert flashed her a smile before he moved to the door, opening it himself.

"I imagine another catastrophe has happened with the building crew, which explains why no one is manning the door," he said ushering everyone inside.

Once they moved into the cavernous entranceway, Temperance found her feet simply wouldn't move as her gaze darted around.

Her attention settled on a curved staircase, one that split in two before it reached the second floor, that second floor sporting a railed galley, although pieces of that railing were missing. She tilted her head back and scanned a high ceiling that had yet to be completely plastered, which exactly explained why a scaffold had been left in the very center of the entranceway.

"I imagine that ceiling would look stunning with a fresco painted on it," she said, turning to Gilbert and raising an expectant brow.

"That's a matter we'll debate at a later date," Gilbert said, frowning as he looked around. "Seems a bit quiet, which is curious, especially since . . ." His voice trailed off as Tobias suddenly dashed into the room, looking the worse for wear with a bloodied lip, mussed hair, and . . . a motley-looking dog scampering next him, and one that seemed to have some type of horn tied with a red bow around his head.

"Do not tell me that mongrel is your idea of a cute puppy," Gilbert said right before the mongrel in question let out an excited yip and made a beeline, not for Gilbert, but for Temperance.

The next second, she was knocked to the ground while the beast tried to lick her to death, the cone attached to his head doing its very best to poke her eye out.

"I knew they would take to each other," Tobias said. "But, sir, we've got a situation in what barely passes for the drawing room. You'd best come see, and . . ." He stopped talking as his gaze settled on Gilbert's brother. "Lord Strafford, you're not dead."

Charles inclined his head. "Good afternoon, Tobias. I see America has already turned you less civilized."

Pushing herself to a sitting position while the large dog of what could only be described as questionable breeding plopped down on its haunches right beside her, Temperance watched as Tobias raked a hand through his hair and shook his head.

"Begging your pardon, Lord Strafford, and . . ." He stopped talking again. "Lord Grantley, Lord Abinger, it's nice to . . ." His sentence faded away. "How long have you been in New York?"

"We've been here about a week," Lord Grantley admitted, looking rather taken aback that a man who'd once been Lord Strafford's underbutler was addressing him so familiarly.

"It's been you and Lord Abinger I've been seeing around town," Tobias said with a shake of his head. "I thought I was losing my wits, but I really was seeing people I'd seen before. Imagine that, but . . . I don't think I took note of you, Lord Strafford."

"I stayed back at the hotel in our rented suite of rooms while my friends traveled around the city, trying to decipher what Gilbert was up to."

Tobias's brows drew together. "And I'm sure you have a reason for doing that, my lord, but an explanation will have to wait until we get matters settled here." He turned to Gilbert. "You'd best follow me, sir, although" — he jerked a head in Lord

Strafford's direction — "you'd best come as well, Lord Strafford, because the concerning situation transpiring in this very house does involve you, albeit indirectly."

Taking the hand Gilbert held out to her, Temperance struggled to her feet, tugging the folds of her skirt out of the dog's mouth before stumbling ever so slightly when the dog then began nudging her with the cone still tied around its head.

"That was not remotely what I had in mind when I asked Tobias to find you a puppy," he said, his attention on the dog that was now trying to divest itself of the cone by shaking his head back and forth.

"He's adorable, and I'm already in love with him," Temperance said, bending over to untie the bow that was holding the cone to the dog's head. She ruffled the dog's fur and bent close to its ear. "Do know that I'll try to refrain from tying a cone around your head in the future, although I do think it was only done to fulfill Gilbert's curious notion that I needed to be presented with a dragon."

The dog licked her hand before she straightened. "I wonder what I should name him, or if he already has a name."

"It's a girl, and no, she doesn't have a name," Tobias said over his shoulder as he started down a hallway.

As she followed Tobias at a rapid pace that didn't allow Temperance time to give the hallway a proper look, she caught glimpses of wonderful molding attached to doorways and numerous swatches of fabric hanging from the walls, clearly waiting for someone to decide which patterns and colors would work best.

"I imagine you'll be able to whip this place into shape in no time," Florence said from behind her, sending Temperance a wink when Temperance turned her head to look at Gilbert's mother.

"Hmm . . ." was all she felt comfortable responding, although given Gilbert's kiss, and the fact that he truly had procured a puppy that Tobias had apparently been trying to turn into a dragon, she was finally beginning to feel rather hopeful regarding her prospects for the future.

Not knowing what they were about to find in the drawing room Tobias had just disappeared into, Temperance braced herself as Gilbert steered her through a doorway. A woman and man, tied to two chairs, both of them looking as if they'd been in a bit of tussle, looked up.

"Charles . . . darling," the woman exclaimed. "Praise the Lord but you're still . . . alive."

Charles stopped in his tracks and drew himself up. "Alice, what in the world are you doing in America, and . . ." He shot a glance to the man tied next to her. "What is your brother doing here as well, and . . . why have you been tied up?"

Tobias stepped forward. "They came to the front door, and since I'd offered to man that door because the butler and under-butler were off trying to find me something better to use to turn the dog into a dragon, since the dog didn't seem to want to have a horn attached to its head, I was the one to open the door after they began banging on it." He shook his head. "Before I could even blink, I found myself staring at the end of a pistol. They then insisted on being taken to Lord Strafford" — Tobias nodded to Gilbert — "and they meant you, if that was in question, now with the former Lord Strafford being alive and all."

"Come to kill me, if I'm not much mistaken," Gilbert said, turning to consider the two people tied to chairs he'd only recently purchased.

"Don't be silly, Gilbert, we weren't going to kill you," the woman named Alice said, the beauty of her face marred by the fact her eyes were flashing with temper. "We'd heard that America is a very dangerous place, so my brother and I simply weren't taking any chances."

"Is that why you knocked me to the ground and threatened to shoot me after I refused to disclose where Mr. Cavendish was?" Tobias asked. "You thought I'd turn dangerous since coming to live in America?"

"Exactly," Alice replied before she shot the dog a disgusted look. "It wasn't very nice of you to encourage that mutt to attack us like it did. Why, we could have been mauled to death and, to make it more frightening for me, you threatened us with the pistol Andrew so foolishly dropped, and then you tied us up." She lifted her chin. "You'll make them untie us, won't you, Charles?"

Charles, instead of doing as his wife asked, was looking her over, his eyes narrowing fraction by fraction. "Not that I believe this is the appropriate time to ask such a delicate question, since I've always believed matters of delicacy should be handled privately, but have you taken to eating vast quantities of food since learning I was dead, or . . . could you possibly be with child?"

Just like that, the room went silent.

Alice beamed a bright smile his way. "I

am with child, which is why I convinced my brother to travel to America with me, not wanting to take on such a task alone in my delicate condition." Her smile increased in brightness. "I knew I needed to disclose my condition to Gilbert posthaste, saving him the bother of packing up his life here in America to assume a life in England."

"Because if you happen to give birth to a male child, Gilbert would no longer be the Earl of Strafford. . . . Our son would be," Charles said, earning a nod from Alice in the process.

"Indeed." She turned her attention to Gilbert. "I knew you'd be disappointed to learn I'm in the expecting way, so . . ."

"I'm astonished you're in the expecting way," Charles interrupted. "Particularly because you know full well that you and I have not been in the same room together, let alone spent time of a . . . ah, close nature, for over a year."

The sound of a pin dropping could have been heard in the silence that followed that statement, until Tobias stepped forward. "Contrary to what your wife has stated, Lord Strafford, she's not expecting. She's just made use of some type of pillow, one I felt while she was pulling my hair after I wouldn't tell her where Mr. Cavendish was."

Charles tapped a finger against his aristocratic chin. "I would imagine your being with child scenario was a backup plan after your efforts to have Gilbert murdered weren't seeing much success."

Alice stuck her nose in the air. "I'm sure I have no idea what you're prattling on about."

"I'm sure you do, as well as knowing that I'm quickly concluding it was you and your brother who put into motion plans for my demise." Charles began *tsk*ing under his breath while Alice deliberately turned her head from him, taking a marked interest in a half-painted wall.

Charles discontinued his *tsk*ing and took a step closer to Alice. "There were five attempts on my life over the past few months in England, attempts I became convinced were perpetuated by my brother." Charles looked to Gilbert. "No offense. I know now you have no interest in the family title."

"None taken, and I might have thought the same if I were in your shoes."

Charles inclined his head before he turned back to his wife. "In case you were curious, I faked my own death. I never fell off my yacht, but instead had Lord Abinger sail me to his hunting cottage off the coast. I then asked him to return to London and make the claim I'd been swept out to sea." He smiled. "What an enjoyable few weeks I had at that cottage without you nagging me, Alice. But because I knew I couldn't stay dead forever, and knew I needed to uncover the truth about who wanted me dead, I decided to sail to America. At that time, I truly did believe Gilbert was the one behind the attacks on my life, and I knew by the time I reached this country he would have somehow learned I was dead. I wanted to see what he'd do with that information."

Florence cleared her throat, drawing everyone's attention. "I sailed home to tell him."

Charles, surprisingly enough, smiled. "I would have thought you'd try to withhold that information from him, Florence, what with your disdain for the aristocracy."

"I was told your death had made the papers, and the ocean that separates England from America isn't nearly as large as it used to be."

"Quite," Charles returned, nodding to Gilbert again. "We've been trying to keep track of you for the past week, and during that time, we learned that someone seemed to want *you* dead. I should have realized then what was occurring, but it's a little hard to swallow — accepting the idea my wife could have possibly detested me so much that she'd want me dead, or that she'd then set her sights on killing you."

He turned to Alice. "If you'd been successful with murdering Gilbert, and even if you weren't, should I assume you were then going to return to London and produce a male child a few months later — one you'd claim was mine, and one I imagine you'd fetch from an orphanage?"

Alice refused to address his question, but Charles didn't seem to notice as he began to pace around the room.

"It would have been relatively easy to convince most everyone the child was mine since we've never let it be known to many people how much we detest each other. I have to imagine you would have then worked it out so you'd retain control over my vast holdings until the baby reached his majority, at which point I'm sure you would have come up with yet another plan, one that would see you continuing to manage matters of the estate behind the scenes."

He stopped pacing. "What a shame that Gilbert was so difficult to murder, wasn't it? I imagine that's what forced you to decide you'd have to do the deed yourself or convince him you really were with child and that he'd need to put his plans on hold until after the birth."

Alice slowly turned her head, her eyes flashing once again with temper. "Gilbert is incredibly resilient, even with us bringing assassins from England who were supposed to be the best in their chosen profession." She let out a laugh that was anything but amused. "Imagine my disgust when I learned those idiots were captured during their second attempt of dealing with Gilbert, and that was *after* they'd failed in their first attempt in Central Park. Because of their ineptitude, my brother and I were left with no other option but to take care of the matter ourselves."

Charles began twisting a signet ring around his finger before he lifted his head and pinned his wife with an icy glare. "What I don't understand is why you'd want to kill me. We barely see each other. You've been free to enjoy the life of a countess unencumbered."

Alice lifted her chin. "You're old enough to be my father. You're also condescending, arrogant, rude, and I could go on and on. You only married me to provide you with an heir, and when that didn't happen within the first year of our marriage, you grew tired of me and found me to be worthless."

"You're saying too much, Alice," Alice's

brother muttered. "We'll likely find ourselves in jail if you continue talking."

"They're not going to have us arrested. I'm a countess, and in this country, they don't arrest aristocrats. They cater to us."

Less than five minutes later, Alice discovered that was not exactly the case when the Pinkerton detectives who'd followed them to Gilbert's house, and had been watching the house from the sidewalk, were summoned inside.

Kicking and screaming, and tossing curses at Charles that left Temperance's cheeks heated, Alice was taken from Gilbert's house, her brother not putting up a fuss at all when he was led from the house behind his sister.

Charles watched them leave, and then, as calm as you please, he brushed a single piece of lint from his jacket and turned to his brother. "I must apologize for the antics of my wife, as well as apologize for believing you were the one who wanted me dead." Then, and before Gilbert could respond, Charles turned to his friends. "While it is early for dinner, I'm suddenly famished. What say we go sample the food at Delmonico's, a place that's been highly recommended, but a place that's certain to disappoint."

Biding everyone a good evening, Charles and his friends quit the room. Gilbert followed them, telling Temperance and his parents he'd be back directly.

Florence took a seat on a linen-draped settee, her husband sitting down beside her. "I think we're going to have to stay in New York for the foreseeable future, dear, if simply to ascertain that no one else wants to see our son dead."

As William nodded in agreement, Temperance moved to join them, pulling over a chair that was also draped in linen. Taking a seat, she smiled when her new dog plopped down over her feet.

"What will you name her?" Florence asked.

Temperance considered the dog for a moment, noticing the scruffy fur, the ear that seemed to be missing a chunk out of it, and the happiness that radiated out of the dog's eyes, as if it had suffered a tough time of it, but finally realized its life was going to be fine because it had found its place in the world.

"I think Happy would be appropriate," Temperance said, smoothing a hand down Happy's thick fur.

"That suits her," Florence said as Happy let out a bark of obvious agreement right as

Gilbert strode back into the room, holding a piece of paper.

"Charles and his friends are off to Delmonico's, where I'm certain he'll enjoy a superb meal but will never admit to that."

"What do you believe he'll do about Alice?" Florence asked.

Gilbert smiled. "He's the Lord of Strafford, Mother. Distasteful as you find aristocrats, they do wield a certain amount of power, and I'm sure Charles will use that power to secure a speedy divorce, as attempted murder is a legitimate reason to dissolve a marriage." His smile widened. "I'm sure the courts over in England will agree that an earl can hardly be expected to sleep at night with one eye open, wondering if or when his wife is going to try to murder him again."

He gave a wave of the paper he was holding. "I found the list and speech I've been working on."

Florence rose to her feet, pulling William up beside her. "We'll just give the two of you some privacy, dear."

Sending Gilbert a smile, and then turning that smile on Temperance, Florence and William strolled from the room, whispering, if Temperance heard correctly, something about grandchildren.

"I've missed your mother," Temperance said, trying to distract herself from nerves that were beginning to jingle.

"I'm certain she, my stepfather, and your parents won't be leaving the city anytime soon, so you'll have plenty of opportunities to spend time with everyone." He bent to look at the paper in his hand, frowning as he scanned the page and, to her amazement, he stuffed the paper into his pocket. "This may seem outlandish, but I'm simply going to try telling you how I feel."

He strode to stand directly in front of her, then bent down on one knee and took her hand in his. "First of all, I'm incredibly happy."

Happy turned her head, let out a yip, then stretched out on the floor, rolled to her back, and with legs sticking straight up into the air, closed her eyes and went to sleep.

Temperance felt her heart melt. "I named her Happy."

"Excellent choice, and remind me to give Tobias a raise since he obviously knew you'd fall in love with Happy on sight." He sobered and gave her hand a squeeze. "And speaking of love . . ."

"I'm not a gentleman prone to wearing my faith on my sleeve, but I've come to the conclusion that God knew exactly what He was about when He allowed you to get abducted and I was sent to rescue you."

"You were supposed to be rescuing Clementine."

"Well, yes, but see, that's why I think people always say that God works in ways we don't understand at first. If you hadn't been abducted, and I hadn't begun to push you to marry me in order to observe the rules of society, well, we wouldn't be where we are today."

"And where is that?"

"Head over heels in love with each other, our friendship still firmly in place, but a friendship that's grown into so much more, or . . ." He suddenly looked worried. "At least that's how I feel. I'm not certain if you're there with the head-over-heels business. But if you are, and if you're now convinced we are well suited to each other, I would be incredibly humbled and honored if you would agree to be my wife."

Fishing a ring out of his pocket, he held it out to her. "This is the ring Mrs. Davenport gave me, but I'm more than willing to get you a different one if you have something else in mind."

Temperance smiled. "Mrs. Davenport has become a wonderful friend to me, and I'm incredibly touched she'd go through the bother of providing you with a ring, so . . . no, I don't have anything else in mind."

"That's a relief, because I'm fairly sure she was looking forward to the day she'd see this particular ring on your finger. I'd hate to disappoint a woman who helped you abandon your stint as a wallflower, as well as being instrumental in getting Permilia and Gertrude to abandon theirs as well. Although she was aided in that endeavor by Miss Henrietta and Miss Mabel, of course."

"Those three ladies do seem to have achieved their goal of taking Permilia, and Gertrude, and me in hand."

"They wish you nothing but happiness, Temperance, and have even taken, along with Mr. Barclay, to threatening me with bodily harm if I don't make you happy, so . . ."

He stopped talking when Happy let out a bark, even though the dog didn't open its eyes and seemed to fall back to sleep a second later.

Looking slightly disgruntled by the interruption, although his lips were curving at the corners, Gilbert returned his attention to Temperance. "Where were we?"

"I think this is the part where I tell you that I'm head over heels in love with you as well, and that . . . yes, I would love nothing more than to become your wife."

Sliding the ring over her finger, Gilbert rose to his feet, pulled her up next to him, cupped her face with his hands, and kissed her.

When he finally eased away from her and looked into her eyes, Temperance saw her future gazing back at her, and it was a future filled with love, laughter, amusement, and happiness.

Closing her eyes for the briefest of moments, she sent a prayer of thanks to God, realizing that He'd known all along that she and Gilbert were always meant to be more than friends. In all honesty, He must have been more than amused as He'd watched them realize they'd been caught by surprise with a love that was certain to last through the ages.

Epilogue

January 14, 1884

Reverend Perry walked down the aisle of Grace Church, appreciating the bright sunlight that was streaming through the stained-glass windows. It had been snowing for days, but the snow had finally stopped, and while he enjoyed the sight of the city blanketed in what he thought of as God's quilt, he cherished this brief respite in the midst of winter.

Taking a seat in the very first pew, he smoothed a hand across the heavy vellum envelope Mr. Barclay had personally delivered to him a short time before, that gentleman beaming in delight about whatever the contents were inside.

Taking some time to simply reflect on the year that had recently passed, Reverend Perry couldn't help but marvel at the ways God had worked to change the lives of three young ladies who'd been certain their days would be spent as wallflowers.

Permilia and Asher had been the first to marry, in late November of 1883, not wanting to wait more than a week to exchange their vows after Permilia's father returned to town. The church had been filled to overflowing with friends and business associates, and Permilia had made a stunning bride, wearing a gown designed by Miss Betsy Miller, a woman who was quickly becoming known as the local designer of choice amongst the social elite. Gertrude and Temperance had been Permilia's maids of honor, while Harrison and Asher had been groomsmen.

The new Mr. and Mrs. Rutherford had immediately left on their honeymoon, but hadn't stayed away long, the demands of owning a department store having them gone not more than a week.

Gertrude and Harrison had been next to marry, although their wedding had been a smaller occasion than Permilia and Asher's. Mrs. Davenport had walked Gertrude down the aisle, and there'd not been a dry eye in the house. The newlyweds had departed on Harrison's yacht for a holiday farther south, but they'd returned two weeks before Christmas, the date Temperance and Gilbert had chosen for their wedding.

That day had arrived with blustery winds and snow, but no one had minded, especially not Temperance and Gilbert. With Happy by their side, dressed in a dragon costume Tobias had crafted, although she'd only tolerated the horn attached to her head for a mere five minutes, Gilbert and Temperance spoke vows they'd created for each other. Gilbert had not even bothered to look at the vows he'd written down, preferring to embrace a more spontaneous attitude, something he later told Reverend Perry he was beginning to enjoy.

Temperance and Gilbert had chosen not to go on holiday after the wedding, preferring to retreat to their new home, one that Temperance was rapidly whipping into shape. Gilbert had insisted on turning one of the rooms into a music room, and they made it a habit to invite everyone to their home to listen to Temperance play. Those gathered together would then repair to the dining room after Temperance was finished, and once there, they were treated to the tastiest of dishes, cooked to perfection — or sometimes not — by former students they'd hired from Miss Snook's school.

Temperance's parents, Anthony and Grace Flowerdew, had reclaimed the fortune Mr. Howland had stolen from them, and subsequently purchased a house three houses down from Temperance and Gilbert. They were determined to make up for the time lost when they were presumed dead, as well as the time Temperance had always longed to spend with them in her childhood. They'd also taken to spending time again with Florence and William Beckwith, both couples thrilled their children had finally realized they were perfect for each other, and both couples, if he wasn't much mistaken, were looking forward to the day they became grandparents.

As for Miss Henrietta, she continued to search for young ladies to take in hand, as well as help the students at Miss Snook's School for the Education of the Feminine Mind find suitable positions about the city. She was not above badgering Asher, Harrison, and Gilbert to take on more employees, and she encouraged all of their business associates to do the same.

Miss Mabel was still enjoying managing the tea shop at Rutherford & Company, still bickering with her sister every now and again, especially when Miss Henrietta would insist Eugene drive her sister to work when it snowed. The last time Reverend Perry had seen Miss Mabel, she'd been leaping out of a fancy sleigh right in front of Asher's store before it had come to a complete stop, yelling something about being in fear for her life before she'd stomped away, Eugene grinning ear to ear. He'd then helped the other occupant out of the sleigh, that being Mrs. Davenport, who'd been delivering a few of her latest designs to Permilia, who'd been selling them at a fast clip.

Mrs. Davenport had also created the wedding gown for Edwina when she'd married her Agent Samuel McParland a week before, and because Edwina, now the face of Rutherford & Company, was rapidly becoming known as the *It* girl about town, whatever that meant, Reverend Perry had a feeling Mrs. Davenport's designs were going to become more in demand than ever.

Miss Snook was continuing her quest of searching out women in need, willing to offer any woman a spot in her school if that woman was agreeable to working hard to obtain the education needed to better herself. Mr. Barclay had taken to escorting Miss Snook around the city, and together, they'd filled the school to the brim, improving the lives of women who'd never thought they'd have a reason to hope.

Miss Mercy Miner had certainly seen her life improve, having been offered a full-time typing position by Mrs. Martin, Gilbert's secretary, who'd gone ahead, on Gilbert's request, and hired all the students Miss Henrietta had originally sent to his office.

Mercy's brother, Eugene, besides driving Miss Henrietta and Miss Mabel around town, had been given the job of teaching the young women at Miss Snook's school how to defend themselves. Many times when Reverend Perry stopped by the school to check on everyone, he'd hear young women shrieking and running around, dripping paint from paperboard swords and wearing shirts streaked with red paint.

One of the most surprising developments had been with Miss Clementine Flowerdew. She'd turned softer over the past few months, and . . . she seemed to have captured the eye, although it was still too soon to know about his heart, of none other than Charles Cavendish, Lord of Strafford. He'd recently invited Clementine, along with Wayne, Fanny, and their Aunt Minnie, to London for a visit. And while Charles had yet to be granted the divorce he was seeking against Alice, Reverend Perry had the sneaking suspicion Clementine might someday achieve that high social status she'd always desired, along with a title she probably never imagined.

As for Alice and her brother, they'd returned to England where they'd been put on trial, found guilty of a lesser charge than murder, and had already been released. London society evidently did not take kindly to anyone trying to kill off one of their earls, though, so Alice had fled to India, where she was expected to live out her life, eased by the fact that Charles, surprising everyone, had settled an allowance on her.

As his thoughts began to settle, Reverend Perry closed his eyes and folded his hands, giving thanks to God for all the many blessings He'd bestowed on so many people. Asking God to watch over these people, as well as to watch over the ones who'd yet to find their happily-ever-afters, he opened his eyes and turned his attention to the envelope he was still holding.

Breaking the seal, he pulled out a piece of thick vellum embossed with a flower design around the edge, smiling as he read it.

Mrs. Asher Rutherford,
Mrs. Harrison Sinclair,
and Mrs. Gilbert Cavendish
Request the Honor of the Presence of
Reverend Benjamin Perry
at the
Wallflower Ball

Held at the residence of
Mr. Gilbert Cavendish
855 Fifth Avenue
to take place on
Monday, February, 4, 1884
10:00
Dress — Formal — But As You Please

With his lips curving into a smile, Reverend Perry shook his head, read the invitation again, and knew that the Wallflower Ball was going to be a ball for the ages. More important, though, he knew that Permilia, Gertrude, and Temperance would never be left lingering against any walls ever, ever, again.

ABOUT THE AUTHOR

Jen Turano, a *USA Today* bestselling author, is a graduate of the University of Akron with a degree in clothing and textiles. She is a member of ACFW and RWA. She lives in a suburb of Denver, Colorado. Visit her website at www.jenturano.com.

The employees of Thorndike Press hope you have enjoyed this Large Print book. All our Thorndike, Wheeler, and Kennebec Large Print titles are designed for easy reading, and all our books are made to last. Other Thorndike Press Large Print books are available at your library, through selected bookstores, or directly from us.

For information about titles, please call:
(800) 223-1244

or visit our website at:
gale.com/thorndike

To share your comments, please write:
Publisher
Thorndike Press
10 Water St., Suite 310
Waterville, ME 04901